Readers who know me as JOSEPHINE COX often ask why I write under two names.

Both the JOSEPHINE COX and JANE BRINDLE stories are drawn from the tapestry of life. They are about ordinary people with dreams and aspirations. People with loves and fears and longings of one kind or another. They are stories of pleasures and regrets, of deceit and friendship. Stories of ordinary and extraordinary people, of a kind that might live down your street; people you have known forever, or you've only just met; people you think you know, then realise you don't know at all. People who fill your lives so completely you would not know how to live without them.

Relationships. Emotions. Situations that bring out the best and the worst in all of us. This is what I write about in both the JOSEPHINE COX and JANE BRINDLE stories. So why the different names, you ask.

Since time began, there are things far deeper than first imagined. Wicked, dangerous things, to create evil and mayhem in any one of us . . . the dark side. These are the sinister stories. As a child, and for reasons I can't say here, I suppressed many frightening feelings. These have now surfaced in the JANE BRINDLE books.

Many JOSEPHINE COX readers enjoy the JANE BRINDLE books. Yet because there may be others who don't wish to delve into that darker side, I was obliged to keep them separate. JANE BRINDLE is my mother's name.

No Mercy

Jane Brindle

First published in paperback in 1992 by
Warner Books

Reprinted in paperback in 1995
by Orion Books Ltd

First published in this paperback edition in 1998 by
HEADLINE BOOK PUBLISHING

A HEADLINE FEATURE paperback

10 9 8 7 6 5 4 3 2

ISBN 0 7472 5754 X

Printed and bound in Great Britain by
Mackays of Chatham PLC, Chatham, Kent

HEADLINE BOOK PUBLISHING
A division of Hodder Headline PLC
338 Euston Road
London NW1 3BH

CONTENTS

PART ONE

The Follower

*'The night was dark, no father was there
The child was wet with dew.
The mire was deep, and the child did weep
And away the vapour flew.'*
William Blake

CHAPTER ONE

'Don't cry, Ellie . . . *please don't cry*.' Looking up at his sister with blue, soulful eyes, the boy shifted himself along the car seat and slid his small hand into hers. For a warm April afternoon, his fingers were surprisingly chilly. His voice, too, had a cold, disturbing edge to it. '*I hate her!*' he said, his gaze reaching beyond Ellie, to where the man was knelt in the grass, his head bent low and his lips moving in a whisper, as though he was taking part in a secret conversation.

For a fleeting moment, the man's eyes strayed back to the two huddled figures in the car. He smiled, but it was merely a kind gesture designed to comfort them. Yet it brought only pain to his watching children, for the smile never reached the man's eyes – dark, familiar eyes that were still haunted and confused. 'Hush, Johnny.' Ellie squeezed the boy's fingers lovingly. 'Please don't say that . . . don't ever say you *hate* her.'

'All the same, *I do!*' he hissed, his baby blue eyes brilliant and hostile. 'Anyway, she never loved me. It was *you* she loved . . . *and him*.' He nodded his head in the man's direction. 'She never wanted me. I heard her say it.'

'You're wrong, sweetheart. Mother *did* love you.' She, too, had heard her mother say on at least one occasion, that Johnny had 'been a mistake'. Ellie had often wondered at the age gap between her and Johnny, but

3

whenever she broached the subject to her mother, Marie, her questions were coolly received.

'Then why did she tell Daddy that she wished I'd never been born? You answer me that.'

'She was ill. We know that now. Don't think about the last few weeks, Johnny. Think about before . . . when she was well. When she made us laugh, and sang you to sleep . . . when she kissed you and loved you better than *any* woman could ever love her son. Think of those times, sweetheart. Don't dwell on the bad times.' For a moment, Ellie was lost in her own thoughts. Strange how no one had realised how disturbed their mother had grown. Strange, and unforgivable. Yet, how were they to know, when only two days before it happened, they were all opening their Christmas presents, bubbling with happiness and making plans for the New Year. Only, when the New Year came, she was gone. And by her own hand, or so they said. Even now, almost four months on, the whole, terrible thing seemed so unreal. 'You know she adored you, Johnny . . . deep down, you do know that, don't you?' Ellie pleaded, her strong amber eyes tenderly bathing his face. He was so wrong, she thought, so very wrong. But then, he was only nine, and had seen things that *no child* should see. Not for the first time, Ellie wondered if he would ever recover from his experience.

For a long, painful moment, the boy glared back at her, his mouth drawn into a thin, spiteful line. Then slowly, his gaze mellowed and he began trembling. 'I suppose so,' he murmured sullenly, 'if you say so, Ellie.'

'And you won't think about that one time when she said something that hurt you . . . something she didn't mean?' The tears tumbled down Ellie's face. She missed her mother so much.

Johnny saw her crying. It angered him. 'All right.' His voice fell to a whisper as he added, 'But it's too late now. You mustn't cry, Ellie.' He tugged at her. 'There's nothing

4

we can do to bring her back . . . nothing *any* of us can do. It's too late, don't you see? *It's too late.*' Something that sounded like a sob broke from him. Yet, when Ellie glanced down, he was smiling. 'But, it'll be all right now,' he told her, nestling so hard into Ellie's side that she winced. 'I won't let any harm come to you, though . . . you'll see, I won't let anyone hurt you!' There was vehemence in his voice. And fear. And something that made her blood run cold.

'Bless you, Johnny.' Ellie inwardly chided herself and hugged him fiercely. 'You make me feel ashamed.' She wiped her eyes. 'Here am I, going on twenty . . . more than twice your age and, of the two of us, *you're* the stronger.' It was true. She had been astonished at her brother's courage, yet it had also crossed her mind how unnaturally calm he had been since that fateful night. It concerned her that he had not shed a single tear. And, though she put it down to her own imagination, Ellie could not rid herself of the realisation that, in unguarded moments, he seemed to be more surly in manner, often spiteful, whereas, before, he had been a bright, busy child, curious and always gentle in his affection. On the two occasions when Ellie had broached the subject with her father, she was told it was not surprising that Johnny had changed. 'Don't forget it was the boy who found her, Ellie. A thing like that will stain his memory for a very long time to come. But, he'll be fine . . . he's young, and strong-minded. You know what the doctor said, Ellie . . . all we can do is reinforce our love for Johnny. In time he will forget, I promise.'

Ellie was reassured by her father's confidence. And when, some weeks ago, he had broken the news to them that he had been offered a post as caretaker of a listed building in the south of England, Ellie agreed that a 'new start' was exactly what they all needed.

She didn't mind leaving college. Her mind had strayed

from studies anyway, and things were not going too well with Barny. Oh, she still loved him, but she needed a little time to think. She needed a breathing space, away from the pressure of college, and a measure of distance between her and Barny, at least for a while, might do more good than harm. She *did* love him. There was no one else; there never had been. Right from that first moment when Barny had screeched his battered old van to a halt after driving it through a puddle and splashing her from head to toe, she had been drawn to him. She liked the way he fussed over her and the charming, if frantic, manner in which he had apologised. 'Like' quickly turned to love over the ensuing months, when they spent every spare moment together; arguing, making-up, fighting and laughing like all lovers do.

After the tragedy, the laughter disappeared, and there settled between them a terrible quietness. The shock of her mother's death, and the awful manner of it, festered between them until it became an unbearable threat to any future they might have had. She could no longer give herself to him. He understood, but bitterly resented the situation. It got to a point when they would meet, only to sit in an unsettled silence in his van, neither of them knowing what to say or how to repair the damage that was tearing them apart. In the end, regretfully, Ellie had finished it. 'We need time away from each other,' she had said. And she was not surprised when Barny did not argue. She missed him, though. And, deep down, she knew that he missed her.

Jack Armstrong got to his feet. He groaned softly as the cramp gripped his knees. He was not a young man, but neither was he old; it was only six months ago that he had celebrated his forty-fourth birthday. So much had happened since then. So much, that it would haunt him until the day he, too, was called to his Maker. Amidst all the shock and grief, one question had surfaced and remained uppermost in his mind – why? 'Dear God in heaven . . . *why*?' He raised his face to the sky, his voice soft in prayer. He found no answer. No comfort. No reassurance. Only a deep sense of horror that would not go away. And a terrible instinctive foreboding that had begun long before his wife had . . . had . . . He could not bear to think on it. He must learn to look forward now, to a new beginning. He had to carve a new life for himself and the children, many miles away from here. A sudden desolation settled on him. In his deepest heart, he was still mortally afraid. On that God-forsaken night when his wife had committed such a heinous act, there must have been wicked, dark forces at work. How otherwise could a sweet and gentle soul enter into so terrifying an ordeal? There was something . . . some awful, crippling thing that had driven her to do it.

Turning his head away from the afternoon sunlight, Jack Armstrong looked across to where his two children were waiting in the car. His warm, blue eyes sought out Ellie's anxious face. He smiled. How lovely she is, he thought with pride. And how very much like her mother – with her strong, amber-coloured eyes and wild, curly hair that tumbled to her shoulders like spilling sunshine. The bitter-sweet pain tugged at his senses. He drew his gaze away. And now, he was looking on the small face of his son. He felt the smile melt from him, and in its place there came a puzzling emotion. For what seemed an age, he continued to gaze on the boy, studying the unruly shock of brown hair and the blue eyes that seemed too brilliant, too vivid, almost *unreal*. But then, those young eyes had seen too much. The pain and regret stabbed at his heart. Reluctantly, he looked away.

'Don't punish yourself any longer.' Ellie had seen her father's suffering. Taking the boy's hand in her own, she had left the car and crossed the neat, pretty churchyard. Deeply moved by his obvious anguish, she urged, in a gentle, comforting voice, 'Please . . . we've all said our goodbyes. Can't we go now?' She tugged at the sleeve of his shirt. '*Please.*' There was desperation in her voice.

'Are we doing the right thing, Ellie?' He bent his head to look directly into her eyes. A shock thrilled through him as he realised again how incredibly like her mother Ellie was; small, petite. He always had to bend his head to look into *her* eyes as well. Regrets for what was lost and for what might have been lacerated his insides.

'It's the only way,' Ellie promised, 'we have to try. We need to . . . forget.' The tears threatened. She choked them back. Not in front of her father and Johnny, she thought. Instinctively, she knew they would be looking up to her. She must not let them down.

There was a moment of uneasy silence. Ellie could see her father's torment. She sensed that Johnny was also watching him closely. When, presently, Jack Armstrong addressed himself to the boy, saying, 'What about you, Johnny . . . do *you* think we're doing the right thing?' Ellie felt her brother's fingers stiffen round her own. She waited for an answer. Her father waited. When the answer came, it was not what either of them expected.

'I want to go now.' Johnny instinctively backed away, his face puckered in disgust and his eyes narrowed as he glanced towards the headstone. '*She smells the same!* The same as when I found her. I don't like that smell. It makes me feel sick!'

'What are you talking about?' Ellie clutched his fingers tightly, drawing the trembling boy to her. There was anger in her voice.

Jack Armstrong stepped forward, impatient yet gentle in manner as he asked, 'Your mother wore a perfume that you didn't like? Is *that* what you mean?' When Johnny hesitated, he demanded, '*Is it? . . . Is that what you mean?*'

Hesitantly, the boy nodded. His father was stunned.

'But that's impossible, Johnny.' Ellie felt her brother's terror. Her voice was deliberately calm. 'Mother never wore perfume. *Never*.' Her anxious eyes glanced upwards to see the same disbelief in her father's ashen face.

'She *did*!' The boy was frantic, tugging to get away, his eyes wild and frightening to see. 'She wore it that night . . . *and she's wearing it now*!' He was screaming. 'Let me go . . . Let me go!' With a determined twist of his arm, he had wrenched himself from Ellie's grasp and was speeding back to the car. Ellie started after him.

'No! Leave him,' instructed her father, 'he'll be all right . . . he's afraid, that's all.' He could have said that the 'perfume' Johnny had smelled on his mother was probably the peculiar stench of blood. He could have warned Ellie that the boy was still reliving the nightmare in his mind and how it was so real that, even now, just standing close to his mother's grave, that same awful stench in his nostrils was just as odious as on that night. Jack Armstrong knew. Because the awful events were a nightmare that he himself was struggling to come to terms with. 'We'll help him,' he told Ellie now, 'you and me together . . . we'll get him well, believe me.' And Ellie did.

From a short distance away, Barny Tyler had witnessed the scene between these three people; one of whom he adored. In a moment he had come forward, a warm, pleasant glow spreading through him when Ellie's face lit up on seeing who it was. Disentangling herself from her father's embrace, she ran towards the tall, slim figure that was Barny, her eager eyes taking stock of how attractive he looked in the open-necked shirt that was almost the same chestnut colour as his thick, wayward hair. He looked much younger than his twenty-six years.

'I guessed you would be here . . . saying your farewells.' He told her apologetically, 'I'm sorry, Ellie. I couldn't let you go without seeing you just once more.' His green eyes bathed her face. There was a kind of sadness in his voice, yet it was tinged with hope. 'Why don't you stay, Ellie?' he asked, 'or is it that you really don't love me enough?'

'*Don't, Barny.*' Ellie felt the frustration rising in her. They had gone over this same argument so many times before. And each time it had ended in ill feeling. 'It isn't a question of whether I love you . . . I *do*! You know that.'

'Then stay.'

'No. It wouldn't work, don't you see, Barny? Things have changed between us. Oh, I know it's my fault. But . . . I can't think of our future just yet. Trust me . . . please.' Now she was convinced that she had made the right decision, not to give Barny the address at their new home; at least not for a while, and maybe *never*.

Suddenly, the fire was back in his eyes. There were times when he understood, and other times when he didn't. Like now. 'I'm asking you to marry me, Ellie,' he snapped, angrily clasping a hand over the small, trim shoulders and gently shaking her. 'I want you for my wife. If you say you love me . . . then *nothing* should stop us!'

Ellie was taken aback by his outburst. This was the first time 'marriage' had seriously entered the argument. It threw her off balance for a minute. But then, she remembered the tragedy that had marred their lives. In her mind's eye she saw it all. And, for now at least, her answer had to be the same. 'I can't commit myself, Barny. Like I said . . . I must have time to myself, time with my father and Johnny. Just now we need each other. I couldn't bring myself to desert them. I'm all they have. *You must see that?*'

'Yes, I do understand that,' he conceded, 'but why must you turn your back on me? I need you too, Ellie. *I love you*, for God's sake!'

Ashamed of the pain she was causing him and unable

to meet the accusation in those pleading green eyes, Ellie lowered her gaze to the ground. She was desperately torn in two directions, with her own future happiness tugging her towards Barny's love, and both her conscience and family loyalty insisting that she owed a duty to her mother's memory. That duty called for her to go south, with little Johnny and her father. Maybe, when they were both settled there? When the two of them were strong enough to come to terms with what had happened? Maybe then, she thought, she could consider her own future with Barny. In that moment something occurred to her, cruelly smothering her optimism. Suppose she herself could not come to terms with what had happened? On that December night in 1955, her mother had been possessed by demons. Ellie had never spoken of her awful suspicions, not to her father or Barny, and certainly not to her young brother. It seemed a sinister, unnatural thing to say, she knew that. But then, what her mother had done was far more unnatural, far more sinister. Only a soul possessed by demons could contemplate such a thing. Her brown eyes darkened with pain as the terrifying images stalked her mind. Horrible images of a broken, bleeding body, of her mother's wide-open eyes, that were dead, and yet were not. Images of a once beautiful face, and of the eerie tricks the moonlight played on it. Ellie visibly shuddered. 'I don't know if you'll ever understand, Barny,' she said in a quiet, trembling voice, 'I have to go with them. I must watch over them . . . for a while at least.'

'You say you love me?'

'I do love you, Barny.' Her heart ached for him; for herself.

'Then don't do it to us.' He sighed as she shook her head, lowering her gaze to the ground and itching to be gone from the awkward situation that loomed between them. 'All right then!' he said sharply, his patience at an end. 'Go if you must . . . but don't expect me to wait forever.' He wanted to shake her. To hurt her. To take her in his arms and love her. 'Let me come with you. Or at least give me an address where I can contact you.'

'No.' She had to resist. She must keep a clear mind.

'But you'll write to me, won't you? Let me visit . . . spend *some* time with you?'

'Later.' She watched his eyes light up, then close in anguish when she added, 'Maybe . . . I don't know.'

'Then to hell with you, Ellie! You've made it plain enough where I stand.' He stared at her a moment longer, hoping in his heart that she would relent. He wanted her so much it was like a physical pain. Just for the merest heartbeat, he felt the tension relax between them. 'Oh, Ellie . . . Ellie,' he moaned. In a moment, they were kissing. Her warmth against him was like a heady wine, stirring his senses and flooding him with hope.

The moment was dashed when she pulled away. 'I *will* write,' she murmured.

'Soon?'

'I hope so.' Ellie saw that he was about to plead once more. She put a gentle finger to his lips. 'Don't . . . please,' she warned. 'Give me the time I ask for. I don't want to promise anything beyond that.'

He took her hand in his. 'How much time, Ellie? For God's sake . . . how long am I to wait?'

'I don't know. I'm sorry, Barny . . . but they're ready. I have to go now.'

'I will find you, Ellie . . . I *will*!'

'If you do, there'll be no future for us.' She glanced towards the car. They were watching, *waiting*. 'Goodbye, Barny.' She reached up to kiss his lips. 'I won't hold you to anything,' she murmured against his mouth, 'but I do love you. Remember that.' Before he could reply, she hurried away. And though her heartbeat was quickened and the urge to glance back was strong inside her, she went on at a faster pace, climbing into the car and cuddling Johnny to her, deliberately forcing Barny from her thoughts. Yet, try as she might, she could not oust him from her heart.

Jack Armstrong drove the car out of the churchyard and onto the main road heading away from the town of Blackburn in Lancashire, and taking them to a small hamlet some twelve miles from Medford in the county of Bedfordshire. He wondered whether he would ever come back. He had made arrangements for her grave to be kept neat and tidy, even though there was something repugnant about that. Especially after the way she had . . . the way . . . she had . . . *No!* It did not do to dwell on such things. They were on their way to a new life. That was what had to be remembered. And only that. He glanced in the mirror to where his children were huddled together. God, they looked so frightened, so vulnerable. A stab of fear shot through him. Things would be all right now he promised himself. A new area, a fresh start and a lovely old house that was steeped in history. A second chance, that's what they were getting. It had to work. He must believe that. There was no reason why life should not begin again for them, was there? What was done, was done. There was no way he could change it. He had better memories, and he had his children. Few men had more. Suddenly his heart felt lighter than it had done for months. He even smiled a little. It would be all right now. They would come through. His optimism was pierced only briefly. And that was when he caught sight of Johnny's sleeping head. The boy. The boy worried him.

From her place in the back seat, where she lovingly cradled her sleeping brother, Ellie was also deep in thought. She had seen the ghost of a smile on her father's face and was heartened by it. It was like a glimpse of sunshine after a storm. For the first time in a long while, a sense of peace and well-being flushed her heart. But, she did not fool herself. There was still a long way to go before the events of the past could be erased.

A loud cry shattered Ellie's thoughts. 'Go away! *Get away from me!*' In his nightmare, Johnny flayed and kicked at the air, fending off someone or something, his face contorted with fear.

'Ssh . . . ssh, sweetheart,' Ellie drew him closer, enfolding him in her arms and brushing her mouth across the top of his head, 'it's all right.' Her words comforted him. Soon, he was quiet again, clinging to her, his slumbers more peaceful. For now.

'He'll forget, Ellie . . . with our help, he will forget.' Jack Armstrong's anxious gaze was conveyed through the mirror to Ellie. 'It will be some hours before we arrive at our new home,' he added. 'I suggest you follow the boy's example . . . get some sleep while you can. Lord knows there'll be more than enough work to do before we're settled in.' His gaze momentarily mingled with hers. When she smiled, he nodded and looked away. 'I've a feeling the place will be in a shocking state of repair.' He reached up to tilt the mirror. Ellie could no longer see his eyes. But she could still feel his pain. His anger.

Tired as she was, Ellie could not sleep. So many questions invaded her mind. Would Barny wait for her? She wouldn't blame him if he never wanted to see her again, but she felt instinctively that it was wise to put time and distance between them. That way, they could take stock of their feelings for each other; recent events had put them under so much strain, there was a very real danger they would drift apart anyway. This way, she felt their long-term relationship had a better chance. It was an opportunity, also, for Barny to strengthen his efforts to find his mother. She had abandoned him as a babe-in-arms almost twenty-six years before. And ever since

Barny had learned that he was adopted, his dream had been to find his true mother. His adoptive parents had emigrated to Australia four years ago. Ellie had never known them because she had known Barny for only a year, but Barny spoke proudly of them all the time. Even in their middle years they were youthful in outlook. Kind, adventurous people. Barny never tired of talking about them. It was obvious that he cared deeply for the couple. But, when they left for Australia, Barny had chosen to stay behind. He was still pursuing the idea of finding his real mother.

All the same, Ellie suspected that he missed them dreadfully, even though she understood he kept in touch by letter. Barny had mentioned to Ellie that maybe, 'When we're married . . . we could join them . . . make *our* new life in Australia?' Ellie had been excited at the prospect. Now, she was numb with shock and grief.

Closing her eyes, Ellie began to relax; the trauma of the last twelve weeks and more had taken its toll. Weariness crept through her like an incoming tide, washing away all resistance. The welcoming sleep invaded her senses, lulling her to quietness, but the questions in her mind would not be stilled. Was Barny's love strong enough to stand the test of time? Was *her* love strong enough? Would Johnny ever again be free of the nightmares that still haunted him? Would her father find peace of mind in their new surroundings? Would *she*?

Suddenly, Ellie felt the tears threatening. Resolutely, she forced them down. There had been enough tears shed by all of them. Bitter tears. Sad, angry tears. But for whom? For themselves? For her dead mother? Where did it all begin to go wrong? Ellie asked herself. Why didn't they see it? Why didn't *she* see it? Surely a daughter should know when her own mother was desperately unhappy, or ill, *or losing her mind*! She hadn't wanted that observation to present itself. But, now that it had, Ellie searched her own tortured mind, recalling, reliving those past few months before . . . before. *No.* There had been nothing. Her mother had seemed content, happier than she had been for a long time; looking forward to the birth of her new baby; even teasing Johnny that he would soon have another sister. Johnny had resented that. 'I want a brother,' he insisted, 'someone to play football with me.' Now, there was no new brother, no baby sister and no mother. In one despicable, destructive frenzy, they had been wiped out for ever. But, *the pedlar!* Ellie suddenly remembered the pedlar! *What about the pedlar?* Two weeks before Christmas, Ellie had passed a bedraggled pedlar on the path to the house.

Old he was, and bent as Methuselah. He made an odd-looking figure as he went away from the house, furtive and badly limping, the brim of his battered hat pulled low over his forehead and muttering beneath his breath while he agitatedly delved into the wicker basket on the crook of his arm. When Ellie laughingly commented on him to her mother, she was told, 'Don't laugh at him, Ellie . . . or you might get struck dead!' But Ellie had laughed, chiding her mother for being superstitious. Her mother had not laughed, though. Not on that particular day, nor on many others following, she now recalled.

Ellie was deeply curious about the old pedlar. Had he somehow frightened her mother? Oh, but surely not! He was strange, scruffy and somewhat alarming in appearance, there was no denying it. But certainly he could not have done or said anything that might have worried her mother too deeply. Ellie smiled at the idea. How foolish she was, grasping at straws and searching for reasons that might explain her mother's sinister deed. The pedlar's call was just a coincidence, she reminded herself. Because, earlier on the morning of that same day, Ellie had come downstairs to find her mother seated at the kitchen table.

She was crying. To Ellie's concerned questioning she had simply replied, 'Being a cry-baby is quite normal when your time is close . . . wait 'til you're expecting, my girl! You'll see what I mean.' They had laughed together, and Ellie was reassured. Now, her mother's words rang in her thoughts like a death knell – 'when your time is close', she had said – *'when your time is close'*. Of course, she meant the birth, Ellie told herself. Of course she did! All the same, Ellie fought off the urge to scream out like Johnny had just done, urging the bad things to – 'Go away – *get away from me*!'

Determined to occupy her mind with other, more pleasant thoughts, Ellie reached into her handbag and withdrew a folded newspaper cutting. She wanted – needed – to remind herself of the new life waiting for them. As she unfolded the cutting, she felt cheered. The advert was still so clear in her mind's eye.

Handyman/Caretaker required to implement minor improvements to a house of historic interest, and afterwards to maintain the house in good condition.

Excellent wages and spacious accommodation offered to suitable applicant, who will have experience of house renovation.

There was a box number, but no name or telephone number. Ellie's father had shown interest in the advert straight away, as 'house renovation' was his special skill. It was how he earned his living. He had always nurtured a love of historic places. The post seemed tailor-made for him. Half-heartedly, he had written away to the stated box number, enclosing references and work experience details. When some time later he was offered the job by post, his enthusiasm grew. He saw it as an omen, a second chance for them all – particularly as the house in question was situated in a place called Redborough, in the south of

England, some two hundred miles away.

'That's strange.' Ellie turned the newspaper cutting over and over in her hands. *This was not the advert*.

'What's wrong, Ellie?' Her father tilted the mirror back again, his quizzical gaze searching her face.

'The advert . . . this isn't the one I cut out of the newspaper.'

'It must be amongst the paraphernalia in your bag.'

Ellie delved deep into her bag, spilling its contents onto her lap. 'No. It isn't here.' She was puzzled. Irritated. 'I can't understand it. I distinctly remember cutting out the advert and putting it into my bag!'

'Well then, you should be able to find it,' her father assured her, spasmodically glancing to the road in front. He sounded anxious, swearing aloud when the rear wheel mounted the kerb and he almost lost control.

Ellie was alarmed to see her father growing increasingly agitated, yet at the same time being convinced that she *had* put the advert in her bag. But she couldn't have done, or it would still be here! 'No matter,' she said, folding up the cutting and returning it to her bag. 'We don't really need it anyway. I hope you remembered to bring the letter of appointment with you, though. You did, didn't you?' She leaned forward, unintentionally awakening the boy. He peered up through half-opened eyes, smiled knowingly, and closed them again.

Jack Armstrong laughed. 'Don't you trust your old man?' he asked. The smile stayed on his face until he had tilted the mirror back. Then it slid away, leaving a grimmer expression shaping his features. Damn and bugger it! Was he going out of his mind? High and low he'd searched for that letter. Last night, and again this morning. He did not find it! And he could have sworn it was safely put away in the pocket of his jacket. But he daren't admit it to Ellie just now. He felt such a bloody fool! Still, it was just as well that he had made a mental note of where they were going. 'They would be expected' it had said in the letter. So, there was nothing lost. No need to worry. But he *did* worry. And he *would*. Until they were safely settled into their new home, Thornton Place.

He had located Redborough on the map. It did seem to be somewhat isolated. Still, there was no going back now! He had already returned the keys of their rented house to the grateful landlord, who had a string of potential tenants willing to pay a much higher rent. He had accepted a month's wages in advance on his new post. So his bridges were all burned. They were on their way now. And there was no place else for them to go. A sense of determination and adventure flooded his soul. It was a time for looking forward, not craving for the past. With this renewed sense of purpose, he began softly singing to himself. Ellie heard it and was both astonished and glad. They had made the right decision; she knew that now. And things could only get better. Please God.

In the pretty churchyard where Marie Armstrong was buried, the air grew clammy; unmoving as the departed who lay beneath the ground. There was no whisper of a breeze, not even the promise of one. Yet, the leaves in the oak tree rustled and moaned, seeming to sigh, 'No mercy . . . no mercy.' Above, the sky was awesome. Like some giant finger had stirred a deep, muddy pool and created a seething, eddying mass.

Rising gently into the air came a sickly sweet perfume, powerful; suffocating. It was the same fragrant perfume that had driven the boy to panic. 'She *did* wear it,' he had cried, *'she's wearing it now!'* It was a warm, lingering scent of summer. The unique and sultry fragrance of lavender.

Slowly, it pervaded the air, stayed a while, then purposely stole away . . . *following* . . . in a southerly direction.

PART TWO

The Stranger

'The motions of his spirit are dull as night,
And his affections dark as Erebus:
Let no such man be trusted.'
William Shakespeare,
The Merchant of Venice

CHAPTER TWO

They had been four, and now they were three. Now they were three, now they were three. 'NO ... NO!' Ellie's eyes popped open; the scream still echoing in her head. She felt the car jerk to a halt and her father's voice, gentle, soothing. 'All right, Ellie. Wake up ... we're almost there.' He climbed out of the car and opened the back door. 'Come out a while,' he told her quietly, 'get some fresh air ... stretch your legs.' He made no mention of her scream. It was too like his own. He understood.

'Why did you shout, Ellie?' The boy was eyeing her suspiciously. 'Did you have a nightmare ... did you?' There was fear in his voice, and wonder. And something much like satisfaction.

'Leave your sister alone, son.' Jack Armstrong leaned his head towards the car, his dark blue eyes condemning as they searched out the boy's face. Sometimes he suspected the child of being deliberately wicked.

'It's all right, Dad.' Ellie wiped the beads of perspiration from her forehead. It was a nightmare. But now it had receded, into the depths of darker, safer places. In a moment she was out of the car. Johnny clambered out and stood beside her, pressing himself close to her. She hugged him tight. 'Yes ... I *did* have a nightmare,' she confessed, 'I'm sorry for shouting like that. It must have frightened you.'

'No. It didn't frighten me.' There was indignation in his

voice now. He raised his face to look at her, but in the deepening twilight he could not see the expression in her eyes. Irritated, he kicked at the earth. 'I *knew* you were having a nightmare,' he said, '*I just knew!*' In his heart he was glad.

'Where are we?' Ellie looked towards her father, who had ventured away a few paces and was anxiously glancing about. Irritated, he told her that the journey was taking much longer than anticipated, especially as the car was 'not performing at its best'. 'But . . . where are we?' she insisted.

'We're lost, that's what!' The boy grabbed Ellie by the hand and tugged at it. 'I don't want to stay here. *I don't like this place!*'

'Don't be silly.' Pushing down the anger inside her, Ellie added in a firm voice, 'You *will* stay here . . . we *all* will. Because there's no place else for us to go. Besides, Johnny . . . we haven't even seen the house yet, and maybe this isn't the place at all.' She was not too surprised when he twisted away from her and climbed back into the car, slamming the door behind him. She lingered for a moment, unsure as to whether she had been too hard on him. After all, he was only a boy, and he had lost so much. But then, so had she! All the same, it was harder for him. The doctor said he must be reassured, and loved. Ellie felt herself weakening. She felt ashamed. But, at the same time she realised that over these past months both she and her father had gone out of their way to compensate the boy for all he had lost. His answer was to grow more sullen and demanding. Maybe they were molly-coddling him too much. Maybe it was time to make him face reality. He was shouting at her now, 'I don't like this place. I won't stay. I *won't!*' His shouts became sobs.

'Leave him be. Don't pamper him.' Her father's voice cut sharply through the night air. The darkness was closing in fast now. 'Come here, Ellie,' he called. Ellie glanced inside the car. Johnny was brooding, huddled in the corner. He turned from her. '*Ellie!*' Her father sounded agitated.

'Is this the place?' Ellie wanted to know, carefully picking her path over the rough ground. 'Soon, we won't be able to see well enough to find our way.'

'Look down there.' Jack Armstrong explained that while Ellie and the boy were sleeping he had seen a signpost some four miles back. 'Redborough . . . five miles, it said.' He had travelled on for what he calculated was five miles, but had become concerned when there was still no evidence of a hamlet, 'or even a single house!' That was when he had pulled off the main road into this rough ground. It was a high point. From here, he had hoped to see what lay ahead.

'Lights . . . street lamps?' Ellie was relieved. A double row of lights ran in a straight line for a short distance, but then the two rows joined in a half-circle at one end, as though round a cul-de-sac. 'Do you think it's Redborough?' She roved her eyes over the area below, looking for other lights; the lights of Thornton Place. But there was only darkness beyond. To the left of the valley there was a dense area. Ellie wondered whether this was a wood, possibly camouflaging the house. She said as much now, pointing to the area in question.

'I don't know any more than you do, Ellie.' Jack Armstrong narrowed his eyes to scour the distance. 'I don't even know if the place below is Redborough.'

'It must be,' Ellie said, thinking her father looked harassed. As a rule he was patient, easy going – except where the boy was concerned. And Barny. Looking at her father now, at the weariness that was on him, she allowed for the impatience in his voice. They had come a long way . . . almost two hundred miles, and they had been travelling many hours, with only a short stop for fuel and a bite to eat.

'Well . . . there's only one way to find out!' Jack Armstrong dropped his hand to Ellie's shoulder, gently turning her in the direction of the car. 'It can't be more than a ten-minute drive to where those lights are . . . and there's bound to be another signpost further on.' He opened the car door and waited for Ellie to get in. 'I've got a feeling that it *is* the place we're looking for.'

'And if it is . . . why can't we see the lights of Thornton Place? Isn't it only a short way beyond?'

'That's what I understood.' He shrugged his shoulders. 'So, we should be able to see the lights, I suppose.' The very same thought had earlier crossed his mind. 'But you have to remember that it's going on for ten p.m. . . . perhaps the present caretakers of Thornton Place are already in bed. They may be fairly old. Or –' and he had been churning this possibility over in his mind '– they could even have moved out. Maybe they got fed up waiting for us. They might be bitter because they've been pensioned off and someone else has been appointed in their place.'

Ellie nodded. It made sense, she supposed. All the same, she was suddenly anxious. 'What if that's true . . . about them being bitter? Old folk can be very stubborn when they've a mind to.' She had no grandparents now; her mother's father had been the last, and he had died three years ago, but she recalled how cantankerous he had been. 'Supposing they've barricaded themselves in? Supposing they won't let us through the door?' Her fears were running away with her. She began to understand why Johnny was so apprehensive.

'Nonsense!' Jack Armstrong got into the driving seat and switched the engine into life. 'Stop being so dramatic, Ellie,' he told her, softly laughing. 'Barricaded themselves in . . . Won't let us through the door.' He shook his head. 'For all we know, they might be sick to their back teeth of living in a big, draughty old house . . . places like that need a lot of work, I might tell you . . . constant attention. It's no easy thing for a *young* couple . . . let alone an old man and his wife. No! They'll probably welcome us with open arms.'

'They won't,' Johnny's voice whispered into the darkness. He knew they would all be sorry for coming to this place. There was something else too! That perfume . . . that sweet, sickly scent . . . the one his mother was wearing when he found her, then again, in the church-yard. They had not left it behind. It was there when he got out of the car just now. He could *still* smell it. Now it was here, right here. In the car. It terrified him. It comforted him. A great weariness took hold of his senses, lulling him, until he could hardly keep his eyes open.

A flood of relief surged through Ellie when she heard the man answer her father's question. 'That's right, mate . . . this 'ere's Redborough.' He was a friendly fellow, stocky and bald, with kind eyes and a jovial countenance. Ellie smiled to herself. It occurred to her that his 'jovial countenance' might be due to the fact that the fellow had just emerged from what appeared to be a Working Men's Club. No doubt he had been enjoying a pint or two of booze in pleasant company; that same 'company' now making its way home in the distance, and singing 'Roll Out the Barrel' at the top of its unmelodic voice.

'Just a private party.' The fellow chuckled when he saw Jack Armstrong glance in the direction of the noise. 'Oh, but don't you go thinking that Redborough's a rough kinda place!' he urged, his face becoming serious. 'We're a quiet law-abiding community, that we are.'

'I'm sure you are,' Jack Armstrong assured him, 'and no doubt we'll all get to know each other in time. Right now, though, we've travelled a long way and all we want is a meal, the chance to freshen up, and a warm, inviting bed. So, if you'll kindly point us in the direction of

27

Thornton Place . . . we'll be on our way.'

At once the fellow was attentive. 'Ah! . . . it's "Thornton Place" you're looking for, then? I did wonder. We don't often get folk pulling in off the main road . . . more often than not they just drive right on by without a second thought for this place.' He bent his back and peered into the rear of the car, looking first at the boy, and then at Ellie. He half smiled. Ellie smiled back. The boy stared him out.

'Is it far . . . Thornton Place?' Jack Armstrong was impatient to be on his way.

'What? . . . Oh, no, it ain't far.' The fellow stretched out his arm, turning his head in the same direction, away from the main road. 'Follow this road here . . . until you come to the very last house. You'll see a block of garages close by. Just beyond there you'll see a lane . . . well, more like a rough track it is . . . don't get used much, that's why. But, it's been wide enough for a horse and cart in the past, or a carriage . . . or a hearse. So, I dare say you'll manage to get this 'ere car along it. Go careful, mind . . . it's uneven and winding – full of potholes. It's not easy to negotiate in daylight, let alone in the dark.' He glanced at the boy again. He was strangely relieved to see that the brown head was lolled to one side; as though in slumber.

'How far is the house?'

'Not more than two or three miles, I dare say. The track runs level for two thirds of the way, then it begins to climb. Thornton Place sits right atop a hill. You can't miss it.' He chuckled. 'Or if you do . . . you'll likely end up in the lake!' He grew serious. 'You wouldn't be the first, though. No, you wouldn't be the first.' He peered into Jack Armstrong's face. He thought it to be a strong face, good and honest. From the man's stern expression, he also suspected a quickness of tongue when riled. 'You'll be the new caretaker, I expect . . . Is that right?' He waited for confirmation before looking into the back of the car again, saying, 'These your young 'uns are they?' This time he did not wait for an answer. 'No missus, eh? Well, I don't mind telling you . . . you'll have your work cut out with that crumbling old relic. And it's no place for children, mate . . . no place for children, and that's a fact!'

'Goodnight to you. And thanks.' Jack Armstrong slid the gear stick into position and the car went slowly away.

'Aye, and goodnight to you,' murmured the fellow as he watched the car draw out of sight. From the back window, the boy's pale sleepy features glared back at him. In the light from the street lamp, the small eyes glittered like jewels. The fellow frowned and pursed his lips while he thought hard on the way the boy had stared him out. 'Hostile!' he muttered, 'that's what he is. *Hostile*. Just like the others. God forbid!' Shaking his head, he went on his way.

'I can't see no "block of garages", dammit!' Jack Armstrong nosed the car out of the roundabout for the third time, his temper rising by the minute. 'The fellow must have been drunk . . . there's no sign of any "garages"!' He stopped the car and looked about. The street was deserted. 'It's like bloody zombie land!' he groaned.

Ellie didn't like her father swearing in front of the boy. She glanced down at his small, bent form lying crumpled across the seat. He appeared to be fast asleep, thank goodness, but he was right when he said they would all be 'sorry for coming to this place'. She was sorry already, and, from the sound of it, her father wasn't exactly enjoying the experience. It was a long time since she had seen him in such a temper, although she knew from experience that he did have a temper. A *vile* one, at that.

Winding the window open, Ellie glanced up and down the street – a narrow, lamplined street exactly the same as the one before, flanked with square, unattractive

29

red-brick houses. There wasn't a soul in sight. Not a dog or a cat. Not even a light burning in any of the windows. Wait a minute, though. There was a figure, a man, leaning against the lamp-post not too far away. So close, in fact, that Ellie's heart jumped with fear. He was looking right at them! Why hadn't she seen him? Why hadn't her father seen him? Strange, she thought. But then, the street lamp threw shadows all around, and the man was tall, slim, seeming to merge with the lamp itself. And he was so still; so uncannily still. He kept looking at them, but he made no move. Now, her father had seen him. 'The man . . . against the lamp-post, Ellie. Ask him how we find the way to Thornton Place.' Ellie hesitated. For some inexplicable reason, she did not want to leave the car. The thought of walking even the short distance up that half-lit, silent street gave her goose pimples. Or was it him? Was it the way he just went on staring, not moving? 'Ellie!' Her father's voice snapped into her fears. 'For God's sake . . . go and ask him which way.' Now, the boy's eyes popped open, willing her to go.

As Ellie made her way along the pavement, her heart was in her mouth and her every step ready for flight. Still he made no move. Always, his eyes were on her. Now, as she stood before him, Ellie could see those searching eyes. Dark and intense they were – and incredibly beautiful, glowing in the soft light, like silken velvet. For a split second, when his gaze first mingled with hers, Ellie was mesmerised. Then she heard her father behind her, impatient.

The young man spoke. 'Lost, are you?' His voice was low, trembling, *enticing*. Ellie was fascinated.

'My father's the new caretaker at Thornton Place,' she explained. 'We were told to find the block of garages, and the track would be just beyond.' She laughed softly, irritated by the effect he was having on her. 'We've been up and down the estate half-a-dozen times ... but well ... yes ... we *are* lost!' For a moment she thought he had not heard, because he made no response. His gaze never left her face; his handsome features remained still, carved into that sensuous, inviting half-smile. She got the feeling that he was quietly taking stock of her. She also felt his strength. She was astonished to find herself drawn to him.

'Thornton Place, eh?' He nodded his head as though in approval, and his smile enveloped her. 'What's your name?'

'Armstrong. My father is Jack Armstrong.'

'*Your* name.' It was like a command, but, loving.

'Eleanor ... Ellie.'

He gazed on her a moment longer, then, 'Tell your father to drive straight on towards the big field ... and the last lamp. He'll see the garages to his left. Follow the track round the back of the garages and keep going straight on. There are no lights to show him the way, and the going is not easy. If he takes his time ... keeps his headlamps full on and his eyes sharp, he'll come to Thornton Place in about ten minutes.'

'Thank you.' Ellie smiled up at him.

For a long moment, he held her gaze fast; thinking how lovely she was, with those warm, honest eyes and that air of vulnerability. But not too vulnerable, he hoped, or she could get hurt. He wouldn't want that. Not that. He watched her walk away. So young, so innocent. Already he had taken a liking to her. 'Don't stray from the track,' he warned. 'It's dangerous.'

As she got in the car, Ellie glanced back. With a stab of astonishment she realised he was gone. She felt a little sad, wondering whether she would ever see him again. Then she inwardly chided herself. He was a stranger! What did she know of him? She didn't even know his name. Quickly, Ellie repeated the young man's directions to her father. As the car pulled away, she leaned forward in her seat, her eyes scouring the road ahead. The sooner they got to Thornton Place, the sooner they could be settled, and get on with their lives. She was angry with herself. She had been too friendly with that young man. Why! He must have thought she was a hussy . . . going weak inside when he turned his dark eyes on her, and giving him her name for the asking. All the same, the sensation he had created in her would not go away. His eyes were so magnificent. His voice so soft, so invasive.

'What else did that man say to you, Ellie?' The boy had come forward on his seat and was trying to see her face.

'What do you mean . . . "what else"?' Ellie was surprised and annoyed by his probing. 'He told me what I wanted to know . . . the way to Thornton Place.'

'You were a long time.'

'I was not!' His insistence infuriated her. And, even without looking at him, she knew he was staring at her. She resented that. She resented his impertinence.

'You *were* a long time. He liked you, didn't he?'

'Your imagination will get you in trouble one of these days, my boy!' Ellie retorted indignantly. All the same, she felt herself wondering whether that was true. Had he liked her? A sense of pleasure rose in her, flushing her face a warm shade of pink. She was thankful that it was dark and the boy could not see. Suddenly, she was thinking of Barny, and her mood was subdued.

Jack Armstrong heard the banter between the boy and Ellie and he had sensed Ellie's embarrassment. More than that, he had suspected that the boy was right. He had seen for himself how the man had gazed down on Ellie's upturned face, how close they had been, and how reluctant Ellie had seemed to draw herself away. It could come to nothing, he was certain. They were strangers, nothing more. Even so, he wondered – not for the first time – whether he had made a wrong decision in accepting this

job and taking Ellie away from Barny. After all, it was
obvious that Barny Tyler adored Ellie. Sure, he wasn't
perfect; but then, who was? No doubt Barny would have
made a good husband and, before the tragedy, everything
had been going the right way for Barny and Ellie. *Now*,
well . . . like everything else, their relationship was in
danger of falling apart at the seams.

'Stay on the track, Dad!' Ellie was thrown sideways as
the car veered to the right.

'Okay, don't worry. We should be there any minute.'
He screwed his eyes up and searched ahead. 'There! . . .
look there!' he yelled excitedly. 'It must be Thornton
Place. It has to be!' At first, the huge shape was like a
shadow in the distance. But as they drove nearer, it
became a formidable thing, looming before them like
some giant sentry standing astride the top of the hill, its
four turrets reaching into the clouds like the fingers of a
mighty hand; the whole awesome structure silhouetted
against a silver sky and filling the horizon so that everything else seemed diminutive in comparison. Even the
gaunt, sky-scraping poplar trees surrounding it appeared
like tiny candles around a shrine.

'It's horrible!' The boy shrank back in his seat.

'You can't really see what it's like in the dark, Johnny,'
Ellie told him. Secretly, though, she had experienced the
very same feelings. The place was huge, frightening. But
then she reminded herself – it was dark and they were all
very tired. No house, however lovely, looked at its best in
the dark hours. It wasn't fair to form an opinion without
first seeing Thornton Place in daylight.

'They haven't gone to bed yet . . . there's a light on in
one of the downstairs rooms.' Jack Armstrong manoeuvred the car onto a level area some way from the
entrance to the house. The deep potholes and overgrown
shrubs prevented him from coming closer. 'Watch your
step, you two,' he warned, 'there's only the light from the

window . . . and the path is a mess of overhanging thorns and loose paving beneath.' He swore aloud when his foot came down on a jutting stone that viciously jabbed his ankle. 'First thing I'll do is make sure there's a clear access to the house!' he snapped. 'No wonder they've been given their marching orders!' He stamped his feet down, squashing the undergrowth beneath.

Ellie followed, the boy's hand tight in hers. The short distance from the car to the front entrance was slow and painstaking. More than once she felt the sharp thorns of protruding branches tearing at her skin. She felt the blood spurt up and begin to trickle. Her father was yelling now, angry, frustrated. 'You in the house! . . . open up for Christ's sake!' He cursed at the ensuing silence, pushing his body forward, breaking the way until now they were at the foot of the steps, broad stone steps that were already crumbling and pitted with small, deep craters. Running up either side of the steps was a thick, ornate railing of black, barley-twisted design. In the half-light it was plain to see that the iron railings were badly eaten by rust and lolling sideways in a dangerous way. 'Don't lean on the railings . . . you'll likely break your neck,' Jack Armstrong told the two bedraggled figures behind him. 'Jesus! How could they let the place get into such a sorry state?' He started up the steps, shouting once more, 'You in the house . . . it's Jack Armstrong . . . the new care-taker. Open up!'

'Perhaps they're not in . . . perhaps they always leave a light on when they go out,' Ellie suggested. She was apprehensive. And she suspected her father felt the same, else why was he yelling like that?

The front door was magnificent, with huge panels carved deep into the oak and a crescent of stained glass over the top. There was an old iron knocker in the shape of a floral bouquet and a wide, impressive border etched around the door frame. Long coloured glass insets flanked the door, and above these were two delightful cherub faces, each riddled with decay.

'You have a point there, Ellie,' her father reluctantly conceded. 'We should have been here hours ago . . . it is possible they thought we weren't coming. Yes. They could have gone out.' He kicked out angrily, stubbing the toe of his shoe against the wooden rail that skirted the door frame. He was worn out, tired from the long journey. For years now there had been talk of a six-lane dual carriage-way that would carry traffic between London and the Midlands, a motorway they said, the first of many. Talk. Just talk!

'They haven't gone out!' The boy stared at the lighted window. At the face there. When Ellie and her father glanced up, they saw only the drawn curtains. But the boy had *seen*. And now he remained silent.

Ellie visibly cringed when her father began furiously rattling the knocker. It made enough noise to wake the dead. But there was no response from inside the house; no movement. 'To hell with it!' Jack Armstrong slammed the knocker against its base, startling the night creatures who could be heard scampering through the undergrowth.

Ellie shivered as the night breeze gained momentum, sighing and whistling in the tree tops like a soul in torment. Curious, she glanced away from the house and into the distance. 'It's beautiful,' she murmured, 'look, Johnny . . . there's a lake.' In the light of the rising moon could be seen a vast stretch of land, dipping away into a valley, interspersed here and there with small spinneys and irregular mounds of what looked like boulders. Nestling at the foot of the valley was a shifting carpet of black and silver water, shimmering like diamonds in the soft moon glow.

The boy gazed at the landscape. He made no comment. He had not wanted to come to this place, and he did not want to stay.

Jack Armstrong appeared not to have heard Ellie's comment about the lake. Instead, he was stretching his neck, searching for a sign, *any* sign, that there was someone at home. At length, he told Ellie and the boy, 'Well . . . I've no intention of staying out here all night!' He began frantically searching in his pockets, crying out when he triumphantly produced a tangled bunch of keys. 'As from today, *I'm* the caretaker here. For all I know . . . the two of them could have cleared off.' He started fitting the keys to the lock, one after the other. 'It won't do no harm to wait inside . . . make a hot drink . . . keep warm. If they have "gone out" for the evening, I'm sure they'll understand. Anyway . . . according to the letter of appointment, the pair of them have been instructed to move into a cottage in the grounds as soon as they've shown me the ropes.'

'What will happen to them?' Ellie wanted to know. 'If they're not being paid as caretakers . . . what will they live on?' She had not seen the letter of appointment. Her father had taken care of all that.

'Search me.' He shrugged his shoulders and began putting the keys to the lock once more; this time with increased deliberation. 'Stop asking questions, Ellie,' he told her, irritated that, somehow, he must have missed the key that would open the door. 'Sorry,' he apologised, '. . . but it's been a long, tiring day. I expect they'll be found another place to take care of . . . something smaller and more manageable I should think. Or they might be got rid of. I wouldn't be at all surprised, after what I've seen of this place. If you ask me, they'd be better employed at *demolition*!' He seemed surprised when Ellie laughed. Slewing round to look at her, he chuckled in spite of himself. 'No matter,' he said, still smiling, 'we'll soon have this place ship-shape.' He didn't admit it, but he was really looking forward to tackling this job. It looked a grand old house; proud but ill used. It deserved better.

'I'm cold.' The boy huddled closer to Ellie.

'Don't worry, we'll be inside in a minute,' Ellie promised him, wrapping her arm round his small shoulders, 'as soon as Dad finds the right key.'

The 'right key' was not found. None of the eight keys fitted either the lock on the front door, or the heavier padlocks which were firmly secured to the back door, and the other two doors that provided access to different parts of the house. Jack Armstrong tried them all.

'What are we going to do now?' Ellie and the boy had waited by the front door while their father had circled the house, searching for a way in, and finding the building to be impenetrable. He had been astonished at the size and structure of the house, which, in his expert opinion, was built more like a fortress than any he had seen. The distance from the ground to the window levels was some fourteen feet high, with the walls themselves being constructed of hard, red brick and strengthened intermittently by thick, formidable buttresses; these structures were knitted deep into the brickwork and thrust upwards for some considerable distance. They were impossible to scale. Besides which, the buttresses were positioned in such a way that they would not afford any point of entry into the house. None of the outer doors was at ground level; each was situated at the top of a steep flight of steps.

In all his experience of old, historic places, Jack Armstrong had never seen anything like it. He was both shocked and fascinated. Here was a real challenge. He was deeply excited at the prospect of knowing the long history of Thornton Place. He knew also that he would not rest until he had unearthed all its glory, its tragedies, *its secrets*. He had stood for a long time, staring up at the hugeness of its make-up, cursing it, touching it. It had touched him, also. Beckoned to his heart like no other house had ever done before. He had long believed that a house could possess a personality, a mood, a soul. Maybe take on the qualities of the man who created it. He had never spoken to anyone of this belief, because he knew only too well that there were those who would laugh in his face. But, he did believe in his heart. And, now that he had seen Thornton Place – now that he had communicated with it – he knew beyond all doubt that he was meant to be here, even though the house had denied him access.

Ellie's father had recently suffered niggling doubts about moving far away from familiar surrounds. He had spent many anguished hours kneeling by his tragic wife's grave, talking to her, seeking reassurance, advice, forgiveness. He had found none of these things. Instead, he had grown more afraid and desperate, for himself, for the boy and, most of all, for Ellie. She was so good, so very strong. And she was like her mother. *Too much like her mother*. Sometimes he would look at Ellie and the memories would come flooding back; good memories, of youth and laughter, and of a love so wonderful that he could feel only joy inside himself. Other times, though, he would see Ellie in the half-light of a lamp's soft radiance, when she might glance up unknowingly and catch him watching her; then her lovely smile would pierce his heart, awakening other emotions in him, and filling him with such bitterness that he could almost taste it! *Somewhere, somehow, he had gone badly wrong*. He prayed that some day soon, here in this place, he would know the answer. And be at peace with himself.

'If there's no way into the house, we'll just have to go back to the car . . . wait it out until they get home,' Ellie suggested. In a way, she felt relieved that her father had been unable to get inside. She hated the idea of the couple coming home to find strangers waiting in their front room.

'You're right, Ellie.' Jack Armstrong accepted there was nothing else to do now. 'Back to the car, then.' He led the way down the steps. 'There's a picnic blanket in the boot . . . you and the boy snuggle up under that. Hopefully, it won't be for too long, eh?'

Keeping close in his father's footsteps and clinging tight to Ellie, the boy glanced back to the house. He expected to see the woman again. He was not disappointed. He glimpsed her small, narrow figure silhouetted in the window. For a moment he imagined it was his mother. In his mind's eye he looked at the image that haunted him; she was small and narrow, just the same. He saw the dark crimson substance . . . bathing the other figure. *Smothering it!* And that perfume. Lavender. He knew the name, because his mother had screamed it at him when he innocently brought home the pretty blue flowers given to him by the old pedlar. It was a shame, because they had such a lovely, kind of floating scent. But she *hated* them! She told him never to bring them near her again. And he never did. But, there was something he could not understand. If she hated the perfume so much, then why was she wearing it when he . . . when he . . . found her? Why was she wearing it today in the graveyard? And even now, it was in the air, right here at Thornton Place.

Johnny glanced back once more before the shrubbery closed in around him and hid the figure from sight. Yes. It was still there. Was it really his mother? Now, he could hardly see for the overhanging branches. He looked away. He knew there would be another time. And, curiously, he was not afraid.

CHAPTER THREE

It was a glorious morning. Even before Ellie opened her eyes, she heard the birds singing. The sunlight streaming into the car touched her face, warming her, causing her to blink as she raised her head to look out of the window. A slight groan escaped her as she straightened her back. It had been a long, uncomfortable night.

Glancing at her watch, Ellie saw that it was not yet 6.00 a.m. Careful not to wake Johnny and her father who appeared to be sound asleep, she quietly opened the door and eased her way out of the car. Somewhere from the vicinity of the house the shrill crowing of a cock shattered the stillness. After that, there was only a deep, brooding silence. Ellie looked into the horizon, scanning the green rolling fields that seemed to stretch away endlessly before tumbling down to the lake. She gasped with astonishment at the beauty of the landscape. Last night, in the light of the moon, it had a special magical quality, dark and mysterious. Eerie, even. But now, in the brightness of morning, there was something about this strange land that was far more enchanting. The shifting clouds created trembling shadows across the fields, making them seem alive. And the sunbeams dancing on the water seemed to twinkle a welcome to Ellie. Going on tremulous steps towards the lake, she felt inexplicably drawn there – as though to the arms of a friend.

Suddenly, Ellie was made to stop in her tracks. There

was something, someone, in the spinney! Laughter. She could hear laughter! And furtive whispering. Now the laughter again, like children at play. She listened. No. It was too early in the day for anyone to be loitering in the spinney, she assured herself. It must have been the wind sighing.

The breeze pursued Ellie, ruffling her hair and making the hairs on her skin stand on end.

The ground was more uneven beyond the spinney. Ellie found herself stumbling, yet still she went on. She *had* to.

'Ellie!' Her father's voice came like the crack of a whip through Ellie's pleasant mood. She stopped and turned round, astonished that she had strayed so far from the house. She could see its monumental turrets rising high above the trees. The sight gave her a degree of comfort. Now, her father was rushing towards her. 'What possessed you to go wandering off like that?' he demanded, slowing to a walking pace as he came nearer. Ellie could see that he was angry. She felt the urge to rebel against him. Then, almost immediately, she was ashamed. Whatever was she thinking of? What was the matter with her? She felt strange; as though events were careering out of her control.

'I was worried, Ellie.' Her father was facing her now, his dark blue eyes clouded with anxiety. 'You mustn't go off on your own like that!' he chided her, 'at this hour of a morning . . . in a strange place. How in God's name was I supposed to know where you'd gone?'

'Sorry, Dad.' Ellie thrust her two hands deep into the pockets of her skirt, her voice full of contrition. 'I didn't think . . . and I didn't want to wake you both.'

'Don't do it again, Ellie. Don't *ever* wander off like that . . . at least, not until we know the area . . . and the folks hereabout.' He hated the way he sounded like an over-possessive father, but, somehow, that awful sense of impending doom *still* had not left him. He was being bloody foolish, he told himself. All the same, none of them really knew what they'd let themselves in for here. Until they did, it was wise to be cautious. 'I've been to the house . . . and the cottage. I thought you might have gone there.' He laid his hand on her shoulder and gently propelled her along.

'Is there anyone home yet?' she wanted to know. 'Did you see anyone . . . have you been inside the house?' So many questions. Her apprehension betrayed itself.

'I've neither seen nor spoken to a living soul,' he said, shattering her hopes. 'As soon as I woke and found you gone, I ran to the house and called. When there was no sign of you, I fled to the cottage.' He was still out of breath, and afraid for her. 'Don't stray again,' he warned. 'And as for getting *inside* the house . . .!' He glanced down at her and shrugged his shoulders. 'You saw for yourself that the keys did not fit.'

'Couldn't you smash a window . . . climb in?' Her heart sank when he shook his head. 'Waste of time . . . even if I broke a window . . . threw a brick or something . . . there's still no way I could get up high enough to climb through.' He stretched out his hands in despair. 'I hate to admit it . . . but I'm beat, Ellie. The way I see it, we'll just have to wait for someone to come back to the house. Surely to God they can't have just *left*! They'd be bound to leave a note pinned to the door . . . explaining.' He shook his head again, lapsing into deep thought. After a while he murmured aloud, 'I don't understand! *Why won't the keys fit?*'

'What about the cottage?' Ellie suddenly recalled what her father had told her. 'Perhaps they've moved into the cottage already!' A great sense of relief washed through her.

'Sorry, sweetheart. When I found the cottage just now, there was no sign of life. There's nobody there, I'm afraid . . . and by the looks of the place, it's been empty for some long time.' He paused and slowed his pace, telling Ellie, in a subdued manner, 'Strange . . . that cottage. It's the loveliest place . . . pretty as a picture. But, there's something . . . something . . .' He shook his head slowly.

'What?' Ellie was unbearably curious, yet she knew instinctively what he was going to say. She had already imagined that the cottage would be delightful. After all, Thornton Place was old and full of character. The cottage was probably built around the same time.

'I don't know!' In an instant her father's mood had changed. 'It might be best if we stay away from the cottage altogether. It was made clear enough by the owners of this place that the cottage was not part of the contract. Besides . . . if the previous caretakers are moving in there, they certainly won't want us prying around!'

For the next few minutes, Ellie walked alongside her father in silence. This was an odd situation, she thought, not at all what she had expected when they set out. Here they were, almost two hundred miles away from all that was familiar, all that they had given up . . . could not go back to, even if they wanted; *which they did not!* There was no one here to greet them. The house was closed against them, and there was no sign whatsoever of the previous caretakers. Besides which, they had been given the wrong keys! And the cottage? That, too . . . empty!

To Ellie's mind, there were two things to be done. Firstly, they had to have shelter until they could gain access to the house. That meant they must move into the cottage themselves; unload the car of their personal possessions and take advantage of whatever comfort was on offer. And, so far as Ellie could see, it had to be the cottage! A thought suddenly occurred to her. Then another, and another. What about food? And bed linen? Did the cottage have electricity? No doubt it had a fireplace, and there were more than enough fallen branches about to kindle up a cosy fire when the evening drew on. It wouldn't be too bad; she was a good home-maker, even if she did say so herself. Her spirits lightened, and she actually found herself looking forward to the challenge. Besides, she reminded herself, it would prob-ably only be for one night, because somebody was *bound* to turn up at the house. At the most it would not be more than a couple of days. That was her second plan of action. Her father would have to contact the owners and explain the circumstances. Their telephone number would be on the letterhead. In no time at all they would send a representative with the proper keys to the house. It was all a matter of time, and patience. There was nothing to worry about. Nothing at all!

Ellie had not realised that her father had strode away in front. She chased after him, thinking he would not be so worried when she suggested their course of action. Yet, she was surprised that he himself had not come up with the solution. As a rule, he was level-headed and quick-thinking. But then, he had been through so much, she reminded herself. No wonder he wasn't thinking clearly. Now, she was full of purpose, pressing down the initial upset and disappointment they had experienced on arriv-ing here. It would all come right. *It must!* She recalled the estate which they had passed through. It couldn't have been more than two miles back along the track . . . three at the most. There was a club there, so there must also be a telephone, and a shop. Her mind's eye roved back to the previous evening; to the first man who had pointed the way; to the rows of houses and the lamp-lit streets; to the dark-eyed stranger who had spoken to her. Her heart leapt at the memory. The dark-eyed stranger! How defined was his image in her memory. Tall enough to gaze down on her, but not so tall that she felt insignificant beside him.

Suddenly, Ellie was not running after her father.

Instead, she had slowed to a strolling pace, all of her thoughts intent on the stranger; on the intimate way in which he had looked on her. His dark brooding eyes that made her tremble inside. And the voice that seemed to open her heart like a pervading spirit. He was there now, touching her mind and awakening her senses until a great longing was created in her; a desperate longing to see him. The prospect sent a delicious frisson of pleasure through her being. *And it frightened her!*

'Where's the boy?' Once more her father's angry voice shattered Ellie's thoughts. It occurred to her that he was angry most of the time, since coming to this place. Quickly now, she ran to where he was standing, impatiently banging his clenched fist on the car roof. 'I told him to stay put!' he snapped, glancing into the vacant back seat, then casting his narrowed eyes all about in every direction. 'Damn and bugger it! . . . Can *neither* of you use your commonsense?' Catching sight of Ellie's reproachful look, he clicked his tongue behind his teeth and dropped his head as though in shame. 'Sorry, Ellie . . . I didn't mean to sound off at you like that,' he apologised, 'it's just that . . . suddenly it's all going wrong!'

Ellie half smiled, reaching up to kiss him. 'I know,' she said softly, 'I know. But, it isn't "all going wrong" . . . it's just a small setback. You'll see . . . we'll be ship-shape and organised in no time at all.'

'You're an angel. What would I do without you, eh?' He smiled also, and Ellie was relieved to see him more relaxed.

'First of all we'll find Johnny, then I'll tell you what I think we should do,' she suggested, hoping her father didn't take offence. Normally, he took a healthy, manly pride in being in charge.

'First things first, eh?' He actually laughed. 'Quite right, too.' Now he was pointing towards the spinney. 'I'll search the woods . . . and the cottage, one more time. You look around the house.' As they parted, he added a warning. 'Just the house! Don't go wandering off.'

'I won't,' Ellie promised, chuckling to herself when she heard his mutterings – 'I'll kick his bloody arse when I get hold of him!' She knew he would do no such thing, though he would no doubt give Johnny the length of his tongue when they did find him. All in all, Ellie could not blame her father for being angry – Johnny should have 'stayed put'. She also might have given vent to anger at the boy, if she hadn't blamed herself for going off, so that her father had felt obliged to come after her. It was she who ought to have 'stayed put' she realised, then none of this would have happened.

Coming into the clearing at the front of the house, Ellie caught sight of her brother almost at once. She opened her mouth to call him; to chastise him. But a deeper instinct stopped her! Her voice whispered low, 'What's he doing?' She went forward on silent feet, but she did not know why. Only that he must not see her. She came softly towards the side of the house, her eyes fixed on that small, solitary figure. It stood quite still, drawn up taut with its hands stiffly to its sides, and its head tilted back, face impassive and staring in the same direction, intent. As though listening to someone. In a moment, Ellie was on him! 'Johnny?' Remaining motionless, he appeared not to have heard. '. . . what are you doing?' His eyes were turned upwards, transfixed. Ellie's heart shivered as she made her gaze follow his. The window. High in the wall. Nothing. No one. Ellie grabbed the small, stiff shoulders, gently shaking them. 'Tell me what you saw,' she urged; quietly though, lest she scared him.

'We have to leave this place.' His voice was strangely hollow, his gaze remained on the window, expressionless.

'Who told you that, Johnny?' Out of the corner of her eye she saw her father approaching. Her voice was desperate now. She shook him harder. His gaze swung to her face; a flicker of recognition. 'Johnny! . . . *Who told you that we must leave this place? . . .* Someone up there? At the window . . . was there someone at the window?' She glanced up quickly, slyly, hoping to see a furtive figure, a peeping face. But there was none. No movement, no sound. The curtains hung still and tattered. The grime was impenetrable.

'What the hell d'you mean by disobeying me, eh? . . . Didn't I tell you to stay in the car?' Ellie felt the boy snatched from her grasp. 'Come on! We've wasted enough time . . . we're going back where the other houses are! Surely to God somebody must know where these people have gone.' He was gripping the boy's hand, marching him along; unaware of the small face that was white as chalk, and the vivid blue eyes that crumpled with pain.

'Wait a minute, Dad!' Ellie yelled, struggling to keep pace. She had to tell him. Johnny started crying; softly at first. Then loudly, the sobs racking his body. 'Stop a minute . . . Johnny saw somebody at the window!' Ellie was frantic. 'Somebody *spoke* to him, I tell you!' She stumbled and cried out; at once steadying herself when she saw her father stop and turn. She realised with a shock that he was like a thing possessed. What was happening to him? *To all of them?*

'What's that you say?' He gripped the boy's hand harder, shaking it viciously. 'For Christ's sake . . . stop that bawling!'

Her words tumbling one over the other, Ellie described what she had seen, afterwards repeating what the boy had told her. ' "We have to leave this place" . . . there was someone there . . . talking to him, I'm sure of it.'

For a moment, Ellie thought he believed her, but, in the next, he was swinging his son round to face him, demanding, 'Is that the truth? *Is it?* Somebody "talking to you"?' The boy shrank from him. 'Answer me! . . . was there somebody "talking to you"?' Ellie knew the moment was lost, because her father was not asking a question. He was issuing a threat!

'I never saw anybody! There was nobody "talking" to me.' The boy was defiant. His stance defensive. Ellie was not surprised.

'Then why did you lie, eh?' He glared at the boy. 'Don't you think we're in enough trouble without you dreaming up such tales?' He waited for an answer. When none came, he leaned down towards the boy, his face set like stone. Through gritted teeth he insisted, 'I asked you a question. *Answer me* . . . why did you lie?'

A voice, low and resonant, issued from the spinney close by. 'He did not lie.'

All eyes turned towards the approaching figure. It was the dark-eyed stranger. Ellie and her father exchanged astonished glances. Her father was clearly embarrassed, but, straightening to his full height and looking the young man boldly in the face, he asked, 'Are you saying there *is* someone in the house?'

'That's what I'm saying, Mr Armstrong.' He half smiled when Ellie's father bristled at the mention of his name. Coming forward, he extended his arm in greeting. 'My name's Alec Harman.' Gripping the other man's hand he shook it just once; a firm, strong handshake. 'I work for Wentworth Estates . . . they own thousands of acres round here.' He gestured widely towards the horizon. 'It's my job to patrol their land . . . keep an eye out for trespassers and the like.'

'Gamekeeper, eh?' Jack Armstrong eyed the cocked shotgun in the crook of Harman's elbow.

'No. We do have gamekeepers, though. My job is to protect the land itself.' He half turned to look on Ellie's upturned face. At once she was aware of how tired and dishevelled she must look – her skirt creased and smudged, and her blouse torn by the sharp thorny shrubs the night before. She saw how incredibly handsome he was. She watched the moist fullness of his mouth as it curled into a smile, showing the even whiteness of his teeth. Beneath the lamplight last evening, he had seemed like no other man she had ever known; magnificent to look on, arrogant and fascinating. Now, in the morning light, with the sun glistening in his rich black hair, and the dark persuasion vibrant in his eyes, he was even more captivating. A flush of pleasure welled up in her, suffusing her face with a soft pink glow. She had to look away, *or be lost for ever*. A moment later, she heard Alec Harman address her father. 'Many acres of land are employed in the production of spruce trees ... Christmas harvest. They're very valuable, and the thieves never give up. You'd be surprised at the lengths they'll go to. We have extensive nurseries ... lakes manually stocked for fish breeding, and various other enterprises underway. Technically speaking, none of the land is farmed. It's a huge area to patrol, but, like I say ... we have two excellent gamekeepers. *My* prime concern is the timber.' He reached forward to touch the boy's unruly shock of brown hair, twisting it round his fingers, ruffling it. When the boy bent his head in a swift, impatient movement, he drew his hand away, lifting it to indicate the house. 'Thornton Place was part of Wentworth Estates for many years ... until three years ago, when it was sold to a private company. I took on this job round about the same time.' He pressed his lips tight together, inclining his head to one side and with his voice tinged with regret he said, 'Such a beautiful house ... such history! I only wish I could have raised the money to buy it.' His smile was sad. *Secretive*. 'But then I probably would never have been able to restore it to its former glory. That would take a man skilled and practised in such work.'

'Why won't they let us in?' Jack Armstrong delved

deep into his jacket pocket to withdraw the bunch of keys. He handed them to the other man. '*Useless!*' he snapped, 'every one of them. I can't understand it.'

Turning the keys over and over in the palm of his hand, Alec Harman made no comment. In a moment, he clenched them tight in his fist, his jaw working in anger and a thoughtful look in his eyes. '*Strange*,' he murmured, looking towards the house. Suddenly his smile returned. 'Keep the keys safe,' he said, pressing them into Jack Armstrong's fingers, 'you never know.' He glanced first at the boy, and then at Ellie, who had followed his every word, watched his every movement. 'I think it's time to meet your predecessors . . . time to introduce yourselves and take up your rightful place in the house.' He beckoned them to follow him. They did. Only the boy seemed reluctant.

'I suppose they're not to be blamed for refusing to let us in.' Jack Armstrong gently but firmly pushed the boy in front of him. 'I don't expect I'll be any different when *my* turn comes to be pensioned off.' His remarks were met with stony silence. Undeterred, he persisted, 'Been caretakers here long, have they?'

'Not too long.'

'Don't want to move into the cottage . . . is that it?'

'Part of it.'

'But they have to move out!' He didn't know why exactly, but he suddenly felt threatened. *Afraid!*

They were at the foot of the steps when Alec Harman turned at the other man's last remark. He said nothing. But his glance was cold. Jack Armstrong met the dark eyes with a challenging stare. For a split second, the tension between them was unbearable.

Ellie quickly sensed the uncomfortable atmosphere and stepped forward. 'We don't want to cause any distress to the old couple,' she said quietly, 'but . . . well, you do understand. My father has been appointed caretaker now. It was made very clear that alternative provisions had

51

been made for the previous occupants.'

'Of course . . . I do understand.' His smile enveloped her. Ellie suspected he did not 'understand' at all. She had a mind to press him further, but she let the moment pass when he added, 'And, of course, it really has nothing to do with me.'

'But you do *know* these people?'

'Only by way of odd-jobbing for them . . . splitting logs . . . clearing the gutters . . . doing what I can to help out. All in my own spare time,' he assured her. He drew his gaze from Ellie and fixed it on her father's anxious face. 'They're not able to keep up with it all,' he explained, 'it would take an army of able-bodied men to cope here. The work is never-ending.'

'We'll manage,' Jack Armstrong retorted. He had taken a deep dislike to the young man, though he did not know quite why. Was it the fellow's arrogant, secretive manner? he thought. Or was it that he was too capable, too sure of himself . . . *too downright attractive to Ellie*? Oh, he had seen the signals between them. What was the name they had for an attraction like that between two people? *Chemistry*. That was it! He had felt the 'chemistry' between them; he had seen it last evening when she lingered with the stranger beneath the lamplight. It worried him. Suddenly, he wished Barny Tyler was here. Barny was not the ideal person for Ellie; he himself had said that the first time she had brought the young man home; but, by God, he'd sooner have Barny Tyler giving her the glad eye any day of the week, than this black-eyed satan!

'You might as well open this door! We're not moving until you do.' Jack Armstrong raised the knocker, fetching it down again and again into the metal base. The ensuing din echoed through the air, sending up a flight of birds from the spinney close by.

Suddenly, there was pandemonium! From the other side of the door could be heard an uproar as determined as the one without; the door trembled beneath the onslaught. Then a voice – a shrill, piercing voice – calling out, *'Go away!'* There followed a burst of laughter, then a scream. 'You won't get in . . . I'll never let you get in. I know who you are. *I know who you are.* Devil . . . Devil!' Protesting loudly through the letterbox that he was no 'devil' but the new caretaker, Jack Armstrong was left in no doubt that he was not welcome here. He despaired of ever persuading the occupants to admit them. 'There's nothing left but for me to involve the authorities,' he said now, turning to Ellie with a weary expression. 'God almighty . . . I'm beginning to wonder if we should ever have come here at all!'

Up until now, Alec Harman had kept his distance, giving in to the other man's demands to 'let *me* talk to them . . . I'm sure I can convince them that the best thing for all of us is for them to move into the cottage. When it comes right down to it, they've no other choice!' Now, however, the younger man positioned himself in front of the door. 'All you've done is frighten them,' he said in an accusing voice. 'I know how tired you must be . . . and how frustrated. But you won't win them over by yelling and creating a din. They will feel *more* threatened . . . *more* convinced that they should barricade themselves in.'

'Then we'll have to let the law deal with it.'

'No.' He turned his dark gaze on Ellie. 'Please . . . give me a little time. Let me reassure them.'

'Ellie . . . Ellie.' The small voice took her attention from the young man. She glanced down. The boy. Of course. She held his hand and raised her eyes to the dark, intense gaze.

'Do what you can,' she said simply. He smiled and nodded his head. Now, Ellie was asking her father, 'Leave him a while. You and me . . . we'll take Johnny and explore the grounds.' When the boy began making muffled sounds, she hurried him away.

★ ★ ★

The pump was archaic and rusted, but to Ellie the water tumbling from it was sheer luxury. Johnny had run on ahead, shrieking with relief when he came across the dark-red building situated on the perimeter of what might once have been a very pleasant courtyard. Inside the long, narrow building was a blackened coal-hole, still containing a spill of shiny black pieces, and beside it a tiny washroom, with white porcelain pan and hand basin. A dry, musky dampness lingered in the air. The only window was situated at the rear of the washroom, its small, square panes shattered yet trapped between a layer of fine, rusted mesh. The tap in the hand basin was jammed tight.

All three took turns in using the washroom; the boy first, then Ellie, and her father last of all. After splashing her hands and face in the tumble of water from the old pump, Ellie instructed the boy to do the same; though reluctant, he did as he was told, following Ellie's example and using the hem of her skirt with which to dry himself.

'I'm hungry.' The boy stared at Ellie. Blaming her.

'You're not the only one, Johnny,' she reminded him. A glance at her wrist watch showed it was only a few minutes before eight o'clock. 'Once we know what's happening at the house, we can begin to make plans,' she told him. 'There must be a shop on the estate. Later . . . we might have to make our way to a telephone there to contact the owners of this place, or, and I hope this will be the case, to buy in groceries and such like. Until then, you'll just have to be patient like the rest of us.' When he began glaring at her from scowling eyebrows, Ellie impatiently shook her head and came to her father's side. He also was scowling – angry with himself for having mislaid the letter of appointment. Without that, the previous caretaker could refuse to acknowledge his right to be there. On top of which, without their cooperation, he had no telephone number, or point of contact with the owners. Unless of course that Harman fellow could help out. Failing that, he would have to telephone the newspaper office . . . *The Chronicle* . . . where the advert appeared. Having recalled the newspaper in which he had seen the advert, he was pleased with himself. But that was before he remembered that there had been no telephone number – only a box address via the newspaper. It was highly unlikely that they would give out the private address . . . especially to someone over the telephone! It was no good. He would have to confess to Ellie that he had lost that damned letter.

As she came nearer, Ellie saw her father waiting. He was obviously agitated. She got the feeling that he was about to confide something to her. 'What is it, Dad?' she asked as he began walking towards her. 'Is something wrong?'

'Ellie . . .' he started. But then, the sound of breaking twigs heralded someone's approach; another voice cut across his own.

'Mr Armstrong.' It was Alec Harman, coming to them on easy, almost casual footsteps. In a moment he was standing before them, the shotgun languishing loosely over one arm, with its long, thick shaft supported by the fingers of his other hand. For one excited heartbeat, Ellie thought he was about to shoot them. His dark smile reached deep inside her. When he spoke, it was to her father. 'I can't linger here. I've done all I can.'

Jack Armstrong moaned softly, nodding his head as though in agreement. 'They won't listen, eh? . . . I *said* I should bring in the law!'

'No need for that.' Alec Harman dropped the shotgun neatly into the bend of his arm, and thrust his free hand into the depths of his jacket pocket. He visibly shivered as a gusting breeze rippled over the land. 'Go to the house. I've explained . . . it's all right.'

'They'll let us in?'

He nodded, glancing briefly at Ellie before turning away. 'The old one is called George. The other called Rosie . . . be patient with them.' He paused and turned, flashing a warning look in their direction. 'Don't frighten them,' he warned softly. Soon he was gone from sight; the sound of his footsteps crunching the undergrowth grew dimmer and more distant, until they too were gone.

'I hope the fellow knows what he's talking about,' grumbled Ellie's father as he went towards the house, 'he's a strange one, and no mistake.'

Ellie made no comment. Instead, she followed the purposeful figure ahead, taking the boy with her and pleasantly meandering in thoughts of the young man whom her father had called 'a strange one'. There was no denying that he was 'strange'. But to her the 'strange' meant *exciting*! It meant darkly handsome, and deeply stirring. She found it impossible to untangle him from her senses. As she and the boy mounted the steps to the front entrance, Ellie hoped above all else that she would see 'the strange one' again.

'Are we going to die here?'

'What?' Jack Armstrong swung round at the very moment he raised the knocker. It clattered to the base with an odd, muted sound. 'What the hell did you say?' He glowered at the boy, who met his startled eyes for a split second before setting his features sternly and deliberately looking away.

'It's all right, Dad.' Ellie also had been struck rigid by the boy's remark. Yet, she still recalled the doctor's warning – 'The boy's nerves are shredded. Give him time.' Suppressing her own apprehension she reached up to touch her father's arm. 'Don't worry.' She surreptitiously shook her head and made an expression that cautioned the irate man. Reluctantly he drew himself round, this time bending to the letterbox and quietly opening it.

'George!' His voice echoed from within. 'I'm not here to threaten you . . . Alec Harman has told you that much, I know. I just want to talk . . . get things straight between us. I've got my two children here with me and we're all tired and hungry. Open the door . . . there's a good fellow.' He waited for what seemed an endless time, until his fingers were cramped from holding open the letter-box, and his back felt like it was breaking in two. Still, there was no sound from within. No response, or even the slightest sign of life. Presently, he straightened up. 'What next?' he muttered, looking round to Ellie and saying again, 'what next, Ellie?' This time he was not angry, nor was he frustrated. The faceless ones had won. Disappointment darkened his eyes.

'Don't be defeated,' Ellie told him, leaving the boy and joining her father at the door. 'You heard what Alec Harman said . . . "Go to the house," he said . . . "be patient".'

'That's all very well. But, he should have waited. He *knows* these people . . . he must be able to reason with them.' He raised both his arms high into the air in a gesture of surrender, afterwards crashing his hands to his head and groaning aloud as he ran his outstretched fingers through his hair. 'That's it!' he said. He started down the steps. 'You two stay here. Don't wander from this spot. I'm going to the estate . . . got to 'phone . . . somebody's got to get that bloody door open!' The anger had returned. Ellie despaired. Suddenly, there was movement behind the door.

'Wait . . . Dad!' Ellie's cry stopped him in his tracks. Slowly, disbelieving, he made his way back. Yes! It was opening. The door was opening. He gestured for Ellie to step away. She did, but only a small pace. She glanced down at the boy, thinking he might be afraid. He was not. His bright blue eyes stared back, intense, unnerving. Now, he was coming up to the door.

'Must we go inside, Ellie?' he asked, sliding his fingers in hers, and waiting, like the others, for the house to reveal its secrets.

'Ssh.' Ellie was astonished to find her heart fluttering uncontrollably. 'It'll be all right now . . . you'll see.'

She did not hear his returning whisper, *'They'll kill us, Ellie . . . they will.'*

Now, her father was tempting the occupant to show himself. 'Nobody here wants to hurt you, George . . . we're only here to do a job, you know that. We have to talk. We need to get this thing sorted out . . . Alec Harman did tell you who I am, didn't he?' The door inched open when he mentioned the young man's name. 'I'm the new caretaker . . . Jack Armstrong. You must have had instructions about me?'

When the door was opened wide, it was to send out a stench so bad, so shockingly evil that both Ellie and her father momentarily turned away. 'I know . . . who you are.' The voice was only a whisper, its owner remaining hidden behind the door. 'The darkeye told me. He said I had to let you in.' A pause, then a soft rush of laughter before the voice went on in that same forceful whisper, 'He won't punish me though. He doesn't know . . . I didn't tell him what I've done.' Again the furtive laughter. The door began to close.

'No! Wait, George.' Ellie sprang forward, touching the door with her shoulder, and softly pleading into the black interior, 'We *have* to come in . . . you said yourself that the "darkeye" told you to let us in.' She wondered whether Alec Harman and the 'darkeye' were one and the same. 'We *can* come in, can't we?' She could hear the other person breathing; feel the trembling on the other side of the door. Fearful, she moved her eyes to see her father watching, confused and apprehensive. She sensed the boy's keen, glittering eyes on her. He would be fine, she promised herself, once they were accepted. Once they were accepted. Strange, she thought, had she really meant that . . .?

'Maybe I *will* let you in.' The whisper was closer now. In the gloom, the claw-like hand reached out, gripping Ellie's forearm. Now it was she who was trembling. But, suddenly, she was not afraid. Only sad, and relieved, and *curious*. The whisper became a frantic hiss, 'Only . . . you mustn't tell him what I did.'

'We won't tell,' Ellie promised. She did not imagine for one minute that the old man had done anything so terrible that Alec Harman would want to punish him. To her mind the old fellow was just afraid of strangers. Cautious and, perhaps, a little batty. Her own thought shamed her.

Now, when the owner of the voice manifested itself, Ellie was riveted with shock. Here before her was a hideous form, bent and decrepit, a shapeless being with ungainly features and wearing what appeared to be a dark, loose shift about its form. The crooked, claw-like fingers were clasped tightly round the two edges of a coarse blanket. Drawing it together over his back and shoulders, he looked at Ellie with pale shifty eyes, all the while fidgeting from one foot to the other and creating little bursts of sound from the back of his throat. After suspiciously eyeing the man, then the boy – who did not flinch beneath his scrutiny – he feverishly nodded his head and chuckled. It was an unpleasant sound.

Ellie was the first to recover. 'George . . . can we come in and talk to you? You and . . . Rosie?'

The pale eyes grew wide as they seized on Ellie's face. 'Rosie!' Laughter again, then a disturbing span of silence, before, 'Rosie's been bad!' The pale eyes shrank to slits in a deep frown. There was instant fear, and suspicion. He pushed at Ellie with surprisingly strong hands, the blanket slithering from his shoulders to the floor. '*Can't come in!*' he croaked. 'You will tell . . . I know you will!' When the door began closing, Ellie felt herself snatched away when Jack Armstrong leaped forward, frantic to stop the old man from slamming shut the door against them. He saw the aged face leering at him; then the pale eyes, looking beyond. At once they became softer, afraid even. He was speaking to someone. 'They told you . . . didn't they?' Tears tumbled from the pale eyes and ran down into the toothless, gaping mouth. '. . . wouldn't listen, you see . . . I was afraid. Don't punish me. *Please* . . . don't punish me.'

'It's all right. I won't punish you. Nobody will ever punish you, I promise.' Alec Harman tenderly took the cringing figure into his arms, all the while soothing, pacifying the unfortunate creature; reassuring him as one might reassure a child. Together they went deeper into the house.

The bedraggled procession went slowly along the gloomy, narrow passage, each purposeful figure occupied with its own thoughts, its own fears. The young man with the dark, silent eyes kept his gaze ahead; he knew why the recluse beside him was afraid of being punished. Or, at least, he suspected. If he had not been so preoccupied earlier with the girl's fascination for him and entranced by those splendid amber eyes that stirred him deeply, he might have realised that there had been mischief made in this house. But, he had *not* realised. And now, he only prayed it was not too late! He could feel the wizened, bent figure trembling beneath his touch. Just for a second he slowed his steps to turn and glance on it. The old man swivelled his pale eyes up to peer into the other one's face and, seeing the condemnation there, he hurriedly looked away. He knew the darkeye had guessed. He also knew he would not be punished this time, because the darkeye always kept his promise. He wasn't sorry, though. Oh no! He had done it for the best, and he would do it again. He wasn't afraid either. It was not his fault if nobody listened.

Suddenly, he was aware of the footsteps following behind, and his whole body stiffened. Strangers. Intruders! Thieves, come to take what was theirs. He knew. He was not fooled. Another thought pierced the hostility in his fevered mind and, for the briefest moment, he relaxed, a small, wild chuckle moving his features. The darkeye had told him to let these people in, and he had done as he was told. But only because he knew that to keep them out would cost him dear. In this place he could watch them closely, the man and the girl. And the boy in particular. He could not be certain, not certain. But, there was something about that one – something about the way he had looked at him. It was the eyes, those shrieking eyes that put him in mind of . . . Oh God above, help me. He shivered inside, trying to shut away that certain look in those staring eyes. Eyes that were too invading, too rich in blueness. When he had looked into that sea of vivid blue, he had seen something there to make him tremble. He had seen the lavender! And now, its scent was all around. *Overpowering.* 'Send them away!' he screamed. 'I don't want them here.' The fear inside collapsed, and he was a child again, hiding from the world. He heard the darkeye's soothing voice and thankfully he leaned into the strength that moved beside him. There was a time when he could not even trust the darkeye, but, that was in the beginning. In the beginning, when he knew the face of the one who tortured him. He knew the face, and all there was to know about the thing that stalked him. But, there had been so much pain, so much fear and running, hiding; *always hiding*. Now, he had forgotten what it was that he was hiding from. There was no face any more. No name. Only the terror. And the smell of lavender. *Lavender*. A small, involuntary cry escaped his lips.

'If you ask me, the old fellow should be locked away.' Jack Armstrong leaned towards Ellie, his voice a soft, astonished whisper in her ear. 'One thing's for certain . . . I've no intention of living under the same roof as that one, not for a minute longer than is necessary. The sooner we get the pair of 'em out of this house and into the cottage . . . the better!'

Although she was loath to admit it, her father's words had echoed her own thoughts exactly. It was plain to see that the old man was sick. Very close to insanity. She had compassion for him, it was true, but she had known enough insecurity these past few months, and she had been made to battle with her own demons, as had her father and the boy. This was a new start for them all. A chance to recover and to grow strong. They could not, *would not*, be made to suffer for others! A great sense of outrage welled up in her, as silently she stayed close to the old man and the one he called 'Darkeye'. They must be made to see the way of things. Smiling reassuringly, she looked on the boy's face. It was set like chiselled marble. His cold gaze scoured ahead; his steps were faultless, determined. Strangely disturbed, Ellie looked away, her eyes glancing about the room they had just turned into.

Only now did the boy seem to relax, his aqua-blue eyes roving the place in which they were standing. He had been angered by the old man's cry, 'Send them away . . . I don't want them here.' He had secretly wished that Ellie and his father would heed the old man's words and take him far away from this house . . . from the demented stranger and his hateful looks. Now, he was very tired, and his stomach was growling for food; he wanted to punish the old man for what he had said. He wasn't sure exactly how, but he could bide his time. He felt the warmth of Ellie's hand in his own. Suddenly, he was no longer terrified by the prospect of living in this isolated place, or of staying in this big house that reminded him of a fort he had once made out of sand when they were holidaying in the North. A sense of loss pervaded his senses when he recalled that his mother had helped him to build that fort with her own hands. Now, she was gone and he was here, in this strange place. But, he was not afraid, not now. Nor was he excited or curious. He had resisted from the start; fought every inch of the way, until he had not known what to do next. Now, though, he was merely resigned to it all.

'Are you going to tell me what you've done?' Alec Harman had the old man by the shoulders. In the half-light of the room, his black eyes glistened as they bore down on the face with its lolloping wide-open mouth and the pale, surprised eyes beneath the shaggy brows. When the head shook frantically from side to side, the spittle from inside its wet, pink mouth slewed into the air.

'Can't tell you!' The narrow shoulders slunk downwards, away from the pinching fingers.

Alec Harman sighed, looking into the wizened features a moment longer. The features became cunning, challenging him with a devious smile. 'Shan't tell.'

'Do you want me to go away, then? Do you?' The black eyes were stiff with anger; threatening. 'Do you want me to leave you . . . alone with these people?' . . . He flicked his searing gaze to where Ellie and her father stood. The boy was half-hidden behind them. Ellie's surprised gaze encountered the dark fury in his glance; it set something alight inside her.

'*What's that?*' Ellie was the first to hear it. From somewhere deep in the bowels of the house emitted a constant dull sound, rhythmic and insistent – like the beating of a heart, she thought with astonishment. The astonishment careered through her when she saw how the sound had affected the old man. He tore himself from the young man's clutches.

'*You said you wouldn't punish me!*' he yelled, the fear

bouncing in his eyes as he backed away. Suddenly, he was scuttling across the room, shrieking and crying all at once. The young man followed him.

'Jesus, Mary and Joseph!' Ellie felt her father's hand grip her shoulder. 'What the hell is that noise?' There it was again, drumming into the air, seeming to echo all round them. In between each pulse, the span of silence was unbearable.

Before Alec Harman pursued the old man from the room, he turned briefly at the panelled door some short way from the huge fireplace. 'I must go after him,' he explained, bestowing his warmest smile on Ellie. 'You'll find the kitchen back that way.' He inclined his dark head in the same direction from which they had come. 'Third door to your left along the passage.' He glanced knowingly at the boy. Now, he was addressing Ellie again. 'You must be hungry . . . thirsty. There is food in the kitchen. Help yourself. Afterwards, make yourselves comfortable here.' Ellie was surprised when the timbre of his voice changed; he was suddenly afraid. 'I must find him,' he murmured, 'or there's no telling what he might do.'

'He was right about one thing,' Jack Armstrong told Ellie. 'I, for one, am famished.' He stretched himself, took a deep breath, and immediately wrinkled his nose in disgust. 'This whole place stinks to high heaven!' he moaned, striding across the room and reaching up to the curtains that were drawn over the long narrow window, shutting out the light of day, rendering the room dim and forbidding. Clutching the edge of each curtain he yanked them back amidst a shower of dust and fabric particles. At once the morning sun tumbled in through the grey, grimy window panes, filling every hitherto dark corner of the room with warm, brilliant sunshine.

'It's lovely!' The transformation was incredible. In spite of the heavy, ornate furniture with its deep panels, fussy alcoves and formidable appearance – every piece coated in thick, layered dust – Ellie thought the room was the most beautiful she had ever seen. It was immense. On the far side was the panelled door through which Alec Harman and the old man had disappeared; the remaining, considerable length of that particular wall was taken up with a magnificent open fireplace measuring some fourteen feet across with the ornate, decorated mantelpiece sweeping up into a back dresser that covered the upper wall and touched the ceiling above. Carved and fluted columns flanked either side of the firehearth, and the interior of the entire structure was so cavernous that a small family could have dwelt in it. There were two windows, both of which were built into the wall on Ellie's left. The windows were long and graceful but, like everything else in sight, were badly neglected and crying out for love. The wall opposite was finished in the same rich wood panels that encircled the whole room, but, on this wall, were hung many paintings. Ellie thought them to be deeply enchanting yet, by the same token, strangely forbidding. The paintings were of various shapes and sizes; twelve in all. Some were depicted in gilt cameo frames, and some encased in oblongs of purple velvet; others were housed in extravagant black frames with silver edging, and the largest of them all was hung centrally in a stark, blackwood frame some six feet long and four feet wide. Ellie found herself inexplicably drawn to the paintings.

For a long, eerie moment Ellie gazed up at the paintings, her heart filled with utter delight, yet stilled by a feeling she could not understand; a feeling of dread. A feeling that she had seen these paintings somewhere before! Yet she knew she had not, for the subject of these paintings was so incredibly beautiful that a body could *never* forget them. There was something unique about them. They had an essence that was disturbingly spiritual and timeless. *Every one of the paintings depicted the same woman*. She was sometimes smiling, sometimes sad. Here, she was mysterious, there she was enchanting. Pensive. Beckoning. And in every one, she was ethereal in her beauty. Ellie could not tear herself away. There was a magnetism there, calling and holding her. Eagerly, her gaze drank in the details; the corn-coloured hair that spilled over the milk-white shoulders, the bright, laughing brown eyes that would not let go, and the features, so exquisite, so unreal yet so alive that at any moment a body might actually hear her laughing.

'She's so . . . bewitching,' Ellie murmured, 'like someone you feel you know . . . or have seen at some time, somewhere.'

'Huh.' Jack Armstrong had also been looking at the paintings. 'A good painting is supposed to make you feel like that . . . or so they say. Yes . . . she certainly has . . . *something*.' He gazed a moment longer, before deciding that he did not particularly like the woman in the painting. At first glance it looked as though her eyes were twinkling with laughter. Under closer scrutiny he decided that the eyes were hard, the 'twinkle' was more like the glitter of marble, or ice; or *death*. No! He must not let himself slide back into the nightmare.

'She looks like you, Ellie.' The boy's voice cut into the air like a knife.

'Nonsense!' Jack Armstrong glanced nervously from the paintings to the boy, then back again. 'Absolute nonsense. The woman in the paintings looks nothing at all like Ellie.' He pointed to the various dresses that the subject was wearing; regal they were, and of the eighteenth century. The lady was also adorned with precious and exquisite-looking gems. In every painting she held a spray of flowers, so tiny and coveted that it was impossible to identify them. But, in each case, the flowers were a deep, vivid blue colour. She was pressing them close to her heart, cherishing them like a mother might cherish a newborn.

Ellie gazed a while longer. She was intrigued, wondering why anyone would want to paint the same subject so many times. She said as much to her father now. His remark set her thinking. 'Only someone who was besotted would do such a thing,' he said scornfully. Ellie gave no answer. She felt sad that her father had grown so hard, so cynical, when the memories of how he had loved her mother were so alive inside her.

Reluctantly she tore her gaze from the woman in the paintings. Her father was right, though. 'Someone . . . besotted.' It was true. The paintings were magnificent, alive and vibrant, as though the artist had poured his soul into them. The passion emanated from every stroke of his brush. So much passion. The kind that fuels a powerful love, *or a powerful hate*! Ellie shivered and hugged herself. In spite of the warm sunshine flooding the room, she was cold in every corner of her being.

Seeing how Ellie had trembled, her father explained, 'These big old houses are draughty . . . need a lot of heating.'

'I'm hungry!' Johnny was fidgeting from one foot to the other. He had watched the others perusing the paintings, and it had irritated him. He saw nothing unusual or magnificent about the woman there; only what he had said: *that the woman had a look of Ellie*. The same colour hair and eyes. Something else, too. Only he wasn't certain about that. Not yet. He might look at the paintings again. When there was no one else around. But no! He would *never* look at the paintings again. He had seen them this once, and he had seen Ellie in them. No one believed him. No matter. It would not change anything.

For a house of such great size, the kitchen was surprisingly small. 'Not much bigger than the one back home,' Ellie had remarked. The remark brought back memories and with them came a rush of pain and regret.

'It's usually the way,' her father said, moving his gaze about the room; a long, narrow place with high ceilings and big wooden cupboards placed here and there. The floor was cold, uneven stone, and the sink by the window was a huge square thing, its dirty white surface eaten with myriads of fine, meandering cracks. The window was small and facing the barn wall; consequently the kitchen was dark in comparison to the room they had just left. From the centre of the ceiling hung a solitary bulb, the incoming draughts causing it to swing gently back and forth on the brown, twisted flex. 'In the days when this place was built, the gentry were not concerned with staff quarters or kitchens . . . only with their own creature comforts,' he added, absent-mindedly opening cupboard doors and peering in. He paused to glance at Ellie, who was stooping to look beneath the sink. 'There's barely enough food here to stop a baby from starving!' He thrust his hand into the cupboard and withdrew a huge platter; on it was a small cooked bird, pale in colour. Stuck to the congealed rivulets of juice were a few dark plumes. 'Fowl . . . pheasant, I shouldn't wonder,' Jack Armstrong declared, setting the platter onto the square oak table against the wall. 'I expect it came from the forest on the estate.' He chuckled, 'The gamekeepers chase off the poachers from outside and, like as not, the worst ones are right under their noses.' He glanced at the door. 'No doubt that Harman fellow keeps his "friends" well supplied.'

'Don't make rash judgements,' Ellie told him. She had sensed his dislike of the young man, and she was instantly defensive.

'Hey!' Her father had seen that look in Ellie's eyes before. 'And don't you go getting ideas regarding that one!' he warned, cursing himself for putting the fellow down. It was a sure way to make Ellie jump to Harman's defence.

Ignoring his warning, Ellie rose from her half-bent

position and, pointing to the underbelly of the sink, she said, 'It smells bad down there . . . like something crawled behind the pipes and died.'

'Here . . . let me take a look.' He lost no time in getting to his knees and examining the area beneath and behind the sink. At first, he reeled back; Ellie was right. The smell was rancid. A thorough investigation revealed only the ancient pipes, corroded with rust, but nevertheless intact. 'Nothing here, sweetheart,' he told her, clambering to his feet, 'the plumbing is ancient, though . . . the entire system needs updating, I expect. All in good time . . . all in good time.'

The cupboards were found to be empty, except for the platter of meat, half a loaf and a basin of margarine. There was nothing to drink. Even the tap refused to part with a single drop of water. 'Not to worry, folks . . . once I'm let loose in the place, I'll soon have it ship-shape.' Jack Armstrong eagerly tucked into the meal Ellie prepared – a few slices of bread, dressed with a helping of the succulent meat. The food was divided equally, half for them and half for the old ones. The meal was sparse, but it was enough to revive all their flagging spirits. Afterwards, Ellie recruited the boy to tidy up the dishes and pile them neatly on the draining-board. 'I'll wash up later,' she said, suddenly remembering the outside pump near the wash-house. She toyed with the idea of taking a pan out to fill, but thought better of it. For now – like her father and Johnny – she would rather not leave the house, in case the doors were bolted against them for ever. The thought was disturbing. But, not so disturbing as being locked inside with the demented George. She wondered whether the wife was just as batty. At once, she chided herself for such uncharitable thoughts.

It was only a matter of fifteen minutes or so before the three of them returned to the big room. Ellie was the first to come into the room, and almost at once there was a scuffling and the sound of raised voices coming from the door near the fireplace.

'They're back!' Jack Armstrong grabbed his children and quickly ushered them to the long wooden settle. 'Mind your tongue!' he warned the boy, who was glowering at the door with a look of defiance. The scuffling intensified. Suddenly, the door burst open to admit a woman of about seventy years. 'He's a bugger!' she laughed, coming forward at a strange, hopping gait and swinging her two crutches along as if they were a natural extension to her capable, big-boned body. One of her legs was a fine, straight limb, encased in black mesh stocking and wearing a pretty navy-blue shoe with a crossover strap fastening at the ankle. The other leg ended in a thick, shapeless stump some way below the knee; a brown sock had been pulled over it but now it had slipped and hung like a deflated balloon as the stump was whipped back and forth by the urgency of the woman's passage across the room. Behind her, and out of sight, the uproar continued.

'Hello,' she said, flashing a smile that enveloped all three, 'what a shambles, eh?' She laughed aloud. 'What a bloody way to greet the new caretaker! Still . . . it's all right now, eh?' She tucked the left crutch further under her arm, then, leaning her weight onto the good leg and the right crutch, she extended a hand to Jack Armstrong. 'I'm Rosie,' she said warmly, 'I'm told that you're the fella who's going to put this old monstrosity back together again?' She looked around, clicked her tongue and returned her attention to the man. 'You won't do it,' she said simply, 'it's a physical impossibility.' When she realised that her warning was falling on deaf ears, she shrugged, shook his hand vigorously and said, 'Never mind all that for now . . . we'll talk later, eh? No doubt there's a great deal you'll want to know.'

'A *great* deal!' he assured her. Quickly and with pride

he introduced Ellie and the boy. 'These are my children.' He paused, then, 'I'm a widower,' he said, quietly.

Ellie had taken an instant liking to Rosie. Their smiles mingled now, and she thought the woman must be in her seventies, but, in spite of the wrinkles and the severed leg, there was a delightfulness about her, a deep sense of joy and youth, and humour. She put Ellie in mind of a faded Hollywood film star, with her long, grey-streaked peroxide hair swept up in a coil on the top of her head. The thick make-up fell into the crevices of her face, and the crimson lipstick painted a mouth far larger and more sensuous than the thin, narrow lips which Nature had endowed her with. Her teeth appeared too white and even to be real, although when she smiled, her whole attractive face was lit from within. It was her eyes that captivated Ellie. Deepest brown they were; akin to those of the woman in the painting, and, for an old lady, they were stunningly alive. Ellie thought they were Rosie's best feature. Obviously, Rosie thought so too, because she had taken immense care to accentuate their beauty; this was evident in the fine, dark pencil lines that traced right round the almond shapes; the lashes were generously coated with black mascara, and above each lid was a brushing of colour. 'So, you're "Ellie", are you?' Rosie took Ellie's small, slender fingers into her own gnarled hands. 'So lovely,' she murmured, her jubilant mood suddenly subdued, 'so very . . . young.' For a brief second, there were tears in her eyes, but then she visibly shook herself, saying brightly, 'You and me, Ellie . . . I hope we'll be good friends?'

'I hope so, too.' Ellie's response was warm and genuine. She really liked Rosie. In fact, she felt so at ease with her it was almost as though they had known each other for years.

'Good! Good!' She winked boldly before turning her attention to the boy, who was quietly skulking in the corner of the settle. 'My word!' she exclaimed, making an expression to match his own, 'it looks to me like you need cheering up, young man!' She raised the tip of her crutch and prodded his shoe with it. 'There's good fishing in the lake . . . I'll show you the best places, if you like.' She frowned, raising her voice slightly to counter the sounds of the struggle still being enacted out of sight. 'Bloody fool!' she muttered now, slewing round and almost losing her balance when Alec Harman came into the room, urging his reluctant quarry before him.

A few moments later, they were all seated, as Alec Harman – occasionally interrupted by the effervescent Rosie – explained the events of the past two days.

Ellie was not altogether surprised to learn of the deep-seated resentment at her father's appointment here. That, in itself, had been painfully obvious from the moment they had arrived. Apparently, old, senile George had tricked Rosie into the cellar on some pretext or another, then had snatched her crutches and scurried away with them, locking the door behind him. Ever since the owner's representative had called, instructing them of the new caretaker's appointment and telling them that they must move into the cottage straight away, old George had been like a soul tormented. 'The old sod even attacked the poor fellow who brought the message,' Rosie told them, 'scratched him real bad, he did . . . swore he were the devil "come to get me" . . . the bloke weren't frightened though, I'll give him that. He stood his ground and said what he'd come to say . . . albeit it were our bloody marching orders!' She lowered her voice and excitedly tapped her crutch on the bare floorboards. 'George were right about one thing, though . . . that fella were a vindictive sod, and no mistake . . . eyes that smiled straight at you, while his hand were plunging a blade through your heart, if you know what I mean.' She clasped her crutches to her, glared at the boy, and shuddered mischievously, making a ghostly noise. When he stared back at her, she chuckled aloud, while secretly thinking the boy's cold eyes were not all that different from those of the man whom George had attacked.

'So, the sound we heard was Rosie . . . down in the cellar?' Ellie asked, growing more relieved by the minute.

'That's right.' Alec cast an accusing glance at the old man.

'The daft bugger!' Rosie burst out. 'I've a good mind to lock *him* in the cellar . . . see how *he* likes it!'

'That explains why nobody answered the door to us,' interrupted Ellie's father, 'but . . . why didn't the keys fit?' To his consternation, no one had the answer to that.

'You were obviously sent the wrong keys by mistake,' Alec Harman suggested. 'But there is a spare set hanging by the front entrance. You'd better keep them safe.'

'Don't you worry, Mr Armstrong . . . or can I call you Jack?' enquired Rosie with a disarming smile. When he merely returned her smile, she went on. 'Right then . . . Jack, what I was about to say was that me and George here . . . we'll be gone soon – into the cottage.' She cast a cursory glance towards the bent head of the old man. 'Isn't that right, George?' He was slumped in a deep, floral armchair close by, rocking himself back and forth, frantically grabbing little clutches of his grey, wispy hair and making small, unintelligible sounds. He did not look up when Rosie addressed him. Sighing loudly, she turned away. 'Poor George,' she said, travelling her eyes round the gathered group, before bringing her gaze to rest on Ellie. 'You don't know half,' she said, her mood suddenly serious. There was pain in her voice as she went on. 'To look at him . . . you'd think he was older than me, wouldn't you, eh?' She scrutinised Ellie through quizzical brown eyes.

'*Isn't he?*' Ellie could not disguise her surprise. She looked again at the old man, thinking how desolate he seemed. How beaten.

Rosie smiled sadly at Ellie's response. 'No, dearie,' she said, gently shaking her head. 'I'm seventy-two . . . and, it will be another twenty years before George is that old.' She saw the look of astonishment on Ellie's face and heard the gasp that went up from Ellie's father. 'That's right,' she said, addressing herself to Jack Armstrong. 'George is not far past the age of fifty . . . perhaps not many years older than yourself, eh?'

'Not too many,' he conceded, thinking it incredible that there were only some eight years between himself and the pathetic, wizened creature who, even now, was wailing like a lost soul.

He exchanged glances with Ellie; his own surprise was mirrored in her face. In a low voice, she asked of Rosie, 'How did it happen? Has your husband suffered an illness?' She found herself intrigued also by the vast difference in the couple's ages. Twenty years was a long time, and, though it did occur more often where a woman might marry a man who was that much older, it was more unusual for it to be the other way round.

The ensuing silence was uncomfortable. It seemed an age before Rosie chose to answer. When she did, it was to deliver yet another surprise. 'George is not my husband,' she informed the newcomers. Her voice was sharper. She rose instantly from the chair and, tucking the crutches securely beneath her armpits, she turned to the dark-eyed young man. He appeared apprehensive, uncertain. 'I think we've talked enough!' she said, wagging her head in Ellie's direction, yet still speaking to him. 'Have you time to show the girl the route to the estate . . . the shortest route, through the spinney?' She turned her head to look on Ellie, who was flustered by Rosie's abrupt change of mood. 'No doubt you'll want to stock up on food and the like?'

Ellie replied, 'Yes . . . that's a marvellous idea.'

Rosie was pleased. Her smile returned and the tension relaxed. 'Good girl.'

Jack Armstrong could not help but feel the situation was being taken out of his control. 'I don't think that's such a good idea,' he objected. 'I'm sure Mr Harman here has other duties to attend to.'

'None that won't wait,' returned the young man. 'The spinney . . . and the route to the shops, are all part of the area I patrol. I'd be glad to show your daughter the quickest . . . and *safest* . . . path to the estate.' His dark eyes flashed up to meet Rosie's gaze. Ellie had the uncanny feeling that they were silently communicating.

Sensing her father's increasing anxiety, Ellie realised that, if she was to have any measure of freedom whatsoever, then she had to put her foot down from the outset. 'It makes sense,' she told him, 'I can order the provisions we need . . . and you can take stock of the place . . . assess the extent of work here . . . begin to make plans.' She saw the twinkle return to his eyes. 'You said yourself there's so much to be done . . . "can't wait to be let loose" you said. We each have our work cut out, Dad. You get on with yours, and let me get on with mine.' Anger was beginning to bubble up inside her. When would he stop treating her like a child!

'All right. All right!' He clapped his hands to his knees, nodded his head and, with a sharp glance at the young man, he said, 'I'm trusting you, Harman . . . against my better judgement.'

'For heaven's sake, Dad!' Ellie hoped he was not going to embarrass her in front of everyone.

'That's settled, then!' Rosie declared, manoeuvring herself round on her crutches, and addressing Ellie's father. 'You and the boy come with me. I'll take you on a tour of this old mausoleum.' She laughed aloud, a look of conniving in her face. 'Show you what you've let yourself in for!' She raised one crutch and prodded the bowed figure in the chair. 'Are you coming?' she asked impatiently. When there came no reply, she raised her voice. 'I'm taking Jack Armstrong and the boy on a tour of Thornton Place. Are you coming with us?'

'No.' The bent figure made no move, keeping its gaze down to the bare floorboards.

'Please yourself, then,' Rosie retorted, adding, in a softer tone, as she leaned down towards the stooped shoulders, 'I've forgiven you, you know . . . for shutting me in the cellar.'

'Won't punish me?' The voice was like that of a child.

'No. So, are you coming with us?'

'To . . . the cottage?'

'Well, yes, I suppose so. It's all part of Thornton Place.'

'Don't want to!'

'All right, George.' Rosie was exasperated now, and rapidly losing her patience. 'But, you'd better get used to the idea of the cottage, because . . . from tonight on, it will be our home.' No response. 'George! You do understand what I'm saying?'

The wizened figure remained motionless, but – though he appeared oblivious to the woman's warning – his mind was in turmoil, quickened by Rosie's words . . . 'the cottage . . . it will be our home'. The thought terrified him, because even here in this big old house with the doors secured against the outside world, he never felt safe. In his heart of hearts, he knew that one day it would find him, punish him, *kill him*. He knew it would happen, as sure as the sun came up of a morning. And yet, he still prayed that he might be spared. The cottage was small and vulnerable to those who would tear it apart to get at him. Rosie knew. The darkeye knew. He was sure of it! And yet, they still intended to make him leave the sanctuary of this house, this fort, where there was no easy way in. They hadn't punished him, though, had they? Not even when he did the bad things. Maybe they really were his friends after all. Surely they would not let it find him? He looked up and saw the smile that passed between them. Maybe they had a plan! A crafty plan to capture that devil and make it pay for the suffering it had caused him. He chuckled inside. Yes! That was it! They had a plan, his friends. He must believe that. He had to trust them. The fear in him subsided a little, but it did not go away. It would never go away. Now, what was it that pursued him? He thought hard, until it seemed like his mind was crumbling. *What pursued him?* Oh! The devil, of course. But what did 'the devil' look like? Why did it mean to harm him, to torture him . . . do away with him? Why. Why. *Why*. Oh, if only he could remember! *Why* couldn't he remember? He could hear them talking now. It made him curious. And what about her? The young one . . . the pretty thing. Cunningly, he raised his head just enough. His eyes locked onto her; secretly regarding her through frowning, rampant brows. He was at first intrigued. Then he was afraid. There was something about her; *something*. Something? The paintings? Was it the paintings? It was no good. He could not remember. Fear would not let him remember. He sighed inside himself. It would get him. One day, it would get him. Oh, how he prayed that when the moment came, it would not be too agonising.

'Take the boy with you.' Jack Armstrong did not intend to let Ellie have all her own way. After all, she was not yet twenty, and it was his bounden responsibility to look out for *both* his children. If he had expected Ellie to argue, he was disappointed.

Holding out her hand to the boy, she told him, 'Hurry then . . . there are one or two things to be brought from the motor car. We'll do that before we go.' She looked at the dark-eyed young man. 'If we have time, that is?' His answer was to offer help. Suddenly, for some reason known only to himself, he was less hostile than before.

'Here, Ellie . . . you'll need this.' Jack Armstrong slid his hand into his back trouser pocket; drawing out a wallet, he extracted four pound notes. 'Don't stint,' he told her. 'If you need more, you've only to ask.' He folded them into her hand. He still did not like the idea of her going to the estate with Harman. He recalled the warning which Ellie's mother had issued with regard to their first-born – 'Our daughter is not a child, Jack . . . nor is she a prisoner. Don't make her one, or you will lose her.' It had been a threat. And one which he had tried to observe.

As Ellie went out of the door, she was tempted to look back. It took all of her will-power to resist; even though she knew she was being watched. All the while they had been talking, Ellie had felt the one called George staring at her beneath those long, tangled eyebrows. The awful sensation he created in her was deeply disturbing, but then she reminded herself that soon only she, Johnny and their father would remain under this roof. The others would be safely installed in the cottage. The prospect brought a measure of comfort. And an inexplicable surge of apprehension. This was a strange, lonely place, she thought. And yet, Ellie felt as though she did belong.

'Oh . . . so, it was Mr Harman who showed you the way, was it?' The shopkeeper had a bright, friendly smile atop a round, homely body. 'Well now, you must consider yourself highly honoured, young lady.' She tip-toed and stretched up to the shelf where the flour was kept. 'There!' The soft, squashy bag tumbled into her groping fingers. Popping the bag of flour to the counter, she lowered her fluffy grey head and momentarily regarded Ellie and the boy through the narrow space above her spectacles. 'He must have taken pity on you . . . what with the three of you having come all that way to find yourselves locked out. As a rule, young Mr Harman keeps himself to himself . . . known for it!' She dipped a chubby hand in the sweet jar. 'There y'are, fella-me-lad,' she chuckled, pushing two barley twists along the counter towards the boy. Ellie forcefully reminded him of his manners when he quickly snatched them into his pocket.

'To be honest, Mrs Gregory . . . I don't know what we would have done without Mr Harman's help. We thought the place was empty . . . it certainly seemed that way. We had no idea that the old man had locked Rosie in the cellar.' It still surprised her that she should be addressing the woman as 'Rosie'. It seemed too quick, too familiar. She was not in the habit of being so bold. But then, she asked herself, how else would she address the woman? The only name she had been given was 'Rosie'. And, funnily enough, it did seem very natural to Ellie. What did not seem natural was the habit of referring to George as 'the old man'. Like Rosie said, he was *not* old. And yet, he was. Age was not measured in years. It was an attitude, a particular look and manner, a state of mentality. In each respect, George was old. *Very* old. In her heart, Ellie silently prayed that such an affliction as that poor creature suffered would never take hold of her. The image lingered in her mind now, of the one called George; of those pale, frightened eyes beneath wild, shaggy brows; of the manner in which he scuttled about, cringing into himself as though haunted on all sides. She inwardly shivered. He was a strange one, wasn't he? . . . a soul to be pitied. But wasn't he also insane? Yes. Yes, he was! *No.* He was not. He was just a frightened, disquieted soul, who dreaded leaving the place he had come to know. All of these things Ellie told herself. Yet they persisted; the other things, the doubts and the questions, nagging in her mind, nagging. *Nagging.*

'Did Alec Harman tell you anything . . . about the couple at Thornton Place?' The little woman weighed out two pounds of best apples and slid them from the weigh-scale into the brown paper bag. She then paused, waiting for Ellie's reply.

'Only that Rosie had taken care of the old man . . . George . . . for a number of years.'

'About three years, I'd say . . . if my memory serves me right. Probably about the time when Alec Harman himself came to these parts.' Mrs Gregory nodded her head thoughtfully, remembering. 'None of us here knows much about that one. Like I say . . . he does tend to keep himself to himself. Lives on the other side of the lake . . . in one of the tenanted cottages belonging to Wentworth Estates.' She stared into Ellie's face, thinking how lovely Ellie was, and wondering why such a beauty should choose to bury herself in an isolated place such as this. What a waste. *What a shameful, wanton waste!* 'What else did he tell you?' she asked quietly, glancing dubiously at the boy.

'Nothing really,' Ellie admitted, recalling how she had given the dark-eyed stranger every opportunity to outline the history of Thornton Place and the part which the odd couple had played in it. He had not been forthcoming. Instead, he had spoken to her of other things, things that mattered greatly to him – the job he loved, the animals that could not be tamed, yet had become his friends. He spoke of Nature, and beauty, sunsets and moonlight over the lake. When he murmured of these things, there was magic in his voice. Pride and awe. And all the while he had talked, he had woven a spell over her. When, at the edge of the spinney, he had pointed out the remaining short distance to the shop, before disappearing into the heart of the woods, Ellie had suffered loneliness such as she had never known. He had made no mention of when he might see her again, and she dared not ask.

'You don't *love* him, do you?' the boy had taunted, goading her with amused eyes and seeming to take pleasure in her confusion. In answer, she had actually laughed, while her deepest heart writhed in the exquisite agonies of a first real passion. Love him? She suspected so. At least, he was vibrant in every corner of her being. She was both afraid and exhilarated all at once. It was a strange sensation. One she had never experienced before. Was it love? Ellie had been made to ask herself. She had no way of knowing. Whatever it was, she wanted it to live for ever. What of Barny, though? Hadn't she been so certain that she loved him? That was true, yes. And, strangely enough, thoughts of him still made her feel warm, and safe. But, it was different, somehow.

'Thornton Place used to belong to Wentworth Estates . . . up 'til four years ago. Did you know that?' Mrs Gregory did not wait for an answer. 'Oh, yes! That were when Rosie and her husband were caretakers . . . looked after the big house for thirty years and more, they did.' She saw the surprise on Ellie's face. It pleased her. 'Didn't know *that*, did you, eh? When George and his wife were brought in as caretakers some four years back, Rosie and her husband moved into the cottage as tenants.'

'George *was* married, then?'

'Oh, dear me, yes! But she was killed in a tragic accident.' Her eyes glazed over as she lapsed deep into her own private thoughts. 'Nice little woman, too, from what I recall. Still!' She forced a bright, cheery smile. 'It don't do to dwell on such things. And you'd do well not to mention it to the poor man . . . he took it very badly. Never got over it. Well . . . you know, don't you? You've seen the way he is. Demented. Old before his time.'

Ellie had been intrigued by the revelations, but, because of them, some of the nagging questions were stilled. 'And Rosie's husband . . . what happened to him?'

'Old age I expect. Same as what will happen to all of us in time . . . if the grim reaper don't get us first, eh? Rosie's old fella died in the cottage . . . just fell asleep one night and never woke up again. He were a great deal older than Rosie, d'you see? Mind you . . . when your time comes, there ain't no better way to go than just falling asleep, is there, eh?'

'Why did Rosie move back into the house?'

''Cause she adored her old fellow and was lonely beyond belief after he'd gone. Because she's got a heart of gold. Because she's always been a worker, and hates to be bored. Because she saw both Thornton Place and George falling apart at the seams. Because . . . well, because she's Rosie, that's why! I don't believe it were just for a share of the wages, because Rosie's been thrifty over the years . . . got a bit tucked away, I reckon.'

'How did she lose her leg?'

'Don't know. Folks round these parts have never known Rosie any other way. She were crippled when she first came to Thornton Place, and she'll not discuss the manner of it. You won't get much change out of Rosie, I can tell you, young lady! She's never been known to discuss her private affairs with *anybody* . . . not even with Alec Harman. And he's been a godsend to that pair at Thornton Place, I can tell you. A godsend!' She shook her head. 'He's a strange one, though . . . a real loner. Been here some three years and never made a single friend . . . oh, with the exception of them two, but, they've been more like a cross on his back than "friends".'

'Why is that?'

Mrs Gregory looked up as though she was considering a reply. Instead, she squashed the two loaves into the cardboard box, saying quietly, 'There . . . I've only to weigh out the potatoes and vegetables . . . oh, and get my Fred to bag you some coal up . . . then your order's done.' She totted up the bill and took the notes from Ellie. 'He'll have the order on your doorstep within the hour. How does that suit you, eh?' She bestowed a warm smile on her two customers, handing Ellie the change and thinking how the Armstrong family had probably bitten off more than they could chew when they had taken on Thornton

Place. The young lady had told her how awful and dilapidated the big house was. Of course it was! Didn't they know why? Hadn't they been told that getting money out of the owners for repairs was like squeezing blood from a stone? Most of the time there was no contact whatsoever with the owners; faceless beings who probably bought and sold things, *and people*, for the money and excitement it brought! Oh, the representative would turn up now and again, no doubt to check on the 'investment'. Like she said to her old fella only the other day, the owners of Thornton Place must be 'city folk' – the kind who play the stock market and speculate to accumulate. But how they could ever 'accumulate' by letting a once-grand old house like Thornton Place fall to rack and ruin was beyond her. She said as much to Ellie now, adding, 'Happen your father can do better than old George and Rosie . . . he's a new face, with new ideas, and the strength behind him to carry them out. All the same, though, if you ask me . . . he's got his work cut out and no mistake!'

'I never wanted to come to this place!' the thin voice piped out.

Mrs Gregory looked at the boy and was irritated when he deliberately avoided her eyes. Suit yourself! she thought, having decided that he was a surly little brat who needed fetching down a peg or two. Oh, but wait a minute. Hadn't the young lady said something about making a new start . . . their mother was not long dead? Well, then. Shame on you, Elsie Gregory! The boy was too young to be left without a mother. It was no wonder he was hard to fathom; no doubt losing his mother had been a terrible thing to bear. A shock to his system that would take time and patience to mend. No mother, eh? She was momentarily reminded of her own mother's death many years before. The old lady had enjoyed a long life and her passing was quick and merciful. Even then, it was a dreadful wrench, because losing your mother was different to losing anybody else. She was special. Always there, from the day you were born. No, she should not be too swift making judgement on the boy. As her old fella would say, 'Keep your tongue still until you've thought things through!'

'It is a shame, Mrs Gregory. I can't understand how anybody could let such a proud old house fall into such disrepair.' Ellie prepared to leave. 'Still . . . we haven't had time to assess what needs doing yet . . . Rosie is showing my father the house right now, and no doubt Dad will be drawing up a plan of action. You can be sure my father won't let the house beat him!' She dropped the change into her purse before taking the boy's hand in hers and walking him towards the door.

'Oh! Wait a minute, dearie!' Mrs Gregory called. When Ellie turned round, the homely figure was scuttling to the other end of the counter, where the postal duties were executed. 'I completely forgot!' She dug beneath the counter and came out brandishing a small package. 'This arrived the other day . . . addressed to your father.' She peered at the name through puckered eyes. 'Mr J. Armstrong,' she read, 'there you are . . . came by special delivery.' She placed the package into Ellie's outstretched hands. 'Instructions, I dare say,' she declared, with a knowing look. 'If them city folk is good at doing anything at all . . . it's giving "instructions".' Her bright, curious gaze lingered a while on Ellie – at the surprise in her lovely amber eyes, and at the way she held herself, so proud and straight. It seemed to Mrs Gregory, at that point, that this young lady had a whole heap of responsibility on her shoulders. It was only to be hoped that they were strong enough to bear up.

As Ellie closed the shop door behind her, the man stepped out of the dark hall where he had been listening to the conversation between his wife and the girl. It had been an interesting and revealing exchange; not one he had wanted to interrupt.

'Oh . . . I wondered where you'd got to,' exclaimed Mrs Gregory, glancing up as the large, slightly stooping figure came into her sight. 'The Armstrong girl's just been here . . . placed a good order, too.' She sighed, roving her eyes over the bald head and the boozy, bloodshot eyes that stared back at her. 'Pretty little thing she is . . . I can't help thinking what a dreadful waste it is . . . her ending up in such an isolated place. I know I should be glad of new, younger blood in the hamlet, but . . . well.' She shook her head, a look of sadness colouring her features. 'It seems such a waste . . . *such a wicked waste*.' When the man gave no answer – other than to put his two big hands on the table, leaning his large frame forward so as to see better through the window at the two figures making their way into the spinney – she became deeply thoughtful and regarded him closer, afterwards following the direction of his gaze. Together the man and his wife watched as Ellie and the boy went from their sight.

Soon, the woman was bustling about her duties – weighing out the beans and bagging them up, or refilling the shelves as far as she could reach with her short, dumpy arms. The man, though, made no move. His bloodshot eyes were intent on the spot where the two newcomers had been swallowed into the spinney. He thought on Ellie's parting words: 'You can be sure my father won't let the house beat him!' He chuckled inside himself. So! The new caretaker of Thornton Place had come here with good intentions, had he? Had it in mind to make a clean sweep right through the old house? To put right the wrongs it had suffered? Was that so, eh? Such fine ideas! What was it the girl had said? . . . 'My father won't let the house beat him!' Yes. That was it . . . 'won't let the house beat him'. He chuckled again, aloud this time. 'Won't let the house beat him.' Well, now, this new caretaker would need to be a special kind of man, because the house had 'beaten' far better men than he! And, if the house had not broken their spirits, there were always the other things. *The bad things*. The things that struck without warning and frightened the gentler souls away. Or, drove them *mad*!

CHAPTER FOUR

August had been a wonderful month. In the dark hours the rain had quenched the dry earth, and during the day the sun had beaten down from a brilliant blue sky. Today, the last day of August, the weather was perfect, with a soft, refreshing breeze skimming the lake and bringing cooler air to the grounds fronting the big house.

Ellie found her labours both pleasant and fulfilling. Beneath the freshly applied coat of green, the doors to the outhouse lent a cared-for appearance to what had been a haven for rubbish, vermin and homeless vagabonds. At last there was emerging a kind of order about the old place.

'By! You're a cracking little worker, my girl . . . I'll give you that.' The cheery voice sailed through the air.

'*Rosie!*' Ellie's face broke into a smile at the sight of the ungainly and now familiar figure carefully picking its way over the uneven ground. Balancing the paint brush on the rim of the paint pot, Ellie stretched her aching back and reached her arms above her head. It felt good; good to be alive. 'Oh, Rosie . . . I do love it here,' she said, 'and do you know . . . I can't imagine any other life than this. It's like I've always known this place.' She waved her arm in a generous half-circle to encompass the house and grounds, the spinney and the satin lake, and the patchwork of fields beyond.

'Hmph!' Rosie's handsome eyes surveyed the panoramic view, until her vision was curtailed by the close proximity of the spinney. 'It *does* look impressive . . . magnificent. Yes, I'll grant you that,' she conceded, sinking to the upturned bucket and stretching out her one good leg. 'You've had it easy so far, my girl!' she warned. 'Don't forget you've only been here four months yet . . . Sunshine, long day-light hours, and you've been blessed by the night showers, without which the earth would be parched for sure.' She had put her two crutches to the ground and now, with a deal of grunting and cursing, she made herself more comfortable. 'Now then,' she started; at the same time retrieving the hessian bag from around her neck. 'Come and sit yourself down.' She put the bag to her knee and vigorously patted a grassy rise beside her. 'I've fetched us a flask of cold tea and a bite to eat.' Rummaging about in the bag she produced a small thermos flask, two earthenware mugs, a brown paper bag containing plump cheese sandwiches, two rosy apples and a plain dark tablecloth. Shaking the tablecloth out, she let it fall to the ground in a tangle and promptly set everything into the uneven folds, all the while clucking and moaning when the imperfections in her body made the movements awkward. 'There ain't nothing worse than old age, my girl!' she told Ellie in quick, breathless gasps, the stump of her crippled leg moving rapidly back and forth with the reflex action of the knee just above. 'Come on! Come on!' she ordered, sending a cursory glance towards Ellie, who had lingered a while, watching a nearby blackbird as it tugged the worms from the newly dug soil. Afterwards, she vigorously wiped her hands and face with the grubby handkerchief taken from the pocket of her dungarees. She felt hot and sweaty. In a moment, she had come to where Rosie was waiting. The blackbird followed, and two mallards appeared from the direction of the lake, all searching for easy titbits.

'Be off with you!' yelled Rosie, reluctant to share the picnic and noisily crashing one of the crutches to the ground as the curious visitors approached. At once they retreated, amidst a volley of squealing, fighting and a furious beating of wings. 'Bloody cheek!' Rosie exclaimed, shaking her fist in the air. Suddenly the blackbird returned, staying just out of reach of Rosie's crutches, from where, remaining motionless as a statue, it stared at them through keen, brilliant eyes. At first, Rosie continued to thump the tip of her crutch into the ground in a bid to frighten the blackbird away. When it defiantly stood its ground, observing them all the while, Rosie took hold of Ellie's hand, digging her bony fingers deep into the flesh and whispering to Ellie, 'Don't move. It ain't the bird that's watching us!' Astonished by the strange action of the blackbird, and the effect it was having on the woman beside her, Ellie did as she was told. She could feel the hand trembling violently as it closed ever tighter about her own – the long, uneven nails slicing into her skin and making her want to cry out. The blackbird appeared lifeless; as though carved out of coal. Only the eyes moved; piercing, darting shafts of liquid black – staring at them. *Staring.* Then, suddenly, it was gone, its wings unfolding from its small slender form and thrashing the air for a brief time, before soaring into the sky and melting with the sun's blinding rays.

For a moment, Ellie was almost afraid to move. Still in awe of what had happened, she looked at the old woman. She was astonished to see Rosie unperturbed by the incident and actually softly singing. When, sensing Ellie's eyes on her, the old woman looked up, it was to say in a quiet voice, 'It was dying.' She laughed, nervously. 'You get to know these things . . . when you've lived in such an isolated place for a long time.' She stared after the bird, which was now only a mere speck on the horizon. 'It's eerie . . . when they stare at you like that. It's as though . . . you can see its very soul . . . yet . . .'

'What are you trying to say, Rosie?' Ellie was intrigued.

Laughing nervously and nodding towards the direction in which the blackbird had flown, Rosie said, 'Gone to its maker, I expect. Like we *all* will one day.' She lapsed into a brief silence, before slapping Ellie on the hand. 'Don't let it worry you, dearie,' she said, 'it's just one of them things. One of them . . . *strange* things we'll never understand.' She glanced sharply about, giving Ellie the impression that, try as she might to disguise the fact, Rosie had been unnerved by the incident. 'Sometimes I suspect this place has too many mysteries.'

'What do you mean, Rosie?' Ellie sometimes felt that, too; in the house, and out here. Especially when she was all alone.

'Oh, I'm just being an old fool,' Rosie told her. She then completely changed the subject, outlining in detail how 'that silly man, George, has kept me awake half the night with his bad dreams and hobgoblins'. When Ellie asked why the old man had not been persuaded to come out with Rosie on such a lovely morning, Rosie rolled her eyes and flung wide her hands in a gesture of helplessness. 'Because he's like bloody Dracula, that's why!' she moaned. 'Afraid the sun might shrivel him up!' They laughed at the idea.

For the next twenty minutes, the conversation between Rosie and Ellie was concerned mostly with what progress had been made at the big house in the past months. Ellie spoke with pride of their achievements, regarding the immediate living areas and the three bedrooms they were presently occupying. The walls and ceilings in these particular rooms had been stripped, repaired and repainted. Rotting floorboards had been taken up and replaced with new timbers, purchased at a discount through Alec Harman, from Wentworth Estates. Ellie had taken immense pleasure in tearing down the old threadbare curtains and hanging the new ones, made up by her own hands from a batch of pretty pink and white floral material, bought in the summer sales in Medford town. It was the ever-helpful Rosie who had remembered the old treadle sewing-machine; triumphantly unearthing it from the mountain of debris in the outhouse. In all, only five rooms had been renovated; the three bedrooms in the West Wing, the big room downstairs, and the kitchen, whose long, wooden cupboards had taken on a new life beneath the onslaught of hot, soapy water and scrubbing brush. One Saturday afternoon, Alec Harman had arrived with a huge tin of wood varnish. 'It's the stuff we use to preserve certain batches of timber . . . special orders,' he explained.

Ellie and her father had a heated exchange of words when Alec Harman offered his help. Ellie had been pleasantly surprised, but her father was immediately suspicious. 'You're not to give that fellow any kind of encouragement,' he snapped. She insisted on being allowed to decide for herself what friends she made in this new place and, 'after all . . . it will be *me* who spends the most time in the kitchen. You have enough to occupy you with the rest of the house!' Grudgingly, her father conceded. Alec Harman applied the varnish, and Ellie was both astonished and delighted with the transformation of the kitchen cupboards.

With the red quarry floor tiles scrubbed and polished, the window dressed in pretty gingham curtains and the lovely old cupboards rich and gleaming again, the kitchen quickly became Ellie's pride and joy; her very own retreat, where she and Alec had spent a few magic hours working together. Being close to him was a great source of pleasure to Ellie, and though he never once betrayed as much to her, she sensed that he also found pleasure in her company. Alec Harman was a man of few words. A man who had stirred something deep inside her; an all-consuming emotion which she could not fathom. He made her curious, certain that beneath those dark, seductive eyes were kept many hidden secrets. He intrigued and fascinated her. He made her feel wanted, yet he constantly and silently rejected her. They had toiled together, shared a meal together and, very occasionally, laughed together. And *still*, she did not know him. Always he held something back, keeping the essence of himself from her. He was a strange man, a loner, unpredictable and irritatingly aloof. She could never be certain of what he was thinking. She was in awe of him; a little afraid of him and yet, when he was close beside her, her every nerve-end tingled for joy. No one had ever made her feel like that before; not the boys she had met during her college years, and not even Barny, who still held a very special place in her heart.

'You're miles away.' Rosie tugged at the short sleeve of Ellie's blue blouse. 'Dreaming of your sweetheart, are you?' she asked, with a knowing smile.

'Sort of,' Ellie replied, gathering her meandering thoughts and thinking how perceptive Rosie was.

'What did you say the young man's name was?'

'Barny Tyler.'

'Aye, that's it. From what you tell me, he sounds a likeable, hard-working fella. So . . . when do I get the pleasure of clapping eyes on this "Barny", eh?'

'I don't know,' Ellie answered truthfully. What she did not reveal was that she had posted a letter to Barny only yesterday, catching the Thursday noon postal collection from Mrs Gregory's shop.

'Shouldn't hide yourself away in this God-forsaken place!' Rosie growled, regarding Ellie through curious brown eyes. 'Lovely girl like you . . . it's a crying shame.' She snatched her gaze from Ellie's lovely face and, viciously ramming a sandwich in her mouth, she tore at it with strong, square teeth, the crimson lipstick from her mouth leaving an ugly, vivid stain on the bread. Ellie's protest that she was *not* 'hiding herself away' was received with a suspicious sideways look, followed by that wide, disarming smile that was Rosie's most endearing quality. 'Well . . . happen you're not, dearie,' Rosie chuckled, 'but there's many a young heart that would carry you off, given half a chance.' She sighed, tore at the bread again, and spoke out, with niblets of wet, chewed bread splaying into the air. 'There ain't too many young men round these parts . . . not now. There's no industry here . . . apart from the big distribution warehouses just beyond the hamlet. That's where most of the folks work round here . . . loading goods to be sent all over the country. But it's a thankless, boring job I'm told . . . the young 'uns don't like it too much, so they move into Medford town . . . working in the railways and brick-yards. The girls go into the factories . . . or become nurses. No, there ain't much here in this hamlet. And you have to remember that the war took its toll of the young men. It might be over ten years since the war ended, but those brave men can never be replaced.' She shook her peroxide head and a sadness came over her. 'Terrible thing . . . war. So many lives.' She eyed Ellie and was suddenly smiling again. ''Course, there's farming . . . but that way of life don't appeal to everybody.' She cocked her head to one side and squinted her eyes to the sun as she looked deeper into Ellie's soft, friendly eyes. 'The Harman fellow's taken a fancy to you,' she said in a quiet, intimate manner.

Ellie felt the hot blush spread over her neck and face. At first she looked away, feigning renewed interest in her discarded apple, but the excitement had been aroused in her. She could not resist asking, 'How do you know that?'

'Aha!' Rosie laughed out loud, tapping her nose and peering more closely into Ellie's embarrassed face. 'I *know*, that's all. And I suspect that his attentions ain't wasted . . . am I right?'

'Don't be silly, Rosie.' Ellie's face was burning like a beacon beneath the old woman's amused stare. 'Alec Harman is . . . a man who keeps himself to himself,' she reminded her.

'Huh! I may be old and crippled, dearie,' Rosie retorted, wiping the back of her hand across her mouth and spreading a crimson veil over her face, 'but I ain't too far gone to know when a man hankers after a woman. True . . . Alec Harman does keep himself to himself, but, after all, he is a man. He has the heart of a man, and the needs of a man. He has eyes that can appreciate a lovely thing like yourself.' She chuckled and leaned forward, making Ellie obliged to meet her knowing gaze. 'Like I said . . . he's taken a real fancy to you. But then, you must know that.' The smile lingered round her mouth. 'Handsome bugger, ain't he, eh? I bet you ain't never seen such a handsome fellow. Secretive and private, yes, with them dark eyes that could melt any woman's heart; even mine . . . if I weren't so long in the tooth and past all things beautiful!' In a swift, unexpected movement she grabbed Ellie's hand. 'You could do worse, my girl!' she chided. 'I know he's secretive . . . a loner . . . unpredictable and even hostile at times. But, deep down, he's a good man. That's all you need to know.' Suddenly her mood was unusually serious as she warned, 'I suspect he's not a man to be used. But, if you treat him right . . . you'll not be sorry, I'm sure.'

'Rosie, you're imagining things.' Ellie wondered at the old woman's words. 'Alec Harman has never given me reason to believe he . . . he . . . "fancies me" as you say. And though I know you mean well, I think this conversation's getting out of hand. Besides . . . don't forget Barny.'

For a long, irritating moment, Rosie ignored Ellie's comment, turning her sandwich every which way and meticulously examining it. Eventually she said, without looking up, 'No, Ellie. Don't *you* "forget Barny"!'

Without knowing it, the old woman had struck a chord in Ellie's conscience. Everything Rosie had said was true. In her innermost heart, Ellie had also sensed Alec Harman's interest in her. Yet, he had never once made a move or said anything that gave credence to these feelings. For a long time now, she had come to realise how close she was growing to this strange, quiet man, with the dark, sensuous eyes that at times appeared uniquely sinister. In his silent, bewitching way, it was almost as though he had woven a spell over her. Sometimes, in the dark hours, she would lie in her bed, lonely and aching for him. But then, she was reminded of the same two things that raced through her mind now – that she had no way of knowing exactly how Alec Harman felt towards her, and, with a pang of conscience, she would remember Barny; his natural, easy manner, the wayward shock of brown hair and those kind, green eyes that were brimming with love whenever he smiled at her. In spite of herself, she missed him so.

Ellie had lost count of the numerous attempts she had made to start a letter to Barny, asking him to understand *why* she had to leave; pleading with him not to turn his back on her completely, and begging him to come here, to Thornton Place, where they could talk through all that had come between them. But, each attempt to compose such a letter always ended in tears. Finally, driven by guilt and loneliness and the need to feel wanted for herself, she had written to Barny, but it was a restrained and polite letter, more to a friend than a lover. In it, Ellie had told him how much he was in her thoughts. She told him of the big house and of the work they had undertaken. She described how magnificent was the area, how isolated the community, and how they still had many months of hard work before the house was recovered from the awful neglect that had brought it so close to being lost forever.

When reading the letter back to herself, Ellie was astonished to find that she had used up almost four pages, describing and praising the house and the surrounding area. She was shocked to find, also, that she had made excessive mention of 'Mr Harman . . . so handsome . . . intriguing'. For this reason only, she had rewritten the letter, omitting all mention of Alec Harman, and trimming back her seeming obsession for both the man and the house. Strange, she thought, how Thornton Place and Alec Harman were so alike; dark, secret beings, that had somehow etched themselves deep into her soul. She wanted them *both*!

'Have the owners paid a visit yet?' Rosie had been regarding the young woman before her, taking pleasure in the attractive study she made and gently enjoying Ellie's petite figure that was almost lost in the paint-spattered overalls and the cornflower-blue blouse that softly billowed in the breeze. She was so young, so very lovely. Her warm, amber-coloured eyes and the wild, pretty hair that held the golden brilliance of sunshine made a body want to reach out and touch the beauty, feel its vitality. Take it to themselves.

'No. Since the envelope was delivered to the shop, we've heard nothing at all,' Ellie replied, simultaneously replacing the flask into the hessian bag. 'It's a funny way of going on. In this day and age, I'm surprised that the owners should choose to pay their employees in such a way.'

'It's not uncommon, though,' Rosie admitted, 'and there's no accounting for the manner in which money-folk behave . . . a law to themselves, that's what they are. Before you came, me and George were paid in exactly the same fashion . . . a special delivery to the shop every six months . . . wages twice a year, and no choice but to make it last over the six months. Sometimes there'd be a bit extra for urgent work, and occasionally there'd be

some small instruction or another from the solicitors . . .
like when we were told of your father's appointment and
ordered to move into the cottage until further notice. It's
a good job I was careful over the years . . . got a bit put by
to see us through.'

'Do you mind living in the cottage, Rosie?' Ellie looked
at the woman, seeing the deep wrinkles incised into her
neck and face, and thinking how, in spite of them, Rosie
did not seem aged. Yet she *was*. Rosie had told them
herself that she was 'past seventy years of age'. There was
something about her, though, something that shone from
inside, belying those long, ravaging years. It wasn't just
her joy of life, or the thick, tinted make-up that she
plastered into the folds and dips of her skin; it wasn't the
crimson lipstick that even now was smeared across the
bottom half of her face, giving her the peculiar appearance of a clown. Nor was it the twinkling dark brown
eyes, that sometimes laughed and sometimes mocked. To
Ellie, it was a more intangible essence. It was not something to be questioned or analysed. Rosie was special.
And Ellie admired her greatly.

'Oh, I don't mind living in the cottage,' Rosie said,
haphazardly slinging the hessian bag round her neck.
'What you forget, Ellie, is that me and my old fella lived
in that there cottage for quite a while afore he died . . .
o' course, that were when George and his missus took
over the duties at the big house. We'd grown old, d'you
see . . . couldn't take proper care of it. When Wentworth
Estates sold Thornton Place to a private buyer, well . . .
me and my old fella were quickly given our marching
orders. Quite rightly, too!' She leaned into her crutches
and hoisted herself upright. A look of sadness tinged her
merry eyes. 'We had some good years in that cottage,
but . . . well . . . there were the other things.'

There it was again! Ellie was convinced that Rosie knew
more than most about the dark secrets which this place

coveted. 'What . . . "*other things*"?' she asked, knowing in her heart that she would not learn the secrets in Rosie's mind; not on this day, and maybe never.

'What did you say, dearie?' Rosie was deliberately evasive, cursing herself for letting slip her innermost thoughts. She had not wanted to alarm the girl. There were things that should *never* be revealed; things that brought terror to a body's soul. And yet, it had been some long time since . . . since . . . The memory made her shudder inside. There had been a spell of peace, when the nightmares had stayed away. But, somehow, Rosie knew they would be back; she could never tell when. *But, they would be back!* Now, she purposefully hurried away, chattering nonsense so as not to hear the girl's repeated questions. 'I must get back to George,' she called, digging the tips of her crutches into the ground as she stumped away at a furious pace. George would be watching for her. *Frantic!* For that poor, haunted soul, the nightmares never went away.

Intrigued, Ellie watched the homely figure depart. What had Rosie meant when she said . . . 'the other things'? Ellie told herself that she had imagined the disturbing implications behind those words. But, if that *was* the case, then why had Rosie been so deliberately evasive? What could she have meant? What 'other things'? Not for the first time after talking to Rosie, Ellie's curious feelings about Thornton Place were strengthened. These past weeks, she had promised herself that she would visit the library in nearby Medford, and unearth whatever facts there were with regard to Thornton Place. Now, more than ever, it was something she intended to do. Something she felt compelled to do. So much so, that she could wait no longer. Tomorrow was Saturday. She needed some new clothes and, in two weeks' time, Johnny would require a school outfit for the new term. She could combine a shopping trip with a visit to the library. She had worked hard and earned a day off. Ellie was sure her father would not object; especially if she took the boy from under his feet. Thanks to the generous salary his employers paid him, Ellie also had been made a small allowance for her labours, so she could afford to treat herself.

Suddenly, Ellie was made to think again on the manner in which her father had been paid. Six months in advance, together with the sum he had already received, and a deal of money with which to begin work on the big house. There had been a typed letterhead enclosed, simply setting out the various sums of money, and welcoming 'Mr J. Armstrong' as the new caretaker. There was the name and address of a firm of solicitors in London, and an instruction that Mr Armstrong should not contact them. That was it! The communication was signed in an unreadable scrawl. When Ellie had pointed out to her father that the letter was unusually short 'to the point of rudeness' his answer was to tell her that 'as long as I'm paid, that's all we need to be concerned about'. He also indicated that the whole thing could be a ruse by the owner to 'manipulate his taxes'. That took the whole thing beyond Ellie's understanding, and so she let it rest. After all, her father was a shrewd and cautious man. If *he* was satisfied with the arrangements, then who was *she* to question them?

When morning became afternoon and the stifling heat became unbearable, Ellie decided to call it a day. After carefully stacking away the tools of her labours in the outhouse, she went to the courtyard, and there she refreshed herself at the old pump, enjoying the cool tumble of water over her face and neck, and ruminating on her plans for the morrow. Her father would not offer any objections, she was sure of it. Ever since coming here it had been his intention to delve into the history of Thornton Place, but, what with all the work, and his suspicions that the owner would soon send out a representative to check on his achievements here, he had devoted himself to the formidable task of renovating the old house. There remained no spare time for trips to the library.

On her way back to the house, Ellie took the wristwatch from her dungaree pocket. It was 4.00 p.m. An hour, yet, before she would put the evening meal on the table. It was already prepared – rabbit pie, baked in the old range the previous evening, and fresh vegetables, bought from the shop and delivered there daily by the farmer in the valley. There was apple tart and cream to follow; the pie made by Ellie's own hands in the loving tradition taught by her mother. *Her mother!* Suddenly, Ellie's mood was one of regret and nostalgia. In her mind's eye she could still see the way her mother had been when the boy had found her. The grotesque thing that they claimed was her mother. The horror of it! 'How could you?' Ellie was astonished at the vehemence in her own voice. *'How could you do it, Mother?'* So fierce was the pain inside her that she had to stop. Leaning against the broad trunk of an ancient oak tree, Ellie gave vent to the pent-up emotions. The tears burst from her sorry eyes, misting her vision of the magnificent landscape which had so often eased the sadness inside her. Lifting her face to the skies, she closed her eyes, taking pleasure in the warm, healing touch of the sun's rays, forcing the offending image from her churning thoughts and trying desperately to compose herself before she came to her father and the boy.

So intent on chasing away the terrors that tormented her, Ellie had not heard the approaching footsteps. Her mind was closed to the outside world. She felt momentarily safe. The sun caressed her face with its softer warmth, and the gentle breeze dried her tears. She remained motionless, eyes closed, her slim, tired body pressed against the bark, and a sense of peace taking hold of her.

Only when his shadow blocked out the sun's warmth did she realise she was not alone. Startled, she snapped open her eyes – scared, restless eyes that shone like topaz in the gentle shade. She was astonished to see his face so close, his dark, searching gaze on her. She opened her mouth to speak, but no words would come. 'Ssh,' he murmured, touching his strong, slender fingers against her face, causing her heart to leap and panic.

'*Alec* . . .' His name died on her lips as his warm, moist mouth pressed into her, sending her surprised senses reeling. All manner of delight surged through her. She raised her arms, sliding them round his neck and drawing him into her, down, down. A small voice inside shouted, 'This is wrong. *Wrong.*' But her need of him was too strong to be denied. At first, his kiss had been tender, enticing. Now it was like everything she had ever craved. His mouth toyed with hers, coveting, touching her ears, her throat, playing with her every nerve-ending until she felt herself clawing into him. Greedily, she clung to his gently moving body – wanting him more than she could bear. 'Love me,' she murmured. 'Love me . . . love me.' She knew he wanted her. Her own desperation was mirrored in him.

Suddenly, Ellie felt him draw back, his black eyes looking beyond her, stiff and reproachful. For a brief second he returned his brooding gaze to look on her puzzled face. She saw the seething anger soften in his eyes; then regret. She glimpsed the intimation of long-hidden secrets and, in the opaque depths of those magnificent eyes, Ellie saw the underlying anguish. She heard it in his hoarse whisper, 'You should never have come to this place.' Then, as suddenly as he had appeared, he was gone, leaving Ellie flushed with humiliation; a humiliation that quickly turned to bitterness when, at the sound of breaking bracken behind her, she swung round. *It was the boy*. That was why Alec Harman had gone. He had seen the boy watching them.

'What were you doing there?' she demanded, her senses still in turmoil and the fury rising in her. 'How long have you been there . . . *spying*?' The word fell from her lips before she could check it. But she was not sorry. Not sorry at all. For what seemed a lifetime, she glared at him, challenging the cold, blue eyes and hating him. Hating herself. When, with the slightest twist of a smile on his mouth, he turned away, Ellie felt the urge to go after him. To shake the truth from him. *To kill him with her bare hands!* Instead, she wept, inwardly cursing her own weakness. He was her 'weakness' . . . Alec Harman, the darkeye! Why did he haunt her every waking thought? *The darkeye*. Alec . . . who was always her lover in dreams, and almost her lover in the flesh. Alec . . . who instilled such passion in her that it made her lose control. Alec . . . who made her afraid, and unhappy. She loved him – if the fire that raged in her could be called 'love'. And he loved her, didn't he? *Didn't he?* But then he had spoken those harsh words to her . . . *'You should never have come to this place.'* Ellie punched her fist rhythmically into the tree trunk, her voice echoing hollowly, 'You . . . should . . . never . . . have . . . come . . . to . . . this . . . place!' The sharp bark edges tore her flesh, sending scarlet rivulets trickling down her wrist. She did not notice. Inside, the emotions swelled – fear, love and hate. They surged through her being, fusing into a tight knot in the pit of her stomach. A great sense of frustration overwhelmed her. She had come here to find happiness and peace of mind. She had found neither.

From a short way off and camouflaged by the overhanging branches in the spinney, Alec Harman had seen how cruelly the boy had taunted her. A wave of savagery ebbed through him. He longed to persuade Ellie back into his aching arms and enfold her to his jealous heart. But he knew he could not do these things. He *must* not. There was too much at stake. Too much that might easily be betrayed. He damned himself for falling in love with the Armstrong girl. That was never meant to be. *It was not part of the plan!*

Alec Harman saw Ellie's pain, and his own heart felt it too. Moved beyond endurance, he almost went to her. *Almost.* But, he was reminded of his dark purpose there, and he kept his distance. As he went away, his proud shoulders stooped with despair, and there was dark bitterness in his heart. He was greatly tempted to retrace his steps and declare his love for her. But then he remembered why he was there. For a while, all had been quiet in this place. Soon, very soon, the evil must be unleashed. It would be foolish to forget his own part in it!

At long last, Ellie returned to the house, mortified by the awful strength of her feelings. She could never recall a time when she had given vent to such powerful emotions. And the boy? How could she have given in to such destructive feelings of loathing towards her own brother? As for Alec Harman, she knew now that he desired her. And, that he was afraid of her. The first realisation had brought a degree of comfort and satisfaction to her. The second puzzled her. Why would he wish she had not come to this place? Why was he afraid of her? Was he married . . . was that it? *No!* Deep inside her, Ellie believed there was no rival for his love. At least, none that was *normal*. What then? The more she dwelt on it, the more curious she became. She also had to admit the truth of her own feelings towards Alec Harman – she loved him, yes. But, she was also afraid. Afraid of him, and afraid of the emotions he could let loose in her. Oh, but didn't love and fear always go hand in hand? Was it that simple? Something told Ellie it went much deeper.

It was evening. Johnny heard Ellie calling, but he had not

forgiven her. He had not forgiven either of them. Squeezing himself tighter into the darkest corner of the barn, he held his breath when Ellie came right inside. 'Johnny . . . I'm sorry, sweetheart.' He stayed hidden. She waited. After a moment's silence, she went away again, her voice calling his name, her footsteps growing distant.

'I saw you,' he murmured, his slitted eyes burning with vehemence, 'you and . . . him.' His voice was bitter. In his tortured mind he was not thinking of Ellie. He was thinking of another. Two others.

Now, when he heard the slight movement behind him, the boy began to look around, quickly jerking his head back when the whisper urged him to, 'Remember our agreement, Johnny. You must not see my face . . . *ever*.'

'I'm sorry.'

'Good boy.' The voice was soft, teasing, barely audible. There followed an interlude of deathly silence, yet underlying it was a great excitement before the whisper came again – this time with threatening overtones. 'You must never ask my name. That would spoil everything. And you must never tell of our meeting . . . but then, they would not believe you, would they?' The voice was smiling now.

'They *never* believe me.'

'Well then . . . you must keep our secret. *Always*.'

'I won't tell. They hate me, I know. Sometimes . . . I hate them too.'

'Only sometimes? You surprise me.'

'I hate . . . her . . . all the time. Because she hated me.' A sob choked him.

'You didn't like what you saw today, did you?'

'*No!*'

'They were bad, weren't they, Johnny?'

A gasp of incredulity. The stranger had said his name! A wave of pleasure washed over him. 'Yes. They were bad . . . very bad.'

'Who else was bad, Johnny?'

Unbearable silence. Now, the pain in his voice. '*She was!*'

'Who? . . . Who was bad?' The whisper became a frantic, muffled scream. '*Who*, Johnny? . . . *Tell me who!*'

'Her . . . my mother!'

A deep, satisfied sigh. 'Was she *very* bad?'

'Yes.'

'You saw . . . didn't you?'

'Yes.'

'*You saw!* . . . Don't ever forget what you saw, Johnny. Keep it in your mind . . . day and night. Dream about it. Keep the memory alive.'

'It won't go away!' There was fear now, and panic.

'That's good, Johnny. That's how it should be.'

'I know.' A deep sob choked him. He clambered to his feet and scurried out of the dark corner. At the door he looked back with big, sky-blue eyes; they were bright with fear. And exhilaration. He squeezed the eyes into puckered holes through which he peered into the blackness. 'Are you still there?' He waited for what seemed a small lifetime. The silence was suffocating. He had to know he was forgiven. That he would not be punished. 'I only want to say I *will* keep our secret, I promise.'

'I know you will.'

'I *will*! I like the games we play. And because you are my friend . . . my only friend. And I love you.' He ran into the evening light, his diminutive form silhouetted in the huge doorway. Then, very softly, oh so deviously, he swung the door to and went quietly away.

'I'm glad you think me a friend.' The mocking words dripped like venom into the gloom. 'But you're wrong, Johnny . . . *This is no game!*' A gentle, silken laugh caressed the air; and the fervent promise issued. 'There can be no mercy, Johnny . . . Not even for you.' A rustle. Then soft, padding footsteps going away. All that remained was the aura of lavender. And the quiet, tortured sound of laughter.

CHAPTER FIVE

Ellie shivered as she took her place at the big oak table in the kitchen. The quarry tiles struck cold through the thin soles of her slippers, and in spite of the watery September sun filtering in through the window, the damp air inside the old house seemed to penetrate her very bones.

'Are we staying here for ever and ever?' The boy was unusually restless this morning, toying agitatedly with the crispy bacon slices on his plate and snapping pieces from his toast with sharp, weasel teeth. When a river of melting margarine trickled down his chin, he reached out a long, snaking tongue to lap at it, his piercing blue eyes raised to Ellie with a look of contempt.

'For heaven's sake, Johnny!' Ellie reached across the table, dabbing at the boy's chin with a tea towel. 'Don't be so sloppy with your food . . . we haven't got much time as it is, if we're to catch that nine o'clock bus. There's no time to change your shirt if you stain it now!' Strange, she thought, how someone else's miserable mood could ruin a body's day even when it was hardly started. 'And cheer up, *do*,' she snapped.

'Hmh!' The ice-blue eyes settled on her face. 'Don't take it out on *me* if he's not talking to you any more,' he said cuttingly, 'it isn't my fault if Alec Harman avoids you like the plague.' He began giggling, surprised and amused by his own remark.

'That's enough! Do as your sister tells you.' Jack Armstrong thrust his chair from the table and sprang to his feet. With hard eyes he glared down on the boy. 'Ellie's put off the shopping trip *twice* on my account!' he said angrily. 'She works hard round this place . . . a bloody sight harder than someone else I could mention . . . spending all hours of the day and night building a bonfire! If you put as much energy into helping with the work that needs doing here, you'd be far better employed.' He stormed towards the door, angrily buckling his trouser belt, and still issuing condemnation even as he closed the door behind him. 'I should think by now you must have emptied every nook and cranny there is, to pile up that bloody bonfire . . . and there's still over six weeks to go before we set light to it. It might be as well if you lay off a while . . . I don't want you collecting stuff that I might find a better use for. Anyway, the darned thing's high enough, I reckon. It's beginning to resemble an Egyptian tomb!'

The kitchen echoed to the sound of the door slamming. Ellie sighed, leaning forward to rest her elbows on the table. 'It amazes me how you have a knack of upsetting everyone around you,' she told the boy, closing her eyes and nodding her head into the palms of her hands. For a short while she gave herself up to the turmoil that churned through her like an angry storm. What the boy had said was true. Since that day when Alec Harman had kissed her with such passion, awakening all manner of demons in her, he had gone out of his way to avoid her. That was two weeks ago. In that time she had seen him on several occasions, stalking through the spinney, or coming from the direction of the cottages. She had even seen him late one evening, down by the lake, silhouetted against the moon like some unearthly phantom.

On that particular evening, Ellie had been awakened by a strange noise . . . like the sound of an animal screaming.

On going outside she had found only a silent, unusually beautiful night – the scent of blossom had carried on the warm air, and, in the iridescent glow from the moon, the landscape took on an unreal and breathtaking magnificence. The sky above was marbled with rainbows of silver and black, against which the treetops moved like dark, meandering shadows, shifting this way and that in the sighing breeze. There were shadows on the ground too, playing hide and seek across the hills and valleys. On the horizon, the lake stretched out like a dark blanket, interspersed here and there with bright, scintillating shapes that danced and sparkled beneath the moonlight. Here – standing astride on the rising mound that overlooked the heart of the lake – was the unmistakable figure of Alec Harman. Tall, lean and strangely brooding, he had startled Ellie when her roving gaze alighted on him. For a long time, she was dearly tempted to go to him, to ask why he was deliberately shunning her, and to confess her love for him.

On impulse, Ellie had even started towards the lake, bent on putting things right between herself and this unfathomable, dark-eyed scoundrel who haunted her waking hours and tormented even her sleep. Two things were seared into Ellie's heart. One – that this man bred fear in her. The other was the disturbing realisation that she loved him. She intended to open her heart to him, to tell him how much he had come to mean to her, and to ask him why it was that he had deliberately avoided her of late. Was it something she had done, or said? Was it because of her father's hostile attitude? Or was it merely that he did not love her? This last thought had come to her when she was only a short distance from him. It had stopped her in her tracks. Shocked her. But then, something else happened in that moment that was even more *shocking*. First came the soft, urgent call, 'Alec . . . Alec, is that you?' It was a woman's voice. Instinctively stepping into the camouflage of the shrubbery, Ellie waited and watched, her heart beating so loudly that she was sure Alec Harman must swing round at any minute to confront her! Soon, the woman was in sight. She was small and slim, with long, thick hair that hung down to her waist. In the half-light it was impossible for Ellie to see the woman's features. But from the quick, sure way she moved, and judging by the sharp, youthful lines of her silhouette, the woman appeared to be both young and attractive. On sighting Alec Harman, she ran towards him, flinging herself into his waiting arms, their lips exchanging a fleeting kiss. Afterwards, there was a flurry of furtive whispering, when the woman handed something to the man. When they sank to the ground, intent upon each other and talking in soft, secretive tones, Ellie could not bear any more.

As she hurried away, all kinds of emotions raced through her; shock, sadness. But most of all, anger! And shame, because in spite of what she had just witnessed, she still could not deny her love for that man. All the same, he had cruelly toyed with her. Used her, and then contemptuously discarded her. Well, two could play at that game, she decided, in her fury. The following morning, she had written a letter to Barny – a warm, encouraging letter, inviting him to the bonfire celebrations. She had written it in anger, posted it in haste, and, shortly after, had bitterly regretted it. Now, though, her wounded heart was warmed by memories of the good times she and Barny had shared. It wasn't too long before she found herself actually looking forward to his visit. The boy had shown little interest in the news, but Ellie's father had declared his full approval, remarking, 'I can't say I haven't been concerned about the way that fellow Harman seemed to have set his sights on you . . . though I reckon he's got the message at last . . . keeping his distance and all. It'll do you good to see Barny again, I'm sure. What I say is . . . better the devil you know, eh?'

Rosie, too, seemed eager to make Barny's acquaintance, although, 'If you ask me, Alec Harman won't like it. Your father's right, Ellie . . . the darkeye has set his cap at you. I can feel it in me bones.' Ellie vociferously dismissed any notion that she and Alec Harman were anything more than 'neighbourly'. She disguised her deeper feelings well, and made no mention of what she had seen at the lake.

Aware that the boy was quietly regarding her, Ellie mentally shook herself free of all unsettling thoughts, and rising to her feet she told him, 'You'd best go and get your jumper . . . it might strike chilly later in the day.' She began piling up the breakfast things.

'Aw, Ellie . . . do I *have* to come with you? I'd rather stay here and build the bonfire!' He thrust his plate towards her and set himself stubbornly in the chair.

'Stop being difficult!' Lately, Ellie had come to realise that he would go to extraordinary lengths to get his own way. They had been at Thornton Place for over four months now, and in all that time Johnny had received no schooling. It was true that the long summer break had meant that the schools were closed from mid-July to early September. And that, in the weeks prior to them closing, Johnny was not recovered enough from the recent trauma to attend school. However, the local school was now opened and the doctor had previously warned Jack Armstrong, 'The boy must resume a normal life when you move . . . attending school . . . mixing with young-sters of his own age . . . it can only do good.' Last week, on the first day of the new term, the headmistress at nearby 'Crawley School' had eagerly received Johnny's enrolment. 'He can start on Monday,' she had told Ellie, proudly giving her a list displaying the items of uniform, and various regulations he would need to be aware of. Now, Ellie reminded her brother, 'You start at the new school on Monday, and we have to get your uniform *today*.' Collecting the pile of dishes into her hands, she pushed them against the wall and covered them with a tea towel. 'These will have to wait until we get back,' she moaned.

'Tell Rosie to do them!'

'Rosie has enough to do,' Ellie retorted, striding across the room towards him, with the intention of plucking him from the chair and propelling him out of the room.

'I'm going! I'm going!' Before she could get to him, he was out of the chair and skipping towards the door, where he turned and grinned at her. 'You might regret taking me to Medford,' he promised her, 'because . . . I won't be pleasant company.' The look of frustration on Ellie's face pleased him no end. She was upset, he knew. And there were times when he tried her to the end of her patience. It didn't bother him. She deserved it! What *did* bother him was the fact that she was wasting his precious time; when he could be building the most magnificent bonfire ever created. And *worse* . . . he dreamed last night that his secret friend would come to the barn today. Because of Ellie, he might miss him. He thought of the games they played . . . hide and seek games, and guessing games. Games where he was allowed to say whatever he liked, against whoever had offended him. Remembering these exciting games, his heart leapt. Oh, the things they said, he and his 'friend'! Wicked and dangerous things! Things that his father would thrash him for saying. But there, in the barn, in the darkest corners, where he and his secret 'friend' huddled from watching eyes, he could pour the black, hurtful things from his heart. And he was never, *ever* punished!

'You go on with you, darling . . . don't worry your pretty head about a thing.' Rosie met Ellie and the boy on the outer steps. 'My! You do look lovely, child.' She inclined her head to one side and regarded Ellie through panda-like eyes.

That morning, Ellie had taken considerable care with her appearance. After much deliberation, she had chosen to wear a pretty, autumn-coloured skirt. The sleeveless blouse was in the same rich amber as her eyes and the short, cream-coloured jacket over her arm matched the shade of her shoes. It was one that she had bought in Liverpool. Straight-cut and smart, it was a favourite of Ellie's – the kind of practical accessory that could be teamed up with almost any colour. Her golden hair had been brushed until the natural curls seemed to have a life of their own, springing and teasing about her face, giving her a carefree and jaunty look that belied the deep, sincere emotions which had shaped her mood of late. Now, when she smiled up at Rosie, her warm brown eyes gave nothing away. 'Why, thank you, Rosie,' she said, already beginning to make her way down the steps. 'We have to rush . . . got to catch the nine o'clock bus,' she told the older woman apologetically. Her eyes flicked to the bent, suspicious figure that had watched her these past minutes through small, hostile eyes. George shouldn't be here, she thought with a stab of anxiety; Rosie had no right to bring him here! Concerned about what her father would say if he knew, Ellie paused a while. 'Perhaps it might be best if you gave it a miss for today, Rosie,' she suggested discreetly. 'I'm afraid there was no time to tidy up properly this morning . . . the kitchen's in a dreadful mess. Take George home . . . I'll see to everything when I get back.'

'Away with you!' Rosie leaned her shoulders into the crutches and dismissed Ellie with a wave of her hand. 'Hurry . . . or you'll miss your bus. Don't worry about the kitchen, either, because me and George here can see to that, once I've done the big room.' She glanced at the boy's upturned face and chuckled. When in return she was greeted with a stern, disapproving expression, she shrugged her shoulders and turned her attention instead to her companion, 'That's right, ain't it, George, eh?' The tousled head nodded frantically; pale frightened eyes peering up through shaggy brows that hung down like two bedraggled curtains across his vision. 'There y'are!' exclaimed Rosie, raising the tip of her crutch and prodding the unfortunate creature, 'he's only too glad to be giving a helping hand.' When the crooked, nervous figure shuffled past them and disappeared into the house, Rosie saw that Ellie had misgivings – it was betrayed in her face. 'He'll be fine,' she chuckled. 'I know it was understood between your father and me, when he agreed a small sum in return for a few hours' domestic help . . . that George should never be allowed into the house . . . but, oh, he'll not be a problem, I promise.' She lowered her voice. 'Like as not, he'll curl up on the sofa and fall fast asleep . . . he had a bad night . . . *a terrible bad night* . . . hardly slept a wink, poor thing.'

'Oh, I don't know, Rosie . . .' Ellie was mindful of her father's strict instructions and the comment, 'Rosie's got all her marbles about her . . . she'll *earn* the two pounds ten a week . . . take some of the drudgery off your back, Ellie. But, only Rosie! On no account is the old man to set foot in this house. I wouldn't put it past him to lock Rosie in the cellar again . . . and lock all the doors against us!' The awful experience had never really left him – to the extent that he had removed the bolts from all the doors, and carried a key in his pocket at all times.

'Come on, Ellie, or we'll miss the bus,' urged the boy, tugging at her hand. He did not want to go into Medford in the first place, but, if they were to go now, there was a chance they could be back by mid-afternoon. If they missed the early bus, though, there'd be no telling when they'd get back! And he had set his heart on finding his 'friend' waiting for him in the barn. 'Don't forget . . . it's a

Saturday. Some of the shops might close early. And if I haven't got my uniform for school on Monday . . . I'm not going!' He put on his most churlish sulk, snapping her hand viciously and sucking his thin lips into an unattractive pout.

'You stop it this minute!' Ellie warned him. Right now, she had her own problems. As for the boy, she now tended to agree with her father that, 'It's time he learned he can't have his own way on everything. Okay . . . so he's young and prone to dwell on . . . unpleasant memories . . . perhaps longer than you or me. I *know* he's suffered badly. I *know* he's only nine years old. I *accept* the experience he went through that . . . that awful night must still torture him. It tortures all of us . . . And I understand how much he needs to come to terms with being . . . the one who found her. It's hard for him, losing his mother at such a tender age. But he's got *you*, Ellie . . . thank God, we've *both* got you!' Somewhat disturbed, Ellie promptly reminded her father that Johnny also had him, didn't he? Her father had made no reply, other than to abruptly excuse himself from the room, saying in a strangely quiet and private voice, 'I have things to do.'

'Go on, Ellie. Me and George . . . we'll be fine.' Rosie chuckled, 'I promise he won't lock you out.'

'Thank God for that!' Ellie laughed, pleasantly astonished that Rosie had picked on the one anxiety that was paramount in her thoughts. The mere mention of it by Rosie seemed to put it safely into perspective. Of course! How could her father be locked out? He had a key with him, didn't he? And there were no bolts on the doors.

As Ellie hurried the boy through the spinney – following a short cut that Alec Harman had shown her – she was frightened by a short burst of laughter from some place not too far away. Gripping the boy's hand, she accelerated her steps, keeping her anxious eyes fixed to the horizon, where the spinney gave way to open land

and there were no dark corners for things to hide in.

'What was that?' the boy asked, glancing nervously over his shoulder, as he struggled to keep up with Ellie's determined strides.

'I don't know,' Ellie told him impatiently, 'an animal perhaps?'

'No.' There was a ring of satisfaction in the boy's tone. 'It wasn't "an animal" . . . it was somebody laughing. It was . . . wasn't it, Ellie?' he insisted, almost running beside her now, and breathless. 'Is it George, eh? Is it mad George?'

'I've already told you, Johnny. I don't know!' She felt his eyes on her, accusing. He had every right to accuse her, because she was a liar. She did know. The sound was 'somebody laughing'. But it was not 'mad George'. Nor was it anyone else the boy knew. But she knew. Oh, yes! She *knew*! Because she had heard that same laughter not very long ago, down by the lake. It was the young woman, she was sure. The same one who had come running into the eager arms of Alec Harman. The same one who had brushed her lips against his. The same one who had whispered with him, and been so secretly intimate. Ellie *hated* her! But no. She could not bring herself to hate. The young woman had every right to love Alec Harman, and to enjoy his love in return. She only wished with all her sore heart that it was she who had won the love of 'the darkeye'. And though she did not 'hate' she felt humiliation and anger because of the way he had led her to believe there might be love between them. The memory of his mouth on hers was not one she could easily dismiss. It was a beautiful and sensuous experience that had remained with her, and would *always* remain with her. Even now, in this moment with the sound of that laughter ringing in her ears, she remembered how it was – how his body had pressed into hers and those black, liquid eyes had coveted her. The anger in her swelled to rage. How could he? How could he tempt her in that way, when all the while he was already promised? No, she could not hate; although there had been times since when she had come unnervingly close. But neither could she forgive. She wanted nothing more to do with the dark-eyed devil. The further he kept his distance from her, the better she would like it.

'You're hurting me!' Johnny's thin wail cut into Ellie's tortured thoughts, as he struggled to release his hand from her fierce grip.

'All right . . . we're almost there now.' The fury still bubbled inside her, but her brother must not know. He, of all people, must never know. Besides which, she accepted that her deeper feelings for Alec Harman must be denied, because they could only bring her more heartache. And she had already been through so much. So very much that all the Alec Harmans in this world could never understand. But Barny understood! He had understood and made sacrifices because of it. Throughout the whole, dreadful nightmare he had been a pillar of strength. He had shown her only kindness and love; wanting nothing more from her but the same. And she *had* loved him. She *did* love him. But, it wasn't the same, was it? The love she felt for Barny could not compare to the soaring exultation she had felt in Alec Harman's arms. When Barny kissed her, he made her feel warm and wanted; kind of 'comfortable'. With Alec Harman, something had awoken in her that she had never before experienced – passion, fire and such deep longing that even recalling the way it was made her every nerve-ending tingle. The feeling was indescribably beautiful, but it was also intensely painful. He was not hers. She could never forget that. Nor could she forget how callously he had toyed with her emotions! Perhaps her father was right. A man like that was dangerous. She would be far better cultivating her love for someone like Barny. That was what her head told her. It wasn't what her heart said.

'The bus is there, Ellie! . . . The bus is already there!' The boy broke free from Ellie's grasp and ran forward towards the shop, shouting and waving his arms at the driver who was presently preparing to depart. Seeing the boy and Ellie rushing towards him, he smiled and waited. In a minute they were on board. The conductor rang the bell, and the big red bus inched its way out of the shop forecourt and into the main road, which would take them the twelve or so miles to Medford town.

Settling back in the hard vinyl seat that struck cold to her thighs, Ellie deliberately quashed the bitterness that had taken hold of her. She chided herself for not having seen Alec Harman's true character before. Even now, she was not quite sure what his 'true character' was. All she *did* know was that he had cruelly led her to believe one thing, when another was the truth. But then she reminded herself that what had happened was probably no more for him than yielding to temptation in a moment of weakness. After all, he had made the caustic comment, 'You should never have come to this place.' That told her how sharply he regretted having taken her in his arms. She bristled inside at his arrogance. They were not intruders here, any more than he was! Although, the way in which Fred Gregory at the shop scowled on her and the boy whenever they went in there, it seemed to Ellie that Alec Harman was not the only one to resent their coming here. The inhabitants of Redborough were not at all friendly. Their narrow-minded, prejudiced attitude infuriated her, but she had managed to rise above all that. Old George, though! Well now, *he* was another matter altogether – what with his continued loathing and suspicion of them, it was too disturbing. It wasn't so much his hostile attitude as the unfortunate creature himself. There was no doubt in

Ellie's mind that he was helplessly and totally insane.

'Look, Ellie! Look!' The boy's shrill voice penetrated Ellie's unsettling thoughts. He was pointing out of the bus window, drawing her attention to what appeared to be a heap of rubble in the middle of a field. Nearby were two excited children, making their way to the 'rubble' and pulling a flat, wooden conveyor behind them; that too was piled high with various bits and pieces. 'They're building a bonfire,' the boy told Ellie. He laughed aloud; a devious and wicked sound that caused two women in front to stare round at him. 'It's a dismal bonfire!' he went on in acid tones, staring back at the two women until they looked away.

'Don't be so cruel, Johnny,' Ellie reprimanded him. 'Those children are every bit as proud of their bonfire as you are of yours.'

He laughed again, twisting his scrawny neck to look at the children once more before they disappeared from his sight. 'They're pitiful!' he muttered, then in such a vindictive voice that Ellie snatched a disapproving glance at him, he said, 'I'll put a curse on them.' He lifted his clear blue eyes and smiled sweetly at her.

'Don't say such things,' Ellie told him in a shocked voice.

'Oh, it's all right. It doesn't matter anyway, because they'll never be able to build a better bonfire than mine.' He looked hard at her, the smile playing about his mouth but never reaching the cold, calculating eyes. 'There's never been a bonfire like mine . . . ever! It's like a castle . . . you know, Ellie? Like the sandcastle mother helped me to build at the seaside.' He squeezed her fingers in his fist. 'You remember, don't you? Ellie? Say you remember.'

'I remember . . . of course I do.' It was all coming back to her. That was the week they spent in Scarborough. She *did* recall the sandcastle which Johnny and their mother had built and, if she remembered rightly, it took them almost a whole day to construct it out of the crumbling, dry sand. The castle was a magnificent creation, with huge turrets, broad walkways, and a labyrinth of deep, meandering tunnels. The huge structure was completely surrounded by a water-swollen moat. Passers-by had stopped to comment light-heartedly on the 'wonderful accomplishment'. She remembered also how devastated the boy had been when the tide came in and swept the thing away.

'I'm trying to build my bonfire exactly like the sand-castle,' the boy told Ellie proudly. 'It's going to have turrets, just the same . . . and a Guy Fawkes tied to the battlements . . . where he must burn to death.' He relished the idea; smiling at Ellie's surprised expression. 'Oh, and there'll be lots of tunnels, too . . . with little hide-aways. Only, nobody but me will know where they are.' He nearly said 'and my friend in the barn'. But he stopped himself just in time. A small burst of sweat shivered down his back at the thought of betraying his precious secret; their precious secret. He mustn't tell his friend that he had almost given their secret away. Oh, no! He must not do that, or his friend might never come to see him again. And the stranger was such a good friend – an exciting and special friend. It was that same friend who had helped him plan his bonfire, right down to the very last detail. Even to the tunnels and the secret hideaways!

The librarian seemed puzzled for a moment, looking at Ellie and the boy through curious eyes, which were magnified three-fold by the strong lenses in her metal-rimmed spectacles. 'So sorry,' she said, folding away the newspaper. 'I've been reading about the Government's plans to build the first Nuclear Power Station in this country. I can't say I like the idea . . . not at all!' When Ellie gave no answer she cleared her throat and looked embarrassed. 'Sorry, dear. Redborough, you say? Oh, yes! . . . Redborough . . . Thornton Place, Redborough.' She glanced away, looking up the stairs that led to the history and research section. 'Funny thing,' she told Ellie, drawing her gaze back and lifting the spectacles from the bridge of her hawkish nose. 'In the fourteen years I've worked here, I can't ever remember being asked about that particular house . . . Thornton Place . . . but do you know, this very day you are the second person to enquire after its history.' She whipped a clean white handkerchief from the open handbag on the desk and began vigorously polishing the lenses of her spectacles, breathing into them with short, sharp puffs and peering at Ellie through slitted, half-blind eyes.

'The *second* person?' Ellie was astonished, her curiosity instantly aroused.

'That's right, dear.' The thin-faced woman returned the metal-rimmed spectacles to their rightful place on the red dent across the bridge of her nose, and smiled at Ellie through the sparkling lenses. 'There was a man enquiring before you. First thing this morning, it was. I distinctly remember because I hardly had time to open the doors before he was asking about this "Thornton Place" . . . wanted to peruse any and all documents relating to it.' She wagged her head thoughtfully and rolled her eyes up until only the whites showed. After a brief interlude of deep musing she looked directly at Ellie, saying with pride, 'Yes . . . a man, middle-aged with a beard, and wearing a brown tweed jacket with a matching trilby.' She almost chuckled, but the restraints of many years' discipline would not allow it. 'I have an eye for faces,' she said, 'I *never* forget a face.' She might also have added that the man was somehow strange, a secretive sort who spoke in a thick whisper and averted his own eyes from hers. He had made her feel uneasy; suspicious even. But she revealed nothing of this to Ellie who, she cautioned herself, might be an acquaintance of the fellow.

'Did he give his name?' Ellie did not know why, but she was suddenly apprehensive. Why would anyone be investigating the history of Thornton Place? True, it was a listed building, and as such could be useful material for students, historians and the like. But, why now? The librarian herself had said she could not recall any previous interest in the house. So, why should someone be interested now? *Why now?* What was more, it was unlikely to be a student who had called this morning, because the woman had described him as being 'a middle-aged man, with a beard'. A lecturer, maybe? Someone who had recently arrived at a nearby college, and was keen on old architecture? Yes, that could be it, Ellie told herself, and she felt more at ease.

'I did not talk long with the man . . . other than to show him where the records department is.' She raised her arm and pointed to the stairway. 'You will need to see the gentleman at the desk there,' she said, already turning her attention to the next customer – a kind-faced lady who beamed at the boy with friendly eyes.

'If you'll just be seated for a minute, Miss Armstrong . . . I'll ask him how long he is likely to be. He took the papers into a cubicle some twenty minutes ago.' The man at the desk was much more to Ellie's liking. He had that disarming, welcoming manner that put a body immediately at ease. She had been both surprised and delighted to be told that the previous person to have enquired about Thornton Place was 'actually *still* in the cubicle . . . studying all the documents available on the house in question, although little has survived over the years, to tell much of its history. As I told the gentleman . . . the one or two documents we do have are very old, and very sparse. To be perfectly honest, I haven't even read them myself.'

Ellie had it in mind to talk with the man who had

shown such interest in the house. It might even be possible that he could tell her a thing or two that she did not know, or that might not be in the documents available. She hoped so, because in her deepest heart she suspected that Thornton Place had a sinister past. There was nothing to substantiate that belief, other than the brooding atmosphere that closed in with the darkness. There had been moments also when Ellie had felt other things about the house – things that touched her deeply, but which she could not explain.

Suddenly, the librarian was back, almost running towards her, a look of horror on his face. 'That man!' he gasped, frantically wringing his hands together, 'do you know him, Miss Armstrong?' His eyes were wide and shocked and a mist of perspiration appeared on his face. When Ellie told him she had no idea who the man was, he put his two hands over his temples and declared in a shattered voice, 'He's gone! There's no sign of him anywhere. And he's taken the documents with him!'

'Why would he do that?' Ellie rose to her feet.

'Excuse me . . . I must report the theft at once . . . those documents . . . irreplaceable. There are no other copies!' He scurried away, down the stairs. Ellie and the boy followed. At the lower desk, there was a degree of confusion. The hawkish-faced librarian insisted that the police should be told. There followed a short, fierce argument, during which it was decided that, first of all, the matter must be reported to the chief librarian at the main Medford branch. 'It will be he who decides whether to involve the police,' declared the irate man from the records desk.

After a brief but detailed telephone conversation with the chief librarian, the records clerk answered Ellie's queries. 'I'm sorry, but there were no copies of those documents . . . an oversight. And we have no other papers relating to Thornton Place.' However, he went on to explain that he would make extensive enquiries on her behalf, 'in due course . . . although the records office in London and other possible sources are very often under-staffed and inundated with work. All the same, I will do my best, I assure you.' Now that he had shifted the burden of the theft onto more responsible shoulders, he appeared less fraught. 'I can promise nothing, though,' he warned Ellie, 'but of course, there is a possibility that the thief will be apprehended, and the original documents returned.'

Ellie thought not. Not after the 'thief' had gone to so much trouble to remove the documents in the first place. But why? Why on earth should anyone want to remove the records of Thornton Place? There was only one answer, to her mind. Those records were taken in order to prevent them from being examined by anyone else. Or by her in particular! But why? What was it about the house that must be kept from inquisitive eyes? She recalled what the hawkish-faced librarian had said – 'No interest . . . for many years . . . then *two* interested parties only that very day.' A disturbing thought flitted across Ellie's mind. It was almost as though that man had known why she was coming to the library today.

Ellie thought hard. It was suddenly important for her to remember who exactly had known. Her father, of course, and Johnny. The only other person in whom she had confided her intention to trace the history of Thornton Place was Mrs Gregory at the shop. And, if Ellie remembered correctly, she had not been too interested; in fact, at the time, Ellie had wondered whether the busy little soul had even heard her, for she made no comment and quickly changed the subject when her husband appeared. Oh, then of course there was Rosie! The only other person who knew Ellie's purpose for going to the library today . . . It crossed Ellie's mind to wonder whether Rosie might have mentioned it to Alec Harman. After all, he was a regular visitor to the cottage, and a firm friend to Rosie and the feeble-minded one. The feeble-minded one! A cold shiver rippled through Ellie's being. No. Don't be foolish, she told herself. But the nagging thought would not go away. The thief had been a man, hadn't he? Yes, she argued with herself, but the description of the 'man' bore no relation whatsoever to the old one. Neither by any stretch of the imagination could it be Alec Harman.

Before leaving the library, Ellie again questioned the records clerk. His description of the thief was exactly the same as the one given to her by the downstairs librarian – 'shifty-eyed . . . nervous . . . middle-aged, with a dark beard, and wearing a brown tweed jacket with trilby in similar cloth.' The thief was a stranger. He had to be, didn't he? *Didn't he?* Her answer was a chilling feeling, and the certain knowledge that, whoever the thief was, he or she was an enemy. He . . . or she! The thought had just popped into her mind. He, *or she*. But that didn't make sense. She was being foolish now . . . letting her imagination run away with her.

'I don't want to stay and watch the ducks . . . I want to go home.' The boy sat on the bank beside Ellie, skimming pebbles into the river.

'We'll be going home soon, Johnny,' Ellie told him, her gaze fixed on the shimmering surface of the water, and occasionally at the ducks that had gathered not far off, hoping to cadge a titbit from the visitors. Her voice was subdued by the thoughts which still disturbed her.

'You're thinking about that thief, aren't you?' the boy asked, feverishly searching the grass for another small stone with which he might frighten away the approaching fowl. 'I think he was a ghost!' he said, with some satisfaction.

'Don't talk rubbish,' Ellie chided. 'I'm not surprised you're always having nightmares!' Suddenly irritated, she clambered down the bank to the path. 'Come on, we'd better get your uniform, and pay a quick visit to the market. If we hurry, we might just catch the two o'clock bus back to Redborough.' She had intended shopping for a new outfit herself, but somehow her enthusiasm had been spoiled by the events of the morning.

'Now. Can we go home *now*, Ellie?' The boy stood impatiently by, while Ellie paid the man on the market stall for the bright yellow chrysanthemums. All around them was a hubbub of noise and busy pandemonium. People thronged this way and that, some rushing to snap up the late bargains, and others who just loitered, turning the artefacts over on every stall, before walking away empty-handed. Above the general din there rose a bevy of shriller voices – market traders eager to dispose of perishable goods before the last shoppers deserted them to wend their way home. Medford being a market town, there were any number of fruiterers and greengrocers, each keenly competing with the others in a frantic bid to offload their respective produce at tempting prices. Ellie took the time to buy a week's supply of fresh fruit and, much to the boy's growing agitation, she lingered a while by the draper's stall, where she chose some pretty floral curtain material, a set of towels and a dozen tea-cloths.

'*Please*, Ellie . . . I'm tired. Can't we go home . . . please?' The boy moaned for the umpteenth time, and protested yet again at the increased weight of the shopping bag which Ellie had entrusted to him.

Ellie nodded, threading a path through the bodies that continued to surge and congregate in little, busy pockets. 'All right,' she conceded, 'I've almost spent out anyway . . . and I doubt we could carry any more, even if I did have the money to buy it with.' She paused, putting the two heavy bags to the ground and flexing her cramped fingers until the blood flowed freely.

The boy waited, impatient, the frustration simmering inside him. His ice-blue eyes scanned the busy scene from every side, quietly noting the faces above him; adult faces – alien to him, and bitterly resented. Suddenly, his unfriendly gaze came to rest on a more intriguing face. It was the worn and grimy face of an old man; a pedlar. The pedlar's eyes were mingling with the boy's, making him curious. And a little afraid. As though in a trance, the boy began his way towards the bent figure, whose smile remained locked into the boy's cool, quizzical eyes. Mocking. Silently beckoning.

In a moment, the boy was standing before the ragged man. Out of the dirt-laden face and the thick, matted beard, the eyes continued to gaze down on him. Eyes like dark, spitting whirlpools. Strange eyes that were both frightening and comforting. Eyes that were old, and yet were not. Eyes that the boy was sure he had seen before. But where? *Where?* When the voice spoke, it was mesmerising. It held a whisper of madness. 'Hello, Johnny,' it said. The boy was not surprised to hear it speak his name. 'See here . . . on the tray.' The brown-clad arms reached out, drawing the boy's attention to the wooden tray that hung from a thick strap around the tattered shoulders. On the tray was a solitary object. A trinket. Tiny and beautiful it was, and vividly blue. The detail was exquisite. The flower was unmistakable. From the tray, and from the man himself, the powerful scent of lavender rose up to insinuate its way into the boy's nostrils. Into his head. Into those innate fears which would never leave him. Instinctively, he reeled back. Yet he was compelled to linger, even though his every instinct urged him to run. His legs were like lead on his quivering body. And, in spite of the fear that trembled through him, he was also greatly excited.

'*Take it.*' The mocking eyes dared him. All around the

sounds of the market-place droned in his ears. He was a part of it all, he and the pedlar. Then they were not part of it at all. It was as though the two of them were in another place, another time. Now, the boy remembered! The pedlar reminded him of another such vagabond. The same one who had come to the house where they had lived before. The same one who had given him the fresh, sweet-smelling lavender that had so terrified his mother. *His mother.* A surge of hatred stabbed through his heart and the tears burned his eyes. She had died . . . left him in that shocking, cruel way. He would never forgive her for that.

'Take it I say!' The voice grew agitated; the brown-clad arms reached out. 'Use it to curse them. *All of them!*' The crazed eyes sought out the trinket, lingering, enjoying. The perfume rose, heightening his pleasure. 'Lavender,' he murmured, 'lavender . . . and poison.' *Lavender and poison*.

The boy was afraid; cold inside, as though something icy had touched him. But now a sense of wickedness took hold of him. He drew his eyes from the pedlar's smiling face, his sly gaze seeking out the trinket once more. He began reaching forward, eager to touch it, to feel the hard, glittering stones. The moment was close. So *very* close. But then the spell was rent apart by Ellie, frantically calling his name. In a reflex action, the boy slewed round to see her rushing towards him. When he turned again, the pedlar was gone.

On the bus journey back to Thornton Place, the boy was tempted to tell Ellie about the pedlar. And the lavender trinket. But the temptation quickly passed. She would not believe him for one thing, and, for another, the thought of keeping it secret was a greater temptation. Yes. He *would* keep it secret! A special secret between him and his 'friend' in the barn. It would be good for him to share the strange experience. It would be something that he himself could offer to the secret meetings. He wondered whether his 'friend' would come today? He never knew when the stranger would be waiting there. When, on the one occasion he had been bold enough to ask, he was told in a frightful whisper, 'That is for *me* to know, and *only me*! Don't ever . . . ever . . . question my movements again.' And he never did.

CHAPTER SIX

'What in God's name is that boy building out there?' Jack Armstrong leaned over on the ladder to look out of the bedroom window. 'He's like somebody possessed. He's got Rosie helping him now!'

Ellie laughed. 'I'm sure Rosie can't be much help,' she said, jabbing the sewing needle into the floral curtain material. Rising to her feet, she carefully draped the material over the chair where she had been sitting. Going to the bedroom window, she also gazed out towards the back of the house and beyond, to the rough pasture land some way from the big barn. What she saw was the boy and Rosie, wending their way from the hedge that skirted the field. They were struggling to bring a huge, fallen branch to the already mountainous bonfire. Seated nearby, on what looked to be a wooden stool, was George – a pitiful, dejected soul, with his arms folded and a look of nervousness about him. Every now and then he jerked his head this way and that, like a bird nervous of approaching predators.

'I've never known a boy scour so far and wide . . . just to build a bonfire.' Jack Armstrong shook his head and resumed his task – that of fixing the lamp shade. 'And why you should have chosen such a frilly, useless thing is beyond me, Ellie,' he pointed out, ducking his eyes from the irritating silk tassels that hung round the shade like a hula-skirt. 'You'll not get much light from this thing!' he

131

moaned. 'You should have listened to what I told you, Ellie . . . glass shades are much better than these cloth things. It's lined, too . . . that'll cut down the light even more.' He pushed the connection home and steadied the shade. 'There you are. Now . . . if you don't mind, sweetheart, I'll get on with replastering the walls in the next room.' He folded the ladder in and carried it across the room towards the door.

Ellie watched him. She was pleasantly surprised at the change in her father since coming to Thornton Place. He seemed younger, somehow; slimmer and almost boyishly enthusiastic. There was a definite spring in his step these days, and his deep blue eyes were quick to smile. She supposed he had found the purpose that would help him forget the sorrows of the past. She hoped so. Certainly he had tackled the daunting task of renovating this old place with such eagerness and energy that he had little time left with which to brood. She was glad, for all their sakes.

All the same, there was one area that still gave Ellie cause for concern. If her father's workload gave him little time for fretting over their recent tragedy, by the same token it left him even less time to spend with his son. It grieved Ellie to see how far apart those two had grown. They never indulged in the usual pastimes which father and son might enjoy – kicking a ball about, or fishing by the lake. The father was always too busy, and the son showed unnatural contempt for such things. The only occasion on which they talked was the hour immediately after supper, when the father would attempt to make interested conversation – enquiring as to the boy's progress at school, and stressing the importance of a 'good education'. On such occasions Johnny was not very forthcoming, seeming to resent what he described to Ellie as 'an inquisition'. Daily, he grew more morose and secretive, withdrawing into himself, and disappearing for hours on end when his school day was over, or at weekends. When questioned by the anxious Ellie, he would claim to have been 'collecting for the bonfire'. And, although it was true that the bonfire had grown to formidable proportions, she had twice seen him come out of the big barn, but afterwards he had blatantly denied ever having been there. Both times she had later gone into the barn and looked around; she was not sure exactly what she hoped to find. In the event, she found nothing untoward, eventually dismissing the incidents as being nothing more than a boy's natural sense of adventure.

'Dad.' Ellie called her father back. She had so much on her mind. So very much she wanted to discuss with him, about the boy; about this feeling she had . . . had always felt . . . that all was not well here. About that man who had stolen the documents to Thornton Place. And, most of all, about Barny Tyler's letter. She had almost made up her mind, but would have liked to discuss it with her father, or with Rosie. In the instant her father swung round at her call, Ellie decided she would prefer to discuss Barny's letter with Rosie, after all. Only a woman, even a much older woman like Rosie, could understand the struggle going on inside her.

'What now?' Jack Armstrong levelled his dark blue eyes at her and stood by the doorway, his arm through the ladder, and a look of impatience about his whole countenance. 'Ellie . . . you know how much work there is to do! You've read the letter that was delivered to the shop with a packet of money last week . . . a letter warning us that the solicitor intends to call before the year's end. Ellie, it's the first of November today!' he reminded her. 'That means he could turn up anytime in the next eight weeks.' He saw Ellie about to speak and put up his hand, saying, 'All right, all right . . . I know he won't expect us to have carried out all the work that needs doing.' He looked round the room and groaned,

'Lord knows it'll take more time than we've had, to even break the back of it . . . but, he *will* expect to see some results for his money.'

'Don't be so hard on yourself,' Ellie told him. 'You've done wonders in the seven months we've been here . . . the bathroom, kitchen and the big room are finished; the worst of the broken roof tiles replaced; all the fencing round the house repaired and most of the front windows made good . . . the plumbing put right . . . and three bedrooms totally renovated.'

'Woa! Hold on, sweetheart,' he laughed. 'I take your point. It's true we *have* done a great deal . . . but there are still another four bedrooms and two rooms downstairs. Still, I could not have done any of it without your help and support.' His son was strong in his thoughts just then, as was the increasing belief that Johnny was useless to him. God only knew how he had tried to reach the boy, tried to communicate with him in the only way he knew, but there had been no real response, no great enthusiasm for either his company or his opinion. That Johnny was a strange one, secretive and impossible to fathom. To his mind, the boy had been so deeply affected by the thing he had found that night – the grotesque and almost unrecognisable thing that had been his mother. It wasn't the boy's fault. Nobody could blame him for being the way he was. He was to be more pitied than blamed. The sad truth was, though, that the boy had alienated himself from his own father. 'Maybe he blames *me* in some way,' he had often wondered; 'perhaps he thinks I should have protected his mother . . . *saved* her, even.' Dear God, how often he had asked himself the very same question. He could not answer it truthfully. Nor could he give the boy any reassurances. It had happened. No one knew why. Let the boy blame him if he must. It was all part of the punishment! He looked at Ellie, at the petite figure in dungarees; the heart-shaped face and wild, corn-coloured hair. He gazed into the smiling, amber eyes that reminded him of her mother, and he was ravaged by pain. 'I do realise how lucky I am to have you,' he said, leaning the ladder against the wall and coming to wrap his arms round her small shoulders.

'And I'm lucky to have you,' she said sincerely, putting her head to his chest. She knew by his mood that he had been thinking about her mother. 'Dad.' She *had* to ask. She desperately needed reassurance.

'Yes?'

'You don't mind, do you . . . about Barny coming to stay for the bonfire celebrations?'

He held her at arm's length, holding her gaze with his own. 'Seeing as I wasn't consulted in the first place . . . I don't have much choice, do I, eh?' He chuckled. 'No, I don't mind.' Before he departed the room, he warned her good-humouredly, 'But don't you go making the fellow any rash promises, will you? I've no intention of losing you just yet!' But, if he *must* 'lose' her, he prayed to God that it would not be to the likes of Alec Harman, a creepy bugger if ever he'd seen one! Still, thank goodness things appeared to have cooled down in that direction, because the Harman fellow had not shown his face in this quarter these many weeks. He couldn't be sure how Ellie felt about the scoundrel, because she refused to discuss him, but she was a sensitive young woman. She knew bad when she saw it. Still, she had seemed dangerously attracted to him. It would come right, though, Jack Armstrong was sure of it. He was surprisingly pleased that she was entertaining thoughts of Barny Tyler. After meeting the Harman fellow, there was no doubt in Jack Armstrong's mind as to who was the better of two evils. Yes. It *would* come right; he had to believe that. Just as long as Ellie wasn't using Barny Tyler to make the Harman fellow jealous!

★　★　★

After her father had gone and she could hear him pottering about in the next room, Ellie remained by the window. She found a certain pleasure in watching the antics of Rosie and Johnny as they shaped the bonfire into a huge symmetrical structure. It struck her as being somewhat disquieting how obsessed the boy had been in making that bonfire. They had celebrated Bonfire Night many times over the years, but Ellie could never recall her brother ever having shown such keen interest. Still, she told herself, in the same way this house had helped her father to forget what had gone before, the bonfire had given Johnny a similar means of escape. She was thankful for that much at least. But what about *me*? she mused. What is there here for *me*?

Ellie had come to love Thornton Place, it was true. But it was an uneasy kind of love, mingled with fear and suspicion which she could not fully understand. In the dead of night, when sleep would not come, she often looked out of this same window – searching the horizon for something . . . *someone*. Was it that she secretly hoped to glimpse the tall, shadowy figure of Alec Harman? He was always there, in her thoughts, in her heart. She loved him. Wanted him more than ever. And yet, she knew she would never go to him. He had his woman and he did not want her. But she was not entirely alone, was she? She also had someone who loved and wanted her. She had Barny. In her mind's eye she could see him standing over her, his green eyes brimming with love, the attractive lopsided smile that had the power to make her heart turn somersaults. Oh, but that was before. What now? *What now?* Her spirit dipped deep inside her and the tears stung her eyes.

'*Ellie!*' Rosie's exuberant voice soared towards the window. Ellie blinked away the threatening tears to focus her eyes on the excited figure some way off. Rosie was waving, inviting Ellie to join in the fun. Ellie shook her head. She did not want company just now. Not even Rosie's. For a moment, it seemed as though the older woman was satisfied, but then she began coming across the field in that peculiar hopping gait, the tips of her crutches carefully avoiding any ruts and rises in the roughened ground. Inside herself, Ellie groaned. Rosie was not one to take 'no' for an answer!

In a minute, Rosie's familiar figure had disappeared behind the barn. Ellie waited for her to emerge again, when she intended calling from the window to explain how she had too much work to do here. When the curtains were hung, there was the evening meal to serve, and afterwards she had to make sure that Johnny did his homework before he went to bed. Besides, it would soon be dark.

Absorbed in keeping her eyes peeled for Rosie to come round the corner of the barn, Ellie failed to see what was happening in the field beyond. The boy was tormenting poor, senile George – jabbing at him with a long branch; each poke more vicious than the one before. The boy's utter enjoyment was evident in the devilment on his smiling face. George was bent forward, his arms folded over his head in a bid to fend off the hurtful thrusts that stabbed all over his frail, crooked body. He did not scream or cry out, but frantically rocked himself back and forth, whimpering like a baby and occasionally squealing when the sharp-ended branch hit home. Suddenly, he slithered from his seat and scurried on all fours into the nearby ditch. The boy did not immediately follow. Instead, his devious eyes watched the unfortunate quarry in its frantic bid to escape him. He smiled at the thin, spreading trail of blood it left behind, and when with a terrified backward glance it fled into the spinney, he followed. He had come to enjoy the games he played in the barn. His 'friend' had taught him well. He liked all the games they played, but there was never any blood; not like *now*. He liked this game best of all!

★ ★ ★

'Nonsense, child!' Rosie yelled up at the window, 'there's a good hour before dark, and you've worked hard enough all day!' She shook her head at Ellie's protests. 'I'm coming up,' she shouted, at once disappearing out of sight as she passed beneath the jutting eaves outside Ellie's room. With a small chuckle, Ellie turned from the window, shaking her head and smiling at the older woman's stubbornness.

The long, awkward climb up the stairs had almost drained Rosie's strength. 'God love us, child,' she gasped, leaning against the door-jamb and peeking at Ellie through mischievous brown eyes. 'I do believe I ain't so young as I fancy.' Refusing Ellie's offer of help, she hobbled into the room and sank heavily into the small, padded chair by the polished-oak dressing table.

'I've told you before . . . you push yourself too hard!' Ellie chided, sitting on the edge of the bed and watching anxiously while Rosie composed herself. 'You stay here . . . I'll go down to the kitchen . . . make us a brew of tea.'

'*Brew of tea!*' Rosie stared at her through shocked eyes. 'Huh! . . . now, if you'd offered me a small measure of something stronger . . . well then, I just might be tempted.' She laughed out loud, playfully prodding Ellie with the flat of her crutch. Ellie laughed too, thinking how, if she were to live to such a grand old age, she might be blessed with Rosie's admirable vigour. She quietly regarded the older woman now – the straight, white teeth that Rosie proudly proclaimed were 'me very own!'; the twinkling eyes that were encased in deep, smudged circles of extravagant make-up; the scarlet mouth so imaginatively enlarged, and the brassy-blonde, waist-length hair that was normally coiled in attractive fashion on top of her head, and which was now hanging in blissful tatters all about her ample shoulders.

'Rosie . . . you look a mess!' Ellie told her, knowing the other woman would never take offence.

'I expect I do!' Rosie chortled, grabbing both hands to her hair and desperately trying to tuck it into some sort of order. 'I expect I bloody do!' She sighed, giving up the effort and letting her unruly hair tumble freely. 'And so would you . . . if you'd been roped in to drag lumps of timber and all manner of debris across half the countryside!'

'You should have refused.'

'Refused? . . . that little bugger won't *let* you "refuse".' She chuckled. 'Besides . . . I thoroughly enjoyed meself. It's been *years* since I helped to build a bonfire.' She was suddenly serious. 'Strange creature though, ain't he . . . your Johnny? What I mean is, he ain't got much to say for himself, has he? Prefers his own company most of the time . . . and no matter what you do for him . . . he's never what you might call . . . friendly.' She shrugged her shoulders. 'Still, I suppose it takes all sorts, eh? It wouldn't do if we were all alike, would it, eh? All the same, I wish the little sod would let me take him fishing of a Sunday afternoon . . . instead of spending every blessed spare minute he's got building that bloody monument!' She jerked her head in the direction of the window. 'I ain't never seen anything like it, I'm telling you!'

'I know,' Ellie remarked. 'I worry about Johnny. Like you said, he does prefer his own company . . . it's not natural, is it? I've asked him to fetch a couple of friends home from the school, but he says he hasn't got any friends at school . . . doesn't *want* any. The headmistress says he's a loner . . . but not to worry because some children take a while to settle.' Her eyes clouded with worry.

'Oh, he'll be all right!' Rosie assured her. 'There ain't nothing more healthy for a young boy than building a bonfire. And he'll soon start mixing with the young ones at school. You'll see. Happen he'll invite them to see his wonderful bonfire go up in flames, eh?' She teased Ellie with the tip of her crutch. 'So stop worrying, won't you? While I've got you to myself . . . there's *other* things I'd sooner talk about.'

'Like?' Ellie was teasing. She suspected what it was that Rosie was curious about.

'Like this young man of yours . . . Barny, if I remember right.'

'Barny Tyler. But, he's not really my "young man". I haven't seen him for nearly seven months, we have recently exchanged letters, but I made it clear from the outset that I was not making a commitment. Deep down, Rosie, I know there is no future for me with Barny.' It was strange how his excited reply to her letter had left her cold.

'So I gather,' remonstrated Rosie with a condemning look, 'and whose fault might that be, eh? Yours! That's whose. I think it's shameful the way you've kept the poor bugger hanging on like that. It's a wonder he didn't return your invitation with a "no, thank you very much and piss off!" '

'Ah, but he didn't.'

'So you say. But it would have served you right, to my way of thinking! From what you tell me, this Barny is a decent sort.'

'He is . . . steady and loyal.'

'But don't you love him?' When Ellie gave no answer but lapsed into deep, troubled thought, Rosie went on cautiously, 'It's Alec Harman, ain't it? He's the one who's stolen your heart from Barny. It's no good denying it to me, child, because I've seen the way you fall apart when he's near . . . the way you look at him. What's more . . . I've seen the way he looks at you.' She shook her head and looked hard into Ellie's troubled amber eyes. 'What I can't understand is . . . if you're so attracted to each other, what's keeping you apart?'

'You should ask *him*! He still comes to the cottage regularly, doesn't he?' The memory of Alec and the other woman haunted her.

'He does . . . says he likes to keep an eye out for me and George.' She laughed. 'The way he fusses, anybody would think we were about to be slaughtered in our beds.' Memory flooded back and a cold hand touched her heart. But she mustn't speak of such things. Not to Ellie. *Not to anyone*.

She lowered her voice. 'Truth is, Ellie . . . I reckon he's been told to keep an eye on us by Wentworth Estates . . . ever since George deliberately set fire to the woods soon after his wife was killed. The poor soul was out of his mind with grief . . . said the devil who'd murdered her was still lurking in the woods . . . waiting to get *him* next.'

Ellie was both saddened and intrigued. 'You never have told me how she died.' Rosie dropped her gaze to the floor at Ellie's comment. When she looked up again, there was pain in her eyes. 'She was crushed to death . . . dreadful it was!' She paused, then: 'She and George had a fierce argument by all accounts . . . nobody knows what it was about. George refused to say, but it was enough to send them at each other's throats, I reckon. Anyway, she told him she was leaving Thornton Place . . . that she loathed it here. There was a terrible storm raging the night she ran out. George pleaded with her to wait, but she wouldn't listen. He went after her.' The memory of it all washed over Rosie. She shuddered, before going on in quieter tones. 'I couldn't sleep that night . . . what with the storm and everything. From the cottage I heard what I thought were raised voices but, I couldn't really tell . . . the thunder drowned everything out, you see. *Oh, but I heard the screams!*' Her panda-like eyes swelled and rolled upwards in her head. 'And what sounded like timber being wrenched from the ground . . . all mixed up it was. Then a silence; a shocking, eerie silence . . . like the whole world had died. To my shame, I daren't go out . . . there had been . . . *noises* . . . before.' She visibly shuddered. 'Alec Harman found George and his poor wife soon after dawn . . . he'd been patrolling the woods . . . assessing the damage when the storm subsided. George was badly hurt but still alive. He was in hospital some time . . . and, well, you've seen what the awful experience did to him . . . it might have been more merciful if he had been killed that night. His wife was pinned under the bulk of the branches . . . the back of her head . . . pulp, they said. She must have caught the full force and died instantly. As for George . . . he has never recovered. He's deteriorated rapidly, until now he can't think straight . . . he's beset by demons and guilt. Haunted by something deeper . . . some awful presence that won't leave him be.'

'But it wasn't his fault.' Ellie had been shocked by the account. This was the first time Rosie had opened her heart. Yet, even now, she suspected that Rosie was keeping something back. 'That's not all, is it, Rosie?' she ventured. 'There's something else, isn't there?'

For a moment, it seemed as though Rosie might confide everything in Ellie, but then she thought better of it. 'No, that was the way it happened,' she insisted. 'Except . . . I have never been able to forgive myself for not raising the alarm sooner . . . when I heard the screams. It's a terrible guilt I've had to live with. Do you know, child . . . you are the only person I've told. The only one who knows that I might have helped on that night, and I did nothing!' She averted her scarred eyes from Ellie, and bowing her tousled head she murmured, 'Now, you know why I'm beholden to him . . . Why I could never let them put him in an institution.'

'Oh, Rosie! Rosie! How can you blame yourself?' Ellie was filled with compassion towards this dear, troubled woman. She had never guessed. How could she? Rosie was a past master at disguising her innermost thoughts. Who could know that beneath that lively, plucky extrovert there was a seething, tormented soul? 'You said yourself there was a violent storm raging. How would you know exactly where the screams were coming from? If you had gone out on such a night, you might have been killed yourself . . . and even if you had raised the alarm earlier . . . who's to say it wasn't already too late . . . she "died instantly" you said.' Ellie was desperate to ease Rosie's awful burden. Suddenly, she recalled something else Rosie had said. 'Besides, how could you be so certain that anyone was in trouble? Didn't you say how there had been . . . "noises" . . . before?' She didn't go so far as to ask what *kind* of 'noises' Rosie had heard prior to the accident. She didn't ask, because she already knew. Hadn't she herself been awakened by strange 'noises' in the middle of the night? And hadn't she, to her own shame, been afraid to investigate? 'I'm glad you confided in me,' she told Rosie, 'and you have to believe that you should not feel guilty.' She pressed her hand over Rosie's bony fingers. 'You're a good woman, Rosie. Please don't punish yourself for something that would probably have happened anyway . . . with or without your intervention.'

'I suppose you're right, Ellie.'

'I *know* I'm right.'

'You'll not repeat what I've told you, will you, Ellie? It's hard enough knowing myself what a shameful coward I am. I couldn't bear it if the people on the estate were to find out . . . I know how quick they can be to condemn.'

'What you've told me about that night will go no further, you can be sure of that, but, please Rosie, do as I ask . . . put the idea of guilt out of your mind. There was nothing you could have done, I'm certain of it.'

Rosie's eyes met Ellie's anxious gaze. She smiled and

nodded. 'All right,' she said. The smile broke into a grin. She was the old, carefree Rosie that Ellie had come to know. Suddenly, there was no sign of the trauma that had momentarily erupted. But it was still there – pressed deep into Rosie's senses, and disguised by the radiance of her smile. The guilt would still go on plaguing her, and the other things. Those things of terror which she could not bring herself to speak of. On that God-forsaken night when George had been sent over the edge of sanity, and his wife was killed, there had been something else. There were the screams, yes. Horrible, unearthly screams that had sounded like nothing she had ever heard before. Not real. *More devil than human.* But, for the sake of her own reason, Rosie had convinced herself that the screams were those of George and his wife, when they saw the tree falling down on them. But, even so, there were other, unexplained things on that night. Things she had never fully understood. Obscure and shadowy images that played in Rosie's mind even at this minute. Of a face peering through the cottage window and looking right at her – a distorted, maniacal face, smudged with blood and smiling wickedly in the blue-white streaks of lightning that danced across it. Then, the awful sound of laughter as it went into the night. For a long time afterwards Rosie had lain in her bed, stiff and hardly breathing, her terrified eyes following the shadows created by the night-light at her bedside. She made herself concentrate on the gyrating shapes that flitted across the ceiling. Outside, the storm was beginning to subside. But not the chaos inside her. Not for a second dare she lower her eyes to the window. Nor dare she close them, because – then – she would see it . . . that grinning, nightmarish face. After an age, sleep had claimed her. In the morning, the sun was shining. The nightmare had gone. And it was only a nightmare, Rosie told herself. She had to believe that.

When George and his wife were found, Rosie made no mention of the face in her dreams. She knew the people hereabouts. She knew of their superstitions regarding Thornton Place. They believed in spectres and tales of long ago. The stories of disappearing trespassers had become legend. Old superstitions died hard. Rosie knew that more than most. They would call her a witch. They would look on her as having been 'affected' by her years of living in that house. The authorities probably would not believe her, because on that morning when she had searched beneath the window, there were no footprints, no trace of anyone ever having been there. The rain had been a deluge. How could she substantiate what she had seen?

No. It was a figment of the night and the storm. A bad and wicked dream. That's all. *That was how Rosie kept her sanity*.

'Have you heard from the library yet . . . about the documents?'

'No.' Ellie saw through Rosie's ploy to deliberately change the subject, but she was relieved all the same. She hoped the conversation between them had finally put an end to Rosie's guilt. 'I telephoned from the shop the other day, but there has been no response as yet from their enquiries. Certainly, the thief who took the documents has not been found.'

'Strange business.' Rosie shifted uncomfortably in her chair until the brown-stockinged leg-stump protruded stiff and bedraggled from beneath her blue-panelled skirt. She tapped it. 'Bloody useless thing,' she chuckled, her familiar merriment spilling over darker, more disturbing emotions. 'Sometimes I think I ought to have it chopped off to the hip-bone.'

'Don't say such a terrible thing,' Ellie reprimanded in a shocked voice. She might have asked how Rosie had been so disfigured, but, somehow, it didn't seem to matter.

Anyway, if Rosie wanted to tell her, she would do so, in her own good time. 'Perhaps the old documents were worth a bit of money . . . maybe the thief knew someone who would pay handsomely for such antiquities.'

'Hmm . . . maybe.' Rosie had wondered about the incident, but as yet she had not come to any real conclusions. All the same, to her mind it was a disquieting thing to have happened. One that had set her thinking.

After a while the talk graduated onto other things; when Rosie congratulated Ellie on how delightful the room was, with its pretty rose wallpaper and new, pink cushions scattered over the patchwork eiderdown, and 'how pretty those curtains will look at the window . . . I can't believe how wonderful that old oak dresser looks . . . like new again. And I think you were quite right not to throw out the old brass bedstead, because it suits this sunny room just fine.' She wanted to know when Barny was due to arrive, and wasn't Ellie beside herself with excitement at the prospect of seeing him again?

In fact, they found such pleasure in each other's company that neither of them noticed how quickly the evening was drawing in. It was only when the boy's footsteps could be heard on the stairs that Rosie struggled from the chair to swing towards the window on her crutches, exclaiming, 'Buggered if it ain't dark!' When the boy came into the bedroom she was craning her neck to see across the field. Already the night fogged her vision. She jerked her head back to ask anxiously, 'Did George come back with you?' When he shook his head, she hurried towards him, the thud of her crutches against the floor like the sound of approaching thunder. When she spoke again, her voice was marbled with fear. 'Where is he, Johnny . . . where did you leave him? Is he still out there . . . in the dark?' The boy's answer was to shrug his shoulders and throw his twig-like arms out in a gesture of indifference. Seeing how futile it would be to question him further, she pushed past, muttering fiercely under her breath, then swearing aloud, 'How bloody stupid can I be? I should never have left him out there . . . not even for a minute!' There was real fear in her voice.

'*Wait, Rosie!*' Ellie stopped only to grab a long, woollen jacket from a peg behind the door, before chasing from the room. 'We'll come with you.' She ran to the room next door, intending to recruit her father. If George had wandered off and got himself lost, they would need a pair of strong arms to fetch him back – George could be painfully stubborn if he had a mind. Ellie was shocked to find that while she and Rosie had been chatting, her father had stopped his work and had gone. She called out, but there was no reply. Downstairs . . . he's probably downstairs, she decided. But, he was not. A swift inspection of the ground floor told Ellie that her father was nowhere in the house. By now, she was frantic, hoping that Rosie would have the good sense to search the cottage first, before making off across the fields in the dark.

'You won't find him.' The surly voice made Ellie turn. 'It's too dark now, and, anyway, I expect the wild animals have eaten him.' The boy stood at the foot of the stairs, one arm hanging limp by his side, the other snaked round the banister. He regarded Ellie through chilling eyes, a smile playing about his mouth as he said, 'There *are* wild animals in the woods. *I've seen them.*'

'All right, Johnny. That's enough!' Ellie had little patience with the boy these days, especially when he showed no mercy to poor unfortunates like George. She would have taken him to task for being so callous in his remarks just now, but there was no time. It was possible that George had gone back to the cottage and was safe. But, she had to satisfy herself. She must catch up with Rosie. 'Go and clean yourself up,' she told the boy, 'there's hot water . . . get a bath and put your dirty clothes in the linen bin.' She was frantically searching for the long, metal torch that her father always kept by the back door. There was no sign of it. It suddenly occurred to her that her father might be in the cellar. She would have checked, but there was no time.

'You won't find old George. I *know*.'

At the door, Ellie slewed round. 'Do as you're told!' she snapped, 'and when your father comes back . . . tell him where I've gone.' She was already hastening towards the cottage, thankful that, as yet, there was still a vestige of twilight to mark her way.

At the cottage, Rosie was beside herself with worry. 'He's not here,' she said, her panda-like eyes big and tearful as they searched beyond Ellie. 'Where's your father?' she asked, her frown deepening and creating cavernous splits in the thick layers of make-up. When Ellie quickly explained that she had not been able to find him, Rosie did not question her further, instead she gave Ellie a curious look before declaring that she must go in search of George. 'There's no time to wait,' she insisted. Ellie agreed; relieved to see that Rosie had a small, silver torch in her hand. She held it out to Ellie. 'You take it,' she said, 'I'll have enough trouble staying upright without being hampered by that.' She would have gone in that instant, but Ellie made her take a moment to put on a cardigan.

'There's no point in you laying yourself open to pneumonia,' she said kindly. Soon after, the two of them ventured out, each taking it in turns to call George's name. There was no response. Only the thick, eerie silence, and the occasional scurrying of a frightened creature that strayed across their path.

As they ventured deeper into the woods, exploring places where Ellie had never gone before, she wondered whether they would find that poor, demented soul and, if they did find him, would he be safe. She and Rosie did not exchange a solitary word during the search for her dear friend. Instead, they concentrated on finding a firm path and keeping clear of thick shrub and overhanging branches; every now and then calling his name and praying to hear his voice. All the while Ellie swung the torch from their path to probe the forest around, then back again. It was pitch-black now. After what seemed a lifetime to Ellie, she was made anxious by Rosie's laboured breathing, then the quiet sobs. When Rosie lost her footing and tumbled to the ground, Ellie quickly helped her up. 'We can't go on, Rosie,' she told her gently. The chill of the evening had penetrated her bones and she found herself shivering. Rosie, too, felt cold to the touch. 'We'll have to go back . . . get help.' She cradled the other woman to her. 'We can't find him . . . not in the dark. Not like this.'

'We *will* find him!' Rosie stiffened in Ellie's embrace. 'He's out here . . . somewhere . . . frightened and alone. I won't go back. We will find him. *We will.*' Rosie was shouting now, screaming his name and threatening him with all manner of punishment if he didn't 'show your face!' In the impenetrable blackness her voice echoed, mocking. Overhead, the tree-dwellers took to the air, screeching a protest that someone had dared to invade their territory. A furry shape showed itself in the shaft of light from Ellie's torch; two glittering eyes boldly stared, before disappearing into the undergrowth. Then came another sound, not the scratching, fleeting sound of night creatures, but a more recognisable sound. The soft thud of deliberate footsteps. 'Thank God!' Rosie cried, 'someone's coming . . . thank God!'

'Dad?' Ellie had been startled by the sound. 'Dad . . . is that you?' Her heart began thumping violently, the rhythm echoing deep inside her. 'Dad! . . . we're over here.' Suddenly the footsteps halted. She raised the torch in trembling fingers, shining the thin, narrow beam into the direction where the footsteps had been. She called once more. There followed another sound, a series of sounds, as though a struggle of sorts was taking place. Then came a stranger sound, inexplicable . . . carried on the breeze like laughter. Or was it?

'Ssh! Not a murmur,' Rosie whispered fearfully. 'Switch the torch off.' Her cold fingers curled round Ellie's arm. Suddenly they were plunged into darkness. For a moment they stood immobile, their bodies stiffly huddled together and ears strained for every little movement. Footsteps again. Going away. And something . . . *a voice*? Hardly audible. 'No mercy . . . no . . . mercy.' In the coal-black night all became deathly silent. For a long, agonising moment neither of them dared to move. Until, at length, Ellie tremulously raised the torch and flicked the switch with her thumb. The shaft of light probed the darkness. Small, fluttering wings hovered and bathed in its glow. From out of the shifting shadows, the two eyes stared right at them. Big, pale eyes, wide open with terror. *Pleading. Silent.* Like a corpse, he remained upright against the tree trunk, the rope tight around his throat and looped to a branch above. His bare, bleeding feet were close together on the stool. Half an inch either way and he would be left hanging; the rope choking the life from his miserable body.

'Jesus, Mary and Joseph!' Rosie's hand flew over her head and shoulders, making the sign of the cross. After the initial terrible shock, when she felt as though her blood had turned to ice, Ellie was the first to move. Lowering the torch so that the light did not blind him, she surged forward, softly calling his name, telling him not to be afraid. The heavy scent of lavender hung in the air. Suffocating. Powerful. 'Dear God . . . what have they done to you? . . . dear God.' Rosie's voice was riveted with shock. Now, they could see the blood staining his face, spreading down his neck and darkening the shoulders of his sweater in congealed, irregular patches. His pale eyes were static, seeming lifeless and staring straight ahead in a fixation of horror. The large, wet mouth was hanging open. Only the tongue moved inside that dark, cavernous place, jerking, twitching, desperate to form the words that would not come. It was all there, in his fevered mind; the obscure images of his tormentors. The pain. The terror they wreaked in him. They had no faces, yet, he knew them. Especially the one who whispered. That one was the worst, the most evil. The devil clawing at his insides. It was long ago, wasn't it? Inside his writhing, decaying mind he struggled to remember. Yes, it was long ago. Too long ago. He thought he could escape, but, like a shocking, persistent dream, it kept coming back. At first he had fought, defied it, challenged it. But always it beat him, hurt him, made him suffer beyond endurance. Now, he had nothing left. No strength, no challenge. No defiance. Or spirit. Only a wish to die, and be *free* of it. Even while it was cutting him, and taunting him, he had begged for that release. But, it would not release him. Not yet. Not until it had wrung the last ounce of suffering from him. Only then would it set him free. It had even robbed him of the courage to end it himself. It would play with him, and haunt him, and hurt him. It had no mercy. Not then. Not now. Not ever.

A sense of joy filled his heart on hearing Rosie's familiar, beloved tones. Suddenly, there were others, all comforting him, all asking him to tell what had happened. Did he imagine the other voice there . . . the whispering voice? Was it one of them? One of them? No it could not be. All the same, he could not tell them. He didn't know how. All he knew was that it was not yet over.

CHAPTER SEVEN

'George, wake up. Here's Ellie come to see you.' Rosie's voice was unusually tender as she leaned over the bed, her ungainly body stiff and hampered by the crutches wedged tight into her armpits. From beneath the sheets a small, unintelligible sound issued; pitiful, like the mewl of a creature in pain. Lanuginous fingers crept out; short, twisted hands that resembled claws, curling over the sheet's edge, clutching until the knuckles bled white. The movements were tortuous and hesitant. Inch by inch the talons drew the sheet down. The head emerged; thin, unkempt hair like wisps of cloud-white candyfloss. Grey, soft skin, criss-crossed with myriads of deeply etched lines, not unlike the pattern of trodden leaves. Bushy eyebrows, low and frowning, hid the eyes within a tangled mess. Deep inside, the soul was still afraid. *Steeped in terror.* Only the familiar, soothing voice could persuade it to trust. 'Don't be frightened, sweetheart . . . it's only Rosie. Look . . . Ellie's come to see you.' The crippled woman smiled down. Only she knew the horror that haunted this poor creature. In the dead of night when the devils came to torment him, she was there. Always there, with him. 'It's all right . . . all right now,' she murmured. The pale eyes peeped upwards. They saw a friend, and the wounded heart grew quiet.

Ellie remained silent. When the eyes flicked sideways to look directly into her face, she was shocked to the core.

Deep, haunted eyes, incredibly pale . . . translucent, they betrayed something of the darkness in the soul. Such pain! Such indescribable solitude and sorrow. Ellie's heart was wrenched inside her when, with tears brimming in those wretched eyes, the old man pleaded, 'Don't . . . let . . . them . . . hurt . . . me . . . again. Please, oh, please. Don't let them hurt me . . . no more . . . no more.' Plump tears slid over the red rims, tracing the meandering crevices in his crumpled face. 'Please . . . oh, please.' He was sobbing now; a soft broken sound that tore through Ellie with savage pain. Devastated, she turned away.

'Ssh now . . . no one's going to hurt you.' Rosie soothed the fear with gentle words. 'We won't let them hurt you . . . never again. I promise.' The eyes swivelled to gaze on her – curious, unsure. They saw the truth there, and the love. A contented sigh. A childish smile. Then *sleep*. Softly the two women stole away, each with a heavy heart. Each feeling hopelessly inadequate in the face of such despair.

'The bastards who did this to him should rot in hell!' Rosie put the small china plate onto the table, while balancing herself on one crutch and eyeing Ellie indignantly. 'They wanted me to leave him there . . . did you know that?'

'In the hospital, you mean?'

Rosie nodded. 'I couldn't do that! What! . . . abandon the poor soul to strangers.' She shook her head so vigorously that the loose coil of peroxide hair tumbled awry. 'He would have pined d'you see? Oh no! I could never have that. Soon as ever they'd tended his wounds . . . I had to fetch him home, to the cottage. The police upset him . . . asking all those questions, but, well . . . they couldn't get no sense from him. I'm not surprised, though.' She glanced surreptitiously towards the senile's bedroom. 'This last business has driven him right over the edge. I don't expect we shall ever know what happened out there . . . what unspeakable things took place, in the dark.' She shuddered, her narrowed eyes gazing at the bedroom door.

Ellie was astonished by the dark vindictiveness in the older woman's considered gaze. She never felt more strongly that Rosie knew something! Knew something. But what? 'Did he say anything to you, Rosie? Is there . . . something you know, that the police don't?' Ellie was compelled to ask.

Rosie's smile was disarming. The curious, secretive manner was no more. 'Not a thing,' she said, deliberately suppressing the dark thoughts that had swamped her mood. She was not altogether surprised by the question; only protective of the knowledge which she kept close. Yes, she did 'know something'. But, it was not what Ellie suspected. Oh no, it was not all as it might seem! But, she must be careful. Ellie was a shrewd and intelligent young woman. Already, she had sensed the atmosphere of Thornton Place. It would be dangerous for her to learn anything. She must not know. Not yet. And maybe never. 'He couldn't tell the police anything,' she assured Ellie now, 'and he hasn't told me anything either. It's hopeless. Still, happen the police will leave him be now, eh? Oh, they'll search out there a while longer no doubt . . . but they'll not find the truth of it.' Like before, she thought, just like the other times. She saw that Ellie was not altogether convinced. 'Hey! Are you deliberately ignoring my plum pie?' she chided good-humouredly and gesturing towards the china plate. 'Nobody makes plum pie like old Rosie,' she chuckled, 'though I do say so meself!' She saw Ellie's lovely face melt into a smile and the relief washed over her. There had been a moment there when she feared that Ellie intended questioning her further, but the moment had gone, leaving only her own determination to guard her words and glances more carefully in the future. She had been careless and that was unforgivable!

When Ellie had given her honest opinion of Rosie's plum pie, remarking, 'It's everything you say, Rosie,' the older woman beamed from ear to ear, afterwards hobbling away into the scullery. Soon she returned, pushing an oak trolley which had barley-twist legs and four large iron wheels. On the trolley was a teapot and tea-set together with more plum pie on a cake-stand, which, like the teapot and tea-service, was all in pretty matching blue chinaware. There was also a bone-handled knife with a sharp, serrated blade, loosely wrapped in two royal blue serviettes; one of which was promptly given to Ellie, while the other was taken by Rosie to be securely tucked into the neck of her dark brown jumper. Belying the trauma of these past days and succumbing to the deep pleasure she always felt in Ellie's company, she smiled broadly, saying, 'I may be a country bumpkin, but I do like to do things properly. Now, you can wait on me, young lady!' She laid her crutches against the back of the old leather armchair and hopped about on the one good leg, until in a moment she was satisfied that she could drop herself comfortably into the soft, squashy seat.

As always, Ellie's offer to help was firmly refused. 'Just get on and pour the tea, sweetheart,' she urged; by now Rosie was seated and looking on Ellie in a grand, authoritative manner. She had very few visitors to the cottage, and this was something of an occasion to be celebrated. She said as much to Ellie now, gratefully accepting the cup of tea being handed to her. 'Nobody ever comes here . . . with the exception of Alec Harman of course.' Suddenly, she was obliged to recount the night when George was found – was it only three days ago? Dear God, it seemed like a whole lifetime. And *still*, the questions were not answered! What could have persuaded George to leave the open field and go so deep into the woods? What hellish fiend had caused him so much suffering ... punctured and torn his poor body all over ... left him helpless as a babe, and terrified with the knowledge that one false move would tighten the rope round his neck to choke the life out of him? Not for the first time, the boy sprang into her thoughts. She did not quite know why, but there was something about his account that didn't ring true. She recalled his explanation now: 'I never saw the old man wander off ... I was too busy building my bonfire. The first I knew he was missing was when I came into the house and Rosie went mad. It's not *my* fault if she can't look after him!' He was adamant, and really, there was no reason to disbelieve him. All the same, Rosie was not altogether satisfied. More and more she had come to see the truly nasty streak in the boy's character. She chided herself for her suspicions towards him; reminding herself of the fact that he had lost his mother and was no doubt still struggling to come to terms with that terrible trauma. And besides, he could not be held responsible for what had happened out there in the woods. What had been done to George was a bad, evil thing! There had been other bad things. Evil visitations, and things of the night that bided here in this lonely place, long before the boy.

Ellie had grown quiet on hearing the name 'Alec Harman'. Her thoughts were sent reeling back. 'Strange, don't you think ... how quickly he was on the scene?' she asked, her amber eyes regarding the older woman with a measure of suspicion. 'Within minutes of us finding George ... Alec appeared out of nowhere.' She would have gone on to remark how he had not seemed too shocked or surprised to see what cruelties George had endured, but she knew how fond Rosie was of the darkeye, so she resisted the urge to speak out. Besides, there was a degree of peevishness in her thoughts just now, because of the deliberate way in which he had ignored her on that night. Her relief on seeing him had been quashed by the deep hurt he had caused when addressing himself entirely to Rosie; almost as though she herself was not there at all. He had asked, in a curiously intimate voice, whether Rosie had 'seen anything? Or anyone?' When, obviously forgetful in her great distress at discovering George so wounded, Rosie had replied that 'no . . . there was no one to be seen,' Ellie gently reminded her of the sounds that had frightened them just before the torchlight picked out the trembling, fearful sight that was George.

'You remember, don't you, Rosie?' Ellie had prompted, 'the sound . . . like someone shuffling . . . then the soft whisper of laughter.' She had been astonished when Rosie denied ever having heard such noises. So adamant was she, that even Ellie began to doubt what her own ears had told her!

Alec had spoken to her then, explaining, 'It could have been anything. Imagination plays strange tricks, and at night these woods come alive . . . foraging creatures . . . breezes through the tree tops . . . a poacher's stealthy footsteps. It all plays on the senses.' In the garish moonlight, his dark eyes were magically translucent. His penetrating gaze disturbed and excited her. There was an arrogance in those black, beautiful eyes, and condemnation. Yet she felt other, deeper emotions, like tenderness. And *love*. In that moment when he brought his dark gaze to bear on her, she had responded in kind – the love she felt towards him, and her deep need of him shone quietly from her face. In that all-too-brief moment the truth rose between them like a glorious revelation. As though afraid of what he had seen in Ellie's lovely features, Alec had swiftly turned away, skilfully attending to George, and afterwards plying all his attentions to what Rosie had to say.

Rosie had plenty to say now, as she dismissed Ellie's remarks. 'It ain't "strange" at all! You heard what he told us . . . how he was in the vicinity, keeping watch for poachers. He explained that, didn't he? Didn't he?'

'Yes, but . . .'

'But what?'

Ellie shook her head. What was it that troubled her so? At the time, she had accepted Alec's explanation without a second thought. Wasn't it only natural that he should be stalking the woods, lying in wait for the poachers? Of course it was! That was his job. 'You're right . . . I'm just a bit jittery,' she said, surprisingly relieved at having discussed her nagging suspicions with Rosie. Of course there was nothing sinister in Alec suddenly appearing like that and, as always, Rosie was quick to spring to his defence.

'Poachers are his enemy, don't you know?' Rosie declared indignantly. 'He's paid to see them off . . . and that means first he has to catch them at it. The thieving buggers creep about in the dark hours, when ordinary folks are usually abed. If he's to get the better of them . . . then Alec must also walk the night. It's the only way.' She eyed Ellie thoughtfully. 'Besides, my girl . . . Alec weren't the *only* one in the vicinity, were he, eh?' Her aged features relaxed into a smile of satisfaction. 'You might as well ask where the others came from an' all!'

'You mean . . . my father, and the man from the shop?'

'Too bloody true!' Rosie leaned forward, dropping her voice to a whisper as she told Ellie, 'Your father were "out for a breath of air" like he said . . . and I'm not surprised after hours of sucking that awful paint smell into his poor lungs.' She paused, regarding Ellie closely. 'He's been working far too hard. I'm glad he's taking today off. Where did you say he'd gone?'

'I'm not really sure. All he said when he left earlier was that he had "business to see to".' She shrugged her shoulders. Ellie was also glad that her father had taken a rest from the relentless workload. 'I expect he's shopping around . . . looking for materials and so on, at the best prices. He said the other day that there were plenty of bargains about, and he had a duty to shop about as it wasn't *his* money he was spending. He'll be back before supper, though, I'm sure.'

'No doubt,' Rosie agreed. 'Now, like I was saying, your father had every right to be taking the air, after a hard day's work. But, that *Fred Gregory*! Now, he's a different kettle of fish altogether!'

'What are you saying, Rosie?' Ellie had been so relieved when all three men had turned up within only minutes of each other. What with poor George in a state of hysteria and lashing out like a thing possessed at anyone who went near him, it would have been nigh impossible to get him back to the cottage without another pair of strong arms to assist. When her father came onto the scene, he and Alec were able to bodily lift the struggling George. It was Alec who spied the bulky frame of Fred Gregory, who was watching from a distance. He answered Alec's call for help – albeit reluctantly. Afterwards, when Alec commented on the fact to Mr Gregory that he was 'straying through the woods at such a late hour', the big man remained silent, later departing in a sour and sullen mood.

'What am I saying?' repeated Rosie, screwing her face into a thousand deep wrinkles. *'What am I saying? . . .* I'm saying it's very strange that Fred Gregory should have wandered such a considerable way from his own patch . . . skulking about here in the dark! . . . I'm saying that I've had my suspicions for a long time about that surly bugger! I'm saying he's probably one o' them bloody poachers that lead Alec Harman a merry dance! Fred Gregory ain't the upstanding, respectable shopkeeper he likes to pretend. To my mind, he's a devious devil. That's what I'm saying, my girl!' She rammed a chunk of plum pie into her wide-open mouth, before leaning back in the chair and quietly gauging Ellie's reaction to her words.

When, intrigued, Ellie questioned her further – not only with regard to Fred Gregory, but also about the other unfriendly inhabitants of Redborough – Rosie indulged in a long and colourful description of 'them as pretend to be what they're not . . . going to church of a Sunday and standing shoulder to shoulder with their neighbours . . . then giving each other a wide berth the rest of the time . . . 'cause they're all afraid of their own shadows, and riddled with suspicion of each other!' When Ellie pressed her further, Rosie feared she had said more than enough. Mumbling incoherently about 'people going missing . . . never found again . . . talk of the supernatural and all that', she cleverly directed Ellie's interest towards other, more controversial issues. 'It's a pity folk won't live and let live,' she remarked, pulling a wry face, 'look at our own Queen Elizabeth . . . forbidding her own sister, the Princess Margaret, from marrying Captain Peter Townsend. Lord above! Whatever next?'

'I suppose it's inevitable that there will always be "stories" and "superstitions" around a grand old house like Thornton Place,' Ellie said, determined to pursue the matter of Thornton Place. She saw Rosie as being a bit of a 'romancer'. It wouldn't have surprised her to know that it was Rosie herself who had started certain rumours, in order to keep nosy parkers away from here. 'Besides . . . such stories will keep people from prying . . . allow you to live here in peace,' she suggested with a deliberate wry smile.

Rosie laughed out loud. 'True! Very true!' she chuckled, taking a great gulp of tea and very nearly choking on it. After that, the conversation changed direction yet again. This time, Ellie showed great interest in the cottage itself. She told Rosie how it was the most picturesque little place she had ever seen. Enthused, Rosie took her on a quick tour; from the parlour through to the tiny scullery, and up the narrow staircase to the two small bedrooms above.

All the rooms were cosy; little open firegrates, diminutive windows and low, heavy oak-beamed ceilings. The furniture also was of oak, small chests and wooden-framed chairs with plump, floral cushions. The beds were unattractive iron monsters, with angled legs and black wrought-metal features top and bottom. Upstairs, the floors were uncovered, except for an odd rush mat here and there. Downstairs, the floors were more comfortable, having large rugs which almost covered the cold stone underneath. There was a small wooden square set into the concrete floor beneath the window. Rosie answered Ellie's curiosity about it with a short, curt reply. 'It's a trap door . . . locked . . . been locked since I can recall. It's nothing of importance . . . just a cellar of sorts I expect.' She left out the other, more disturbing rumours. Rumours which told of underground excavations that ran from Thornton Place to the cottage, then from there out to the woods and beyond. The secret passageway was said to have been created some hundreds of years ago by an evil and powerful man whose followers practised witchcraft and sorcery. Children and innocents would disappear without trace and, as a result, suspecting locals would rise, incensed and baying for blood, launching attacks on Thornton Place and dragging out anyone found there. These 'devils' were hanged, drawn and quartered without mercy. Unspeakable atrocities had been committed, evil deeds on which legends were built to this very day. Superstition and fear bred in its own evil and, over the years, the rumours had been stilled by a communal silence which was even more harrowing. Rosie chose to say nothing of all this. Instead, like so many others, she deliberately suppressed such unsettling thoughts. After all, there was no evidence, there never had been. There were only frantic whispers, fuelled by certain real tragedies. Now, the whispers were themselves too fearful to acknowledge, and so there remained only the awful silence, and the deep-rooted suspicions that continued to grow and fester in the darker recesses of the mind.

Tragedies were never forgotten. Some were too horrible. Some too recent. These were the ones that returned again and again to haunt and to terrify. For the while, all innocents must be watched over. Until the day when all evil was gone, and those responsible removed forever.

The hands moved quickly. Soon, the casket was unearthed. In another moment the lid was wrenched off to reveal the stiff, used body. In its arms the smaller shroud was curled towards the hard, unyielding breast. There was no comfort there. Not now. Not before. There had been no time.

On the cold night air, the labourer's breath eased out in a murmur of contentment; the murmur became a sound of soft laughter, betraying the unique satisfaction within. Satisfaction and soaring exhilaration on recovering that which was most coveted. Long, sinuous fingers stretched out, tracing the cold, still lines of a face that was still exquisitely beautiful. At first the touch was tender, almost reverent. Whisperings of love moved inside a sorry heart. Tears fell dropping onto that cold, silent face, spilling over the closed eyelids. In the shifting moonlight it seemed as though the corpse itself was crying. The sight was jolting. Anguish returned, with a deep, black vengeance. Now, the touch was harsh. *Cruel*.

With grasping fingers, the lifeless form was painstakingly eased from its resting place and wrapped into the blanket. Afterwards, it was placed roughly to one side while the labourer worked on, ensuring that the grave appeared undisturbed, as before. No one must know. No one must suspect that she was gone. Not yet. Not until she had paid in *full*!

CHAPTER EIGHT

It was November 5th. A cold, grey day when even the birds were reluctant to sing. There was a stillness in the air, a sense of impending excitement. There was no indication of the awful tragedy already brewing.

Ellie emerged from the spinney; she made an attractive figure in her long black coat, knee-length boots and cherry-red beret with matching scarf. There was a vitality about her, an exuberance that lit up her strong amber eyes and lent a radiance to her whole countenance. To the man idling close by, Ellie was a feast of loveliness; a cruel reminder of lost youth, unrequited love and misspent opportunities. Unobserved, he remained partly hidden by the edge of the spinney, slyly following Ellie's path towards the shop, his eyes growing more bitter and resentful with her every step. When, unaware of his presence, Ellie went inside the shop, he turned away, stamping his great boots with anger as he pushed his large, ungainly body along a little-used bridleway through the thickest part of the spinney. He felt the need to be alone, to isolate himself, to curl into some dark, undiscovered corner where he might come to terms with the crippling frustration inside him. It was either that, or take out his bitterness on some poor, innocent soul who might happen across his path!

★ ★ ★

'Fred! . . . Fred, where are you?' Mrs Gregory returned from the room behind the shop, her round face bright red from all the shouting. 'There's no telling where he's gone,' she told the elderly man beside the counter. 'He always disappears when I need him most!' She tutted loudly, packing the last item of groceries into the old fellow's carrier bag and handing it over the counter to him. 'Don't you worry, dearie,' she told him with a flustered smile. 'Soon as ever he comes back, I'll get him to fetch your paraffin straight away.' Her smile belied the anger that still bubbled inside her, since the early-morning row between her and her man. More and more these days the burden of running this shop fell heavily on her shoulders.

'You'll not let him forget, will you?' the old fellow reminded her in a worried voice. 'I ain't got above a spoonful o' fuel left . . . and the nights are getting too cold for my old bones. I can't afford coal . . . besides, it stinks more than paraffin!'

'Like I said . . . soon as ever he comes back.' She took out a thick, black ledger from beneath the counter and made an entry. 'There! . . . one pound three and sixpence. Pay me on pension day . . . same as usual?'

'Aye.' He nodded and began ambling his way out of the shop. Now, when he caught sight of Ellie lingering some way off, he stopped to eye her up and down. 'You're from the big house, ain't you? . . . Armstrong? . . . daughter o' the new caretaker?'

'Yes.' Ellie came forward, ready to make friends.

'You must be mad! *All of you!*' He backed away, inching towards the door and regarding her through suspicious eyes. 'They're still there . . . somewhere in that devilish place . . . I know they are. Folks don't just disappear.' He shook his head and cast a fearful look towards Mrs Gregory. Without another word he hurried from the shop, occasionally glancing back and muttering incoherently.

'What did he mean?' Ellie asked suspiciously.

''Tain't nothing for you to worry your head about. He's an old fool . . . riddled with age and confused about most things.'

'Who was he talking about when he said . . . "Folks don't just disappear"? . . . I want to know, Mrs Gregory.' Ellie would not be so easily put off. Not this time.

'It were all a long time ago.' The round face grew concerned beneath Ellie's determined gaze. 'It happened long before you came . . . don't really concern you . . . not your fault. It's best you don't pry too deep into things of the past . . . things we can't change.'

'What "things"?' Ellie stood her ground. 'I won't be satisfied until you tell me.'

Mrs Gregory sighed. She knew a determined young woman when she saw one. 'All right . . . but you'll be none the wiser for knowing,' she warned. 'It were my intention not to gossip about things that might frighten you and your family because, well, to my mind some things really are best left alone.' She peeped at Ellie, hoping to see a change of heart there. She was disappointed. 'All right . . . all right! It's a disturbing story, sure enough. Happened about the same time as that poor man's wife was killed in a storm . . . as a matter of fact, if I remember rightly.' She paused to look deeply into Ellie's face. 'You do understand how a tale can change out of all recognition, with the telling of it over the years?' Ellie nodded, her expression serious. 'And it's a fact that some people get too excited by their own accounts . . . add a bit . . . get the facts all wrong. To my mind, that's just what happened here.' She shook her grey head and lowered her eyes. 'But it were bad! There's no denying that. First the children. Then a man of God!' She looked to the ceiling and made a hurried sign of the cross on herself.

Ellie recalled the old man's words. 'Folks don't just

disappear.' She asked now, 'These "children" . . . and the "man of God" . . . are you saying they . . . they . . . ?'

'Murdered, some say!' The grey head shook slowly from side to side. 'Nobody knows . . . except them as had an evil hand in it.' She shuddered. 'The priest was a stranger to these parts. He came into this very shop . . . stood where you're standing now and asked directions to Thornton Place. He didn't say why he was going there, and it weren't my business to ask. I recall him very well. A nice, homely soul, with that gentle, kind way a priest has. Not a young man . . . not old, either. Well, I sent him on his way and he thanked me generously. He had one of them little black cars that priests travel about in.' Here, her voice trembled and her eyes grew moist. 'They found the car some days later . . . down by the lake. Now, I made it quite clear that he was to turn off the track long before . . . dangerous. I told him! "Make sure you turn right when you come to the fork in the track, or you'll likely end up in the lake" . . . them's the very words I spoke to the priest. But, he didn't end up in the lake, because the frogmen searched every blessed inch of it. The authorities crawled over every square yard of the grounds, the woods, the house and barns . . . like a creeping black blanket over everything in sight, they were. The priest was never found.'

'Had he been to the house? . . . spoken to anyone?' Ellie was both shocked and intrigued.

'No. According to the police, he just disappeared. The only person he spoke to . . . was *me*.' The thought had disturbed her ever since. It disturbed her now. 'Of course, they found out who he was from the Church authorities. By all accounts, he came from London way . . . 'course he weren't married . . . priests ain't allowed that, and he had no family to speak of. In fact, he was a quiet, private man on his own. Lord only knows why he was making his way to Thornton Place!' She threw out her hands in despair. 'It's a sure fact that the priest ain't telling . . . 'cause it's like he's been snatched from the face o' the earth!' She peered at Ellie, adding in awesome tones, 'Just like the children.'

'Children?'

'Two. Boy aged what . . . nine, ten years old. His sister some two years older. It were on a day not unlike today. They went into the woods to collect chestnuts. Day went, night came . . . but not the children. The alarm was raised and every adult from every house joined in the search. Like the priest . . . they were never found . . . not to this day. Their parents went almost out of their minds . . . lived just round the corner here. Soon after, they moved on . . . couldn't bear to stay.' Being herself familiar with the awful events these past years, she felt curiously surprised to see the blood drain from Ellie's face. 'I've told you!' she chided. 'I said some things are best left alone.' She felt no sympathy for Ellie; only irritation that her own tongue had run away with her, after she had vowed to her husband that she would never speak of the atrocities again. 'So there you have it. A priest, and two children who ventured into the grounds of Thornton Place . . . to be swallowed up and never heard of again!' She experienced a strange satisfaction in ramming home the awfulness of these happenings.

'Have the police given up?'

'They say not. But they ain't been round these parts in many a while. Still . . . if you ask me, there's nothing else to be done. At the time, they drafted in extra manpower. They set up an investigations office in the Club over yonder, and they followed up every lead . . . even the calls from bloody cranks. No! To my mind, they exhausted every avenue. Them three unfortunate souls are gone to their maker if you ask me. They'll not be coming back no how.'

'What makes you so sure they were . . . murdered?'

Mrs Gregory tapped her breast, saying quietly, 'I just know, that's all. In here . . . I just know. Oh, there's plenty who say they heard screams on the night the children disappeared . . . devilish screams . . . shrill and terrible enough to wake the dead.' She made a frantic sign of the cross on herself. 'But I put that down to folk's hysteria. All I know is . . . they won't be coming back. *Ever!*'

Ellie had it in mind to question her further, but, at that point, another customer came into the shop, a hard-faced woman of some forty years. She barely glanced at Ellie. Instead, she busied herself in choosing the greenest cabbage with the plumpest heart from the window display. Mrs Gregory exchanged brief words with her, and afterwards proceeded to fill Ellie's order. Her quick change of mood was astonishing. With a light-hearted smile and cheerful banter regarding current affairs – ranging from 'the turmoil in Suez' to . . . 'this young American, Elvis Presley . . . sending folks wild with his music' – she seemed desperate that the other woman should not know of the previous conversation which had taken place. In fact, when Ellie left the shop a few moments later, she could have sworn that Mrs Gregory gave a sigh of relief.

Wending her way back through the spinney, Ellie began thinking about what the little woman had told her. A priest and two children, all disappeared without trace. *How? Why?* Her mind reeled. Mrs Gregory had explained that no stone had been left unturned in the search to find them. The house, the woods and grounds all meticulously gone over. The lake scoured by divers. And still, not a shred of evidence as to what awful fate might have become them! Ellie turned the account over and over in her mind. Strange. So strange. What could have happened? Perhaps they were not 'murdered', as some had suggested. Perhaps they were not even 'missing'. Maybe they had just gone of their own accord . . . run away.

Children did that sometimes. So did adults. But – a priest? No. Kidnapped, then? No. There would have been ransom notes in that case, and no doubt the police had covered every possibility, however remote.

Deep in the heart of the spinney, Ellie set down her shopping bag and seated herself on a fallen tree trunk. At once, she felt at peace with herself. She had been deeply troubled by the little woman's revelations but, here, in this private, special place, all such troubles seemed irrelevant. Above the tangled tree-top branches, the grey sky peeped in here and there, not intruding, never overwhelming, merely comforting from a distance. Against this patchwork awning, the criss-crossed and interlacing patterns appeared like dutiful sentries holding hands. Shadows played between the trees, creatures scurried on their way, and in the air was a sweet, pleasant smell of fallen leaves, decaying bracken and the last blossoms before winter. All around, the rust and golden colours of autumn made a splendid sight. As far as the eye could see, the trees ringed the heart of the spinney, upright and ageless, some naked, some clinging to the last vestige of foliage until, inevitably, they too were stripped bare.

Here, in this quiet, beautiful place, Ellie felt safe, comforted and immune to all that tormented her. Lately, she had been torn apart by so many upheavals – the loss of her mother and the awful manner of her going, the devastating grief that had threatened to tear the family apart, the terrible guilt, and, finally, in their bid for a new life, leaving everything familiar behind. Not for the first time, Ellie wondered whether they had made the right move in coming to Thornton Place. It was true that her father seemed a great deal happier, but, there were still moments, unguarded moments, when the strain showed in his face. As for Johnny, he had withdrawn into a strange little world all of his own; it was the boy she was becoming increasingly concerned for. She had already spoken to her father about the possibility of taking Johnny to see the local doctor. 'Do as you like, Ellie . . . I don't suppose it would do any harm, although I do believe the boy plays on your sympathies to a certain degree.' It had saddened Ellie to see how little her father really cared. As for her own entanglements, she could see no satisfactory solution. Alec had stolen her heart. She had stolen Barny's. Someone was going to get hurt. Engrossed in deep thought, Ellie was startled when he spoke out.

'You should never linger in these woods.' Alec Harman had come on her from behind. Now, he stood a little way off, his long, lean legs astride, the jackboots barely visible above the layers of fallen leaves and, as always, the shotgun broken over the crook of his arm. In the khaki, knee-length great-coat, with his thick, black hair falling attractively to his ears, he was strikingly handsome. Formidable. His dark, sultry eyes remained intent on her. She waited for him to speak, perhaps with a little more tenderness. When at length he moved, Ellie felt sure it was to come closer. Her heart leaped at the thought of his nearness. When, with suddenness, he cut off in another direction, she called out, her boldness surprising even herself.

'Alec! Don't go.' For a second it seemed he had not heard, or had chosen to ignore her. But then, he stopped and turned, a look of satisfaction in his black eyes. He came forward, a quiet intimate smile softening his classic, angular features. Ellie rose to her feet. She could feel herself trembling. Now, he was looking down on her, his eyes caressing her face. 'Ellie . . . oh, Ellie!' It was a murmur of love, a cry from the heart. A sigh that betrayed the agony inside him.

'Why have you deliberately avoided me?' Her voice was barely a whisper. Tremulous, she waited for his answer.

'I think you know why.' His dark, enigmatic gaze melted into her. 'You go against my better instincts. You have the power to distract me from . . . my work.' Muted visions invaded his mind. Visions that created pain and regret. Visions of mayhem and wickedness. Torturous visions that haunted him, and would go on haunting him. Unless he made himself do what was required.

'I love you.' Ellie met his gaze with honesty. In uttering those words, she had bared her soul to him. When, without a gesture of acknowledgement, he continued to browse his black, caressing eyes on her upturned face, she felt the embarrassment sweeping into her like a red, burning tide. Quietly, she turned away, reaching down to collect her belongings. She was suddenly afraid. She loved him, but she did not understand him.

'I'll walk some of the way with you,' he offered, taking up a place alongside as she started on the homeward path. Gently, he took the bag from her hand. She did not resist. Like before, he had caused her to feel deeply unhappy yet, at the same time, exhilarated by his very closeness. She was unsure, lost for words, her emotions confounded by him.

'Why don't you arrange for Mr Gregory to deliver your orders?'

'He does deliver the larger orders, but I enjoy going to the shop . . . occasionally meeting the people who live in Redborough.' She suspected he knew how unsociable these people were. 'I like walking through the spinney. It's so peaceful, so very beautiful . . . especially now.' She glanced about, not daring to look on his face.

'Peaceful, yes . . . sometimes. And beautiful. But not *safe*. You should never come through these woods alone.'

'Why do you say that?' Mrs Gregory's words still seared her mind. 'Is it because of the children . . . and the priest?' She winced when he gripped her arm, swinging her round to face him.

'Who told you?' His eyes glittered like black jewels.

'Mrs Gregory. She said they had disappeared . . . never been found.' Even though his fingers were hurting her, she wanted him to hold her for ever. As though he sensed what she was thinking, he abruptly released her.

'She told you that?'

'Yes.'

'She had no right to frighten you in that way.' The dark eyes clouded over. He was lost in his own, disturbing thoughts.

'What do *you* know of it all? Do you think they were . . . murdered?' His strange reaction had made Ellie curious.

'It happened before my time here.' His statement was uttered in controlled anger, yet, there was something else in his voice. Some deeper emotion that Ellie could not fathom. She was amazed when he swiftly changed the subject. 'I expect you're looking forward to seeing Barny Tyler. It's today, isn't it?'

'That's right.' She had been surprised by his comment. Now, she was sad. 'I expect Rosie's been chatting with you?' She felt oddly betrayed, irritated that Rosie had discussed her private business with him. She wondered how much more Rosie might have revealed.

'It wasn't Rosie.'

'Oh?' A sense of relief washed over her. 'Who then?'

He smiled. 'It doesn't matter.' Her eyes still questioned him. He relented. 'It was the boy.' The moment he had said it, he was filled with regret. He hadn't wanted to mention the boy, that spiteful child who treated Ellie with such contempt . . . sneering at her behind her back, telling him things only because he believed it would stir up trouble.

'Johnny?' Ellie could not hide her amazement. 'I didn't know he had taken to speaking with you. He doesn't even like you!'

'Children never do what we expect. I dare say he had his own reasons for telling me.'

'I see.' Ellie began to realise the boy's motive. He could be so cruel.

'Did you mean what you said just now, Ellie?' His dark gaze drew her to him.

'I don't know what you mean,' she lied.

'Yes, you do.' He saw the rush of shyness to her face; it endeared her to him all the more. 'Don't let yourself love me,' he warned in a quiet, lonely voice. 'I can only bring you heartache.' He raised his long, gentle fingers, touching her face, tracing the full, lovely line of her mouth. 'Save your love for the young man who obviously adores you. You loved him once. You must still love him.' He bent his head and placed his mouth over hers. His kiss was tender, tantalising. Yet, somehow final.

Ellie's instinct was to hit out; to tell him he knew nothing of what she felt. Instead, she stabbed at him with a spiteful tongue, wanting to hurt. 'And what about her! Do you love her? Do you bring her "heartache"?' She delighted in the shock etching his face.

'Who? What are you talking about?'

Her smile was shockingly wicked. He had the power to create spite in her, and she loathed him for it. 'I expect you thought your secret was safe! But I saw you . . . and no doubt others must have seen you. By the lake . . . you, and the girl!'

He reeled back, his face chalk-white and his eyes wide with shock. Ellie detested herself. 'You're wrong!' he protested, 'there is no "girl by the lake".'

Undeterred, Ellie rounded on him with renewed vigour. 'You are lying!' she told him. He had used Barny against her. Now she had an appetite to play him at his own game. 'I don't like the way you do things, Alec Harman. We may not be right for each other. You may not feel the same way towards me, but at least I'm honest. I don't pretend that Barny doesn't exist, nor do I hide my feelings behind some obscure reasoning like you do ... when all the time you're playing a dangerous game. What is it? ... Can't you make your mind up about which one of us to have?' There was no stemming the pent-up fury now. 'Well, let *me* decide for you! I love you, yes ... I won't deny that. But I'm not so blind that I can't see what a hypocrite you are. My father was right ... you are "trouble". And you were right just now, when you warned that you could only "bring me heartache". You're clever, I'll give you that, and you're devious. But from now on I'll know enough to stay away from you. And yes, I am "looking forward to seeing Barny". More than I realised!' Deeply stirred by the curious pain in his black eyes, she snatched the bag from his hand and took to her heels, ashamed and afraid that he might see the blinding tears that ran down her face. Throughout her astonishing tirade, he had not uttered a single word in his own defence. Nor did he come after her now, as she sped her way homeward.

He remained in the place where she had left him. A solitary figure, with bowed head and scarred eyes that followed her out of sight. After a while he went on his way, his heavy heart a tumult of emotions. How could he tell her? She would be shocked if she knew the way of things. Things that must remain secret. Things that would only frighten her. Awful things that she would not understand. It was enough that these things ruled his life. The only thing that mattered, for the moment, was the purpose that drove him. She had no part in it. She would be better off not knowing!

'I must have those keys!' The whisper grew agitated, menacing.

'I don't know where else to look.' The boy was close to

tears. His 'friend' was dissatisfied with him. He did not want that.

'Think, then. Where would anyone keep a set of keys that they never use?'

'I . . . don't . . . know. I think Ellie put them somewhere safe.' He was trembling now. 'In her dressing-table drawer?'

'No! . . . I've already searched there, damn you!'

'*You!* . . . Were you inside the house?' The boy was incredulous. 'You came . . . into the house . . . and no one saw you?'

'Don't question me. I've warned you . . . never to question me.'

'I forgot.'

'The keys were sent by mistake. The people who sent them want them back. Get them, Johnny. *Find them!*'

'I will.'

'You must. Do you understand that, Johnny? *You must bring me those keys!*'

'Will you punish me if I can't find them?' He smiled. He was confident that his 'friend' would never hurt him.

'Don't come back without them, will you, Johnny?' The voice trembled.

'No.' The smile slid from his face.

'Good boy. I would not like it if you failed me.'

'I won't.' A sense of excitement took hold of him. 'Can I just ask you something? . . . not about you!'

'Ask.'

'Have you been to see the bonfire?'

'Oh, it's *wonderful*, Johnny.'

'I haven't "failed" you there, have I?'

'You have done well.'

'Did you go inside? Under the ground . . . to our special place?'

There was a long, uncomfortable silence. When the whisperer replied, it was with soft, pleasing tones, but there was underlying savagery. 'I can't do that, Johnny.'

'Why not?'

'Enough!'

The hiss of fury momentarily unnerved the boy. 'I don't mean to ask so many questions,' he murmured. The soft, issuing sigh comforted him. The urge to turn and look was strong.

'No matter. I have something for you. No! Don't look round! You can't take it with you now, Johnny. It isn't quite ready. Later, though. Before dark.'

'Is it a present?'

'If you like. It isn't really for you, though.'

'Oh.' Disappointment. Then curiosity. 'What is it?'

'It's a face.'

'A . . . face?'

'For your Guy Fawkes effigy.'

'But he's already got a face!' Resentment betrayed itself. He had made a splendid rag face for his Guy, and he was proud of it.

'It won't do, Johnny! When he burns . . . he must be wearing this special face. *I want to see it suffer.*' A low, insane chuckle, then sweetness. 'You do understand, don't you, Johnny?'

'I suppose so.'

'You haven't told anyone about our secret place, have you? Oh, I do hope not!'

'You mean the underground one? No. I would never tell our secret . . . I would never tell any of our secrets.'

'That's very wise. We must not share *anything* with . . . them. We know, don't we, Johnny? We know every inch of that magnificent bonfire . . . the tunnels . . . our special hidey-hole.' A deep, soft sigh, then, 'We've been clever, Johnny . . . you and I. You haven't forgotten the sandcastle, have you?'

'I can't ever forget that.'

'Of course not. She built it with you, didn't she?'

'Yes.' Sadness. And anger.

'It's our secret.'

'Yes.'

'Go now, Johnny. But, remember, *I must have those keys*!' The whisper hardened.

'I'll try.'

'That isn't good enough. Did you not hear what I said! I MUST HAVE THEM!'

'I won't fail you.' Now, as he crept away, there was real fear in the boy's heart. But it was only a small fear. Not as overwhelming as the delight that coursed through him. He would search for those old keys, but he wasn't sure whether he could find them. After all, hadn't he heard his father only the other day, asking Ellie where she had put them. He was really angry when she couldn't remember. Still, he would do his best to find them. If he failed, it would not matter. This was just another game. And he suspected his 'friend' was only teasing.

'For goodness' sake, Johnny! What are you up to?' Ellie stormed into the big room where the table was set for a special lunch. She had taken a great deal of time and trouble to make it look extra nice. Spread with the deep green cloth and dressed with the best cutlery and white china, it made a splendid sight. She had purposely bought a new set of four slim wine glasses, and pretty patterned napkins, which were neatly rolled into attractive wooden rings. There were logs in the open fireplace, all arranged and ready for lighting, and the cumbersome oak furniture gleamed from Ellie's tireless polishing. With the upper walls now emulsioned in elegant tones of soft creams with the brown panelling below, and the heavy floral curtains drawn at just the right angle, the room was pleasant and inviting.

'Why don't you light the fire now?' the boy demanded. When Ellie came into the room, he had been on his knees beside the big dresser; the contents of the bottom drawer spilled out over the mat. On seeing Ellie, he sprang to his feet and immediately rounded on her, his back arched and his neck stretched towards her in a gesture of defiance. 'It's *freezing* in here . . . I was looking for some matches to light the fire!' His face was cunning. His manner brazen.

'It isn't your place to light the fire, and well you know it, young man!' Ellie reprimanded. 'If you're cold, go into the kitchen . . . the stove is lit there. Or go upstairs and give your father a helping hand. Goodness knows there's enough work still to be done.' She looked at the mess on the floor, at the drawers, all opened and showing signs of having been rifled. 'You weren't "looking for matches" were you?' she demanded. 'You know perfectly well where I keep them . . . in the spice cupboard by the kitchen door.' She stared at him with quizzical eyes. He seemed uncomfortable beneath her deliberate gaze, and the colour flamed his cheeks. 'What are you up to, eh? What are you really looking for?' To her mind, the boy had been behaving in an even more irritating manner than usual. Earlier on, he had followed her every move, showing an unusual interest in where she kept things that were seldom used, mumbling something about 'rusty old keys and things'. She had been too busy to pay him any heed, but now she was made to recall his odd behaviour, because here he was, obviously desperate to find something.

'I want to know, Johnny,' she told him firmly. 'What exactly were you searching for?'

'I told you! Matches. I was looking for the matches, so I could light the fire!' He knew now why his 'friend' didn't like being questioned. It was like somebody was peeping into your mind. 'You go away!' he yelled, running at her with his arms held stiffly in front. He wanted to hurt her. He hated her!

Startled by the vehemence in his voice and the look of loathing on his face as he stormed towards her, Ellie was momentarily taken aback. When he thudded hard into her, she winced, breathless, struggling to keep her balance. Having the advantage of weight and height, it was no difficult thing to fend him off. 'What in God's name is the matter with you!' she yelled. Though he kicked and struggled like a caged stallion, she held him determinedly, her strong fingers coiled tight round his thin wrists.

'Let me go! You let me go!' The words spat viciously into her face.

'What is it, Johnny? What's wrong with you?' Ellie asked in a kinder voice. She saw how the boy was boiling with anger. She felt his loathing of her. But she sensed that, underlying all of these obvious sensations, there was another. Fear. Real, awful terror. It made her blood run cold. 'Tell me what you're afraid of, Johnny . . . I won't mind about you searching the drawers and making a mess. And I'll forget about the way you behaved just now. But, you must tell me what's frightening you, Johnny. I only want to help you.' Was it possible that, even now, after these many months, and even here in these new surroundings, the boy was still haunted by . . . by . . .?

'I'm not frightened of anything!' His aqua-blue eyes blazed from his white face like luminous beacons; the colour was cold, but the emotion was vividly intense. Ellie could feel him trembling with rage. 'You don't frighten me! And I don't care if you punish me . . . you can tell *him* what I've done, if you want to!' His eyes flicked upwards.

'Don't be so sure I won't tell! And don't speak of your father in that tone of voice.' Ellie resisted the urge to turn him over her knee and whip his bare legs. For the first time since he was born, she wanted to make him cry. *Really cry!* Not pretend, or shed crocodile tears, but really cry. Through the outrage that stormed her mind in the face of his despicable behaviour, there spiralled a warning – 'No, Ellie,' it shouted, 'he's only a boy. Don't expect him to behave like a man, or to cry like one. He's still afraid. Alone. Unhappy. How can a small boy cope with all of that?' Her heart flooded with love and compassion. Ellie slid her arms round his small shoulders, holding him tight to her in a warm embrace.

Suddenly, he was calm, looking up at her with softer eyes, his voice low and asking, 'You won't lock me in my room, will you, Ellie? . . . Not tonight. Not Bonfire Night.'

Startled by his abrupt change of mood, Ellie murmured in a smile, 'Why do you say that? . . . No one has ever "locked" you in your room!' He made no reply, but when Ellie's concerned gaze mingled with the ice-blue, challenging stare, a thought struck her. A hard, cruel and astonishing thought that seemed to rivet her to the spot. She did not know him! The small, unpredictable creature who was her brother. *She did not know him!* Shaken, but chiding herself for entertaining such thoughts, she released her hold on him. 'Clean up the mess,' she said, 'afterwards, you know where to find me. It might be a good idea if you and I had a long, quiet talk.' Her manner was serious. She would not let this matter be so easily forgotten.

Silently, he went across the room and sank to his knees. In a moment, he was rocking back and forth, softly singing, oblivious to Ellie's continued presence.

'Remember now,' Ellie reminded him. 'When you're ready to talk, I'll be in the kitchen.' The incident had unnerved her. She could not remember a time when the boy had been so vicious. Later, when he had calmed down enough to reflect on it all, she would make every effort to get to the bottom of it. For now, though, she had other exacting things to occupy her. A glance at the grandfather clock in the corner told her it was almost noon. According to his latest communication, Barny was due here in less than an hour. Although the pork leg was done to a crisp and the vegetables almost prepared, there were still a great many things to be done. Besides the special lunch she was preparing for Barny, the food for the bonfire celebrations was also her responsibility, although Rosie had graciously offered to help. On top of all that, she so much wanted to look her best for Barny; after all, they had not seen each other for almost eight months. She wanted to make a good impression. She felt she owed him that much at least. Maybe there would be time for a drink and a quiet chat before the family sat down to their meal; although Ellie suspected that Johnny and her father would be impatient to eat, after being made to await Barny's arrival. No doubt Barny also would be hungry after his journey. No matter. There would be time enough later for a 'quiet chat'.

At twenty minutes past one, Ellie was beside herself with anxiety. There was still no sign of Barny. The meal was ready. The boy was scrubbed and moaning about the stiffness of his new shirt and Jack Armstrong, having been cajoled from his work upstairs, could be heard merrily whistling in the bathroom. Much to the boy's consternation, Ellie had taken up pacing the floor, constantly going to the window that overlooked the front of the house from where she peered expectantly out. When there was still no sign of Barny, she would come to the fireplace and stand a while, before enacting the whole procedure over again.

'He's not coming. He doesn't want you any more.' The boy muttered under his breath, grinned at Ellie, revelling in her distress, and kicking his foot against the chair front. Inside, he was fuming. She had no right to make him wait for his lunch! She shouldn't keep him here against his will. Not when he should be looking for those keys. A sense of panic squeezed at his heart. He had searched and searched; in her dressing-table drawers and through the drawers in the big room; even in his father's big old tool-box! The keys were nowhere to be found. Not even in the kitchen cupboards, or amongst the paraphernalia in the outhouse. He had even rifled the pockets of his father's discarded overalls, but the rusty old keys weren't there, either. In fact, he had begun to despair of ever finding them. There was only one other place he could think to look, and that was in the small wooden box that Ellie kept on the mantelpiece above the fireplace. He knew she kept little things in there – like the bills and a small amount of money for emergencies. Soon as ever he got a chance he would ransack it, but it wouldn't be easy, he knew. Firstly, there seemed always to be someone in the room, either his father, or Ellie, or Rosie doing the duties for which his father paid her. And besides, the mantelpiece was so high from the ground, he would need to stand on something to reach it. There were plenty of chairs in the room, but they were so heavy it would be difficult for him to drag one all the way across the room to the fireplace. Of course, there was one thing he could do. And that was to tell his friend where the keys might be. It would be easier for him to come into the house at night, when everyone was asleep. He was so clever, so very quiet, that no one would hear him. Frustrated by his own futile efforts, the boy was increasingly convinced that here was the best solution. He glared at Ellie now. If it wasn't for her, he could sneak out right now to see if his 'friend' was still in the barn. 'I'm not staying in much longer!' he told her now, in a louder, bolder voice. 'Your "boyfriend" isn't coming. It's true . . . he doesn't want you any more.'

Ellie swung round from the fireplace, a scathing retort on her lips. But it was Jack Armstrong who spoke. 'That's enough!' he instructed, striding into the room, his angry eyes seeking out the boy. 'I swear your tongue gets more wicked by the day. The least we can do for your sister is to put on a welcome for her young man who – when all is said and done – is our first real visitor to Thornton Place.'

'But I'm fed up. And I'm hungry. It isn't fair that I have to get all dressed up and be kept waiting for my food. I want to go out and see to my bonfire,' he lied. 'Anyway . . . I don't think he's coming, else he would have been here by now.' He rose to his feet, defiant. 'I'm not staying here . . . I've got things to do!'

'You've got far too much to say for yourself, that's what you've got!' came the brisk retort. In two strides, Jack Armstrong had confronted the boy, grabbed him by his shoulder and forced the small, squirming figure back into the chair. 'You'll stay put, like the rest of us. And you'll show a bit more respect towards your elders . . . or you can forget the privilege of enjoying that damned bonfire tonight. One more word out of you, and you'll be up them stairs so fast your feet won't touch the ground!' He stared down on the boy, not moving away until he was satisfied that his message was thrust home.

'It is strange, though,' interrupted Ellie, 'Barny was adamant about the time he would be arriving.' She *was* concerned, but her real motive for attracting her father's attention away from the boy was merely to separate them. The awful animosity that had festered between them greatly saddened her. In this instance, though, she knew her father to be right. The boy needed reminding of how to behave. Lately, even she had despaired of him.

'Oh, he'll be here any minute.' Jack Armstrong crossed the room towards her. In a way, he reluctantly agreed with the boy. Rather than forming a welcoming committee and being required to sit at the best table in a stiff, uncomfortable shirt, he himself would be far happier to snatch a quick lunch and afterwards get on with the workload which stretched before him, never-ending. Besides, he wasn't all that keen on any man making up to his Ellie and posing a threat to take her away. But, to his mind, Barny Tyler was the lesser of two evils. Rather that young fellow than the sinister, darkly handsome rogue, Alec Harman! His hackles rose even at the thought of the man. He had not yet been able to put his finger on what it was about Alec Harman that raised such suspicion and dislike in him, but there was something. Something. Some devious, hidden thing that was positively disturbing. Ah, but then again, it might be just that he had seen how Ellie had been so drawn to the fellow. That in itself was deeply distasteful to him! Now, as for the other one, that Barny Tyler, well, she was not so smitten with *him*, thank God.

There was no doubt in Jack Armstrong's mind that one day in the not-too-distant future, some randy charmer would take Ellie from him. He bitterly resented the prospect, often vowing that it would happen only over his dead body. Ellie was special. She deserved only the best. There was none more loyal, none lovelier. He looked at her now, a petite and perfect figure in a lavender-blue blouse and dark, thigh-hugging skirt. Slim shapely legs, pretty ankles and small feet dressed in black patent-leather shoes with high, flattering heels. Her hair positively glowed, like waves of cascading sunshine, and there was an excited sparkle in her lovely amber eyes that sent a thrill through him. She was his. *Ellie was his!* And it would need a stronger man than he to wrench her away.

The impatient knock at the door was an unwelcome intrusion into his thoughts. He saw Ellie's eyes light up as she rushed to open the door. He resented her pleasure. He hoped it would not last too long.

On opening the door, Ellie had been surprised to see how little Barny had changed; the tall, lean figure easy and attractive in brown slacks and green polo neck jumper; the lop-sided smile and unruly shock of chestnut-coloured hair, and the sea-green eyes that lit up with joy at the sight of Ellie. 'You don't know how good it is to be here with you,' he said, reaching out to take her small hands into his. 'Oh, Ellie . . . I've missed you so.' The warmth of her shocked through him. It had been so long. So very long. His heart urged him to pull her close, to kiss that full, soft mouth and to murmur all of those loving words which had kept the thought of her alive in him, and which, even now, were trembling on his lips.

'I've missed you too, Barny,' Ellie told him, squeezing her fingers against his, but making no effort to draw herself closer to him. She had been pleasantly shocked to find that she really had missed him. But it was still too soon to know. Underlying memories tingled inside her. Memories of love and unbridled passion. Warm, happy memories, of laughter and companionship. Now, as she looked on that familiar, handsome face, all of these memories came rushing back to fill her with pleasure. Yet, overriding these more reassuring emotions were other feelings, deep and disturbing. Feelings created in her by Alec Harman; this persistent image always lurking, firing her blood, haunting her day and night, and spoiling every other sensation inside her. Even though she had reminded herself time and again that her love for him was not returned. He had made it clear enough that he did not want her; that he bitterly resented her presence here. He had deliberately lied about secretly meeting that girl down by the lake. He was everything her father had warned; devious and 'strange', a 'charmer who could only break her heart'. The more Ellie recalled the nature of the man, the more she made herself despise him. 'I'm glad you're here.' She closed the door behind Barny, adding with a warm, sincere smile, 'I hadn't realised just how much I had missed you.'

'That's good to hear,' Barny replied softly, his two hands on her shoulders and his quiet, searching gaze tender on her face. 'But is the love still there?' He felt her stiffen beneath his touch and was at once afraid. 'Forgive me, Ellie, but . . . for me . . . nothing has changed. Nothing ever will.' His gaze mingled with hers. He saw the pain in her eyes, and the doubt. He saw something else that kindled a tiny hope in him; a certain vulnerability, a gentleness towards him that lit his soul. She did still love him, deep down maybe, but it was enough. It was a promise that what they had before was not altogether lost. Wisely, before she might feel threatened, he changed direction. 'What a splendid house!' He lifted his gaze from her face. 'But . . . more like a fortress than a house,' he remarked, 'and so far off the beaten track. Do you really enjoy living in such isolation?'

Going along with his timely observations, Ellie was grateful that he had not pressed her harder on the matter of their relationship. She could not deny there was still a vestige of love for him in her heart. Nor could she dismiss the fact that he had stirred a deal of happiness in her. Glancing sideways at him as they went down the passage towards the big room, she could not help but feel safe beside him. He had a particular way about him that made her feel proud, and *wanted*. That, most of all. Not needed in the way her brother and father needed her, but wanted for herself, as a person, as companion and confidante. As a lover, and wife. Her lonely heart warmed towards him. He was twice the man Alec Harman could ever be! Alec Harman. Alec . . . Alec. His name pulsated through her like hot lead. It took all of her self-control to thrust him from her senses. Barny was here for such a short time. Tomorrow, he would be leaving. In the few, short hours they could probably snatch together, there was so much to put right between them, one way or another. *One way or another*. Suddenly, she felt weary, drained of all emotion, and afraid for the future. She had been reasonably secure. Now, all the old doubts had begun to rear their intrusive heads and she felt the ground shifting beneath her.

★ ★ ★

All through lunch, Ellie felt Barny's eyes on her. Surprisingly, she found herself eagerly responding. She would glance up to his intense, loving gaze with a smile that was too intimate, too encouraging. Inch by inch, she pushed all thought of Alec Harman from her heart, filling the painful gulf with Barny. The feeling was good.

'How's the construction business?' Jack Armstrong also had enjoyed Barny's company. It was somehow reassuring to have a man about with whom he could converse. Certainly, there were few 'men' round here to speak of. The senile was lost in a sorry world of his own; Fred Gregory was surly and unsociable, and Alec Harman was downright unfathomable. Besides, even if Harman wasn't secretive and solitary, Jack Armstrong would have gone to great lengths to ensure that the fellow never came too close to Ellie!

'The firm's doing well. We've just landed a lucrative contract – council – a big new housing project in the Liverpool redevelopment zone,' Barny explained. 'With luck, it could be one of many.'

Still bitter about the earlier unpleasant scene between himself and his father, the boy was unforgiving. In spite of Barny's continued and good-humoured efforts to draw him out of his dark, sullen mood, he remained aloof, occasionally glaring at Barny from beneath frowning eyebrows. Inside, he was simmering with hatred. When at last the meal was over and he was allowed to go, he did so with a begrudging 'Thank you' to Ellie; given only because his father insisted; and without a single backward glance. His first intention was to go upstairs and strip off the irritating, stiff-collared shirt. Afterwards, he would go to the barn, to see his 'friend'. The thought was exhilarating. There was so much to talk about. So many bad words inside him that he must share. So much wickedness and black feeling that he had to spill out, or it would suffocate him! His 'friend' would understand. He *always* understood. Oh, but what about the keys? He would have to confess that he had not found them! Still, he had an idea where they were, didn't he? In that box on the mantelpiece. There, there! He hadn't really failed his friend after all, then. Everything would be all right, he was sure of it. He would go to the barn, and there, in the pitch-black, where no one else could see them, he and his 'friend' would talk, and curse, and make plans, just like they always did. Oh, his 'friend' meant everything in the world to him. He shivered with anticipation and pleasure, as he wondered what unspeakable delights his 'friend' had in store for him tonight.

All the same, even in the midst of his deepest pleasure, there was an undercurrent of chilling terror. That was the fun of it, the game, the excitement of never really knowing.

The boy waited, pressing himself hard against the outer wall of the barn, his heart beating furiously at the prospect of being discovered. He must never be seen to go inside the barn, in case the observer had a mind to follow. Time and again, his 'friend' had warned him of this, and he had paid very special heed. He was loath to share his secret with anyone. He never would! And he must always be careful not to do anything that could frighten his 'friend' away. It was because of such danger that he was hiding now. Hiding from Ellie and Barny Tyler as they went slowly towards the old courtyard. Ellie was softly laughing, her eyes sparkling as they glanced up at the man's face. Laughing, she was! Laughing in a way the boy had not heard for a long time; ever since . . . ever since. He could not bring himself even to think it! He did not want to remember. Ever. *Ever!* Suddenly the word sprang from his angry heart and cried from his lips. '*Mummy.*' He tried to stop the tears from spilling over, but the tide of emotion that swept up inside him could not be stopped. He was crying noisily now, his small figure stick-like against the barn, stiff and unyielding, while the tears burned his skin like searing caresses. There raged through him such violence, such loathing, that he wanted to maim, to kill. To make someone suffer like *he* had been made to suffer. *Her!* He wanted to know that *she* had suffered. She looked as though she had. He let his mind's eye look on the awful image just once more. He saw it all; the horror and the misshapen thing that was his mother. Yes. She looked as though she had suffered. A deep sense of satisfaction came over him. He smiled. But then, the perfume overwhelmed him. He twitched his nostrils in disgust. But no, the perfume was not now offensive to him. Not any more. Not since he had spoken to the pedlar. Not when it reminded him of his 'friend'. He sometimes smelled of lavender. It was pleasant, when you got used to it. Unaware that he was being watched, the boy slid discreetly into the barn.

Satisfied, the silent observer stole stealthily away.

Inside the barn, the boy came away from the light, immersing himself deeper and deeper into the bowels of that huge, formidable space. In the vast lofts above could be heard the pattering of claws, scurrying this way, then that way, and intermittently pausing. The boy smiled, imagining the sharp, pointed ears and the thin rat faces, listening, *guarding*. They were afraid of him. He liked that. For a brief moment, he was tempted to collect the shovel from its hook on the wall. He could creep very softly up the ladder and take them by surprise. Trap them! The thought of bringing that heavy shovel down and seeing the furry bodies wriggling beneath was almost too much for him to resist. He paused. The scuttling of claws was stilled. The listening silence was unbearable. He wanted to. Oh, how he wanted to. 'Another day,' he murmured threateningly, 'another day . . . you won't escape so easy.'

He smelled it right away, that sweet, delicate perfume. 'Are you here?' he asked, projecting his voice into the gloom. 'I can't see anything.' Normally, he could sense the presence, vaguely identify a shadowy bulk pressed into the corner. 'I can't hear you,' he said, feeling his way forward to the small, narrow stool. This was his place, carefully positioned so he could not easily look round. Grunting with approval, he felt the sharp, wooden edges and prepared to seat himself squarely onto its surface. It was so dark. Beneath his feet was a tangle of discarded paraphernalia. Always, he had a dread of missing his footing, when he might fall amongst it and be set upon by all manner of creatures. Things of blackness that would eat into him without mercy. Sometimes – probably afraid that the boy might scream and bring others running – a hand, a cold, gloved hand would reach out and guide him in. Not this time, though. Not this time! Tremulously he crept forward, his small, groping fingers sliding round the hard, familiar edge. But then something unfamiliar! He gasped aloud. Startled, he drew back. There was . . . something . . . there. 'Is that you? Are you playing games with me?' If so, he didn't like it. Not this time. When there came no reply, he waited a moment. Silence. 'You *are* playing a game,' he said. Deeper silence. He chuckled. The sound was a mixture of enjoyment and fear. He went forward, hesitantly this time. Creeping fingers searched again. The hard, wooden edge. That was the same sensation. 'Be brave, Johnny . . . it's only a game.' Trembling fingers moved along. There it was! 'Ugh!' He cringed with repulsion. Reluctantly, he secured it between his fingers, a crinkled, slimy object, clinging to him like a second skin.

Softly moaning, the boy carried the object into the half-light near the door. 'What is it?' he asked aloud, thinking his 'friend' would hear, but never expecting an answer. It was all part of the game. He looked more closely. As big as both his outstretched hands, it had a particular shape. A strangely familiar shape, but he could not tell. It bothered him. Scared him. It was like a mask. The backing was hard against the palms of his hands, but the material stretched over it was unlike anything he had seen before. Paper thin, kind of greyish, and crinkly to the touch, it made him shudder. The object was punctuated by three holes, two widely spaced at the top, and a thin, wide gash below. The holes were clumsy and jagged, as though they had been ripped into the material. Like a knife thrust through his mind, the boy suddenly realised what it was. 'It's a face. *A face!*' He laughed softly, turning to the black void where he suspected even now his 'friend' might be lurking. 'It is a face, isn't it?' he whispered. Secretly, he thought his own rag face was better, but he dared not murmur such treason. 'It's good,' he said proudly, turning the gruesome object in his hands, 'I like it.' He noted the loosely rolled ear-pieces that hung either side of the face; obviously that was how it was meant to be secured. The greyish face was wrapped right around the backing, tight in some places, not so tight in others. Long, floating pieces of hair hung from the high forehead, draping over the hollow eyes and brushing against the vicious gash that was the mouth. All along the edges, tiny globules of rolled-up material hung, suspended like ripe warts. Fascinated, the boy held it up to the incoming shaft of light, at once crying out with excitement at the transformation. The eyes came alive, and the grey matter glowed gently in the shadowy light, each fold and crinkle taking on a sinister texture – almost as though it was breathing. The face seemed so real. *So horribly familiar.* Shaken, the boy dropped it out of the light. Even then, he could still feel the empty eyes looking at him. 'I'll come back later,' he told the blackness, 'when I've put the face on . . . I'll come back and tell you what it's like.' His voice was small now, and uncertain.

At the door, the boy hesitated. Should he tell about not finding the keys? No. Better wait until later. He wasn't really sure whether his 'friend' was there. There was plenty of time anyway, before the bonfire was lit. And he had a great deal to do; there was the Guy's face to be secured, and then he was to be hauled up to the top of the bonfire onto his chair. Ellie had promised that he could count all the fireworks again; even though he was not allowed to light them! And he had promised himself that he would scour the spinney just once more, to collect any fallen branches. He remembered what his 'friend' had said. He recalled the very words. 'Make sure you cover the entrance well, Johnny. We wouldn't want anyone finding our special hidey-hole, would we?' *No!* That was their very special secret. After whispering a promise that he would be back later, the boy hurried away, a sense of adventure thrilling through him.

'We'll have to get back, Barny . . . it's almost dark.' For the first time in a long while, Ellie felt at peace with herself. Here across the open fields, on the highest point above Thornton Place, she and Barny had found a measure of contentment in each other's company. From the high hilltop, all of the vast acreage belonging to Wentworth Estates could be easily surveyed; in one direction, sheets of rippling green stretched away towards the spinney. In the foreground stood the imposing house that was Thornton Place. At the farthest point was the lake, cool and slumbering, bounded on all sides by an undulating landscape that was now cloaked in the gold and brown hues of autumn. Soon, all the leaves would have fallen and the trees, stripped of their garments, must stand, shivering and unhappy throughout the biting winds of winter.

'It's magnificent!' Barny seemed not to have heard Ellie's remark as he gazed, enchanted, over the scene below. 'I can understand now how you love it so.' He turned his gaze on Ellie, smiling but silent. Her beauty took his breath away and filled his heart.

Amused and pleasantly embarrassed, Ellie softly laughed. 'You didn't hear a word I said, did you?' she asked.

'Of course I did,' he protested, bending towards her and pushing the tip of his nose into hers. 'Only . . . I don't want to go yet. I don't *ever* want to go.'

'We must.' Ellie was suddenly disturbed by the havoc he was creating in her. The tip of his nose was warm, soft and squashy against her chilled face. His green eyes were too darkly handsome, too smiling, too searching. She was acutely aware of the gentle rhythm of his breath against her skin. His mouth was too close, too attractive and inviting. Suddenly, his arms were round her, strong yet tender, pulling her down, drawing her to him. She did not resist. She did not want to. The sight of the lake had strengthened the painful memory of Alec Harman and the girl. A confusion of emotions welled up in her, bitterness, jealousy, need. *Need*. Barny. 'Oh, Barny.' But, it *wasn't* Barny who she loved. She must not encourage him too much. It was unfair. 'I do love you so.' His voice was murmuring low in her ear, turning her heart, fanning the passion within her. His fingers reached out, moving swiftly, warm on her skin, enticing, touching, tormenting. 'Barny . . .' His mouth covered hers, then, 'Ssh . . . all I want is you, my darling.' She felt her clothes move against her tingling skin, his weight was on her now, his nakedness fusing with hers. Soft, warm lips over her breasts, teasing the hard, erect nipples, murmuring, always murmuring, 'Oh, Ellie . . . Ellie, I love you so.' Now, he was inside her, firm, demanding, the compulsion tearing away every emotional barrier. She needed him, needed love. 'Barny . . . Barny.' Gentle, probing thrusts, sending waves of delicious anguish through her. Her senses reeling, she clung to him, moving with him. Passion devoured her. Softly groaning, she kept him there until the waves of exhilaration became a tide that over-whelmed them both, lifting, carrying them along, gaining momentum. Now it was a frenzy that knew no bounds. Gloriously, the tide burst, wonderfully spent, peacefully lapping over them.

Arms locked around each other, they followed the path to Thornton Place. Few words were spoken; each was lost in quiet, reflective thought. Night was closing in. Ellie quickened her footsteps. *Shame and regret were closing in, also*.

Back on the hilltop, a solitary figure continued to watch them. A dark, brooding heart was filled with sadness, and envy, and a need so powerful that it threatened to swamp all reason. Sighing, lonely, the figure bowed its head and turned away.

'Forgive me, Ellie . . . I've hurt you, haven't I? . . . spoiled our chances together?' Barny was stricken with remorse, yet he would cherish their time on the hilltop for the rest of his life. He stood by the table in the kitchen, wishing that Ellie would pause in her work, cursing the bonfire that obliged her to spend the time leading up to it in preparing the food. He needed to talk with her. *Intimately*. Away from prying eyes and listening ears. He was desperate to make amends; to strengthen the bond between them. He had come to Thornton Place with the hopeful intention of securing Ellie's promise to be his wife. Instead, he was afraid he might have gone too far. 'All I can say is that I'm in love with you. But, you know that, don't you?' His green eyes were beseeching.

Ellie raised her face to his, momentarily feeling his anguish. 'I know you do, Barny,' she said. A rush of compassion seized her weary heart. Putting down the knife and wiping her hands over the tea towel, she turned from the mound of chestnuts and potatoes. 'I love you too . . . I *must*, or I would never have allowed myself to . . . to . . .' She half smiled and lowered her eyes. 'I wanted you every bit as much as you wanted me,' she murmured, the pink flush of self-consciousness burning her face.

'Then you *do* love me!' Barny was beside himself with relief. 'It wasn't just the moment . . . you felt the same?'

'Barny.' Ellie was afraid of what he might construe from her admission just now. She had to stop him. 'Yes, I *do* . . . love you,' she admitted, '*but* . . .' She would have gone on to explain how it was not enough. Her love for him had been influenced only by other, long ago memories. This afternoon she had been swept along, against her better judgement, all of her emotions a tangle, jealous of Alec, wanting to hurt him, moved by Barny's nearness and the persuasion of his manner. Desperate in her need. *He was a wonderful lover*. Up there on that hilltop, he had awakened something in her that she would always thank him for. He had made her see that it was *Alec* she wanted. Alec who she would *always* want, even in spite of the knowledge that he was all she despised. She and Alec were not meant to be, she knew that. But, after today, she knew also that she and Barny were not meant to be, either. His coming here had been a mistake. She must make him see that; let him down lightly. But not tonight. Tomorrow would be soon enough. Barny was wise; a good man. He deserved someone who could return all the love he had to give. As for Alec Harman? Ellie hoped he would stay out of her life. If she never saw him again, it would be too soon!

Ellie might have said all this and more. If only the untimely, or perhaps *timely*, entrance of her father had not prevented it. 'Ellie, sweetheart . . . I've had enough of plastering that damned room.' He came to the table and stole a chestnut. After skilfully peeling it, he smiled at her, saying, 'I thought I might take your young man on a tour of our delightful grounds.' He glanced at Barny and winked. He made no mention of the fact that he had overheard the conversation between his daughter and this young man. Nor that he had sensed Ellie's reluctance to commit herself to marriage; a reluctance he heartily approved of. It was painfully obvious to him that Barny Tyler had been on the verge of proposing, and he couldn't have that, could he now? What was the old saying? . . . 'All's fair in love and war.' That was it. An apt description of *this* particular situation. Love. *And war.* All was fair!

'But it will be dark within the hour!' Ellie pointed out, glancing up at the big wall clock. 'And Johnny's still out somewhere. I was hoping you'd find him for me.' She wrinkled her nose, gesturing towards the sink and saying with some disgust, 'When you've got a minute . . . that sink smells really bad again.'

'Check the sink . . . find the boy! No problem at all.' He popped the raw chestnut into his mouth, twisting his lips sideways to speak. 'I reckon the sink needs a thicker layer of concrete beneath it . . . . I've noticed that the dressing I put down is crumbling. Don't worry. I'll get round to that tomorrow. For the moment, me and Barny will take a stroll towards the lake . . . kill two birds with one stone so to speak . . . while I'm showing him around, we'll keep our eyes open for the boy. No doubt he's still scouring the spinney for wood to pile on that monumental bonfire!' Before Ellie could protest, he slapped the flat of his hand on Barny's back and began propelling him towards the door. 'Come on fella-me-lad,' he said in jocular voice, 'we'll make our way down towards the lake . . . spectacular!' He kept up a good-humoured banter until he had seen Barny safely through the door, when he turned to praise Ellie. 'That's a proper feast you're creating there, sweetheart . . . hot chestnuts, baked potatoes . . . fresh bread rolls . . .' He stretched his gaze beyond her to the table-top. 'Where's the succulent ham I saw this morning?'

'Rosie took charge of that,' Ellie replied with some amusement. She knew her father's devious little tricks, and had quickly suspected him of having engineered this little 'outing' just to separate her and Barny. Another time, she might have reacted in a very different way but, on this occasion, what she truly felt was gratitude. All the same, lingering beneath her resolution to send Barny away for ever, Ellie felt a murmuring of doubt. Was she doing the right thing?

'Huh! So, Rosie thinks you can't cook a ham properly, is that it?' He chuckled, closing the door on his last words. 'We shall just have to show her what an indispensable treasure you are, shan't we, eh? . . . we shall have to show them all!'

'What the hell was that?' Jack Armstrong jerked his head round, peering towards a spot some way further along the lake's edge. He and Barny had been walking back towards the spinney, discussing Thornton Place and exchanging conversation with regard to each other's workloads, when the older man had cried out in a loud whisper. Grabbing his companion by the arm, he urged him to a halt. 'There . . . did you see that?' he asked, frantically gesturing ahead.

'No . . . I didn't see anything,' Barny replied, straining his eyes towards the spot. 'There's nothing there, Mr Armstrong,' he assured the older man.

'There bloody well is, I tell you. Look!'

Barny peered harder into the darkness. 'Probably a night creature,' he said. He was disturbed to see how nervous the other man was.

'I wouldn't mind betting it's my son . . . sneaking about . . . up to no good!' In the half-light, his face was chiselled with anger. 'He's beyond me. Since his mother . . . well, the boy just seems . . . wrong somehow. He's never been the same. I can't fathom him. I've tried,

God only knows, I've tried, but . . .' He shook his head. 'He's changed.'

'I understand.'

'Do you?' Jack Armstrong turned his anxious gaze on Barny's concerned face. 'I don't think you do, young man . . . certainly, *I* don't. Both Ellie and myself . . . *we've* had to cope. Why can't he? Tell me that!'

'He is only a boy.'

'He's weak, that's what he is.'

Barny gave no answer to that. Instead, he merely nodded his head. He knew from past experience that Jack Armstrong was a very strong-minded man. Look how desperately he had made every effort to discourage his and Ellie's growing relationship in the early days. Oh yes! If Ellie's father set his mind against you, he could be a formidable enemy. It struck Barny in that moment how it was not only the boy who had 'changed'. So had Ellie's father. The previous Mr Armstrong would never have allowed a suitor to get too close to his daughter, let alone invite one to stay under the same roof . . . even for a single night! He really did seem different somehow. More approachable and . . . fulfilled. Less aggressive. Barny supposed that the awful tragedy which had taken Marie Armstrong from her family had touched each one of them more deeply than even they themselves could realise. Now, he could sense the other man's agitation. 'If you like, we'll go and investigate,' he suggested.

'No need. It *is* the boy . . . I just know it. Two of us coming on him would give him warning . . . send him into hiding. That won't do. If it *is* him . . . prowling about . . . deliberately frightening folk, then he has to learn not to.' He looked at Barny, suddenly realising how harsh he must sound. 'You don't know him like I do,' he explained in a whisper. 'Like I said, he's changed . . . developed a nasty, cruel streak . . . likes to hurt things . . . people. Such wickedness must be nipped in the bud.' He began to stride away. 'I'll see you back at the house. Tell Ellie I suspect the boy is up to bad tricks . . . tell her I'll fetch him back.'

'Let me come with you.' Barny started after him. 'Two pairs of eyes are better than one.'

'No! Get back to the house. Turn round and follow the footpath through the spinney . . . you'll find it easily enough, if you keep your eyes peeled.' He laughed. 'Don't stray, though . . . the spinney is said to be haunted.' His laughter lingered on the breeze, long after he had disappeared from sight.

'Huh! It's easy to see where the boy gets his "cruel streak" from,' Barny murmured, beginning his way towards the spinney. He had spoken too soon. Jack Armstrong had not changed at all! A strange sensation came over him. A disturbing sensation, to do with Ellie. It occurred to him that the sooner he could take her away from here, the better. Wait a minute! What was he saying? Surely to God he wasn't saying that Ellie was in danger from her own family? No, *no*! The idea was preposterous. All the same, he had been greatly unsettled by Jack Armstrong's erratic behaviour just now. And, he had not seen anything move back there, nor, he suspected, had Jack Armstrong. Why, then, had Ellie's father rushed away, leaving him in the middle of nowhere? Why had he made such a cruel jibe about the spinney being 'haunted'? And, most of all, why was he so obsessed with the idea that the boy was 'prowling about . . . up to no good'?

Barny reflected on his own situation. Here he was, creeping through the spinney like a nervous kitten, fear bubbling in the pit of his stomach, as the trees closed in about him. He found himself smiling, as he wondered what Ellie would have to say.

Behind him, the other man pressed on his way with soft, purposeful steps.

★ ★ ★

'I thought you were never coming to see me. I hate it when you aren't here . . . when you don't come to see me for weeks and weeks.'

'I can't *always* be here, Johnny. I have . . . other things to do.'

'Oh!' Now his heart was black with envy. He so much wanted to ask what 'other things'? But he knew his 'friend' would be angry. Instead, he said in a peevish voice, 'I put the face on my Guy Fawkes . . . just like you wanted.'

'I know.'

'Do you?' He was astonished. 'Have you seen him . . . on top of the bonfire . . . in his big armchair?'

'Of course, Johnny.'

The boy chuckled, excited. 'Oh . . . did you like him? Did you see how well the face fits? I had a bit of trouble fixing it, but, in the end I did it. Strange, though . . .'

'The face looks perfect, Johnny. But . . . why do you say it's . . . "strange"?'

'Well, I didn't see at first . . . not until I stretched it over the Guy's *old* face . . . you know, the one I made out of rag, and Ellie stitched the two brown buttons on . . . for eyes.'

'Go on.'

'Well, the buttons popped through the jagged holes . . . in your face, and . . . and . . .'

'Yes, Johnny?'

'*It looked like Ellie!*'

In the blackness, in the menacing silence, the boy waited. He had been startled at the discovery. He wanted his 'friend' to be startled, too. The minutes passed. It seemed like a lifetime had gone before the whisper settled his fluttering heart. 'You're wrong, Johnny. Not really "like Ellie". Think again.' A low, harsh chuckle permeated the brooding atmosphere.

Disappointed, the boy thought hard. The face did look like Ellie! He had seen it with his own eyes. But his 'friend' was waiting. He thought frantically now, aware of the irritated breathing behind him. Who else? Who else did the face look like? Oh, please! *Who else?* In his feverish mind, a spiral of light wormed its way through his thoughts. The tension broke. He sighed, then softly laughed. Of course! Of course. 'The paintings! *The woman in the paintings.*'

'Clever Johnny, but . . . not quite right. The woman in the paintings, though . . . she is very beautiful, isn't she?'

'I don't know. She's . . . old, I suppose.'

The whisper hissed at him, depleting his newly found confidence. '*No!* She may be older than you, Johnny, but she's young. She can never, ever grow old. When you are an old, old man, Johnny . . . she will *still* be young. And exquisitely beautiful. Do you understand, Johnny? *Do you?*'

'Yes, yes, I think so.'

'Good. That's good.'

'Did you see the paintings when you came in the house, before?' When there was only silence to answer him, he said boldly, 'I wish you would come and see me . . . in my bedroom . . . when you come into the house.'

'Oh?' A surprised laugh, then, 'Would you *really* want me to come into your bedroom?'

'Yes.'

'You want to see me so much, don't you, Johnny? You do!'

'Yes. Yes. I do!' His heart was almost bursting with anticipation. 'I wouldn't tell. Honest! I would never tell.'

'I couldn't let you tell. *Ever.*'

'Can I see you? Please?' His voice was breathless. He was sorely tempted to turn round. Hopefully, he shifted a little.

'No. You must not see me. I can't allow that.' A low, devious chuckle, then. 'But, you can touch me. Would you like that?'

'Oh, yes. *Yes!*'

The wait was excruciatingly long. In the dark, the small, furtive sounds excited the boy's expectation. What was his 'friend' doing? What was he doing? Suddenly, the excitement was too painful to contain. 'Can I touch you? *Can I?*'

'Yes, Johnny. Reach out . . . I'm here, waiting.' A warning. 'Don't try to look round, though. I wouldn't like that.'

'I won't, I promise . . . I'll keep my eyes shut all the time.'

'That's a good idea, Johnny. Yes . . . a good idea. Shut your eyes. Then, when you touch me, it will feel better. You can . . . imagine . . . what I'm like, can't you?'

'Now?'

'I'm ready, Johnny.' The whisper had changed. It was trembling, excited. Like the boy.

Cautiously, the small, probing fingers reached out, groping the darkness, eager to make contact. Something brushed fleetingly over his arm. Soft and velvet it was; like a gloved hand. Tenderly, it guided the hungry fingers. Oh! Exhilaration coursed through the boy as he felt a new sensation beneath his fingers. Warm and soft. Pleasing to the touch. 'Is that you?' he cried, his fingertips lingering, enjoying.

'Ssh . . . be silent, Johnny.'

Tremulous, his hand continued to explore. With his eyes tightly shut, the boy could see deep into the dark recesses of his own mind. All kinds of images gyrated before him; each one pleasant to the eye. Loving. *Naked*. Sometimes, when he was in bed, he liked to . . . touch himself. To rove his hands all over his body. It was his own, special secret. He never told *anyone*, not even his 'friend'. It was always good. It excited him. Like now. The smooth silkiness was the same. The curves, the softness. And the hardness. He wondered, should he tell his 'friend' that he sometimes touched *himself* like that? He opened his mouth to speak, but was silenced by his 'friend's' cries. Soft, frenzied cries that jerked into the darkness, heightening the boy's deep-down sensations. At first, he feared that his 'friend' was in distress. But then came a rolling sigh, and the soft, soft sound of laughter. Now, his fingertips touched only the cold, black air.

'Did you like touching me, Johnny?' The whisper rose above the other sounds – rustling, hurried sounds, amidst a flurry of movement.

'Yes. But . . . I would really like to touch your face. May I . . . soon?' Suddenly, he felt so alone.

'No. I don't think so.'

'Why not?'

Anger now. 'Don't forget what I told you!'

'I'm sorry. I didn't mean to question you.'

'The keys! Have you brought me the keys, Johnny?'

'I . . .'

'Have you brought me the keys?'

'I tried. Honest, I tried . . . I looked everywhere.'

'Are you saying you failed me, Johnny?'

'I think I know where they are.'

'But you failed me. I am disappointed, Johnny.'

'In the big room. In the box . . . on top of the mantel-piece.' He was frantic. He had never heard his 'friend' so angry. 'That's where they are. I'm sure of it.'

'I did warn you not to fail me, Johnny.'

'I looked everywhere! I searched the outhouse . . . the kitchen and the bedrooms. I crept into Ellie's room and went through all her things. They weren't there. They must be in the box . . . on the mantelpiece, but, I'm not big enough . . . I can't get the chair there . . . someone will see me. You'll have to go into the house . . . at night.

When everybody's asleep.' A sob caught in his throat. The perfume was suffocating him. It seemed to be wrapping itself round his whole body. Suddenly, he was cold; bitterly cold, and shaking from head to toe. He wanted to run from that place. But the perfume was filling his head. It was uniquely pleasant.

'I can't forgive you, you know that, don't you, Johnny?'

'Yes.' The game would not permit it.

'I don't want to . . . hurt you.'

'No . . . please . . . don't.' Terror began to press up inside him. He tried to push it down. Instead it grew. Consuming him. 'Be quiet, Johnny,' he whispered inside himself, 'it's only a game.' But, in his fearful heart, he knew that, *this time*, it was no game.

'You do realise I shall have to punish you?'

He could not answer. His tongue was thick in his throat. He was paralysed with fear.

'I can show you . . . no mercy. You do understand that, don't you, Johnny?'

What happened next sealed Johnny's fate. The creeping fear swelled up inside him, flooding every corner of his being. He could not speak, could not breathe. In his mind, the words towered like dark executioners . . .'*No mercy*'. A mountainous dam burst inside his head, rushing all reason before it, drowning all caution. With an agonised cry he slewed round! 'Don't hurt me!' he pleaded. In that fatal split second, he saw. *He saw*. 'You!' Astonishment coursed through him. Riveting shock lit up his big round eyes like two brilliant blue pools. 'YOU!' Incredulous, he instinctively began to back away. Faster, faster, stumbling, mortally afraid, his heart pounding, yet not beating at all. In the dark, he could hear the soft, insane laughter. The pad of footsteps. Deliberate. *Pursuing*. Now, he was running, blindly, desperate in the belief that if he did not make it to the door, he would never again see the light of day. Behind him, the laughter permeated the air. In the darker distance the voice, not whispering now, but soft, threatening. Unbelievably familiar. 'You should not have looked, Johnny! Now, it's too late, but . . . I could never have spared you. Not you. Not them. None of you can be spared. You do understand that, don't you, Johnny?' The voice was too close. In the silent chaos of his mind, the boy was screaming. Now, he could see the door, only an arm's reach away. In his excitement he fell, his fingers scratching the ground, his legs like jelly. Must get up . . . get away! He was crying now, hot bitter tears filling his mouth, blurring his vision.

'Go away! Leave me be!' On his feet now, he bolted towards the door.

'I can't do that, Johnny. You know I can't do that.' A harder edge to the voice. Fury. Revenge. Sounds of shifting debris underfoot. Slipping. Tumbling. 'You won't escape me, Johnny!' Frantic now. Close. Too close. 'There's no place you can hide. I know every inch of the spinney . . . all of its secrets. I know the house, too, Johnny . . . better than anyone!'

Bursting through the door, the boy ran and ran. The voice followed him. 'Nowhere to hide, Johnny . . . I'll find you . . . find you.'

Violently trembling, his mouth and throat squeezed dry and the blood in his veins like clotted ice, Johnny went on blindly, instincts taking over, and all sense of reason submerged. He had to hide! *Hide*. HIDE. *Into the bonfire he went*. Deep and deeper, right into the heart of that slumbering terramorphous structure. Created by his own hands, it opened to receive him, persuading him deeper. Down. Down. Into the very bowels of its existence. The small, terrified figure crawled on all fours, feeling its way through the inner arteries. In his wake, all that had been disturbed closed in again. He was safe. Oh, how he wished Ellie was here. Sometimes, he wanted to hurt her, and he *did* hurt her, he knew that. But almost every time he was sorry. He did love Ellie, better than anyone. She was his friend. Not the other one. Not now.

From behind, the sound of settling objects came to him like soft, comforting sighs. In the pitch-black he pressed forward, momentarily disorientated. He paused. Hot and trembling, with his back crooked, he listened. All around him the debris heaved, shifting, sighing. Deeper into the labyrinth he went. Small, groping fingers felt the way, tracing the earth contours, searching. Ah! *There*. The ground opened. Quietly, thankfully, he slid into its depths. Enfolding. Suffocating. But safe. *Safe at last*.

Above, seated high on its pinnacle, the figure remained still and regal, monarch of all it surveyed. In the moonlight, ragged pieces of vapoury cloud drifted lazily, creating shadows, bringing the earth to life. Two brown button eyes seemed to twinkle and a face, so long devoid of life, might be smiling. *Watching*.

Below, all was still and silent. Save for a lone, sinister figure that came forward now, closer, a look of satisfaction on its face. A low, evil chuckle, then, 'You did not fail me after all, Johnny.' Soft and pleading, the voice went on, 'But you mustn't be afraid . . . you are not alone. Not now, because . . .' Eyes raised, admiring yet stiffly accusing. 'She is with you.' Pain. Oh, so much pain. Then, anger. 'She is so wicked, Johnny, but, so very beautiful, don't you think?' The softest of laughter. 'The sandcastle. Do you remember the sandcastle, Johnny? Oh, but of course you do! How could you forget? And here you have recreated it so magnificently. It's yours, Johnny. And hers. It's only justice that the two of you should find that sandcastle again . . . feel the same joy that you felt then. But afterwards . . . oh, after you have experienced such joy, it must all end. You, Johnny . . . both of you must pay the ultimate price. Later . . . the others also will be made to suffer. It has to be that way. You do understand, don't you, Johnny?' The grating sound alarmed the stillness, and at once there was a flicker of light. The flame fluttered in the breeze, held too long. Mesmerised. Fingers burned, a whisper of pain. But no panic. No sensation now, other than a deep-down satisfaction. And a mad, almost unbearable halcyon of pleasure. Quickly, another flame, yellow and gyrating in the blackness. The figure leaned down, choosing the point of ignition most carefully. The fire must not rage away too quickly, nor be detected by anyone for a while yet. A few moments. A few, precious moments, that was all. Now, it was done. The sound of a lullaby softly sung, while long, strong fingers dipped into pockets and drew out the dried lavender petals. When they fluttered down into the pyre, the singing intensified. Then, the voice broke. Tears came. But no regret. *No mercy*. Swiftly, the figure went into the night, into the darkness, where plans were best made. Plans. Lots to do. It was not finished yet. Not yet. Not until the very last one!

'But . . . where's Johnny?' On hearing her father come into the house, Ellie had rushed from the big room and into the kitchen, where Jack Armstrong was already taking off his muddied boots. 'It's almost seven o'clock!'

'You mean he hasn't come back yet?' Jack Armstrong looked up, his brow furrowed with anger. Frustrated, he told her, 'That's it! The minute he comes in, he's straight off to bed!'

Regretting her impatient remarks, Ellie tried desperately to make amends. 'I expect he's still scavenging for the bonfire . . . lost all track of time. He'll be home any minute, I'm sure.' But she was worried, and furious with her brother. It was as though he deliberately set out to antagonise his father.

'It's time he was taught a lesson.' Jack Armstrong eased his feet into the flat brogue shoes and straightened his back with a groan. Dark blue eyes, brilliant and accusing, stared hard at Ellie. 'He's a selfish, wicked little bugger!' The words spat out. 'We both know that, only we've given him the benefit of the doubt, because . . . well, because . . .' He wiped the back of his hand over his face. He was sweating. Uncomfortable. 'He doesn't care a sod for anybody but himself! *Look at me!*' he snapped, throwing his arms wide to reveal the scratches on his neck and hands, 'grovelling through the undergrowth like some bloody animal! He was there . . . I know he was there. Probably watching from a distance . . . laughing. Time and again I called after him, but . . . devious little devil . . . he toyed with me. Like he was playing some bloody game!'

'Are you sure it was him?' Ellie knew that the boy was capable of being so spiteful. And her father was right. They had let him get away with it for too long. She loved him, though. How could she help it, he was her brother after all.

'Of course I'm sure!'

'Look . . . you go and run a bath. I'll get you something to eat. If he's not back soon, me and Barny will go and look for him.'

'He got back all right, then?' There was an element of surprise in his voice.

'He did.' Ellie gave a small laugh, but her expression was reprimanding as she told her father, 'No thanks to you, though.'

'What d'you mean?'

'You know what I mean,' she retorted, the smile gone from her face, 'deserting him . . . in the dark . . . down by the lake.'

'Oh.' His features crumpled into a satisfied smile. 'So, he told you, did he? . . . came running to you like a little lost boy. Afraid of the dark, was he?'

For a moment, Ellie was taken aback by the underlying savagery in his voice. 'No. He did not. As a matter of fact,

I had to drag it out of him. I might have guessed, though . . . when he came back without you.' Shades of bitterness coloured her thinking. She had not forgotten how it used to be. In the past, whenever some young man showed an interest in her, her father had done his level best to deter him; even resorting to underhand tricks and incursive comments, much the same as now.

'He told you *why* I left him, did he?'

'Yes. He said you went after Johnny.'

'There you are, then. And I tell you what, Ellie . . . if I'd caught the bugger, he would have felt the flat of my hand across his legs and no mistake!' He shook his head and lapsed into deep thought. 'Honestly, Ellie, I don't know what we're going to do with the boy. I don't mind telling you, he's beyond me, and that's a fact.' He brushed past Ellie. 'As for Barny, well . . . it wasn't meant. I'm sorry. To be honest, I'd rather see you wed him than some others I could mention.' He turned and kissed her on the forehead. 'Friends, are we?'

Ellie nodded. She felt the need to put her father straight on a particular matter, before it all got out of hand. 'Don't be so quick to marry me off,' she warned, 'not to Barny, or to . . . anyone else for that matter.' Alec Harman sprang to her mind; handsome, dark-eyed Alec Harman, who was never far from her thoughts. Or from her heart. Yet she loathed him. Didn't she?

'Oh!' Jack Armstrong could not disguise his pleasure at Ellie's words. 'I see.' He nodded his head approvingly. 'Quite right. You're far too young to get serious, sweetheart. Play the field . . . enjoy life before you tie yourself down.' A strange and distant look clouded his eyes as he murmured, 'Sometimes we make a wrong decision, and have to go on paying for it . . . willing and praying that it will all come right in the end. But, it never does.' Realising that Ellie was watching him curiously, he gave a nervous laugh. 'Still . . . it doesn't do any good crying over it, does it, eh? What's done is done, isn't that right?'

'Yes, Dad.' Ellie was convinced that he was reflecting on her mother, and the possibility that he had failed her – failed all of them. Or, he was regretting the move to Thornton Place. On both counts she believed that he had done the right and only thing. To her mind, he had been a good husband and a good father. There was no earthly reason why he should ever reproach himself; unless it was on the issue of his fraught relationship with Johnny. But then, at times the boy tried even her to the limit. 'We mustn't dwell in the past. There are better times ahead,' Ellie promised, 'we have to look forward . . . to the future.'

'The future?' Something akin to scorn crept into his expression. 'Yes, you're right, sweetheart.' He spread his fingertips into her hair and ruffled it the way he used to when she was small. 'If only your brother was more like you,' he said in a tight, emotional voice.

'Give him time, Dad,' Ellie pleaded, 'just a little more time.'

He made no response, other than to gaze at her through sorry eyes. In a moment he had turned away, going from the room with bowed shoulders.

'You'll feel better after a hot bath,' Ellie called after him, 'meanwhile, I'll get you a bite to eat.' After that, she intended to recruit Barny to help find the boy. And when she *did* find him, he would get the length of her tongue, and no mistake!

When Ellie came into the big room where she had left Rosie and Barny merrily chatting, Barny was the first to address her. 'I hope you didn't make too much of your father going off the way he did,' he told Ellie. 'Did he find the boy?'

'Afraid not,' she said, looking from Barny to Rosie, who was finishing off the dregs in her tea cup. 'Dad's upstairs . . . having a hot bath. I'm just about to make him some sandwiches, then I intend to find Johnny . . .'

'Not without me!' Barny assured her. 'Like I told your father . . . two pairs of eyes are better than one.' Suddenly, the pit of his stomach was curling over with that same uncomfortable feeling he had experienced earlier. For no reason he could truly fathom, he was afraid for Ellie. 'Besides,' he said in a stern voice, 'I'm not about to let you wander the night on your own.'

'There you are, you lucky thing,' Rosie chuckled. 'Oh, what wouldn't I give for a handsome young man to escort me on my way!'

Ellie looked at Barny and they both laughed aloud. Smiling at Rosie, Barny told her in a flirting manner, 'Never let it be said that I would ever allow a good-looking woman such as yourself to walk home unescorted. Whenever you're ready . . . I'm at your disposal.'

'Go on!' Rosie chided good-humouredly; she had taken a real liking to Ellie's young man. 'You only want your wicked way with me!' Her merry brown eyes glanced at the big old clock against the wall. 'Good Lord!' she cried, struggling from the chair and fighting to wedge the hard wooden crutch beneath her armpit. 'I've been here almost an hour!' In her frantic efforts to balance herself, she almost fell over.

Barny sprang to his feet, steadying her and warning, 'Take it easy, old girl . . . what's the panic?'

'George! I've left him alone for too long at once.' She leaned into Barny's strong, helping hands. 'He sleeps most of the time, but if he wakes and finds me gone . . . the poor bugger won't know what to do!' she explained.

Ellie understood. Holding the old woman by the arm, she said in a quiet, comforting voice, 'He'll be all right, Rosie. He's sure to know where you are.'

'But you don't understand!' Rosie was altogether composed now, but still greatly troubled. 'He's taken to . . .

wandering off. If I'm not there to watch him, he sneaks out of bed . . . out of the cottage. Oh, he's no idea what he's doing, or where he's going, but, well . . .' She shook her head and looked beseechingly at Barny. 'He's ill, d'you see . . . convinced in his poor, sick mind that some "awful devil" means to "root him out and do away with him".'

Barny was about to say how sorry he was, he had no idea. But, in the split second when he half turned his head to glance at Ellie, something distracted his attention. Through the window directly behind Ellie, the night sky was ablaze. 'What the hell is that?' He stretched his neck to see beyond the window.

Curious, the two women followed his gaze. In that moment, Jack Armstrong came rushing into the room shouting, 'It's the bonfire! The bugger's lit the bonfire!' He gestured to Barny. 'You come with me, Tyler,' he ordered, then, looking at Ellie, he said, 'take Rosie home, sweetheart. We'll find the boy, but first that fire has to be watched . . . controlled.' His mood was dark as he and Barny left the house. 'The little sod!' he called back to Ellie, 'if this is his idea of a game . . .'

'Don't let your temper get the better of you,' Ellie shouted. But he was gone.

'What's wrong with Johnny, Ellie?' Rosie wanted to know, as she and Ellie negotiated the path to the cottage. 'Has he always had a streak of . . . rebellion in him?' She was tempted to say 'wickedness', but thought too kindly of Ellie to hurt her. As for Johnny, surely to God he must have *some* saving grace?

'No, I don't think so,' Ellie answered, her heart heavy with worry. It wasn't often that she saw her father in such a vicious mood; although she had to admit that lately he was more prone to such moods and that, more often than not, it was her brother who triggered them. 'Johnny was always strong-minded, even as a baby, but I wouldn't say "rebellious" exactly.' A coldness settled over her as it all came flooding back. 'He began to change soon after our mother died . . . He became withdrawn on occasions . . . violent on others. He suffered the most awful nightmares. The doctor did assure us that he would get over it all. In time.' There were moments when she could have gladly thrashed her brother, and other moments, like now, when her heart went out to him.

Rosie went into the cottage first. The lamp was burning softly; the logs were still partly ablaze, sending out a cheery warmth to greet them. All was silent. Rosie began hobbling towards the bedroom. She called 'George' just once before saying to Ellie, 'You never did tell me about your mother, Ellie . . . how she died.'

'No.' Ellie had not been able to bring herself to talk about it. She could not talk about it now. 'I never did.'

Conscious of Ellie's reluctance, and partly understanding it, Rosie did not press the matter. Instead, she pushed open the bedroom door. 'George.' Her voice was gentle, loving. 'It's only me. I'm sorry I've been so long, but I'm back now, come to take you to see the bonfire,' she chuckled. 'That little bugger Johnny has lit it afore he should have done. By! He's in for a spanking when his dad gets hold of him, that's for sure. I can't help but say it serves him right, though.' In the half-gloom, she hobbled towards the bed, cursing beneath her breath because the authorities had not seen fit to install an electricity supply into the cottage, when they ran the cable from Redborough to the big house. 'Penny-pinching weasels!' she muttered. Now, as she approached the bed, she sensed that something was wrong. What she had taken to be George beneath the eiderdown seemed suddenly too perfectly round, too neat altogether.

In the few moments while she waited, expecting to help Rosie with the transportation of the senile to enjoy the bonfire, Ellie busied herself by putting a few small logs on the fire, just enough to keep it going until late evening. There was nothing worse than coming away from the intense heat of a bonfire, through the damp chill of a November evening, only to find that the house was cold and unwelcoming. Warming her hands and lost in thoughts of Barny, Alec and her family, she was not unaware of Rosie's voice calling out to George. She wondered whether taking George out in the bitter night air was a wise thing, but Rosie had revealed how George was so excited about the bonfire and how adamant she was that she would keep her promise and take him to see it all 'go up in flames'.

'Ellie! He's not here!' Rosie's shriek startled Ellie. But then, as she started forward, another sound drew her attention. Crying. Pitiful, like the wail of a newborn. Coming into the room, Rosie heard it too. Her knowing glance was drawn to the small oak dresser. She looked at Ellie and put a stiff, forbidding finger to her lips, silently entreating Ellie to stay quiet. She went towards the dresser, clumsy in her eagerness, her warm, brown eyes marbled with both fear and relief. 'Are you hiding behind there, George?' she teased, 'you're never afraid of Rosie, are you?' The crying stopped. The dresser moved slightly. 'It's all right, love . . . you come out now. There's only me here, and Ellie. You're safe. Quite safe.'

'Won't hurt me? . . . punish?'

'You know I won't.' She gestured for Ellie to help shift the dresser forward. 'The bonfire's lit,' she coaxed.

'Yes . . . bonfire . . . lit.' There was no surprise. No excitement. Only fear. Ellie and Rosie exchanged glances. It was not the response either of them expected.

'Well then, you don't want to miss it, do you?' Rosie asked, 'so, come on out, and we'll take you to see it.' Together, she and Ellie inched the dresser out.

'No!'

'Aw, come on, George, you know how much you want

to see it burn,' Rosie reminded him. He was clearly visible now, a wizened, terrified thing crushed against the wall, his huge pale eyes overhung by long tangled brows and his frail, wasted body trembling from head to toe. 'What on earth made you hide?' Rosie pressed, 'you must have known I wouldn't be all that long.' No answer. 'Were you frightened . . . is that why you hid?'

'You . . . left . . . George.' The voice was heavy with tears, but the eyes were dry, bulbous. Accusing.

'I know.' Rosie reached out. 'I'm sorry.'

'Won't leave . . . again?'

Rosie smiled and shook her head. 'No, I won't leave you . . . for as long . . . again, but you know I must leave you now and then. I can't be with you every minute of every day.' She could see he was not satisfied. 'All right then,' she conceded, 'I won't ever again leave you in the evening, after dark. Is that what you want?'

The unattractive face half smiled, the head nodding, dripping with sweat. Inch by inch the senile gave himself into Ellie and Rosie's keeping. As they helped him into the armchair, he began mumbling, telling them in a fearful whisper and all the while glancing furtively towards the window, 'Don't leave . . . me. Bad things. Bad . . . things happen . . . when you . . . leave me.' He bent his head forward, repeating softly, 'Bad . . . things.' His narrow shoulders were hunched up, his ungainly head buried down, hiding. Only his eyes were raised upwards, staring and awful.

Rosie shook her head, looking at Ellie with a forlorn expression. Returning her attention to the pathetic creature in the chair, she asked kindly, 'Don't you want to see the bonfire?'

The head jerked upwards, narrow, suspicious eyes glaring. The head shook vigorously from side to side, cringing now, burying itself deep into the hunched shoulders. 'No, oh . . . no.'

'That's it then, Ellie,' Rosie said, 'he doesn't want to leave the cottage, and I've promised.' She looked like a disappointed child. 'Never mind,' she added, with a sudden smile, 'you go ahead. Me and George . . . we'll watch it from the window.' The bonfire was just visible from the cottage window – a pyramid of light in the distance.

Disappointed, Ellie hesitated.

'Go on, Ellie,' Rosie urged, awkwardly propelling her towards the door.

'All right then,' Ellie agreed, 'I must admit I am worried about Johnny.' She groaned. 'I wish to God I'd never allowed him out of my sight.' Even as she said it, she realised how impossible it would have been to keep him in. When Rosie promptly reminded her of that fact, she felt curiously relieved. 'Once I've got him safe and sound, me and Barny will bring some of the food over . . . share it with you and George.'

Rosie was delighted. 'That's a marvellous idea,' she chuckled, 'we'll look out for you. Oh, and don't worry about the boy,' she said, balancing precariously on her crutches in order to hug one arm round Ellie's shoulders, 'boys will be boys I expect, and there's no accounting for them.'

When Rosie had seen Ellie away down the path, she came back into the cottage, her expression stern and suspicious. There were certain matters about which she must question George. Serious matters. Like, what did he mean when he said, '*Bad things happen when you leave me*'? And, why had he been outside, tonight, in the dark, wandering about? There would be no use him denying it. Not when she had already seen the mud on his bare feet. And the telltale guilt in his eyes!

Ellie could not draw her gaze from the Guy Fawkes' features. For long, agonising moments she had stood in the full heat of the fire, looking upwards at the macabre figure seated above. In the hazy illumination from the fierce, colourful flames that licked at its feet, the rag creation appeared almost human. *Alive*. There was something uniquely beautiful about the effigy, yet it seemed somehow ugly, and sinister. It was the face which drew Ellie's fascination. In the dancing, flaming shadows, it was incredibly lovely. Poignantly sad, and familiar. Familiar. *Familiar*.

'What is it?' Barny had been quick to notice Ellie's disquiet. Instinctively, he put his arm round her. Her body was stiff and unyielding. 'Ellie!' She continued to stare upwards, mesmerised, as though in a trance. Gently, he shook her. 'Ellie, are you all right, sweetheart?' The look on her face was one he had never seen before. It shook him to the core. 'ELLIE!' His voice became sharp; authoritative. She turned. But her mind's eye was still looking up, up to the effigy. To the face she had recognised. No. It could not be. It was impossible. Her mind was in turmoil. 'Take hold of yourself, Ellie,' she shouted inwardly, 'take hold of yourself! You're imagining things.' Yes. That was it. She was imagining things. It was always the same when she was worried; memories rolled in on her; painful, persistent images filled every corner of her being, making her so afraid, so vulnerable. These things were always with her, even in her deepest dreams. It was always worse when she was worried – about her father, about Johnny. And right now she was desperately worried. Johnny! Where was he? Why had he lit the bonfire in defiance of his father's wishes, and afterwards gone into hiding? Why oh why was he so hell-bent on clashing with his father at every opportunity? Where was he? Where in God's name was he?

'It's Johnny isn't it?' Barny asked now, drawing her closer and filling with pleasure when she let herself be cradled to his heart. 'You're afraid of what your father will do when the boy comes home?' His lips were murmuring into her hair. He loved her so much. And, for some reason he could not yet fathom, he sensed that she was in danger. 'It's all right, sweetheart. He'll come back when he's ready, and your father will be so relieved that he'll just pack him off to bed and that will be an end to it.'

'If you think that, Barny, then you don't know my father.' Ellie pulled away from him. 'This time it's once too often,' she warned. She did not explain how the bad feeling between those two had got steadily worse over these past weeks, until now it had deteriorated to such bitter loathing that she feared some kind of awful confrontation was unavoidable. If it came to a confrontation, then she would have no choice but to side with Johnny. After all, he was only a child. In her heart she knew how confused and unhappy he was.

'No. You're wrong, Ellie,' Barny gently assured her, 'they are father and son. It can be a tricky relationship at the best of times, but, well . . . they'll work it out, you'll see.'

'Oh, Barny, I hope you're right,' Ellie answered. When he took her hand in his, she felt needed. Loved. It was a good feeling. In spite of her intention to let him down as kindly as she could in the morning, tonight she felt lonely and afraid. Tonight, she was worried; unusually apprehensive. Slowly, hesitantly, she raised her eyes. Now, the chair was consumed by fire, a mass of flames. The flames leaped upwards, caressing the figure there. Just for a moment – the briefest and most painful of moments – Ellie's anxious gaze fell on the face. It was burning. Curling horribly. In its final death throes it looked down on her. A sad, pitiful look that tore at Ellie's heart. There was something. Something . . . deep inside. Hurting. Remembering. In the chill of evening Ellie felt the hot, stinging tears against her skin. It was her own mother's face that had gazed on her! The bright, sparkling eyes; the same unique beauty. In that poor, sad face she had seen

her mother. *Her mother*. Dear God! Ellie steeled herself
inside. Was she going mad? Would she never be rid of the
awful memories! The horror! She forced herself to watch
the effigy burn. Now, it was gone. Gone for ever. Still, she
was not comforted. Deeply disturbed, she turned away,
roving her anxious gaze towards the house and beyond to
the spinney. When she saw the tall, familiar figure leaning nonchalantly against the big barn wall, her heart
somersaulted. Alec! In the half-light he was unmistakable; the lean, great-coated figure, darkly handsome and
strangely formidable, he quietly surveyed the scene
before him. Ellie's fascinated gaze lingered a moment
longer. Then, heavy-hearted and regretful, she looked
away. When, unable to resist the temptation, she
returned her glance, he was gone. And with him the
spiral of joy that had lit every corner of Ellie's being.

'You're quite certain there is nothing else you can tell
me?' the constable said kindly, eyeing Ellie with concerned yet quizzical eyes, 'any little thing at all, that
might have slipped your memory? A remark . . . something? The slightest inclination as to whether your
brother might have run away . . . or where he might be?'
  'No. Nothing.' Ellie had searched her mind time and
again through the long, anxious night. She could think of
no reason why Johnny had not come home. She had
deliberately shrugged off the most obvious thing – that of
the bad atmosphere which had erupted between Johnny
and his father earlier, and the possibility that the boy
feared punishment for staying away too long and prema-
turely lighting the bonfire when his father had expressly
forbidden it. But then, Johnny had disobeyed his father
before; many times. And, on each occasion, he had never
been afraid to face the consequences. Why now? Ellie
asked herself. Why should he be afraid *now*? What in
God's name had possessed him to stay out all night?

Where could he be? Was he lost? Hiding? Deliberately staying out of his father's way until tempers had cooled?

'So, you would agree with your father's views when he came to the Station this morning to report his son missing – there was no apparent reason as to why the boy should run off.' He began scribbling in his notebook. 'There were no rows . . . arguments of any kind that might have upset the boy.' When Ellie hesitated in her answer, he raised his eyebrows and peered down at her. 'Well, Miss Armstrong?'

Meeting his gaze with strong, steely eyes, Ellie resolved to keep her own counsel with regard to the animosity between father and son. In her deepest heart, she felt instinctively that it had no bearing on the boy's disappearance. In spite of herself, she could not help but recall Mrs Gregory's words – 'Two children . . . missing. Never found again.' Her heart lurched with fear. 'I can think of no real reason why Johnny should choose to go missing, and on Bonfire Night too, when he's worked so hard for weeks, to build the precious thing!' She was beginning to tire of all the questions. Wasn't it the constable's job to find the boy? Ellie said as much to him now, adding with a degree of reluctance, 'Isn't it true that there have been *other* children missing from these parts?'

The constable's expression was grave. 'I'm afraid that is true,' he conceded quietly, 'but I really don't think it's wise to dwell on such matters . . . it was some time ago after all.' Seeing how distraught Ellie was becoming, he smiled, saying, 'Look here, Miss, I'm sure we'll find your brother safe and sound. Boys get up to all manner of pranks, as well you must know.' He was saying one thing and thinking another. Even before Ellie had mentioned about the previous incident when the two children had disappeared, the issue had already been raised, in his mind and in the minds of others. However much he reassured the young lady with regard to her brother's disappearance, he would not . . . could not . . . rule out the possibility that the two incidents might somehow be linked. Although he sincerely hoped they were not!

Having established when Ellie last saw the boy, the constable enquired as to who else was in the house at the present time. 'It's important that I speak to everyone,' he explained.

'There's no one else in the house. My father's been out ever since he returned from the Station . . . he's taken Barny with him. They're searching the grounds now.'

'Barny?' The constable scribbled in his notepad.

'Barny Tyler.' Ellie was reluctant to expand on that, but when it was obvious that the constable required more, she told him quietly, 'A guest, well . . . more a friend of the family. He and I were considering marriage at one time.'

'I see.' More scribbling into the notepad, then, 'So there are just the three of you living at Thornton Place . . . your father, brother and self?'

'That's right.' Ellie's patience was fast running out. 'Constable, with due respect, don't you think you should be out there looking for Johnny?'

'I didn't come here alone this morning, Miss,' he said with a smile, 'there are two of us. Constable Rogers is already out there . . . scouring the area.' He did not want to alarm Ellie by pointing out that the Station Officer considered this particular situation serious enough to warrant two constables; especially in view of the previous disappearances. He turned his attention to the woman in the chair. He knew her of old. 'Now then, Rosie, you say you can't throw any light at all on the situation?'

She shook her head, looking up at him with worried, nut-brown eyes, the multitude of wrinkles surrounding them seeming more deeply etched this morning. 'Sorry,' she said, 'but, if I'm to tell the truth, I reckon the little bugger's hiding . . . taking delight in worrying everybody half out of their minds!'

The constable merely smiled and nodded his head. It was a known fact that Rosie could be cantankerous as hell when she took it to mind. It was part of her charm.

With the constable's departure, Ellie grew increasingly anxious. Until Rosie told her sharply, 'Come on, my girl! It's no use you staying here, crucifying yourself . . . imagining all manner of terrible things.' She scrambled from the chair and hobbled across the room to Ellie. Fastening the large bone buttons on her tweed coat, she told Ellie, 'Get your overcoat . . . you and me will have a look around. I wouldn't mind betting he's holed up in that spinney somewhere. There ain't a soul alive as knows them woods like I do. Come on! We'll flush the little bugger out.' She nodded her head in approval when Ellie made off towards the kitchen. 'That's it, my girl,' she declared, 'you get your coat . . . and when we find that brother o' yours, I hope you'll give him the thrashing he deserves!' When Ellie turned to say something, Rosie rightly anticipated it. 'Oh, it's all right. I know you feel you should stay here in case the boy comes back, but we'd both do more good out there . . . helping to find where he's hiding! If he does decide to come back, well enough, but . . . he's not likely to run away again just because he finds there's nobody here, now is he, eh!'

Ellie had to agree. And to tell the truth, as she and Rosie left the house to go in search of Johnny, she felt better already. Anything was better than just waiting. It was too nerve-racking.

Intent on their purpose, neither Rosie nor Ellie saw the furtive movements behind them. Swiftly, the figure slunk away towards the house. Plucking the key from a pocket, it quickly opened the front door and went stealthily inside, then on into the big room. There, it made straight for the mantelpiece. Long, trembling fingers reached up to grasp the box. Inside lay the rusty old bunch of keys. 'So! The boy was right.' The laughter was soft. *Insane*. Quickly now, the keys were taken, the box replaced. On silent feet, the intruder departed the room. There was nothing else here. Its mission was done. Oh, but wait! Into the kitchen. Always wary, listening for the slightest noise that would betray someone's approach, the figure remained perfectly still, head cocked towards the main door. Nothing. Safe. There was time enough. Down onto its knees; probing fingers searching beneath the sink. The smell. Awful, *deathly* smell! Again, the quiet, chilling laughter permeated the air. 'They don't know.' The murmur was pleasant, self-satisfied. 'Fools!' Even so. Even so. Beneath the thrusting fingertips, the concrete began to crumble. The stench was thick, suffocating to the senses. Danger. Confusion and panic. Think. *Think*. The trembling hands rummaged through the sink cupboard, withdrawing the bottle, spreading the liquid like a blanket over the offending ground until the blinding smell of bleach filled the air, disguising the corruption beneath. It was enough. For now. Things were moving swiftly; time running out. And still there were things to do. Dark, satisfying things that could not wait. Grinning with delight, the intruder fled the house; footsteps swift and determined, a black crazy heart bent on destruction.

One more grisly deed, and then softly to the cottage; with the emaciated bulk cradled gently in strong, loving, loathing arms. The key slid into the ancient lock, the trap door raised. The stench floated up. No matter. Now, it was pleasant. Soothing. All was well. Silently, the footsteps went down, down, down. Into the cloistered bowels of the earth. Reverently, all that was left was laid to rest. Unclean and defiled. Ravaged to the last. One fleeting kiss. Then goodbye. But not forever. Oh no! Not forever. That would be too painful. Too cruel.

Emerging into the daylight, the figure went on its way,

merging into the surroundings with astonishing boldness. It was done. Now there must be no suspicion. Everything must be as it was. Suddenly, it turned, its gaze drawn to the cottage, to the watching face there. Satisfaction. Yes. He was there. Good! Pale, haunted eyes peeped out beneath ragged brows. In the space of the fiercest heartbeat they stared at the figure, now incredulous, now in fear. Suspicion. Disbelief, then realisation. And stark, naked terror. With a gasp of horror, the face withdrew. The figure remained a moment longer, in its tormented heart there was a deeper sense of achievement. Delight. All was well. All was as it should be. But not yet finished. No. Not yet.

'That's it then!' Jack Armstrong flung himself into the armchair. 'We've searched high and low . . . I can't think where else to look.' He stared at the ceiling, pushing his long fingers through his hair and sighing noisily. 'Where the hell is he? What's his bloody game, eh?' he demanded, looking at Ellie with hard, bitter eyes.

Ellie stared back at him, saying nothing, for there was no answer to her father's question. She felt numb inside. Guilty. It was as though Johnny had disappeared from the face of the earth. Like the others. Just like the others! But then, she had suspected that he had sneaked back when everyone was out searching. At least, neither she nor her father could account for the spill of bleach beneath the sink.

'He can't just have disappeared.' Barny swung round from the window, where he had been scanning the area fronting the house, but to no avail. 'What about friends . . . from his school?'

'No.' Ellie shook her head. 'The constable raised that question, Barny, but . . . Johnny never made any friends. He was not one for mixing.' She smiled sadly. It was enough to bring him to her side. 'Barny . . . we need to talk,' she told him, 'before you go, there are things I need to tell you.' Her voice fell to a whisper. Afraid to hurt him, she lowered her eyes. There was too much pain in her heart.

'Look . . . I want to have a word with the constable while he's still poking about.' Jack Armstrong clambered to his feet and brushed past Ellie, touching her intimately on the shoulder as he went. He sensed her deep distress, suspecting that she was about to give the young man his marching orders. He was glad. 'In the outhouse, wasn't he? . . . the constable?'

'I reckon so.' Barny had just seen the uniformed figure making off in that particular direction. He had seen someone else, also – a lone, purposeful figure, standing some way off near the spinney and looking towards the house. He described the same to Jack Armstrong now.

'Sounds like that bastard Harman!' came the sharp retort. 'What the hell is he creeping about for?'

Instinctively, Ellie sprang to Alec's defence. 'Perhaps he's heard that Johnny's gone missing, and he's come to help.'

'Be buggered for a tale!' At once he regretted his temper, adding quickly, 'Sorry, sweetheart, but you know how I feel about that one . . . creepy sort if ever I saw one . . . gives me the shivers!'

'Is he a neighbour?' Barny was not about to admit it in front of Ellie, but the lurking fellow had given him 'the shivers' as well.

'You could say that.' The other man laughed and glanced sideways at Ellie. 'Or you could say he was a rival of yours . . . hankering after our Ellie here.' One glance at Ellie's face told him he had gone too far. It was in his mind to apologise, when the front door burst open to admit the constable.

Looking straight at Ellie's father, his face stiff and sombre, he said quietly, 'I think you had better come with me, sir.'

'What do you mean?' Jack Armstrong's face drained white as he stared at the portly, upright figure.

'It's . . . your son.' It was the tone of his voice that told it all. 'I'm sorry . . .' He nodded sadly, standing back and gesturing the other man towards the door. Slowly, Jack Armstrong came forward. The constable looked beyond him to Ellie and Barny. 'It would be better if you were to stay here . . . inside,' he told them.

Shocked to the core, Ellie remained motionless, all manner of emotions raging through her. In the distance she could hear Barny – strong, reassuring; he was beside her, and yet he seemed a million miles away. The constable's words echoed like the tick of a clock in her mind. 'Your son . . . I'm sorry . . . I'm sorry.' She heard the door click shut. It felt like a dam bursting inside her. She darted forward. 'Johnny!' She had never been so afraid. Out into the open air she went, running, vaguely conscious of the activity around the bonfire ashes; Constable Rogers, Alec Harman, Rosie . . . they were all there, the other constable and her father coming into the scene, across the debris of the bonfire. Alec Harman and Rosie were sternly ushered away and kept at a distance. Now, only the portly constable went close enough to examine the spot. He still wasn't certain. Ellie's tear-filled eyes searched her father's face. She saw him peer down, heard him cry out. His anguish tore her in two. Fear pushed up like a huge wave inside her. Afraid to look, yet knowing she must, she lowered her gaze, her vision blurred by the hot stinging tears that spilled down her face. Now, she could see the charred and blackened thing that lay half in, half out of the deep scar in the earth. Her distraught mind saw the remnants of a shoe – a child's shoe, distorted, pathetic. Horrified, she wanted to look away, but could not. Further down, part of it covered in earth, were the unmistakable head and shoulders of a carcass. Instinctively, Ellie knew beyond a shadow of doubt. It was Johnny! Terror welled up in her, his name falling from her lips even as her senses slipped away and the blackness enfolded her. Then, mercifully, she knew no more.

If Ellie had only seen the nightmare still to come, she might have prayed never to open her eyes again.

PART THREE

If Only . . .

CHAPTER NINE

It was January. The day was bright and crisp, with little evidence of the recent snowfalls. Above, the sky was a wide, slumbering blanket of puffy, chalk-white clouds, nudging and snuggling together and plumping themselves out, until it seemed as though they might begin dropping to the ground one by one. Two red-chested robins sang to each other, and nearby a hare sat bolt-upright, its ears alert and its glittering eyes darting at every tiny sound. Entranced, Ellie paused a while on her journey across the field.

'Beautiful, isn't it?' Alec Harman appeared as if from nowhere, straddling the pathway and looking at Ellie, his voice warm and smiling, his whole countenance betraying his pleasure at seeing her. 'Out here, everything is so natural, so very peaceful, don't you think?' Ellie had been quietly surprised when he had suddenly appeared like that, but she quickly recovered her composure.

'It *is* lovely,' she agreed, a pleasing flush of delight creeping into her heart. 'All the . . . sad, unhappy things do seem a million miles away from here.' She glanced at the bunch of white chrysanthemums in her hand, and, suddenly, it all came flooding back. But then, it was never far away. How could it be?

'The flowers?' Alec's dark gaze fell to the blooms. 'You're going to the churchyard?' There was sadness in his voice. There was guilt, also.

Ellie nodded, and began walking on. A short distance away, over the hedges, the tall gothic church spire soared upwards like an accusing finger pointing to heaven.

'Do you mind if I walk with you?' He took up a place alongside her; soft, sure footsteps, clinging, like a shadow.

'No.' As always, when he was near, Ellie was uncertain, a little afraid. Somehow she never felt safe in his company. What she felt was nervous and threatened. What she felt was his brooding presence, like dark, simmering secrets. What she felt was a deep, stirring passion that took hold of her, creating turmoil in her heart and suffocating every vestige of reason within her. What she felt above all else was fear. Fear of him, fear of herself, and fear that he might beckon and she could not find the strength to resist. Everything decent in her, everything she had learned over the years, and all of her instincts warned Ellie against this man; this strange, haunting man whose black eyes bewitched and disturbed her. She must not let herself be persuaded by him, nor must she forget that he had lied about the girl by the lake. If he lied about that, he would lie about *anything*. She must be on her guard against him, against that devastating charm and that slow, easy smile that lit up her world. 'Be careful, Ellie,' she told herself, 'or be lost forever.'

During the next five minutes or so, while she and Alec trod the same path, Ellie deliberately kept her distance, although she was acutely aware of his closeness. She spoke few words, and when she *was* obliged to converse, it was with an aloofness that belied the confusion in her heart. They talked of the countryside, of the weather, about the remarkable Rosie and the pathetic hermit George had become. They discussed Thornton Place and the fact that only the other day a representative had come from the solicitors, afterwards leaving more than satisfied with the progress being made on the house. They talked about the withdrawal of Britain and France from the

Suez, and lamented the demise of Humphrey Bogart. All Ellie's personal, secret questions remained locked away, secure, unexposed, simmering beneath the surface of her cool, friendly exterior. More than once, when their glances mingled, Ellie sensed the deep dangerous current of emotion that ran between her and this man.

'I'll leave you here, then.' At the entrance to the churchyard he smiled on her, his dark eyes seeming to plead. When she merely nodded, he lingered a moment longer, his gaze intense and searching. Feeling herself responding to him, Ellie quickly turned away. When the sound of his boots, stamping the earth, died away in the distance, she slowed her own pace to risk a glance over her shoulder. At once, she bitterly regretted having done so, because there, some way ahead of Alec Harman's tall, striding figure, there was another. It was a girl. The same girl Ellie had seen down by the lake. Muffled against the cold, and looking attractive in a long, fur-collared coat, she waited for Alec Harman, smiling radiantly as he approached. In a swift action that took Ellie by surprise, he jerked his head round to glance in her direction. Quickly, she looked away and stumbled on, pretending not to have noticed. A few seconds later, burning with curiosity and partly hidden by the old cedar tree, Ellie looked again. What she saw intrigued her even more. The girl had run to meet Alec Harman. Far from being pleased with her obvious pleasure on seeing him, he seemed angry, nervous that they might be seen. When she raised her face, her lips puckered in a kiss, he grabbed her by the arm and shook her angrily. The girl snatched herself away, the tenderness in her face replaced by indignation. She said something to him, and he at once began striding away. The girl followed. An argument erupted. Exasperated, he raised his hand; Ellie instinctively drew back with a gasp, certain that he was about to strike the girl. Instead, though, he rested his hands on her shoulders and smiled down on her, shaking his head and murmuring. Then he bent to kiss her forehead. She laughed and snuggled into his arm, then the two of them went on their way, adoring in each other's company.

Sadly, Ellie resumed her path. And not for the first time since she had sent him away, Ellie's tortured thoughts turned to Barny. Even though she had severed all ties with him, she still could not help but wonder whether she had done the right thing. She knew in her heart that there could be no future for either of them together. Yet, she also knew that she would always love him, just a little. In her mind's eye she recalled the terrible trauma of that day in November. 'Dear God, was it really more than two months ago?' she asked herself. The shock of it all had never left her. It was as real to her now as it had been on that day. Every moment, every sight, sound and word was magnified in her mind; the constable's face when he came for her father, the shock of realisation, and the awful implications when she saw the look on her father's face as he stared down into the ashes, the gasp of horror, the cry that sounded like a muted scream. Rosie and Alec Harman, staring, unbelieving. Her own searing sense of horror, and the unbearable pain, the grief that she carried *still*; then the dark, silent abyss opening before her, sucking her down, *down*.

Falling to her knees before the mound of earth that signified her brother's grave, Ellie closed her eyes, unaware of the tears that oozed from beneath her eyelids to spill down her face. 'Johnny . . . just a boy.' All the heartbreak was in her voice, quiet agony for his passing; for the awful manner of it. Thoughts of her mother throbbed through her. Memories that brought their own pain and echoed the horror of her brother's death. Regret tore at her heart. The questions were there, always there. But no answers. No, never the answers.

After a while, Ellie went into the church to pray, and to

kneel before the altar. She yearned for peace. There was none. There were no answers here, either. Disillusioned, she returned once more to her brother, to tell him that, in spite of everything, she had loved him, and loved him still. She wanted him to know that his father would come soon, one day when the pain had subsided, when he was stronger of heart and ready to forgive. But then, there was the awful guilt. That, more than anything else, was the hardest thing of all. She wanted Johnny to know these things, to understand.

As Ellie drew closer, she was at once aware that someone else had been here. In these last few moments while she was in the church, a visitor to the grave had placed a sprig of dried flowers at its head. Lavender. The scent was everywhere – oil of lavender, sprinkled, still glistening wet in the clear, cold light of day. Quickly, Ellie glanced about. In every direction there was only silence and solitude. No sign of any living soul; only the souls beneath the ground, long ago quiet and peaceful, beyond all earthly pain and fear. Unbeknown to Ellie, there was one, though. One tortured and forlorn being, whose soul was neither dead nor alive, neither quiet nor peaceful. It was driven by revenge, haunted by sadness, and tormented almost beyond endurance by its lonely vigil. Its mission was to exact a terrible punishment. To watch. To plan. To wait patiently, as it had done over many, long, haunted years. There was no hurry. Everything would come right, in time. All of those who belonged must pay the price. One by one. One by one! Sad, mad eyes peered out from the hiding place. In its black, unhappy heart, the sight of Ellie was like a spear of pain. Yet the watching soul dared not cry out. Not now. Not then. Not ever!

Strangely disturbed, and touched by the creeping sensation that, even now, someone was quietly observing her, Ellie stood a moment longer, her anxious eyes gazing all about. Only silence. Not even a bird sang. Curious,

Ellie glanced down, searching for a sign that might betray the visitor; footsteps, maybe? She was disappointed.

The snowfall was long gone, so now the ground was hard underfoot, rugged and narrow walk-ways between the rows of graves, interspersed here and there with wild growing tufts of grass and protruding weeds. The churchyard was not always best kept. It was a matter for regret.

Coming into sight of Thornton Place, Ellie's quiet mood was lifted by the approach of that familiar, welcoming figure, Rosie. Rosie, always there, always ready to listen, a warm and cheery being who had helped Ellie through her darkest days. Enlightened of heart, she quickened her steps towards the other woman, who stood waiting, a strange yet lovable sight, with her ungainly figure leaning crookedly into the crutches and her peroxide hair hanging in scruffy tangles about her ears. Even from a distance, the two large round smudges that were her eyes were easily distinguishable. Now, as Ellie drew closer, she could hear the plaintive song that Rosie was softly singing. It was a sad, haunting melody that she had never heard before. Intrigued, Ellie had it in mind to question the old woman about the song, but then Rosie looked up and began calling as Ellie came nearer. 'Where the hell have you been?' she demanded, her voice sailing through the air. 'I've finished my duties long since . . . thought you might be back to sup a drop o' tea with me . . . have a natter and such like.' Ellie was before her now. 'You know how I enjoy having a chat with you, Ellie,' she moaned. 'There ain't nobody else I can talk to, is there, eh?'

'I'm sorry, Rosie.' Ellie threw out her hands in a gesture of helplessness. 'But you knew where I'd gone, didn't you?'

'Well, yes . . . but it were no thanks to *you*, my girl!' Rosie scowled and manoeuvred herself about on her crutches. 'If your dad hadn't told me you'd tekken some flowers to the churchyard, I wouldn't have known *where* you were!' She cast Ellie an accusing sideways glance as the two of them picked their way over the stiff ground. 'You know, Ellie . . . you need to be careful,' she warned, 'it ain't sensible to wander about so early in the morning when . . . there could be all manner o' curious folk stalking the woods and places hereabouts.'

Rosie's words set Ellie thinking on the strange event at the graveside. Who on earth could have put those dried lavender sprigs there? It was a puzzle to her . . . like so many other things at Thornton Place. Suddenly, she felt the need to confide in Rosie, but not now, not here in the open. 'Rosie . . . come back to the house and I'll make you a cup of tea . . . we can have that "chat".' She touched the older woman on the arm, adding in a quieter voice, 'There's something I want to tell you, and other things I need to talk about.'

'What "things"?' Rosie turned her head and looked at Ellie with quizzical, panda-like eyes.

'Just . . . *things*, Rosie.' Ellie's fingers moved inside her coat pocket, tracing the sharp, straight edge of the envelope there. A feeling of sadness came over her. The letter had arrived that morning. It had been a shock.

'I'm sorry, darling,' Rosie said, shaking her head slowly, 'I *can't* come back to the house. You know I daren't leave George for too long at a time.' She paused, staring at the ground with serious eyes. 'That's why I especially wanted you to be there this morning . . . why I was so glad to see you making your way back. Oh, Ellie . . . you don't know the half.' She laughed – a hard, dry laugh without mirth.

'What's the matter, Rosie?' Ellie had never seen the other woman in such an odd mood.

'Aw, I don't know.' Rosie was suddenly wary. 'It ain't nothing really.' She shrugged her shoulders. 'I expect I'm getting old,' she said in a weary voice, 'but . . . well, suddenly it's all too much. This place . . .' She raised her face to the skies. 'Sometimes it can be so lonely, Ellie. Then there's George . . . you know, I've grown very fond of the silly old bugger!' She laughed, but Ellie saw the tears in her eyes. 'I'm afraid . . . he won't be with us much longer.'

'Why do you say that?'

'Just a feeling, that's all.'

Rosie's unhappy mood weighed on Ellie, heightening her own misgivings. 'I'm sorry I wasn't there when you needed me this morning,' she said tenderly.

'Well, you're here now, ain't you?' Rosie retorted. 'And being as I can't come back to the house, what about you coming with me now, to the cottage?' She chuckled, the low mood seeming to have passed, 'Then we can cry on each other's shoulders, eh?' She seemed her old self again.

'All right.' Ellie welcomed the idea, although she could not rid herself of the foreboding that murmured through her, at the prospect of being so close to the other inhabitant of the cottage. Try as she might, Ellie could not bring herself to feel comfortable in his presence. Oh, she had visited him and shown compassion at his awful decline. And she really did feel a deep sympathy for that poor broken creature. But, somehow, he frightened her. He had frightened her the very first time she had seen him, when he reluctantly opened the door of Thornton Place to them. He had frightened her every time he shuffled that twisted, crab-like body towards her. He frightened her when he stared at her through pale, hang-dog eyes that had no real substance, and he frightened her when he spoke of 'bad things' . . . and . . . 'devils who mean to find me'. Grasping hands that were reminiscent of 'claws'; festering 'secret thoughts' that roamed his crazy mind and whispered on his face; all of these things frightened Ellie. And she was mortally ashamed. 'Of course I'll come to the cottage,' she said, determinedly.

'Good!' Rosie quickened her peg legs, a genuine smile wreathing her aged features.

'First, though . . . I must let Dad know I'm back, and make sure he had a good breakfast.'

'Your dad ain't there.'

Ellie was astonished. 'Not there? Where is he, then?'

'Took off soon after I arrived this morning . . . I reckon he couldn't have been too long behind you, gal.' Rosie coughed in the cold, biting air and paused to draw her coat tighter about her. 'I don't suppose he's gone far, though . . . into Medford, to the shops, I expect. Perhaps he didn't intend going out at all, only, well . . . he said he had to do some'at about the stench under the sink . . . concrete it again or such like.' Rosie wrinkled her nose and made a face. 'By! The bugger does stink, though! It's allus been a problem, but, well, it's got worse of late and there's no denying it!'

Ellie could not deny it either. In fact, it was she who had asked her father to see what he could do about it, especially now the layers of concrete were crumbling so badly. 'I don't suppose he had the good sense to have a hot breakfast before he went out?'

'Nope!' Rosie declared with some impatience. 'I did try to persuade him, but your dad's like all other fellows . . . bull-headed! He said he couldn't stomach food . . . not until he'd stopped that foul smell from filling the kitchen. So there you are, my gal.' Her homely face beamed from ear to ear. 'When he gets back, it'll take him a while to do that job, so we can count on a good half hour afore you need start panicking. Right?' She stopped and looked Ellie in the eye. 'Ain't that right?' she demanded, half afraid Ellie might still refuse.

'Go on with you,' Ellie laughed, 'let's get in the warm. My bones are chilled through to the marrow!'

Happy in each other's company, the two women quickly made their way to the cottage, where Rosie switched on the wireless and began singing along with the recent hit tune 'Cherry Pink and Apple Blossom White'.

In his bedroom, the senile lay apparently deep in slumber, immobile. Unknowing. But beneath the calm exterior was a mind that was wickedly alive; a boiling, seething mass of terror. And a wounded heart that cried out for justice.

Sleep was impossible. Lying in her bed, Ellie turned this way and that, the events of the day coursing through her troubled thoughts, giving her no peace. Images paraded across her mind, like a macabre carnival; Alec Harman and the dark-haired girl, the lavender sprigs on Johnny's grave, her mother . . . that bloodied mess, and the innocent beside her, her father and his changeable moods of late . . . creating the same distance between them that had cruelly separated him and Johnny; the awful way in which Johnny had died, and the verdict of 'death by misadventure' which to Ellie's mind only emphasised the awful, tragic waste of a young life. These past months she had tried to alleviate the loss and pain by reminding herself how utterly miserable the boy had been since that fateful night when he had found the remains of his mother. At times it seemed to Ellie that he would never get over it, and yet, by the same token, she had not stopped hoping and praying that he would. Instead, he had sunk deeper and deeper into a terrible despair which seemed to strike at the very root of his personality, corrupting all that was decent and normal inside him. Yet, even so, Ellie grieved for the boy; for what he had endured. He was only a boy, and he was her brother. Her heart had already been heavy with the loss of her mother – so vital and lovely, so full of life and laughter. Now, the boy's passing was almost more than she could bear. On top of which, her father was a changed man; moody, morose, quick to temper and strangely secretive of late, preferring to keep his own company. Ellie mourned, also, for that special intimacy that was lost between them. Nothing was the same. Nothing would ever be the same again.

Gasping when her bare toes touched the cold linoleum, Ellie got from the bed, pulling the pink nylon dressing gown over her shivering form. On silent footsteps she crossed the room, coming to stand before the window. Noiselessly drawing back the curtains, she looked out, her serious amber eyes scanning the dark shapes in the landscape. It was so magnificent. So primeval. Almost as though mankind had never touched it. Quietly slumbering, the tall trees stood proud and majestic over all; the sky was a mingling of grey and silver, with shifting, tumbling clouds moving lazily in the soft moonlight. Against this magnificent background, the spinney spread upwards like a fine lacy tapestry, and the lake made a ghostly brooding picture, black as night, sinister and terrifying. Ellie shivered. The unknown was always terrifying.

Of all the persistent images that had kept Ellie from her sleep, that of Alec Harman and the girl was the most disturbing. He, above all others, had crept insidiously into her heart. Now, in spite of the knowledge that he did not want her, she could not free herself of him. She loved him. It was as simple, and complex, as that. Here was a man to whom she might gladly surrender herself, if it was not for her sense of pride, and the bitter belief that the consequences would be too much of a price to pay. No other man had turned her emotions inside out in the same way, making her love and loathe at the same time. But then, she had never met any other man like Alec Harman. There was Barny of course, but these two were as alike as chalk and cheese. Feeling in the depths of her dressing-gown pocket, Ellie withdrew the letter. It was from Barny. A long and agonising letter that had touched her deeply, revived memories of the laughter they had shared, the good times they had enjoyed. Bright, happy times that were over forever; lost in the mist, destined to fade over the years. Suddenly, Ellie saw herself, old and lonely, like Rosie. It was a sobering thought.

Unfolding the letter for the umpteenth time, Ellie reflected on the conversation that had taken place between herself and Rosie. She had worried for the older woman, thinking her to seem more tired and unhappy than she had ever known her. Of course, Rosie had rejected any idea that she was suffering from some lurking ailment, declaring boldly, 'I ain't never had a day's proper illness in the whole of me life, Ellie Armstrong!' Though she did admit that 'my old friend George is a source o' trouble to me, gal'. She had taken Ellie in to the senile's bedroom. It was an unsettling experience; he appeared unaware of their presence, lying almost lifeless, like a marble effigy. Not once did he make any sound or open his eyes. 'The poor old sod's like that most of the time, these days,' Rosie explained, 'just lies there like he were an empty vessel, and it does upset me. Oh, but he has nightmares! Such terrible nightmares . . . crying and thrashing . . . demented. At these times he's inconsolable. It takes me ages to quieten him down.' Ellie knew how badly it was affecting Rosie. It was obvious that she was not the same exuberant, carefree character she had been. It occurred to Ellie that it might be a blessing in disguise if the Good Lord saw fit to relieve the senile of his suffering.

By the time Ellie was set to go back to the house, though, Rosie's spirits were somewhat revived. 'By! You've done me old heart a power o' good!' she told Ellie. 'Ain't it amazing what a good old chinwag can do, eh?' Ellie had hugged her affectionately. She did like Rosie; liked her a lot. And it was true what Rosie had said; it was amazing how much better a body felt after sharing the things that troubled. They had talked for almost an hour; about George, about the boy and the way his death had seemed to affect Jack Armstrong so deeply that he refused to discuss it with anyone; even with Ellie. They recalled how shocked and afraid the inhabitants of Redborough had been, and how the more superstitious of them claimed it was 'the same badness that took the others . . . that tainted Thornton Place and everyone connected with it'. Rosie had dismissed such speculation as 'out and out nonsense!' Ellie agreed, but could not forget the mysterious disappearance of the priest and the two children. When Ellie described how someone had placed a sprig of dried lavender on Johnny's grave, Rosie thought little of it, saying, 'Folks on the estate might be a peculiar lot . . . afraid o' their own shadow some of them . . . but I suspect their hearts are kind enough. No doubt one o' the more sensible and sympathetic put the lavender there. Think no more of it, Ellie gal, 'cause it don't mean nothing untoward.' And, strangely enough, Ellie was reassured by Rosie's words.

The letter from Barny was a different matter altogether. Rosie could only say, 'It's up to you, Ellie gal . . . follow your instincts.' Now, in the moonglow through the window, Ellie roved her troubled gaze over the unfolded page. In the half-light she was unable to see the words clearly, but it was no matter, because what Barny had said was emblazoned in her mind, written on her unquiet heart. It was a long, sincere letter from a man who finally realised that his love for a certain woman was impossible. It was a final letter, asking for nothing and offering nothing. The sentiments were honest and endearing. And, not for the first time, Ellie was made to reflect on the value of what she had thrown away:

Dearest Ellie,

Why didn't you tell me that you had fallen in love with someone else? There I was, desperately trying to keep alive what we had going for us, when all the time you were losing your heart to Alec Harman. I would be a liar if I said it did not matter because it does. You're a lovely young woman, Ellie, and I expect it will take me a while to get over you, if ever.

I don't blame you, Ellie. These things happen and we don't seem to have a say in who we fall in love with. The only thing I beg of you is to be sure before you make a final commitment to this man. After all, you can't know him too well after such a short time. But he does love you in return; even a blind man could see that. I had not realised, Ellie, not until you collapsed at the bonfire and Alec Harman almost knocked me aside to get to you. When he carried you inside the house, he was beside himself with worry . . . as we all were. I hope he treats you well. I pray you will be happy.

A short while ago I had a plea from my parents to join them. While there was even a faint hope that the two of us might get together again, it was out of the question. Now, however, I feel it will be the best thing for all of us.

Thank you for all the wonderful memories, sweetheart. Forgive me for intruding on your grief, but I hope enough time has passed since your loss for you to begin a new life for yourself. I am only sad that it will not be with me. But, as I say, things don't always turn out the way we want them to. I hope they do for you, Ellie. I'm sure they will.

God bless,
Barny.

'Oh, Barny . . . what have I done?' Ellie pressed the crumpled letter to her breast, the tears tumbling down her face. She wondered what her answer might have been if Barny had asked her to go with him now? She was tempted to travel north this very day and beg him not to leave. But then she bitterly chided herself. Barny was too decent to be used as second best! He was right. She *did* love Alec Harman. But, he was wrong about Alec Harman returning her love. It was true that he had carried her back into the house, and, if Rosie's account was gospel, it was also true that he was greatly concerned about her, but, 'love her'? No. Much as she wanted that to be true, it was not. Otherwise, why was he meeting that girl, and blatantly denying it? Why did he avoid coming to the house or seeing her? And why, after he had carried her back into the house, did he hurry away? Not once since that fateful morning had he sought her out. Yes, he had enquired of Rosie as to her well-being, but – like before – he kept his distance, treating her as Johnny would say 'like the plague'. He was a strange and unpredictable man. Barny was wrong in thinking her happiness lay with Alec Harman, because it did not! But then, it didn't lie with Barny either and, much as she did not particularly like the idea of him going to the other side of the world, neither did she have any right or reason to persuade him to stay. In her mind's eye, Ellie recalled the moment of Barny's departure after the funeral. Before leaving her, he had waited to satisfy himself that she was fully able to cope. There was no ill-feeling. Just a mutual acceptance that their time together was over. Afterwards, Ellie had watched the small, battered van chug away, taking Barny out of her life. And, in all truth, she could not deny the murmur of regret in her heart, nor the fact that when he went, a small part of her went with him. Now it was final. He was leaving for good, and she would never see him again.

Subdued and weary of heart, Ellie climbed back into bed. With the letter against her pillow, she lapsed into a deep and fitful sleep.

Many miles away, in the north of England, there was

another lonely and unhappy being who gazed out of the window, watching the night sky and dreaming, much as Ellie had done, his thoughts mentally spanning the miles between himself and the woman he loved.

After great deliberation and an agonising of heart, Barny had made up his mind. He had fully accepted that Ellie no longer loved him and, as much as he would have wished it otherwise, he had forced himself to come to terms with the fact that he was shut out of her life forever. He had lingered far too long in the hope that all would come right between them; now, he knew it never would. Ellie loved another. There was nothing he could do about that. But, in spite of the fact that she had rejected him for Alec Harman, he felt a certain duty to protect her. There was something about the Harman fellow that disturbed him; so much so that he could not go away with peace of mind until he had satisfied himself that all was well. Ellie's father had taken a deep dislike to Alec Harman, and though Barny reminded himself that Jack Armstrong had a habit of belittling any man who dared to cast an appreciative glance in his daughter's direction, this time he himself had suffered the same misgivings with regard to Ellie's suitor.

Barny Tyler turned away from the window, went cautiously across the room and switched on the light. Everything was ready for his long journey; his bags were packed, and he had already said his goodbyes to friends and colleagues. It had been his intention to depart quickly and quietly. A new life was waiting and now he longed for it to begin. He was lonely. Only now did he realise how very lonely he had been. He had prayed that Ellie would find happiness and a new life. Now, it was everything he himself craved. First though, he needed to check out this Harman character – make certain he really was all he claimed to be.

Barny had been toying with the idea. Now, the idea

gained momentum. Plans quickly began to take shape. The woman called Rosie would be the one to talk to. She probably knew Alec Harman better than most. Look how the two of them had huddled together just before Johnny was found, and even before that, at different times, Barny had seen them deep in conversation together. After the funeral, during which Alec Harman had stayed at the back of the church, it was *he* who escorted the old, crippled woman home.

Unable to sleep now, Barny got dressed and made himself a mug of coffee. He felt more at peace with himself now. Before anything else he must make sure that Ellie was safe.

Afterwards, he could go on his way with a clear conscience. First thing in the morning, he would get things underway. He would need to recover his van from the auctions; it was just as well the sale hadn't already taken place. Besides, he didn't see any problem in selling it down South. It might be old and battered, but it was a sturdy, reliable little vehicle. Suddenly, all the niggling doubts he had entertained about Alec Harman bubbled persistently to the surface, telling him unreservedly that he was obliged to resolve the issue, or never again know peace of mind. He knew he could not have Ellie's love, but that must not deter him from doing right by her. He owed it to himself. And, most of all, he owed it to Ellie!

CHAPTER TEN

The letters arrived just before 10.00 a.m. on Tuesday, January 24th, just as Jack Armstrong came down for a short break from his labours. He had been up with the lark on this fine, bright morning and now – after a back-breaking session when he had finally stripped the last bedroom of its many layers of emulsion – he was more than ready for the hearty breakfast put before him by Ellie.

'Any post?' he asked, settling himself in the chair and scouring his eyes over the front page of the newspaper. Scanning the headlines, he snorted and pushed the paper aside, saying with scorn, 'Harold Macmillan! For my money, Rab Butler would have made a much more acceptable Prime Minister.' Jack Armstrong was not a man for politics, but, like every Englishman, he felt he was entitled to his opinion. Seeing Ellie return with the post, he asked whether there was anything for him. 'Not that I'm expecting anything but *bills*!' he moaned.

'Well, *this* doesn't look like a bill,' Ellie told him, handing over the small square envelope with the copper-plate writing on the front. Intrigued, he opened the envelope, took out the letter and began reading. Absorbed in her own correspondence, Ellie did not see how her father's expression changed from one of curiosity to one of incredulity.

'Well, about time too!' Ellie remarked on perusing her

own letter. 'The library have uncovered part of the history of Thornton Place. They'll have a copy ready for me on Saturday.' She wandered across the room, intent on the letter in her hands. When in a moment she swung round to impart the details to her father, she was astonished to see his chair empty and his breakfast untouched. Going along the passage, she looked into the big room; there was no sign of him there. There was no sign of him anywhere on the ground floor, and a quick search of the upstairs rooms told Ellie that he was nowhere in the house. Puzzled, but not altogether surprised by his behaviour, she looked out of the bedroom window. Yes, there he was, leaning against the wall of the big barn, his head bent towards the letter, his whole attention riveted by it. Even as Ellie watched, he crumpled the letter in his fist, his eyes remaining downcast and a look of desolation about his whole countenance.

Unaware that Ellie was observing him from the bedroom window, Jack Armstrong angrily punched his fist against the barn wall. 'Damn and blast! . . . Damn. Damn!' he muttered. Just when you thought there might be a chance to forget the past once and for all, it had a nasty habit of creeping up on you unawares. The letter had been like a pair of cold hands round his throat; a chilling reminder that he was still not free of the spectre that haunted him. Now, he wondered whether he would *ever* be free of it. Perhaps not until he himself was rotting meat for the worms!

The letter had been a bolt out of the blue. His first instinct was to ignore it, to try and shut it out of his mind and pretend it had never happened. Yet, even as he dwelled on this possibility, he knew it was out of the question. The very content of the letter demanded that he must act on it, and quickly! Black anger flooded his uneasy thoughts. There were people roaming this earth who were not fit to draw breath. *Monsters!* Creatures

252

without substance, without soul. So much filth that contaminated everything it touched. *Damn them to hell!* Because of them, he had been dragged, screaming, back into the past. Because of them, he had no choice. It was clear what he must do. And he would not shirk from doing it; however unpleasant the consequences! Besides, the last thing he wanted right now was police crawling all over the place!

'You're . . . going away?' Ellie could see how upset her father was; how agitated he had been since returning to the house a few moments ago. 'It's that letter, isn't it? Something in the letter you got this morning has worried you . . .'

Her words were cut off as her father retorted, 'It doesn't matter! You don't need to know the why and wherefore. All you need to know is that I'll be leaving this afternoon, and probably won't be back for a couple of days.' He began pacing the room, his fists clasped together behind his back and a look of anguish in his deep blue eyes. 'Leave me, Ellie,' he told her, 'I need to think . . . to work things out.' He groaned aloud. 'Dear God! Why is it when you think it just might start to come right . . . it all begins to go wrong?'

'What is it?' Ellie placed herself in front of him. 'I'm not budging until you tell me.' When he made as though to turn away, she clasped her small, firm fingers round his wrist, saying quietly, 'Look, Dad . . . there are only the two of us left now . . . all we have is each other. Trust me, please. These past weeks we seem to have drifted further and further apart . . . we don't confide in each other any more. Tell me . . . I may be able to help . . . what was in the letter that's upset you so?'

It seemed ages before he replied, when in fact it was only a moment; a moment of panic during which he cursed himself for betraying his anxiety to her. He had to think quickly! Ellie must not know the contents of that letter. What then? For Christ's sake what was he to tell her? He had seen the fiery determination in her lovely amber eyes. He knew she would not be satisfied until he had given her some sort of explanation – confided in her. In his frantic mind there rose the germ of an idea. It was enough! 'We've got a problem, sweetheart,' he said, his warm, sincere smile a clever mask for the devious and cunning wile beneath, 'nothing for you to worry about, though. I can handle it, believe me.'

'What? What can you "handle"?' Ellie needed to know. She stood her ground, eyeing him, daring him to cut her out.

'All right then, but . . . like I say, I can handle it.' He sauntered over to the settee, where he dropped himself down with the easy attitude of someone who was suddenly at peace with the world. When, as he expected, Ellie followed him and stood looking down, anticipating, he went on. 'The letter was from the solicitors in London. It seems the owner is contemplating selling Thornton Place,' he lied.

Shocked, Ellie sat beside him, eager to lessen what she knew had been a real blow to her father. 'But it won't make any difference to us, will it?' she said, 'I mean . . . you did sign a contract?' Suddenly, she could see them being homeless. It was easy to understand why her father had been so wrought up over the letter. After all, the last time the house had changed hands, Rosie and George were thrown out; although of course they had the cottage to go to. She and her father had nowhere!

'As far as I'm concerned, they'll have a real fight on their hands if they reckon *me* to be a pushover. I'm sure it won't come to any kind of fight, though.' He had to find a way of convincing Ellie that the situation was important enough for him to take time out to deal with it, yet be careful not to burden her with a deal of worry. 'Look . . . don't mention any of this to Rosie, or to anybody else,' he warned, 'we don't want folk panicking that there's going to be a full-scale eviction.'

'You're sure it will be all right?'

'Of course.'

'But . . . you didn't seem so certain after reading the letter,' Ellie insisted. 'I saw you out there . . . you looked devastated.'

'It was just the initial shock. After all, when you're told the roof might be sold over your head, you don't stop to think,' he lied. 'Don't you worry . . . we're safe enough. But, as I say . . . it needs me to go to London and remind them of the contract. I'll rest easier when I have more information.'

'You could telephone, or write.'

He shook his head. 'No. It won't do. When you're dealing with something like this, Ellie, it's best to confront it . . . put your case first, before they deliberately overlook you.'

'Yes, you're right.' Ellie had to agree. 'How about if I came with you?' After the recent happenings, she welcomed the prospect of a few days away. Excitement grew in her, but it was cruelly quashed with her father's firm refusal.

'Not this time, Ellie.' Before she could argue, he departed the room.

It was 4.00 p.m. when Ellie saw her father off in the old car that had brought them to Thornton Place almost a year ago. The car had been little used since then. Her father rarely went out, being happy to stay within the vicinity of Thornton Place, and whenever Ellie went into Medford, she preferred to go by bus from the shop.

'Expect me back the day after tomorrow,' he told Ellie. She was pleasantly surprised when he took her in his arms and kissed the top of her head, just like he used to in the old days.

As she watched him go, the daylight was already

slipping into that prolonged grey period before the night smothered everything beneath its black mantle. 'Take care,' she shouted. A spiral of joy rose in her heart, dispelling the sad uncertainties that her father's unpredictable moods had thrust on their once close relationship. At long last, Ellie prayed that the dark clouds which had overshadowed their lives might really have a silver lining after all.

At the top of the steps, she turned to watch the little car disappear out of sight. 'Hurry home, Dad,' she murmured. 'I do love you.' It was with a lighter heart that Ellie went back into the house. Here, she set about her work with a song on her lips, and a hope for the future that she had not experienced in a long while.

Ellie could not have known that her hope would be short-lived. She could never have envisaged that when her father embraced her just now, it would be for the last time. And even in her worst nightmares, she could not have foreseen the awful carnage that was to come.

Engaged in deep conversation, Rosie and Alec Harman did not at first hear the knock on the cottage door. When it sounded for the second time, they were immediately alert, afraid of who it might be, and loath to be discovered here, in the shadowy lamp's glow, furtively whispering for fear of being overheard. It was late, dark outside, and Rosie was not expecting anyone. 'I know it isn't Ellie,' she said in a soft, harsh voice. 'She would never come across here after dark . . . alone. And it can't be Jack Armstrong, because, when I went over to see Ellie this afternoon, she told me her father was going away for a couple of days.' She smiled, a knowing, intimate smile. 'But of course you know that, don't you?'

Alec Harman made no answer, other than to return her smile, his black eyes glittering in the flickering lamplight. The knock came again, insistent and ruder. 'Whoever it is, they won't go away,' he murmured, 'you'll have to answer the door.' Silently, like a cobra, he uncurled from the chair, his lithe, handsome figure towering over her.

'Stay quiet then!' The crippled woman grabbed the two crutches which were leaning against the chair arms. Scrambling from the soft, sucking depths of the chair, she thrust the hard wooden artefacts into her body and hopped into a steady gait. '*In there!* Hide in the bedroom!' she told him. At once he nodded and slipped away, going softly into the bedroom and noiselessly closing the door behind him.

Preoccupied with thoughts of who could be calling here so late, Alec Harman only glanced at the bed, at the misshapen and bulky thing that was silhouetted by the incoming moonlight. He could not see the face, nor the pale, spacious eyes that peeped from it; peeping at him, following his every move, and behind the eyes the swirling maelstrom of thoughts and images that had taunted a sanity for so long. Like a dark, tempestuous storm, it had been all-consuming, turning daylight into blackness and serenity into chaos, but, even in the midst of such a destructive storm, there were brief interludes of clarity and light. It was like that now, in the farrago of the old man's mind . . . blinding confusion reigned for most of the time, but then there were split infinities of shocking calm. He knew. Then he did not know. He recognised. Then he did not. A name sprang to mind . . . a face . . . a certain time. And suddenly they were gone. All gone! Silently, he watched, and prayed, and tried so desperately to remember. He would. He knew he would. Soon, he must leave this world. He was not sorry; there was no great longing left for him; no joy, no kind, warm emotions. No love, no satisfaction of the body, or the soul. He wanted to leave. But, before he did, there was something . . . something . . . some urgent and necessary act he must carry out. What though? What must he do? *Kill?*

Was that it? Maybe. But who? And why? Think, oh think! Try to remember. Struggling, always struggling. Oh, now the light was gone, and everything was blanketed in darkness again. Don't move, though! Lie very still. Watch. And listen. Someone was in the room. Be careful now!

'Why, Mr Tyler!' Rosie had cautiously inched open the cottage door, her old heart fluttering. Now, as she blinked into the dark night, it was with a surge of disbelief that she recognised Ellie's young man; or at least the young man who had once set his cap at Ellie, only to be disappointed. 'Whatever brings you here at this time of a night? . . . it's gone ten o'clock . . . folks like me are usually tucked up in their beds long afore now.' She regarded him through small, narrowed eyes, thinking what a handsome thing he was, with them sea-green eyes and unruly mop of thick, earth-coloured hair. Still and all, she had been glad when Ellie sent him away. It left the door open for Alec. To Rosie's mind, there could be only one man for Ellie. And that must be Alec. Rosie had set her heart on it, and she would not take too kindly to being disappointed. Oh, there was no denying that, in spite of herself, she had reluctantly taken a liking to Barny Tyler, but, when everything was taken into consideration, he had only got in the way of things. Some very well-laid plans had been almost ruined because of him!

'Did I give you a fright?' Barny asked, his brows furrowed in an apologetic expression. 'I really didn't mean to . . . only . . .' He glanced about nervously. ' . . . I'm leaving to join my parents shortly and, well . . .' He lowered his gaze and shifted uncomfortably from one foot to the other. 'I'm sorry,' he said. 'I should not have come. I feel foolish . . . it was just that I had something playing on my mind, a niggling worry.' He thrust his hands deep into his overcoat pockets and nodded, as though he had come to a decision. 'Look . . . it doesn't matter . . . now that I'm actually here, standing on your doorstep at this time of night . . . well.' He gave a small, embarrassed laugh. 'Forget I was here,' he said, beginning to turn away. 'I'm so sorry to have disturbed you.'

'No, no . . . you look frozen to the bone,' Rosie protested, opening the door wider. 'You get yourself inside, young man. Whatever brought you here must be important to you, or I'm sure you would never have come knocking on my door.'

'Well, yes . . . it did seem important,' Barny conceded, stepping gratefully out of the cold night air, 'but, like I say . . . I'm not so sure now.'

'Well, I am!' Rosie closed the door and ushered Barny into the parlour. Suddenly, she needed to know why he was here! Had he seen something on his previous trip to Thornton Place? *Did he suspect?* It was imperative that she should know. The fact that Alec was in the next room, hopefully listening, gave her a comfortable feeling. 'Sit yourself here,' she suggested, deliberately persuading Barny into the chair seated on the left of the fireplace, nearest to the bedroom. 'Warm your toes by the fire while I fill the kettle.' She went into the scullery. Barny's gaze followed; he was curiously fascinated by the easy manner in which she swung that cumbersome body along on those crutches. He believed Rosie to be a good woman. Ellie had explained the crippled woman's absolute commitment to the one called George. Such love and devotion was very rare. It was to be much admired. Hoping she did not think it too intrusive of him, he told her so the moment she returned to the parlour.

'Away with you,' she chuckled, allowing him to take the small blackened kettle from her and squash it onto the glowing coals. 'George is a dear. Oh, I know there are those who say he's past all help, and there are others who think *I'm* the mad one for looking after him, but . . .' She lowered her gaze to the fire. 'He's so helpless, you know. Fate has not been kind to him . . . long before his mind was failing, there were *other* misfortunes.' She looked up now, her quiet eyes observing him. 'You should have seen him when he first came to Thornton Place. Handsome he was, a tall, commanding figure. But, even then, he was not a happy man. Soon after, his wife was killed . . .' She glanced towards the window. 'Out there it was . . . in the spinney. He was devastated . . . adored her he did. He was never the same after that. He had a breakdown . . . then it went from bad to worse, until . . . well . . .' She pursed her lips in anguish, as though suppressing a great weight, but the tears sprang to her eyes, gently brimming there.

'How did it happen?' He was curiously hurt to see this old woman racked with such emotion. '. . . His wife . . .?'

Suddenly, Rosie was softly laughing. 'Look at me!' she cried. 'Pouring me troubles all over you . . . and you already burdened with your own . . . or you wouldn't have come aknocking on this 'ere door so late of an evening.' She shuffled to the edge of the chair and eyed him with bright, quizzical eyes. 'Now then, fella-me-lad . . . enough of *my* problems . . . let's have it, eh? What's on your mind?'

Barny looked at her for a moment, thinking how few people there were in the world like Rosie. He felt ashamed, wishing he had not come here. Besides this caring woman's burdens, his own anxieties seemed unreal. 'You'll no doubt think I'm being overcautious,' he said tentatively.

'We'll see. First, though, I need to know what's plaguing you to such an extent that you felt the need to come and talk with me about it.'

'It's Ellie.' There! It was said, and in all truth he felt the better for it.

'Ah.' Rosie chuckled, 'I thought it might be.' She

nodded her head, a seriousness emerging in her expression. 'Go on,' she urged.

With her panda-like eyes bearing down on him and her whole attention riveted to his every word, Barny found it difficult to start. Suddenly he realised how ludicrous his fears would sound to her. How could he say that he believed Ellie to be in some kind of danger? He had no evidence of it, nor did he really understand the nature of that danger. And how could he bring himself to voice his misgivings with regard to Alec Harman? Sure, he was a sullen, moody man, but that in itself did not make him a threat.

'Well, I'm waiting, young man,' Rosie insisted. She had sensed his quiet agonising, and was all the more intrigued because of it.

Seeing that he had little option after coming so far, and believing the crippled woman to be a close and valued friend of Ellie's he told her what was on his mind; how he had made all the necessary arrangements to join his parents, given up his job and burned all his bridges. 'I had hoped there might be a future for me and Ellie, but . . . it's Alec Harman she loves. I don't like the idea, and if it wasn't for the fact that I know everything is finally over between Ellie and me, neither hell nor high water would prevent me from making it as difficult as possible for Harman.'

'You don't like him?'

'Not in the slightest.'

Rosie smiled. 'Is it "dislike" of the man himself? Or is it jealousy that colours your opinion of him?'

'Some . . . maybe, yes!' he reluctantly agreed. 'What man *wouldn't* be jealous? *I love Ellie!*'

'What makes you so sure it's all over between you?' Secretly, Rosie was thrilled. She let her mind's eye rove over the man in the bedroom. She could imagine the delight Alec was feeling at Barny Tyler's words.

'If you know Ellie, then you'll know she's a strong-minded and determined woman. After the boy's funeral, I knew there was no chance for me with Ellie. She told me straight enough that it was finally over . . . Oh, I've seen it coming for a while. It began to go wrong soon after her mother . . .' He paused, shifting uncomfortably in the chair. Determined, he went on, 'Well, all I know is, there's no going back, not now. Not ever. Believe me, Rosie . . . Ellie loves Alec Harman. There's no one else.'

'And you're unhappy about her choice of man?'

'As I said. I don't like him. He's unsociable, morose and sour of mood. Besides, there's something else . . .' Barny's enthusiasm for the subject was growing by the minute. In the heat of the moment, all his inhibitions were swamped. Everything that had been on his mind was suddenly pouring out. He spoke about his fear that Ellie had been blinded to Alec Harman's true character, and that she was being drawn into a future of uncertainty and unhappiness. He himself believed Alec Harman to be shifty and suspicious in nature. He drew on a particular night for example – the night when Jack Armstrong had gone by way of the lake, in search of what he thought was the boy, 'skulking about in the dark . . . frightening people . . .' 'I believe it was more likely Harman!' he suggested. Then he shivered. 'It's just a feeling, and I could be wrong.'

'I think you are . . . *very* wrong.'

Jolted by Rosie's response, he said quietly, 'I sincerely hope I am, Rosie. Tell me, though, what do you know of his background? I understand you know him as well as anyone.' He had been made to exercise caution. In the heat of the moment, he had nearly forgotten that Rosie was well acquainted with Alec Harman.

'Better than anyone,' Rosie corrected, 'and I can tell you with hand on heart that you have misjudged him. He is sullen and morose, as you say. And, in his job, it might seem that he's "skulking about".' She shook her head gravely. 'He's a good man, Barny . . . believe me. If Ellie was to put her future in his hands, she would be safe enough. You see, like you, I believe she does love him. I also believe that he loves Ellie. If it came to it, he would make her a fine husband.' She could see how her words were like blades through his heart. His pain did not deter her. 'I love Ellie very much, you know. Do you think I would let any harm come to her?'

'I'm trusting you, Rosie . . . there is no one else I can count on.'

'I know. Believe me, when I say you can go on your way with a quiet heart where Ellie's well-being is concerned . . . go to your parents. Build your new life . . . maybe with a new love. I'll look over Ellie . . . you have my bounden word on it.'

'What of his background?'

'I'm told he comes of a good family, solid respectable people.' She leaned forward and clasped her gnarled fingers over his clenched fist. 'Like you said, Barny . . . Ellie's a strong-minded, determined soul. She'll walk her own path. I don't have to tell you, either, that she won't be dictated to. No woman will . . . especially in matters of the heart.'

Barny nodded, his smile tinged with regret. 'You're right, of course. I dread to think what she'd do if she knew the two of us were sitting here, discussing her like this!'

'She wouldn't take kindly to it, and that's a fact!' Rosie conceded. She shifted her attention to the kettle, which was boiling and spitting, sending little spurts of water into the coals and causing them to fizzle deliciously. 'There! A brew of tea, that's what we want!' She twisted herself about, and collected the tea towel from the chair arm. Wrapping it thickly round her bony knuckles, she prepared to lift the kettle from the fire. 'You *will* stay a while, won't you, Barny?' she asked, secretly thankful when he declined. 'Oh,' she groaned, looking at him with sad eyes, 'still . . . I expect you've a lot to do, what with going abroad an' all . . . that is where Ellie said your parents are . . .? Besides, you're no doubt ready for your bed, eh?' She hoisted the kettle out and put it carefully on the trivet in the hearth. 'You're stopping in Medford, I expect? There ain't nowhere else round these parts for a body to stop.' Suddenly, an unpleasant thought occurred to her. 'You're not . . . staying with Ellie, are you . . . at Thornton Place?'

'No. Ellie has no idea that I'm here, and I would be grateful if you didn't mention it to her.'

'O' course not, dearie . . . if you're sure that's what you want?'

'I do. Like as you say, she would not take kindly to my interfering.'

'Still, she's a fortunate young woman to warrant such concern. I am sorry it didn't work out for the two of you,' she said, with a small murmur of genuine regret. 'Life's full o' disappointments, but if a body's strong enough, it'll get over it.'

Barny nodded but gave no answer. Instead, he rose to his feet. 'I'll be on my way. Thank you for your reassurance. I could not have gone without it.'

'You know I'll watch out for her, don't you?'

'I believe she has a friend in you.'

'You'll be all right?'

'Like I said, I've already burned my bridges. Regrettably, Ellie is just one more.'

'When d'you leave?'

'Soon. But for now, I'd best be making my way back to Medford. I won't trouble you again.'

'Oh, it were no trouble, dearie. I'm only glad I were able to put your mind at rest. Be assured, Ellie won't come to no harm.'

'You're a good woman. A fine friend.'

'I do me best.'

In the moment before she closed the door on him, there was something Rosie needed to know. 'You remember the day the boy went missing . . . when you and Jack Armstrong went off looking for him?'

Puzzled by a question that seemed to have no relevance to his purpose here, Barny cast his mind back. 'Yes, I recall it,' he replied, a deep frown accentuating his strong, attractive looks.

'Tell me, Barny. Was Ellie's father with you the whole time?'

'Well . . . yes.'

'In your sight? The whole time?'

'I reckon so. We strayed away from each other now and then, I suppose, but that was only to be expected. We were searching for the boy, after all. On the whole, though, I think I can honestly say Ellie's father was in sight most of the time. Why do you ask?'

Rosie's face beamed broadly. 'Oh, no reason. Just a thought.' She certainly did not intend to reveal her deep-down suspicions. Nasty, uncomfortable suspicions that centred round Jack Armstrong. 'No matter,' she said, 'you go safely on your way, Barny Tyler. Good luck and God bless.'

'Goodbye, Rosie, and thank you again.'

'Did you hear all of that?' Rosie whispered, her panda-like eyes bright with apprehension.

'I heard.' Alec Harman's face was set in a stiff, anxious expression as he stared down on Rosie. 'I didn't think Barny Tyler would be much of a problem. I was so obviously wrong.'

'He's suspicious about you. That could be very dangerous!'

'He's going away, though. Isn't that what he said?'

'That's what he said right enough!' Rosie shook her head slowly, her smudged eyes regarding him, making him think. 'Can we trust him, I wonder? Something tells me he wasn't altogether satisfied. He's nobody's fool.' She bowed her head, saying, 'I don't like it . . . we've come too far not to see it through.'

'What are you saying, Rosie? Are you suggesting I should . . . have a quiet word in his ear?' He laughed softly. The idea was amusing to him.

'I don't rightly know.' Rosie smiled, touching him tentatively on the arm. 'Did you hear what he said about himself and Ellie?'

'That they were through?'

'That . . . it was you she loved?'

'In a way, I wish that was not true.' His heart soared at the realisation that Ellie truly loved him, but, he had not expected it, not 'planned' it that way. It only complicated matters.

'And you love her?' Rosie's smile was teasing, tormenting.

'Enough, Rosie!' he chided, going across the room towards the door. 'We have too much to do! You know this is not the time for "love".'

At once, Rosie was mindful of other issues. Important issues that must take precedence over all else. 'What about Barny Tyler? What if he doesn't "join his parents"? . . . what if he decides to hang around these parts a while longer?'

'You think he will?' Alec Harman's black eyes glinted brilliantly in the dying glow of the fire.

Rosie shook her head. 'I don't know. If he does, though . . . snoop about . . . watching . . . suspecting, well . . . it could ruin everything!'

'Don't worry.' He opened the door and stepped softly into the night.

'You'll deal with it?'

The door closed on his answer, given quietly and gravely, without hesitation. 'If I have to,' he said. Then he was gone, into the dark, bent on his own purpose. There was no going back now!

From the bedroom window, the senile watched as the tall, shadowy figure merged with the blackness, until finally it was part of the spinney and he could see it no more. 'Oh . . . let me remember.' The soft, awesome whisper permeated the quiet of the room. 'Please . . . let me remember!' Round, pale eyes grew moist, tears highlighted the terror there. Bent and cold, he shivered in the darkness, the moonshine lightening his shrunken features, creating shapes and shadows, making him appear gruesome. In his small, unhappy heart he prayed, asking that death might release him from the prison that was his mind. 'If only . . .' The haunted murmur was a cry for help. 'If only I could remember . . . if only . . .' Events rippled through his thoughts – of Alec Harman hiding in this very room . . . hiding from someone who had knocked on the door . . . a stranger? No. Not a stranger. Who then? Somebody . . . come to see Rosie. When the stranger was gone, pale curious eyes had seen from the window. Then, voices. In the other room . . . talking, afraid. The same, curious eyes watched Rosie's friend go into the night. 'Oh!' He had a gun. He *always* had a gun! So afraid now. So *afraid*! 'Why can't I . . . oh . . . if only.' Ssh! Ssh! *Too late*. The door's flung open. Can't hide, not now.

'Jesus, Mary and Joseph!' Rosie's sharp eyes sought out the cringing figure pressed into the wall by the window. 'What are you doing out of your bed?' She swung forward at a furious pace, the hard tips of her crutches creating chaos against the floor. 'Into bed with you!' she cried. 'Whatever possessed you?' She stopped, sighing noisily when he scuttled past her. Whimpering like a wounded animal, he clambered beneath the eiderdown, sliding out of sight, his every limb quivering with fright.

'What in God's name am I to do with you?' Rosie went towards the bed in a quick, hopping gait, where she looked down on the misshapen bulk. 'I never know what you'll get up to next,' she said in a soft, surprised voice. Leaning down, she tugged at the corner of the eiderdown. In the gloom she could just make out the claw-like fingers that sprang out to grasp it from her. She tugged. The crooked fingers tugged harder. 'All right . . . all right, but don't you go getting out of your bed again this night,' she warned in a severe voice. 'Get some sleep. We'll talk in the morning.' No response. 'Will you do that for Rosie?' When there came an indistinguishable sound from amongst the bedclothes, it was enough to satisfy Rosie that her words had been heeded. 'That's right,' she murmured lovingly, 'do that for Rosie . . . sleep now. Sleep well. Don't be afraid, sweetheart.' She waited a moment, moving away only when she imagined the hard, regular breathing to mean that he was slumbering. Bone-tired and craving sleep herself, she softly drew the curtains, closed the door, and made her way upstairs. Tomorrow, she and George would talk. She suspected he had things on his mind.

Afraid to rear his head from the safe blackness beneath the clothes, the senile heard the door close and he knew that Rosie had gone to her bed. Rosie would not hurt him; he felt that. Yet, he could not talk to her. The words just would not come. He had tried so hard, tried and tried until his head hurt. Tried to remember! Those things . . . out there in the night . . . bad things! And people . . . evil, wicked people. Oh, if only . . . if only he could remember. *Remember!* Do something. Stop them, before it was too late. He tried so hard, so very hard, but he could never pluck that certain awareness out of the swirling blackness where he was blind forever. But he must keep on trying. *He must!* Like before, always like before, the effort was too much, dragging him down, smothering him. Like a soothing tide it lapped over him, covering his terror with sleep, deep penetrating sleep, stilling the awful fear that lurked in every corner of his being, soothing, for a while. Only for a while.

It was done! A sigh of deep satisfaction rose on the night air, warm breath created a spiral of grey vapour in the bitter-cold stillness of the darkest hour. Eyes that had seen death, that had seen awful, wanton destruction, that had remained aloof to it all, observed this new experience with chilling detachment. A heart was gladdened by the sight; a stiff, unyielding heart that knew no mercy. *No mercy.* Only loathing, and a warped sense of justice. It had felt such terrible things, cruel awful things. It was driven by them, haunted by them. And these atrocities would go on. They must go on. *Until the heart itself was stopped!* Inch by inch, the vehicle was sucked under. Now, it was only a stiff metal sheet shimmering in the moonlight. Slowly at first, then with delicious swiftness, the waters lapped over, lapping, caressing, embracing, until the thing was altogether gorged. All that remained was a spurt of rising bubbles. Like silver spheres, they momentarily danced over a watery grave, and then they were gone.

Satisfied, the watcher stooped to the ground, grasping the lifeless form and swinging it, effortlessly, onto one shoulder. On swift, silent footsteps the watcher stole away. One more who had paid the price. One more. But there were still others. They had not been forgotten. They, too, must pay. In a while. A very short while.

An uneasy quiet hung over the cottage. Silently, practised and sure, the intruder entered. It took only a moment for the trap door to be unearthed. Carrying its grisly burden, the figure descended. Soon after, it was creeping away into the night. Unobserved. Unrepentant. Already scheming. Into a fevered mind there crept an image. The image reflected a painting; a woman. The image agitated, causing unbelievable pain. The pain subsided, and in its place was a merciless loathing. The loathing writhed intricately with the fiercest love. The images faded. Another emerged. The image was Ellie! Soon. Very soon.

'Fred! . . . is that you?' Mrs Gregory sat up in bed, her small puffed eyes heavy with sleep. She had been woken by something . . . a noise, a nightmare. 'Fred . . .' Her hands fumbled for the light switch. Shockingly the light spilled into the room. There was no sound now, only a disturbing eerie silence. A glance at the empty space in the bed told her that he was gone; she stroked the space with the flat of her hand. It was cold. 'Long gone!' she muttered. She was angry; afraid.

Sliding from the bed she wrapped the candlewick dressing gown about her short, dumpy figure and went downstairs. All the doors were locked and bolted, with the exception of the back door, which was locked but not bolted. The bolt had been wrenched back. 'You fool! You bloody fool,' she murmured, shaking her greying head. For one insane moment, she was tempted to slip the bolt home. It would serve him right, she thought. But no. Whatever else he was, he was first and foremost her husband. Disquieted, she returned to her bed. But she could not sleep. Instead, she lay waiting for him, listening, into the early hours and beyond. Through the open chink in the curtains, she watched the fidgeting clouds on the horizon, she saw the moonlight dip away and the silver edge of the sun paint the sky. And still he was not home. 'Oh, Fred Gregory, what a fool you are,' she mumbled, 'will you never learn?' Clambering from the bed, she went to the window, throwing back the curtains and scouring her weary eyes over the landscape. 'One day,' she tutted, 'one day . . . you will be caught, and punished!'

CHAPTER ELEVEN

Morning had risen. The sky was shot with brilliance; the sun loomed large and bright, like a silver shilling against a blue-tinged backcloth. It promised a warmer, light day. Beneath, the earth was awakening. Birds were singing, creatures scurried on their way, and in the rushes that skirted the lake, moorhens and water rats could be seen bobbing in and out, oblivious to the quiet, thoughtful figure that sat hunched on a boulder not too far away.

Alec Harman's dark, brooding eyes were scarred by his tortuous thoughts. Thoughts that brought their own particular brand of fear. Thoughts that dictated what he must – and must not – do. Painful, merciless thoughts which all night long had pierced his soul and disturbed his peace of mind. So often in these past months he had been gravely tempted to abandon the sinister purpose that had brought him to Thornton Place. All night long he had been crucified by thoughts of Ellie. Her delightful image rose in his mind now; her heart-shaped face, magnificent amber eyes that were both wistful and strong. The way she looked at him, wondering, curious gazes that betrayed both her fear and her love. She had suffered so much pain. Her pain was his. But he could do little to ease her suffering. One part of him cried out to love her, to be free to love her. The other – more disciplined – part of him knew that he could not be free; not yet. The reasons were two-fold. Firstly, he believed that to betray his deeper feelings for Ellie would put her in danger. Secondly, he had made a promise long ago. It was a promise that obligated him to secrecy; a promise that sentenced him to things of the dark. Wicked, evil things. There could be no freedom, no life or love for him. Not yet. And maybe never!

He had ruminated long and hard on Rosie's warning. If the Tyler fellow had been suspicious of him, then how much longer would it be before others began to cast questioning glances his way? Rosie was right. Time was running out! Evil forces were pressing all around, urging him on. But, Ellie! What of Ellie? A dark and devious plan sketched itself on his mind. He smiled. Yes! Yes, he would do it. It would not be pleasant, or kind, but he would do it. He must!

Hurt by the wickedness of what he now planned, Alec Harman raised his eyes to gaze across the lake. On the other side, too far away for him to see, walked the very person who was paramount in his thoughts. Steeped in disharmony, Ellie wandered aimlessly along the perimeter of the woods. Her father had been gone almost forty-eight hours now. She missed him. She missed her small, tormenting brother. She missed her mother. Her mother. Even now, over a year later, Ellie could not imagine what devilish thing could have driven that gentle, loving person to such incredible extremes – incredible, and heartsickening. In spite of the love Ellie had known for her mother, she could not find it in her to forgive that last senseless, hideous act.

Far away on the horizon, the thin spiral of greyish smoke twisted its way upwards, to be lost in the clouds that were now suddenly gathering; an ominous indication that the weather might possibly turn for the worse. Her gaze transfixed by the curling smoke, Ellie deduced that it was probably from the Lodge. The Lodge was Alec Harman's home. Ellie's heart soared at the thought of him.

Day or night, he was never very far from her thoughts. She paused a while, entranced by the gyrating smoke line and wondering about the kind of man he was, curious also as to his home. Was it like him – dark and secretive – or was it merely a place for him to return to after his nightly wanderings? Was it a home without a heart? Was it warm and welcoming? Or was it like Alec Harman, aloof and inaccessible?

Ellie was fascinated by the thought of him on a winter's day, sitting by the fireside. She could not envisage the whole picture in her mind. Would he be alone? Was the girl with him? Formidable and tantalising, he was not the sort of man who would fit so easily into a scene of domesticity. Ellie was both amused and sad. In her deepest heart she had tried to justify her love for him, but it was beyond her understanding. It had happened almost without her realising it. One moment he did not exist in her life. The next moment he had infiltrated every small corner of it. She felt it was hopeless. Then he had gazed on her with black, sultry eyes, and all of her resistance had crumbled like so much sand. She had told herself that he did not love her, that he was toying with her affections; like a cat might play with a mouse before ending its life. But then, she had felt the swirling undercurrent that drew them both in, threatening to drown them. There was too much passion smouldering beneath that cool exterior of his; too much wanting, too many unspoken words that told her volumes. There was too much she did not understand. And there was danger! All of these things Ellie knew. But they were not enough to stifle her love for him; only enough to make her cautious, and to keep her distance.

Deliberately suppressing thoughts of Alec Harman and dwelling instead on the fact that her father must soon be home, Ellie retraced her steps along the lake edge and afterwards through the spinney, and on towards the house. Rosie would be there by now, Ellie reminded herself. It was enough to bring a smile to her lovely face.

'What d'you mean . . . I "needn't keep up with the work" if I don't want to?' Rosie was most indignant, eyeing Ellie with astonishment. 'I ain't complained have I?' she demanded. 'So what sort o' comment is that to make, eh?'

Ellie was at once repentant. 'I only thought the work might be getting too much for you, that's all,' she protested, 'and with the restoration well underway now . . .'

'You don't bloody well want me no more!' Rosie interrupted. 'Is that it? Is it?'

Ellie sighed noisily. What she thought was a helpful suggestion to ease Rosie's lot had only served to raise Rosie's hackles. 'Look . . . the tea's made . . . and there's apple pie,' she pointed out, bringing the tray to the kitchen table and afterwards drawing out two chairs. 'Please, Rosie . . . come and sit down,' she pleaded with an apologetic smile. 'I'm sorry . . . honestly.'

'And so you should be,' retorted the older woman, drying the last plate and flinging the cloth onto the wooden rail by the sink. When she seated herself at the table, her face was a study – reminding Ellie of a child in a sulk. 'It ain't as if what I do is heavy work,' Rosie went on, 'a bit o' dusting and dishwashing . . . little routine jobs that let you get on with the bigger jobs, like curtain hanging, painting and scrubbing down. Oh, I know very well that you and your dad are ploughing through it all like nobody's business . . . and it's heartening to see the old place coming to life, but you ain't finished, not by a long chalk you ain't! And when the inside's all done, there's the outside to be seen to . . . the outer walls have centuries o' grime on 'em, then there's the grounds, which have been so neglected these past years – they're nothing but a wilderness. Y'see, my girl,' she said with satisfaction, 'you've more than enough work to keep you going another year, if my reckoning's right.' Having said her piece, she plied her full attention to the task of slicing a piece of pie and pouring herself a cup of tea. 'You can't do without me, and the money your dad pays me is very welcome,' she said, settling herself down to enjoy a well-earned break, 'so let that be an end to it!' She had her lips wrapped round the pie when a thought suddenly occurred to her. Withdrawing the pie from her mouth, she looked at Ellie with injured eyes. 'Unless o' course you're telling me I'm fired?' she asked in a quiet voice.

'Oh, for goodness' sake, Rosie!' Ellie had been first mortified when Rosie was offended by her half-hearted suggestion that she might like to give up her few hours' work a day; then she had been amused at Rosie's indignant attack. Now, she was afraid Rosie was taking the whole thing far too seriously. 'You know perfectly well I would never do any such thing. I only wondered whether you might be glad to give up the work . . . I'm sometimes afraid it could be too much for you, what with George the way he is.' Beneath Rosie's accusing stare, she felt guilty and exasperated. 'I love you coming to the house, Rosie . . . I look forward to your company, you know that.'

'Hmph!' Rosie bit off a huge chunk of pie and glared at Ellie. 'You've got a funny way o' showing it then, that's all I can say . . . asking me if I want to quit me job!' Her words were muffled, hampered by the serious matter of chewing the pie. She bit off another chunk and continued staring at Ellie with a wounded expression. Feeling misjudged on her kindly intention, Ellie stared back. It was a case of who was the more indignant. Suddenly, Ellie felt an irresistible urge to laugh. She did her utmost to suppress it, but she could not stop that delicious bubble of gaiety from rising up in her. Her eyes began to twinkle, and the corners of her mouth insisted on curling upwards. A small noise escaped her; a little laugh.

Startled, Rosie glared harder, but it could not last; she giggled, then laughed aloud.

Ellie rose from her chair and came to the old woman's side, where she lovingly embraced her. 'Rosie, oh . . . Rosie. You old devil. You've been having me on!' she laughed, rocking Rosie in her arms.

'Happen I have . . . and happen I ain't,' Rosie teased.

But it was settled. Ellie would never again raise the question as to whether the work was too much for Rosie and, if it ever did prove to be so, Rosie would be the first to admit it. 'But I ain't ready for no knacker's yard yet!' she declared indignantly, 'and don't you forget it, my girl!'

Afterwards, the conversation took a completely different turn when, in a quiet, serious voice, Rosie asked, 'Have you any regrets, Ellie . . . about ending it all with that young man o' yours?'

Ellie became uncomfortable, but her reply was instant. 'No. It was not meant to be.'

'Just so long as you have no regrets, child.' Rosie had been tempted to mention Barny's visit to the cottage, but in the light of Ellie's answer she thought better of it. She had not forgotten Barny Tyler's words, though – that Ellie loved Alec. She thought of Alec now, and of the secret that bound them. It created in her a need to know. 'And what about Alec?' she asked softly. 'Do you love him?'

It took a moment for Ellie to reply; Rosie's abrupt question had come as something of a shock, causing a turmoil in her. Presently, she treated the older woman as a friend, a confidante. 'Yes.' Her eyes appraised Rosie, seeking something . . . approval, disapproval, a warning. Instead, the old woman merely smiled and nodded. Then she sipped her tea. Ellie ventured further. 'I love him but . . . *I wish I didn't.*'

Rosie's panda-like eyes grew big and round, questioning, puzzled. 'Why?' she asked, her hand poised in mid-air, with the tea cup almost to her mouth. 'That's a strange thing to say,' she remarked softly.

'It's the way I feel, Rosie.' Ellie had reached the point of no return; she had to go on. 'He intrigues me. Sometimes, when he looks at me with those black, beckoning eyes, I see things there . . . *disturbing things*. They frighten me.'

'What do you mean . . . "disturbing things"?' Rosie was also a little afraid.

'It's as though he wants to tell me something . . . a secret, maybe, I don't know, but . . . once or twice when we've crossed each other's paths and stopped to talk, he seems to have something on his mind.' Ellie was shocked to find herself thinking of Johnny. 'Like a little boy . . . like Johnny – *hiding* a secret . . . yet wanting to share it. But, he never does.'

'That's because you're imagining things, I expect.' Rosie disguised her anxieties beneath a warm-hearted smile. So! Alec had been on the verge of confessing all to Ellie! That would have been most unwise. She understood what he had been trying to tell her back at the cottage . . . 'This is not the time for love!' He was right. There were other things, more urgent, to be dealt with. And yet, her old heart was sore because she knew how deeply Alec was attracted to Ellie. It was a hard thing to see two young people so in love, and to know how wicked and evil was the reason for them being kept apart. Alec was right on another count also – time was running out!

'I believe he loves me, Rosie,' Ellie persisted, 'but I can't trust him. Deep down I believe he's just a charmer . . . likes to flirt. *I don't need that kind of heartbreak.*'

'You could be right. He's certainly a good-looker.' She had to discourage Ellie. It was for the best.

'I *am* right. I saw him down by the lake, and again on the path to the church. He was with a girl.'

Rosie was instantly on her guard. 'A "girl", you say?'

Ellie nodded, raising the painful memory in her mind.

'Nineteen . . . twenty years old, with long dark hair. Very lovely, she was.' She had seen how Rosie's face grew paler with her every word. It troubled her, made her curious. 'Do you know the girl, Rosie?'

'No. Not at all,' Rosie quickly assured her. Too quickly, Ellie thought. 'The description doesn't immediately bring anyone to mind,' she lied. Alec had obviously been very careless. She would have to caution both him, *and* the girl.

'They were very close,' Ellie remembered. 'You see why I can't trust him; can't allow myself to be drawn towards him.'

Rosie gave no answer. Instead, she abruptly changed the subject. 'Are you expecting your father home today?'

Surprised by the swift change of direction, Ellie answered, 'I certainly hope so, Rosie. He's been gone almost two days.'

'Aw, it'll do him good . . . a change o' scenery does us all a world o' good now and then,' she sighed. 'But there ain't much chance o' me taking off . . . not that I'd want to,' she added. 'I'm content to end me days here.' She chuckled, 'That's if the landlord will let me.' When Ellie expressed her opinion that no one would be so callous as to turn Rosie and the senile out, Rosie shook her head. 'Happen you're right,' she said, 'I don't think they will, or they'd a' done it afore now.' She was chuckling again, struggling to right herself on the crutches. 'But I'll not give 'em a chance, eh? I'll keep up with me rent, so they ain't got no excuse to kick us arses out! Now then, my girl . . . you see what good purpose me wages goes to, don't you, eh?'

'Aw, go on with you,' chided Ellie, beginning to clear away the crockery, 'don't you start again!' Rosie laughed, but her face grew serious at Ellie's next words: 'Is George any better?'

''Fraid not, sweetheart. He ain't no better at all. If

anything, he's worse.' She recalled how he had begun sneaking out of his bed, peering out of the window, and screaming in his sleep . . . just like he used to. He had changed in other ways; he'd become secretive and deceitful. These days he was very hard to fathom – worse than she had ever known him. 'He's wasting away in front o' me eyes, and there ain't a thing I can do about it,' she told Ellie in a sad voice. 'Some'at's plaguing him . . . eating away at his mind. Poor sod, if only he could remember, we might be able to talk it away.' She sighed. 'But, to be honest, Ellie, I reckon it's all some garbled fancy . . . some'at and nothing.' She went away shaking her head, an odd, cumbersome figure yet surprisingly graceful. Rosie's agility on those crutches never failed to evoke Ellie's admiration; she was always put in mind of a seal . . . ungainly and slow on land, but capable of gliding with incredible speed and grace when assisted by the support of water.

For the next few hours, Ellie busied herself upstairs in the big front bedroom. Here, her father's ladder and work tools were exactly as he had left them; surprisingly, though, he had not tidied them away like he normally did. The emulsion brush was still dipped in the paint pot, and already a thin crust of paint was beginning to form all round it; the old chequered shirt he used for a wiping cloth was slung haphazardly over the ladder steps, and the wall he had been working on was left as though in a hurry, with the last application of emulsion running in slow, congealed drips to the skirting board. It was well into the afternoon by the time Ellie had made good the wall, washed and cleaned all the brushes, and put everything neatly away. Feeling satisfied with her work, she indulged in a long, hot bath and a change of clothes, after which she made her way down to the kitchen, where she put the kettle on for a hot drink. Her throat felt parched and her head was spinning. The smell of paint always did that to her. Something else was buzzing in her head as well – something that quietly worried her. Why had her father left his workplace in such a mess? It was so unlike him. For as long as Ellie could remember, he had always taken a great pride in the order of things – 'a good workman takes care of his tools of trade,' he was fond of saying, and it was a principle he never failed to keep. *Until now!* Ellie attributed it all to that letter. He had certainly been put out by it. She smiled, thinking how she would not like to be in the shoes of that solicitor when her father confronted him. He had a temper, and that was a fact.

Ellie was just about to take the tray into the big room, where she intended to relax a while. Afterwards, she would return to the kitchen and start the evening meal. A glance at the clock on the dresser told her that it was already three o'clock. Only now, did she feel a murmuring of uneasiness inside her. She had expected her father to be home before now. It consoled her a little to remind herself that it was a long and difficult journey to London; first the drive into Medford, and the fact that getting the right train connection was hit and miss; then all the rush and planning at the other end. Ellie knew how much her father hated the thought of travelling on the underground, so it would have to be a bus or a taxi that carried him to the solicitor's office. As far as she knew, he had not had time to book into a hotel, so that in itself might have proved to be a problem. Then, when he felt satisfied that he had done what he set out to do, there was all the paraphernalia in reverse. She imagined he would be tired when he got home. Still, a hot bath and a good meal would soon put that right, she thought.

Ellie collected the tray of tea and cheese sandwiches, and began her way out of the kitchen. It was then that the knock came on the door. Curious, she put the tray down on the table and hurried to see who the visitor was.

If it was her father, why didn't he let himself in? And it wouldn't be Rosie; anyway, Rosie also had a key. Who, then?

Anxiously, Ellie opened the door and her eyes widened in astonishment to see a particular face staring back at her.

'Miss Armstrong?' The dark-haired girl stepped forward, a look of apprehension in her eyes – large, luscious eyes that seemed to see right through Ellie. When Ellie replied that yes, she was Miss Armstrong, a look of relief washed over the girl's handsome face. Now it was replaced by a sense of urgency, her voice urging, 'Alec Harman sent me. He needs you.'

'Alec . . . he sent you?' Ellie was shocked. She felt uncomfortable beneath the girl's eyes; felt herself being studied, assessed.

'He's hurt. A short while ago, I found him at the Lodge.' The girl's face was chalk-white and she was obviously in a state of distress. 'I think his legs are broken.' There were tears in her eyes. She began to babble now, her words tumbling one over the other, telling Ellie how Alec Harman had been working in the attic. 'He fell . . . dear God, I don't know if his back is broken . . .' She seemed on the verge of hysteria.

'Have you alerted the doctor?' Ellie felt sick in the pit of her stomach. '. . . Rung for an ambulance?' The questions came thick and fast as Ellie ran into the kitchen to get her coat. The girl did not answer any of her questions. Instead, she went on about how Alec insisted on her going for Ellie, how he was adamant that Ellie had to be fetched straight away . . .

'He said I wasn't to take no for an answer,' the girl told Ellie in a breathless voice. 'He said I was to make sure you came with me, and that you were not to tell anyone.'

Ellie was already scribbling a note for her father, explaining where she had gone, when she was pulled up sharp by the girl's warning. 'But that's impossible!' she protested, finishing the note. 'My father will be frantic if he comes home and there's no sign of me.' Another thought occurred to her. 'Besides . . . I think we should get Rosie to come with us. After all, she knows Alec much better than I do.'

The girl had followed Ellie into the kitchen. She shook her head frantically. 'Alec was adamant,' she said in a frightened voice. 'You were to come with me straight away, and you were to tell no one!'

Ellie was puzzled. 'I don't understand,' she said, doing up the buttons on her coat and slipping her feet out of the flat shoes and into her ankle boots. 'That doesn't make sense! You say he's hurt . . . probably both legs broken . . . and he doesn't want anyone but me to know?' She propped the note to her father against the kettle where he was sure to find it. 'Why? Why would he insist on such a thing?' She shook her head and went from the kitchen. She did not see the girl surreptitiously snatch the note and stuff it quickly into her coat pocket. Together, Ellie and the girl left the house. The girl stayed slightly ahead, leading the way. Ellie asked again, 'You haven't answered me . . . why would he insist on such a thing?' In the heat of the moment she had not really stopped to examine the situation properly. Something curious tugged at her senses. She felt increasingly uneasy. Suddenly, she had half a mind to turn back. She stopped, causing the girl also to stop and turn. Their gazes mingled; the girl with a look of apprehension on her face, and Ellie's sincere amber eyes resolute, suspicious. 'Why would he insist on no one else knowing?' she demanded. 'And why would he send for me . . . not for Rosie?'

The girl fidgeted. There was fear in her dark eyes, and a visible mental struggle in the wake of Ellie's repeated questioning.

'I won't go another step until you answer me!' Ellie's

expression was stern. The girl began to relent.

'You must believe,' she pleaded, 'he has his reasons.'

'Well?' Ellie kept her ground. She meant what she said. Her every instinct was in uproar now. She had to know what she was letting herself in for.

'There are things you should know,' the girl went on reluctantly. Alec had warned her that Ellie might not be so easily persuaded. 'Alec has . . . something to tell you. He says you must know now, before it's too late.'

Shock stabbed Ellie's heart. 'He's not . . . dying, is he?' She felt the colour drain from her face when the girl gave her answer in a quiet, darkly serious tone.

'I believe he might be.' The girl saw how her words had affected Ellie. She sensed the depth of love which Ellie had for Alec. It was a weakness that she knew she must play on. 'It's only natural that Alec would want you by his side,' she said in a more confident yet probing voice. 'He loves you, Ellie Armstrong.'

'I'm not sure . . .' Ellie was desperately afraid. Surely to God, fate would not be so cruel, she thought. First her mother, then Johnny, and now Alec? No. Oh no! It couldn't be. She wanted with all of her heart to rush to him, to comfort him and tell him how he could not die because she needed him oh, so much. She was torn in two directions – her deeper instincts told her there was something wrong here, something the girl was keeping back. And yet, dare she risk refusing to go on? Supposing she returned to Thornton Place, right now. Would she be able to sleep this night? Wouldn't she be tormented with worry and guilt? Could she be so callous as to turn her back on him when he was lying injured? One thing she had to know. Regarding the girl with stiff challenging eyes, she asked, 'What are *you* to Alec Harman?'

The girl was already prepared for such a question. She had been warned, and now she must play the part. 'We were lovers, I must confess that,' she replied in a quiet, reticent voice, 'but it's over. It's been over for some time now . . . ever since *you* came on the scene I've felt him growing away from me. I'm no fool. I know it's finished.'

Ellie felt embarrassed and curiously defensive. She was reminded of her relationship with Barny, and of how she too had 'grown away' from that relationship, when Alec came on the scene. Suddenly, all the doubts were suppressed beneath her desire to go to him, to talk with him and comfort him. In newly determined mood she began striding on, telling the girl, 'We must hurry. It will be dark shortly. Is there a short cut? . . . will we get there before the ambulance?' Anxiety took over, and a simmering disappointment that she had been so reluctant. 'Who's with him now? . . . you haven't left him alone, have you?' Without waiting for answers, she pushed on. Now, the girl was in front again, leading the way. An awkward silence descended. There was no need for words as they pressed ever onwards, through the spinney, skirting the lake, keeping to the little-used track that led directly to the Lodge, and to Alec Harman. The daylight became less intense, greyness began creeping over all. The silence was ominous, broken only by the scrunch of leaves beneath their hurrying feet. In spite of her earlier doubts, Ellie felt as though she was rushing towards her destiny. And now, at long last, she went willingly. Longingly.

Twilight descended, pushing away the remaining vestige of daylight. Soon, very soon, the blackness would envelop everything. The evening grew quiet. A breeze began softly whispering, stirring the air, carrying every sound. From the old barn the voices floated out, hushed and tender murmurings that spoke of retribution, and of love. *And insanity*.

'Hello, Johnny. I've been waiting for you. You've been gone a long time. Are you angry with me?'

'Yes. You *burned* me! Why did you burn me? I thought you were my friend.'

'Oh, but I am. I *am* your friend. You must believe that.'

'How can I?'

'You must.' Soft laughter, then, 'You haven't forgotten the things we talked about, have you, Johnny?'

'I don't want to think about them now. You burned me. *Why* did you burn me?'

'You don't forgive easily, do you?'

'No.'

'Not even me . . . your friend?'

'Not even you. Not now.'

'But we understand each other, you and I, don't you see, Johnny?'

'No. Why did you burn me?'

'It was a bad thing, wasn't it?'

'Oh, yes, it was a very bad thing.'

'As bad as . . . the others?' Soft now, persuasive. Clever.

'I don't know.'

'Yes you do, Johnny. *Think!*'

'I can't remember.'

'Yes you can!' Anger; impatience.

'You burned me!'

'And you can't forgive me?'

'*No!*'

'Of course you can, Johnny.'

'*Never.*'

'But . . . I love you.'

'You lie. You lied to me before. I thought you were my friend . . . my only . . . friend.' Anguish. Sobbing now.

'Oh, please . . . don't cry, Johnny.'

'I don't want you for my friend any more.'

'Ssh . . . ssh now. Let me hold you. There, Johnny. I'm so sorry. So very sorry. I promise I will never hurt you again.'

'Promise . . . never, ever hurt me again?'

'Ssh. Lie softly, Johnny. I do love you. But, not them. I hate them, but, it isn't really your fault.'

'Why did you burn me?'

'To punish you, of course.'

'I didn't deserve to be punished.'

'Oh, but you did!'

'Because of the keys?'

'That was only part of it. I didn't punish you for the keys . . . not really. Not altogether for the keys.'

'Why then?'

'For what you did . . . with her!' Pain. Such unbearable pain.

'What? What did I do?'

'You played, Johnny. You laughed in the sunshine together, and made a sandcastle.'

'I remember.'

'You were so happy, you . . . and she. She held your hand. She kissed you . . . embraced you. She loved you so much, did you know that?'

'I think so.'

'Oh . . . she did, Johnny. She adored you. I didn't like that. It hurt, oh, so very much.'

'Were you jealous?'

'Oh, yes . . . yes!'

'*Why?*'

'You're forgetting our agreement!' Anger. 'Never ask me questions about myself.'

'But you forget . . . I know who you are. *I saw your face.*'

'That was very wicked of you, Johnny.'

'I'm not sorry! You were wicked to burn me. Was that why? Was it because I saw your face?'

'Like the keys, it was only part of the reason.'

'Was it really because she loved me . . . my mother?'

'*She loved you too much!* That was so painful. I had to punish you, Johnny. I had to punish her also.' A small hard laugh. 'But you saw how I punished her, didn't you, Johnny?'

'*You!*' Deep, dark silence, then, 'Was it you who,

who . . .?' It was too awful to contemplate.

'Yes, Johnny. *I killed your mother. And the other one.*' The voice trembled. '*I hated that one most of all!*'

'It was . . . horrible.'

'No, Johnny, it was incredibly beautiful. All was as it should be.'

'That perfume?'

'Lavender.' A long, satisfied sigh, then, 'It had to be lavender. I anointed them . . . said a prayer over them.'

'Were you sorry afterwards?'

'Not "sorry", Johnny . . . glad. I was so happy. But, you see, it wasn't finished, though. There were others. They were all part of it. They could not be allowed to live. It was not over, Johnny.'

'Is it over now?'

'Not yet. Soon, though . . . very soon.'

'Are you going to kill again?'

'Oh, yes, Johnny.'

'Can I watch?'

'If you really want to.'

'I do.'

'That's good, Johnny. I knew you would not fail me. I want you to watch! It's only right that you should be there.'

'When? When can I watch?'

Soft, crazy laughter. 'Don't be impatient, Johnny. We have to be very careful, all the time . . . careful. There are eyes everywhere . . . watching, waiting to trap me. I'm clever though, Johnny. I move with the shadows.'

'Tonight?'

'*Tonight*, Johnny. When the shadows are large and black enough to hide us, that is the best time to punish . . . to kill. *Tonight*. Be patient, Johnny. All is as it should be!'

Outside, only the breeze could be heard, a fluttering sighing through the leaves. The dark shadows deepened, the night closed in. Soon, soft, stealthy footsteps disturbed the air, but softly, oh, so softly, urged on by a heart that was blacker even than the darkest night.

'*Alec!*' The girl flung herself into his arms as he came into the room. 'I'm so glad you're back . . . I was frightened. I don't like it here, in the dark.'

'Ssh, it's all right now.' He held her away from him. 'There's no need for you to be frightened,' he told her, his black eyes smiling down on her anxious face. Releasing her, he took the gun from the crook of his arm and propped it carefully against the wall. From upstairs there sounded a series of shouts, followed by a loud thumping noise. His smile deepened. 'You brought her here, then?' When the girl nodded, he asked, 'Did it prove difficult?'

'Some. She was suspicious, though. It was her love for you that decided her to come with me.'

'You think she *really* loves me?'

'Very much.'

Suddenly his face grew serious as he gripped the girl by her arms. 'I didn't want to frighten her this way, Laura, but it was the only way.'

'Are you sure?'

'I'm sure. I had to get her away from the house. I'm sorry to have involved you, but she would never have agreed to come with me.' His face was suffused with pleasure. 'You know how I feel about Ellie,' he said softly, 'I wasn't altogether sure that she felt the same way towards me . . . it was a gamble.'

'If she's in danger, you had no choice. I'm glad I was able to help, but I was so afraid.' Her voice began trembling again.

'Ssh . . . you'll be all right. I truly believe that you were never in any danger, or I would not have asked you to help.' He went to the door and took down her coat from the hook there. Returning to the girl, he began draping the coat over her shoulders, urging her to put it on. 'You *might* be in danger, though . . . if you stay here. The Land-Rover's outside. I want you to leave straightaway. Get right away from here.' He frantically fastened the buttons of her coat and propelled her towards the door. 'Go back to Medford, and stay there until I come for you!' he ordered in a stern voice.

'I'm afraid, Alec. Do you really think it will happen *tonight*?'

He nodded, opening the door and gently pushing her out into the night. 'Something bad will happen tonight,' he told her, 'I know it. Ellie is the one. But, I've got her here. She will draw the badness to her.' His face was grave as he added, 'It has to stop. It has to stop tonight.'

'Be very careful, Alec!' She clung to him. 'For God's sake, be careful. I'm afraid for both of you.'

'Don't be.' He pressed the keys into her hand. 'Get away from here, Laura. Now!'

'I'll pray for you,' she said. A brief kiss, then she fled into the night. Only when he was satisfied that the girl was safely on her way did he close the door, slipping the bolts home, and afterwards stalking through the house to check that every door and window was secure. Then, he went upstairs to stand outside the room where Ellie was kept. During a brief lull in her vehement and noisy protests at being first tricked, then locked up against her will, he called her name. 'Ellie. Ellie, it's me . . . Alec.'

Nothing stirred, no sound was heard, then, in a quiet, controlled voice, 'Open the door, Alec. Please let me out of here.' Ellie had never been so afraid in her whole life. The girl had shown her up here to this room, indicating that Alec was in here, lying twisted and broken, mortally injured. Once Ellie had set foot inside, the door was slammed and bolted. It was a prison. *A nightmare!* The one small, narrow window afforded no way of escape, her cries went unheard. There was no telling how long she had been imprisoned here and, when she made herself think calmly, it was to realise, with shock, that Alec Harman and the girl had conspired to take away her freedom – to hurt her. But why? *Why?* That was the most terrifying part. During the seemingly endless time in the dark, she had recalled her father's words with regard to Alec Harman . . . 'There's something strange about that one . . . something sinister.' Was her father right, then? Was Alec Harman insane? Carefully, with this in mind, she pleaded in a firm, calm voice, 'Open the door, Alec . . . please. My father will be waiting . . . he's bound to come looking for me.'

'He may come "looking for you", Ellie,' the answer was returned, '. . . and he may not. In either event, I will be ready.'

'Don't keep me here against my will. Don't do that.'

'Believe me, Ellie . . . I must. I'm sorry I had to trick you that way, but I had to get you away from Thornton Place.' He paused, not wanting to frighten her any further, but she had to know. He hoped she might understand. He knew she would not. 'You were in terrible danger there, Ellie.'

'I'm in danger here.'

'I hope not, Ellie, but . . . I can't be sure. I have to keep you safe. I dare not take any chances.'

'Let me out!' The terror rose in Ellie; it betrayed itself in her cry.

'Trust me, Ellie . . . I love you.' His words only made her accuse him all the more, made her plead . . . calmly . . . then with panic, made her kick and thump at the door. He felt her fear and it broke his heart. He wanted to go in there and take her in his arms, make her safe, reassure her. He dared not. Steeling himself against her anguish, he turned away. Downstairs, he re-checked all the doors and windows and switched off the lights, then, with the shotgun poised and loaded across his knees, he sat in the tall-backed rocking chair, facing the front door, watching. *Waiting*. Behind him, the logs crackled in the firegrate, the flames sending long, lazy shadows up the wall. Outside, the breeze had died down. Save for Ellie's muted cries, the night was quiet, brooding, loath to yield its darkly kept secrets. Ssh! There! *What was that?* Yes! There it was again . . . a low, scratching sound. Every hair on Alec Harman's neck stood up, prickling against his skin, beads of sweat broke out across his temples. There was no denying what he had heard. Someone was out there! Trying to get in . . . wanting to get to Ellie. He would not let them. Ellie must not be harmed, even if her safety cost him his own life! On sly, silent footsteps he went slowly towards the door, stealthily, one by one he drew back the bolts, holding his breath, afraid that he might be heard. It had not been his intention to go from the house; he had planned to wait until the intruder gained access, then he would be ready. Now, though, his every nerve-ending was screaming out, there were writhing snakes eating at the pit of his stomach. How could he wait? His whole being was on a knife edge, his instincts screaming, 'Attack! Attack! . . . get it before it gets you!'

With excruciating slowness, he inched the door open, his life's blood boiling in his veins, his breath pulsating in his throat, almost choking him. Easy . . . go softly. On tiptoes he padded forwards, the dark night embracing and chilly to his face. At first he could see nothing through the blackness. Then a movement! The smallest of movements . . . to the right of him, a sliver of moonlight falling on the curve of a shoulder, a head, bent towards the window intent on peering in. Easy now . . . go easy! Like a snake with its belly to the ground, he slithered along the wall, closer, as yet unseen. His grey-blue breath made gyrating patterns in the bitter night air. The clouds drifted away, uncovering the moon. *Now! Now!* Before the head was lifted and the eyes swung to see him. With deadly speed he surged forward, part-running, part-leaping. There was a sickening thud as he pitched himself at the quarry, a kind of breathless gasp, soft cold flesh beneath his fingers and a soaring desperation in his heart, fury mingling with terror. A primeval, deep-down yearning to kill! Surprise had been his advantage. The intruder was pegged to the ground, his large plain features shaped by fear, his hang-dog bloodshot eyes stared up. In the cold moon glow his face took on a silver-blue tinge. It was a bad face, a guilty, frightened face. Alec Harman stiffened with astonishment. It was Gregory's face!

Mesmerised, the face stared up, the eyes bulbous, wet and stark in the folds of flesh. 'I didn't mean no harm . . . I swear to God,' he whimpered. His breathing was erratic, his chest pumping up and down as though it might suddenly burst open.

'Gregory!' Alec Harman's fists remained locked onto his quarry. He could feel it trembling beneath him. Fred Gregory! He was not the one Alec Harman had expected. It occurred to him now that he might have been wrong. Such a prospect did not sit easily in his frantic mind. Like a fleeting macabre procession, the trail of images passed through his mind now . . . the missing children and the priest . . . George's wife . . . the attack on old George . . . the bonfire. It was too much! He flicked his eyes shut, trying desperately to banish the awful sight of the boy, charred and blackened. He had tried so hard to believe it was as they had decided – 'an act of misadventure' – but he couldn't accept such a verdict. The images seared his mind, his heart, his very soul. He glared down at the man in his clutches. Dear God, he had been so sure! Had he been so wrong? Another image . . . of tyre tracks impressed into the soft, damp earth! Tyre tracks, leading down to the water's edge, and then disappearing into the moving blackness there. And footsteps. Large. A man's footsteps – shallow impressions, then cutting deeper as though the weight had become two-fold. Like a physical pain, the memory of that young man spiralled in his thoughts – a young man come to see Ellie, an old battered van . . . the tyre tracks. He feared the worst! Anguish rose up in him like a vindictive tide. He had thought to handle it alone. He was a fool! In the distance, beyond his mind, he could hear Fred Gregory pleading. Bitterly, he began shaking him, demanding in a harsh voice, 'What the hell are you doing here?'

'I weren't doing no harm! Just stalking a wild deer . . . or a fat-bellied rabbit.' He struggled to get upright. Harman kept him down.

'You damned liar!' he hissed. 'You were looking in the window, that's what you were doing.' He tightened his grip on the fellow's shirt collar, twisting it until it bit into the thick, leathery neck like a hangman's rope. 'You'd best tell the truth, Gregory . . . or I'll not answer for the consequences!'

'Honest to God, you've got to believe me. All right, so I was looking in the window. I saw the girl and Ellie Armstrong earlier . . . I was curious, that's all. Nothing more. So help me, I was just being curious.' His words were choked, his big plain face growing redder by the minute. Suddenly, he was crying, blubbering like a baby, the tears rolling down his face.

Alec Harman had to think fast. He must decide. He prayed it was the right decision. 'Get up!' he ordered, releasing the big fellow and watching his every move. Surprised but grateful, Gregory scrambled to his feet, both his hammer hands round his chafed neck, soothing the soreness there. With narrowed eyes, he glowered at the other fellow. His silence was ominous. Harman sensed the undercurrent of loathing, but his decision was made. He had little choice. 'Take to your heels, man,' he said, glancing furtively from side to side, his watchful eyes minding the door. Ellie must be protected at all costs. 'Get the police! As fast as you can . . . there'll be murder tonight if you don't.' Gregory made no move. Instead, he continued to glower at him, as though he had not heard. Harman gripped him by the shoulder, twisting him away. 'Run, man! *Fetch the police*, you bloody fool! There's a maniac loose in these woods.' He silently prayed he was not making a grave mistake in letting the fellow go.

'What d'yer mean . . . a maniac?'

'Never mind. All you need to know is that someone out there means to commit murder this very night. Do as I say . . . get the police!' He lowered his voice. 'And I shouldn't take too long about it. He's probably watching us even now. For God's sake, man . . . Run for your life!' It was enough. The big fellow inched away, his loose, pale eyes peering all around. In a moment he was gone, his large bulky shadow merging with the night. Satisfied, but not completely, Alec Harman swung away. He was only a few steps from the doorway when the blow was struck – a heavy, merciless blow that thudded against his skull like a sledge-hammer, sending him reeling against the door, where he crumpled to the ground like a felled ox.

'Is he dead?' The voice was curiously small, squeaky, like that of a child, yet – not like a child.

'Oh, I don't think so, Johnny.'

'Aw . . . I thought you said I could watch you kill.'

'You will, Johnny. He has to die, just like the others. Only not yet. Not yet.'

'Soon, though?'

'Oh, yes. Soon. Very soon.'

When she heard the footsteps mounting the stairs, Ellie ran to the door, beating at it with her fists and demanding to be released. Her terror was heightened by the fact that no light filtered beneath the door. Before, when Alec Harman had come to the door, a light had been switched on somewhere outside the room. Strangely, now, all remained in darkness. Only the thin shard of moonlight lifted the blackness. The footsteps came nearer, nearer, faltering a little, but determined. Curious, and suddenly filled with a terrible dread, Ellie backed away from the door. The key was inserted. She cringed in the corner, her heartbeat thumping inside her like the tick of doom. The footsteps were different! It was not Alec Harman, nor was it the girl. And yet, somehow, somewhere deep in her senses, the footsteps echoed with murmuring familiarity. 'Who's there?' she called, her voice sounding strange, even to her own ears. No answer. Slowly, the door was pushed open. There was no place for Ellie to go. Her legs were paralysed beneath her, mortal fear pressing her down, down. She knew she had to try, had to try . . . had to try! But she could not move. Like a rabbit caught in the headlights of a car, she was mesmerised by the oncoming figure. It was only a flicker of moonlight, the briefest glance, but, in that split second when he raised his arms to smother her with a blanket of darkness, she thought she recognised his face. Her horror-struck senses refused to believe what she had seen. In those few frantic moments when she struggled, fighting for her very life, the last voice she heard before her senses slipped away was the voice of her dead brother. What it said was chilling. What it said was, 'Kill her now. *Now!* . . . You promised I could watch.'

CHAPTER TWELVE

It was the earliest hour. In the drawing room of the vicarage, two men were deep in conversation; one an officer of the law, the other a man of God.

'Of course we will follow up your complaint, vicar.' The police officer wrote hastily into his notepad before returning it to his pocket. 'And you say you contacted . . .' He paused, his brows furrowed. Dipping into his pocket, he drew out the notepad again, quickly consulting his notes there. 'Mr Armstrong?' he finished, retaining the notepad in his chubby fist.

'I did.' The vicar looked distressed, his hands wringing one over the other and his bright blue eyes beseeching the officer. 'You will go gently, won't you?' he asked. 'Mr Armstrong was ill with grief at the loss of his wife. I would hate to think I was the cause of bringing him even more pain.' He began pacing the floor, his footsteps silent against the plush blue carpet. 'But you see . . . I had no choice. None at all,' he said apologetically.

'I'm sure you didn't, sir,' agreed the officer, 'but . . . you say he did not reply to your letter . . . didn't contact you in any way?'

The vicar shook his head. 'That was when I decided to bring in the authorities.' He lowered his gaze to the carpet and shook his head sadly. 'A terrible . . . terrible thing,' he murmured, '. . . who would want to desecrate a grave?'

The very idea was too incomprehensible.

The officer also looked shocked. 'It's a sorry fact that some people are capable of anything,' he told him.

'What will you do . . . exhume the body?'

'First things first . . . we'll need to establish the facts . . . get authorisation where necessary . . .'

He replaced his helmet and moved towards the door. 'Our first port of call will of course be the deceased's next-of-kin . . . Mr Armstrong.'

'You'll talk to him? Explain, that his wife's grave has been tampered with?'

'With all respect, vicar, we don't know that for certain yet. But yes, we *will* arrange for someone to call on Mr Armstrong, at . . . Thornton Place, Redborough.' He shook his head and furrowed his brows, lapsing into a brief interlude of deep thought. 'Hmm . . . Redborough. Can't say I've heard of the place, but then again, I've only ever been south once, and that was on a six month course with the London Metropolitan.'

'I had not heard of Redborough either,' rejoined the vicar. 'Had it not been for an arrangement made between Mr Armstrong and our ground-keeper for him to take care of the grave, well then, I might not have so easily located the address. As it was, our good fellow gladly offered it. According to what Mr Armstrong told him, Thornton Place was somewhat "off the beaten tracks".' A thought suddenly presented itself. It tempered a part of his anxiety. 'Ah! . . . of course that could be why he has not responded to my letter. Perhaps the mail is not so regularly delivered. What do you think?'

'We'll soon know,' the officer promised, after which they parted company; the vicar to his Godly calls, the officer to his ungodly ones. And neither of these two realising what horrifying developments they would cause to unfold.

'I'll take you home again, Kathleen,
To where your heart will feel no pain
. . . where the hills are fresh and green
. . . take you home again, Kathleen.'

The plaintive tones floated from the radio. Inspired, Rosie hummed along, hopping from one end of the tiny kitchen to the other as she prepared old George's breakfast – a piping-hot mug of tea, two thinly buttered slices of toast, and a lightly boiled egg; that was it! All ready now. The song had ended. A voice intervened, harsh and penetrating to the ear, announcing news from Monaco of Princess Grace and her first-born child, a girl.

Rosie switched the radio off, and brought out the trolley from underneath the wall cupboard. First, she put the empty tray on it, then one by one she put the breakfast items onto the tray; it was a difficult exercise, being hampered as she was by the two crutches always in the way. Rosie, however, had mastered the task through years of practice. Soon it was done, and, hoping against hope that he might for once be able to eat his breakfast . . . or at least a good part of it, Rosie trundled the trolley before her, out of the kitchen, through the cosy parlour and into the room where the senile slept. She shivered. As yet, she had not kindled a fire, and the cold morning air wrapped itself round her like a clinging vapour. The curtains were not drawn back either, so only the lamplight from the kitchen showed her the way.

At the bedroom door, she manoeuvred the trolley to one side while she lifted the latch and pushed open the door. Normally, Rosie would have gone straight into George's room on waking, but this morning she had done the unforgivable – she had overslept! It had been a bad night with little sleep, when all the worries and fears of these past years had come to torment her. Alec had promised it would soon be over.

She hoped so. Oh, she hoped and prayed so!

'Breakfast, sweetheart,' she called out, propelling the trolley ahead of her. When there came no answer, she tut-tutted, smiled a little and made her way across the room in the semi-darkness. At the window she grasped the curtains one by one and slid them back. The daylight poured in. She peeped through the glass, shivering aloud and remarking, 'By! It looks sharp and bitter out there, George. You're in the best place . . . warm an' cosy in your bed.' She swung round, gasping with astonishment when she saw that George was not 'in his bed'. The bed was empty. The shock of it momentarily silenced her, numbing her brain. Then, a murmur, 'George.' She went clumsily forward to the bed, bending down to run her hand between the sheets. Cold. Stone cold – as though it had not been occupied for many hours. 'George . . . George!' She glanced round the room, her brown panda-like eyes half smiling. 'You bugger, George . . . are you playing games with me again?' Since he had been more or less confined to his bed, George had nurtured a real liking for 'playing games'.

Rosie searched everywhere. George was definitely not in the cottage. His outdoor clothes were gone and she was at her wits' end. Exhausted and beside herself with worry, she dropped into the armchair, her frantic mind casting back to when she had last seen George. 'Last night . . . soon after Alec left,' she told herself. She had gone in to say goodnight. A cold hand gripped her heart. She should have realised! Recently, he had seemed very distant to her, steeped in thought, ranting a little and demanding to know why he 'couldn't remember'. He had been saying that a lot of late . . . 'couldn't remember'. Remember what? Time and again Rosie had talked with him, but to no avail. Her efforts at conversation had been disturbing to her, but more disturbing to him. Something was plaguing him. It was plaguing him more than usual last night, after Alec left. Rosie wondered now whether George might have overheard the conversation that had taken place between herself and Alec. If so, it could have alarmed him, could have sounded 'strange' to him. Suddenly, she was afraid. Suddenly, she was suspicious again, being made to recall other times when she had been suspicious . . . the children . . . the priest . . . George's own wife. No. *No!* Whatever was she thinking of? He was not the one. *How could he be?*

Now, she was out of the chair, hobbling back and forth across the room, her mind in turmoil. 'Take hold of yourself, Rosie gal,' she said softly, 'you thought all of that through once before, remember! And didn't you decide that . . . George was not the one!' A horrible realisation spread through her. 'Dear God above, let me be wrong . . . let me be wrong!' She had to find him. She prayed that she had not innocently put Alec in danger. Oh, and Ellie! Ellie! Alone in that big, sprawling place. George knew every inch of it . . . every nook and cranny . . . every way out, and every way in. Every way in! Terror rose like a tidal wave; her voice rose with it. 'George! . . . *George.*' She was screaming now, rushing from the cottage and going towards the house, tumbling and slipping, and calling out to Ellie, 'Stay inside . . . don't let him in! *For God's sake, Ellie, don't let him in!*'

Behind her, the cottage door swung back and forth. Fingers clutched it, held it still. The intruder entered the cottage with a pitiful burden breaking its back. Silent, broken and bloody though it was, the seemingly lifeless form was somehow still breathing, not yet devoid of life, but dangerously near. Softly, the cottage door closed behind them. Another opened. Down, down, deep into the earth. As deep and unlovely as hell itself. And yet, it appeared as heaven, and calm and gratifying to the crazed mind that now perceived all of its work. It had been a long and painful road. Now, all was as it should be. The sound of gentle laughter echoed through the cottage. The scent of lavender pervaded the air. A voice breathed, soft, satisfied. 'Yes . . . all is as it should be.'

After a while, the cottage door opened again. He came out. This time he was alone, having deposited his burden amongst the gruesome victims of his insanity. In the star-shine the smile lingered on his features, the eyes glittered, alive with madness. On quiet, urgent footsteps he went towards the house. The paintings! He must have the paintings.

A short way from the house, he saw Rosie standing at the top of the steps. Slipping surreptitiously into the long shrubbery, he watched, biding his time. Presently, her ungainly familiar figure came down the flight of steps; even from this distance it was obvious that she was crying. It was a saddening sight that touched his wicked heart. He knew how unhappy she would be if only she knew . . . if only she knew! He did not intend her to know. All the others deserved to be punished. It was only right. But not her. Not Rosie. He felt he could never hurt her.

'George . . . Ellie . . . for God's sake answer me!' Rosie searched and called, the tears rolling down her face, smudging the make-up round her eyes. The bright crimson gash that was her mouth turned down at the corners, heightening the comical effect. Now, she passed within only feet of him! He watched slyly, glad that she had not detected his presence. If she had suspected, he would be obliged to kill her. Unawares, Rosie went on, still searching, desperately hoping that, even now, Ellie might be unhurt.

When it was safe, he hurried into the house. He would collect the paintings and return to the cottage, to his secret there. As he stole silently in through the door and along the passage, he did not know that, in the very same moment, a stranger's car had drawn up outside. Now, when the knock came on the door, his guilty heart almost leaped from his chest. But then, after the initial burst of fear, he became calm, unruffled. Tip-toeing into the kitchen, he peered out. Another shock. It was the police! No matter. He was safe enough. No one had any cause to suspect. Boldly, he opened the door. 'Why, good morning, officer.' His smile was all deceiving. 'What can I do for you?'

The officer met his smile with a serious face. 'Mr Armstrong?' His voice was quiet, not threatening. 'Mr . . . Jack Armstrong?' His gaze roved the man, curious at what it saw there.

'Yes, I'm Jack Armstrong.' The smile slipped away, eyes darkened with panic. 'It's not bad news is it? My daughter?'

'No. No . . . nothing like that, sir.' The officer saw how badly affected the other man seemed. Strange too, how he had not envisaged 'Mr Armstrong' to look anything like this fellow! Still, it was not for him to draw conclusions. He was here to deliver a message, to pursue a certain complaint. That was all. The Station had received notification from up North, and he had a job to do.

'Come inside, officer.' He stepped aside, closing the door. Together, they went along the passage and on into the big room. He might have been tempted to 'do away' with the law-man, only there was another in the car. It deterred him.

Outside, the second officer was alerted by Rosie's distressed calls. Inquisitive and concerned, he got out of the car and went to investigate.

Almost out of her mind with worry, and fearing the very worst, Rosie was already beginning to make her way towards the path that would lead her up to the shop, and, God willing, to help. She knew now that she must not delude herself any longer. She had been frantic on finding that Ellie was not in the house. Where was she? 'Oh,

Ellie! *Ellie!'* Rosie's anguished cries echoed through the spinney. She was beside herself with terror at the thought of what might have happened. She blamed herself. How could she have let compassion and pity blind her to the awful truth all these years?

Help. She must get help. And quickly! She knew in her bones that something terrible had happened to Ellie.

There was another who sought to protect Ellie. He, too, had his suspicions. He, too, prayed it was not too late. Unobserved, he went softly towards the big barn; a weary and bedraggled figure, beset by nightmares of a kind that stayed alive even in the daylight hours. He knew now, knew for certain. And the knowledge filled him with the worst kind of horror.

As though waking from a deep sleep and pressed down by unseen hands, Ellie shifted, softly moaning, every corner of her body racked and sore. Layer by layer the darkness lifted; now it was twilight, now it was grey, like swirling, misty fog. She forced open her eyelids, leaded weights that hurt, resisted. It would be so easy to lie there, to surrender to the all-enveloping blackness . . . so easy, drifting away, the pain gossamer light. Oh, so very easy. Too easy. Death was too easy. Too final. She struggled, trying to hitch herself into a sitting position against the wall, cold and damp she could feel it beneath her fingertips. The shudder rippled through her. The effort was too much. Wait, wait a while, let the life flow back into your stiff, sore limbs. She moved herself inch by inch, painstakingly, onto her side. Eyes open now, looking round, searching. There was nothing to see. It was all deathly silent, and dark, oh so dark. Wait! *Voices.* She could hear voices. Thank God. Oh, thank God! Something was wrong, though. Horribly wrong. She was imagining, hallucinating, her senses were playing tricks on her. The voices, distant, murmuring, now and then laughing softly; one sounding uncannily like that of her dead brother, the other like that of *her mother*! *No! No!* How could it be? On and on they went, conversing together, infiltrating her mind until she thought she was crazy. She cried out. Suddenly, all was silent again. A brooding, awful silence that crept right through her. Determined, she pulled herself up; leaning against the wall she listened. In the cold, biting air the sweat trickled down her face, erupting on her back in wet, sticky patches that mingled with the cold moistness of the wall. Summoning every ounce of strength left in her, she struggled to her feet, violently shivering, mortally afraid. And it was dark, so dark. So cold. Suddenly the darkness was relieved by a low, flickering light. Candles, a glowing circle in the distance. There were people there. A stab of hope and gratitude pierced her terror. Slowly, with a fast-beating heart, she moved forward. The room was spinning, she was spinning; light-headed still and mesmerised by the garish brightness, she went towards it on slow, faltering footsteps.

From a distance they watched, smiling, welcoming eyes, beckoning to her, willing her ever onwards. At last, at long last. The smile was beautiful, madly, madly beautiful! Only the heart was ugly, yet satisfied, content a while, the evil simmering beneath the surface. 'Don't be afraid,' the voice whispered, 'don't be afraid.'

The voice was soothing to Ellie. It was familiar, yet, it was not. With every step she feared the darkness would descend to swallow her. The voice urged her on; she called to it. When it answered, she was filled with joy. It was her father! Eagerly, she went on, towards the circle of light, to her father, to safety. Now, she could see him. He had his back to her, strong broad shoulders, a voice, his voice, coaxing, 'Hurry, Ellie. Hurry, sweetheart. Don't be afraid.' Only a heartbeat away now. She reached out, loving fingers, touching. Laughing, he slewed round to face her. *Barny!* Their eyes met – hers scarred with horror, his boring into her, wild, insane. *Barny's eyes! Barny! Barny!* The shock tore through her like nothing she had ever known. The face was Barny Tyler's, the voice was her father's. The scream began in the pit of her stomach, pushing up, suffocating, trapped inside. Then, like hell unleashed it left her body, splitting the air, time and again. She could not wrench her terrified eyes from that mad, delighted stare. She backed away, her screams stilled; now the silence was deafening, unearthly. Her mind was in chaos, fragmented. She had to get away, get away. *Dear God, help me!* In her haste she stumbled, the blackness rose in her, smothering her senses. Suddenly he was on her! 'Oh, Ellie. You disappoint me. Don't run away. Not from me.' His voice was strange to her, but the hands, that gentle, loving touch, so familiar, so disturbingly familiar. Trembling, she felt herself being lifted, turned, made to look into those smiling green eyes. 'You mustn't be afraid, my lovely.' His voice was the strangest whisper. She struggled, but there was no escape. The cold green eyes stared into hers, smiling, always smiling. His long, strong fingers closed about her throat, the two thumbs meeting across her Adam's apple, gently squeezing. Desperately she fought, clawing at his hands, kicking out, but she was no match for his maniacal strength. 'No, no, Ellie . . . don't fight me,' he murmured, all the while smiling that handsome, charming smile that now hardened into a devilish grimace. His fingers closed tighter, tighter until they were an iron collar round her throat. All thought fled her mind. Only greyness now. Then darkness, closing in, suffocating. She felt her arms drop limply to her sides; inside her head the blackness was bursting, spitting out in starlike bursts. In her heart she knew it was too late, too late, all over. The tears rose but could not flow – like her, they were trapped.

'*No!*' The scream issued into the darkness, bouncing across her fading thoughts. Suddenly, she felt a thud, then a different kind of pain as she was viciously flung to the cold, hard ground. She rolled over, smacking her head into the wall. She felt the blood spurt, trickling down her temple, salty in her mouth. Her eyes popped open, unseeing, then through her fading senses she saw – shadows in the flickering light, intertwined like sinister dancers, writhing, madness there. Madness. Her pained, dimming glance looked beyond, drawn to the halo of light, to the lifeless figures seated round the table, her father, and Alec, both of them bloodied, oh, and a child . . . a boy . . . his face strangely melted like a mask, and beside him another . . . a woman with her hair the colour of Ellie's, but she had no face! In her arms was the smallest bundle . . . a tiny infant?

Confused, in the grip of hysteria, Ellie's shocked glance flicked back to the man, her father? Was it really her father? No. Not him, or he would help. Ellie's eyelids closed; the gruesome images persisted. Darkness caressed her, uplifting, lapping over her. Until she knew no more.

'Jesus Christ!' The officers burst into the cellar, horrified by the carnage that unfolded before them – the macabre scene illuminated in the halo of candle light, Ellie broken and bloody, seemingly lifeless, and the old senile, fighting for his life but losing it inch by inch as the steel blade plunged time and again into his writhing body. Above him the green eyes went on smiling, even while the long, strong fingers drove the blade home, and with each vicious thrust his rasping voice accusing, 'You were never my father! You lied. You deceived me! Marie Armstrong was my mother. She had to die! They all had to die!' When the old man slid away, cocooned in a cradle of his own blood, the smile fell from Barny's face. With a chilling scream he dropped to his knees and took the dying man in his arms, rocking to and fro, in anguish. When the officer closed in he looked up, singing the softest lullaby, the tears rolling unheeded down his face. His heart was heavy with pain, oh, such pain. He had never been free from it. And now it was too late. Much too late. The officer's hand reached out. The singing stopped. Green eyes smiled. With one last defiant stare he challenged. He knew it was over. He knew what he must do. The knife swiftly pierced his heart. The smile was incredibly beautiful. Then dim. And still. No more pain. Only peace. At last. At long last.

When they reached the one called George, he was clinging to the smallest vestige of life. He was crying.

'All right, old fellow . . . be still now.' The officer spoke softly, with reverence. Death was all around him. When the claw-like hand beckoned him closer, he leaned forward, the warm, sticky smell of blood churning his stomach. He had sent for an ambulance. It was a futile gesture, he knew. 'Easy, old fellow,' he murmured, 'what are you trying to tell me?' The claw-like hand drew him nearer, the large lolloping mouth made a curious gurgling sound. The blood spilled out, the words spilled out. His confession was not for himself, but for the one who had caused so much loss and suffering, and yet had also suffered. For the only son he had ever known – *Barny*. His confession was for Barny.

CHAPTER THIRTEEN

Mrs Gregory shook her grey head and scooped the sweets from the jar. 'It don't bear thinking about,' she told Rosie. 'Such horror . . . no, it don't bear thinking about.' She tipped the sweets from the scales and into the paper bag. 'Whoever would have thought that Barny Tyler was the senile's adopted son . . . that Marie Armstrong was his real mother!' Her eyes grew wide at the implications. 'And Ellie . . . his half-sister.' Undeterred by Rosie's cursory glance she went on. 'What a wicked, wicked thing.' The thought of it all was too much. She dabbed at her eyes, saying, 'And you've no idea when the authorities will allow the dead to be buried?'

Rosie's brow creased into a deep frown and a look of disgust spread over her features. 'They won't allow it yet,' she replied, leaning on her crutch and fishing in the pocket of her coat. Presently she withdrew her purse and took the coins into her hand, counting them onto the counter in a careful fashion.

'But it's been two months now!' exclaimed Mrs Gregory, collecting the coins and spilling them into the till.

'Aye. An' like as not it'll be *another* two months afore they've finished with . . . what they term as "evidence".'

Mrs Gregory tutted. 'No, dear me no, like I say . . . it don't bear thinking about. Them poor little children – oh, and a man of God!' She hastily made the sign of the cross on herself. 'And the letter that old George sent to the priest after his poor wife was . . . murdered . . . asking him to come straight away like the old friend he was . . . that were still in the priest's pocket?'

'So I believe.'

'Poor George, that sorry old thing, he must have been desperate to have sent a letter like that. I understand he sent for the priest when he suspected it was Barny who'd killed her?' She paused. The thought was chilling to her.

'George's wife was murdered by Barny.' The condemnation was bitter in Rosie's voice. 'Murdered! That's what!' She stuffed the bag of sweets in her pocket. 'Butchered, like the rest of 'em.' She stared at the other woman, her panda-like eyes swimming with tears. 'George, too,' she murmured.

Mrs Gregory regarded Rosie with concerned eyes. 'Look here, Rosie, you must never reproach yourself where he was concerned. You're a good woman, and you looked after him like nobody else could.'

Through the window, Rosie saw Mr Gregory's van pull up outside the shop. 'It's good of your husband to take me back to the Lodge,' she said with a half-smile. 'I hadn't intended to make my way this far . . . just felt the need for a breath o' fresh air . . . time on me own, to think.' Her thoughts had not been pleasant, recalling as they did the account of old George's confession to the officer – an awful catalogue of terror that went back to the day George and his wife told Barny that he was not really their son. From that day on, the boy had grown into a monster, his terrible secret loathing fed by the insane desire to kill, to maim and punish those he held responsible. He had traced Marie Armstrong, the woman who had given birth to him when she was little more than a child herself. He traced her, seduced her and when she was close to bringing his own child into the world, he killed her, slitting her wrists even while she writhed in labour. When the child was born, the ritual was mercilessly repeated. Afterwards, Barny had cleverly removed all trace of his presence there, out in the field where he had lured her. Suicide was never questioned. Only her sanity was in doubt; a sanity that had been sorely strained by the pedlar who paid her a visit, a ragged pedlar who raised so many things from her past – secret things such as having borne an illegitimate child; things that had haunted her; things she deeply regretted. Barny had been that pedlar, her tormenter. She never knew.

Mrs Gregory gestured to the ungainly figure at the steering wheel. 'He'll be only too glad to take you back.' She chuckled. 'He's a changed man is that one,' she said, 'got taught the lesson he deserves, the night Alec collared him at the Lodge. Frightened the life out of him! I don't reckon he'll be so quick to go poaching them woods again in a hurry!' She put a comforting hand on Rosie's arm. 'Thank God Alec and Ellie have recovered! What will you do now that George is gone and Alec Harman's mending in leaps and bounds? The rumour is that he will be moving out of the area soon. He'll be giving up the Lodge then . . . and, as you've been staying there, along with his sister Laura and young Ellie, well, what will you do?' A look of horror washed over her features. 'Surely to God you'll not go back to the cottage?'

'I could never do that.' The very idea was unthinkable to Rosie. 'Besides, as you must have heard, the cottage and Thornton Place belonged to Barny Tyler. It was all part of his devious plan to entrap first his adoptive parents, then Ellie and her family.' Rosie sighed. 'Of course, when old George sensed the evil in Barny, and deliberately went through emigration procedures . . . never really intending to go . . . well, he did put Barny off his trail, but, sadly, only for a while.'

'So I gather!' exclaimed Mrs Gregory. 'And wasn't it true that Barny put an advert in the papers to deliberately entice his victims to Thornton Place?'

Rosie nodded. 'The irony of it all is that he bought the place with money he got from his share of the construction company. It was George's gift to him, long before he truly suspected Barny's evil nature.'

'You know Rosie, I wonder how many more might have died, if Alec Harman had not been determined to find out why his uncle . . . the priest . . . had so mysteriously disappeared.' She put her hand to her breast and took a deep breath. 'It really don't bear thinking about!' She watched as Rosie opened the door and began manoeuvring her way out. 'But what *will* you do when Alec Harman moves away?' she persisted.

Rosie smiled, a whisper of contentment lightening her eyes. 'We all have homes to go to.' She laughed quietly, eyeing the other woman mischievously. 'Well, now, I'm surprised you don't know already,' she teased. 'Alec's sister, Laura, will return to London and her secretarial career. Alec has a small farm in the West Country, which has been well managed these past years by an employee of his. I'm to be the housekeeper there. I shall be travelling to the farm this very week. Alec won't be seen there for at least a month, because he'll be far too preoccupied . . . with other matters.' Her smile deepened at the other woman's obvious frustration. But she had said enough. She was not a woman who liked to gossip – although she had found a wicked delight in teasing the curious Mrs Gregory just now.

'Will you be sorry to leave this place . . . the Lodge . . . the lake, everything you have come to love?' Ellie gazed up at the man who walked quietly beside her. She loved him so. Not a single day or night had passed during his long stay in hospital, when she had not given thanks for his safety. Life without him would have no meaning for her.

He stopped, drawing her deep into his arms. For a long,

wonderful moment, when the strength of their love bound them close, he gave no answer. Together, they looked out across the shimmering lake. It was a chilly March day. The wind sighed, rippling the waters until they shivered. In the far distance could be seen the skyward-reaching chimneys of Thornton Place. It made a formidable skyline. Tenderly, Alec placed his hands on Ellie's shoulders and turned her to face him. When she looked up, his dark eyes enveloped her. 'There is nothing here for me,' he murmured, 'only bad things . . . painful memories for both of us.' Suddenly he was back in the cellar, bound and gagged, propped in the chair, helpless while the madman related his awful plans – of how he meant to torture Alec before finally ending his life, and he told of other things, delighting in the telling, eagerly revealing how he had been given away as a child wrapped in a lavender-scented shawl, how he had exacted revenge, but, in all his well-laid plans had not foreseen that he would come to love Ellie. Alec was to be 'punished' because he had 'watched . . . made me nervous . . . the children saw me with the priest, sadly, they could not be allowed to live'.

'I love you, Alec Harman,' Ellie whispered, touching his fingers with her own. 'Home will always be where you are.'

He gazed a while, drinking in her loveliness, the small, heart-shaped face, the hair that shone like gold, and the warm amber eyes that looked on him with so much wanting. In his heart he knew he would never need more than this woman, whom he adored. It hurt him to see the lingering sadness in her eyes, the same sadness that was echoed in him. Together, they would overcome it. Together, they could find the joy that had almost eluded them. His gaze softened. 'You'll never regret promising to be my wife?' he asked.

'Never. Not for as long as I live,' she murmured. She

had lost so much. So very much. And yet, she had found Alec. It was enough. His answering smile warmed her heart. Then his arms tightened about her. Here she was safe, as safe as any woman could be. She raised her lips to his. And all the bad things were gone.